Other books in Margaret Daley's
Men of the Texas Rangers series

Saving Hope
Shattered Silence
Scorned Justice

SEVERED TRUST

Book 4 of Men of the Texas Rangers Series

Margaret Daley

Severed Trust

Copyright © 2013 by Margaret Daley

ISBN: 978-1-4267-6186-7

Published by Abingdon Press, P.O. Box 801, Nashville, TN 37202

www.abingdonpress.com

All rights reserved.

The persons and events portrayed in this work of fiction
are the creations of the author, and any resemblance
to persons living or dead is purely coincidental.

Published in association with the Steve Laube Agency.

Library of Congress Cataloging-in-Publication Data

Daley, Margaret.
  Severed trust / Margaret Daley.
    pages cm. — (Men of the Texas Rangers series ; Book 4)
    ISBN 978-1-4267-6186-7 (Binding: Paperback / Trade Paperback) 1. Texas Rangers—
Fiction. 2. Youth—Drug use—Texas—Fiction. I. Title.
  PS3604.A36S48   2013
  813'.6—dc23

                                                                        2013014482

Printed in the United States of America

1 2 3 4 5 6 7 8 9 10 / 17 16 15 14 13

To my husband, Mike, who is the love of my life

Thank you Steven, Jan, Vickie, Miralee, and Kimberly for your help

Prologue

Standing at the gravesite, I stare at the coffin, my mom inside. Dead. I don't understand. Why did she do it? Leave me and Dad?

I glance at my father next to me, tears running down his face, and my own stay clumped in my throat. An ache spreads through my whole body.

Memories of a few days before, of trying to wake up Mom, send the terror through me all over again. I close my eyes, not wanting to remember, only to picture her sprawled on her bed, an empty bottle of pills next to her.

I rub my hands across my face, trying to scrub the image from my mind.

As the crowd thins, my aunt approaches Dad. "I have some ladies from the church lined up to bring food over. Are you sure you don't want Bob and me at your house today? As they bring it, I can take care of it for you. You won't have to worry about anything."

"No. I want to be left alone. Cancel them."

"I know you're hurting. You shouldn't be alone at this time."

My dad leans forward, his face inches from my aunt's. "Don't tell me what I need. I need her."

My aunt pulls my father away a few steps and lowers her voice, but not enough that I don't hear what she says. "Paige was sick. She didn't mean to kill herself."

Dad jerks away from my aunt, grabs my hand and tugs me toward the car. People try to stop him, but he ignores them.

"Mom killed herself?" I ask as he drives toward our home.

He doesn't say anything.

"How?"

Still silent.

"Dad?"

He pulls into the driveway and twists toward me. "She didn't want to be with us. She took sleeping pills so she never had to wake up."

Mom? Leave us on purpose? No, she loved me.

"Go to Tommy's house and play with him." He pushes open his door and stomps to the house.

I don't know what to do. Tears finally flood my eyes. I blink and climb from the car. Instead of going to Tommy's across the street, I trudge toward the porch. I need Dad. I need to understand.

When I put my hand on the doorknob and turn it, a loud blast coming from inside, like a car backfiring, echoes through the air.

1

Fingering the necklace, Jared had given her for her seventeenth birthday, Kelly Winston cracked her bedroom door open. When she peeked out, her mother strode toward the staircase. Releasing a swoosh of air, Kelly snuck down the hall to her mom's bathroom and pulled out the middle drawer where she kept her supply of medicine.

Kelly picked up the first bottle, a painkiller her mother had started taking last winter after her car wreck. Kelly shook one into her palm. She grabbed the next bottle, not sure what these pills were, but she pocketed several of them anyway, then moved on to the next medication, an old one for anxiety her mom had taken when Dad divorced her and moved away. She took three of them.

"Kelly," her mother yelled from the foyer downstairs.

She shot straight up, her heart pounding, but she didn't hear any footsteps approaching.

"Your date is here."

She drew in a deep breath to calm her rapid heartbeat and quickly closed the drawer. "Coming, Mom."

She stuffed the pills she'd taken into her jean pocket and hurried from her mother's bathroom before she came looking for her. When Kelly saw Jared standing next to her mom in the foyer, she smiled and nodded once.

His mouth curving up, a dimple appearing in his left cheek, he winked at her.

"When are you going to be home?" her mother asked as she walked toward the kitchen.

"The party lasts until midnight so after that."

"Don't wake me when you come in. I'm exhausted and hope to go to bed early."

"I won't," Kelly said, right before closing the front door. It was so easy to stay out when her mother took a sleeping pill. Mom would be out until tomorrow.

"What did you get?" Jared rounded the front of his Porsche.

After sliding into the front seat, she dug the dozen pills out of her pocket and laid her palm out flat to show him. "Painkillers, sleeping pills, and an assortment of others. Is that what you wanted?"

"You did great. This will be fun."

"Are you sure your friends will be okay with me coming?"

"You're my girlfriend. We've been dating for over two months." At the stoplight, Jared looked at her, his blue eyes gleaming with male appreciation. "You're the most beautiful girl at Summerton High School. I'll be the envy of every guy at the party."

Though his words flattered her, Kelly's nerves tensed throughout her body. This was her first pill party. She'd heard of them from some of the other girls. She'd always wanted to be a part of the in crowd. Tonight she would be. Finally. All because Jared Montgomery, a hottie and a senior, had started dating her when she became one of the junior cheerleaders—after years of honing her skills and dieting constantly.

When Jared parked behind a warehouse, Kelly glanced at some of the other expensive cars. A few she recognized. "The party is here?"

"Yeah. This place isn't in use right now. Perfect for what we want to do. Ready?"

She nodded, laying her quivering fingers on the door handle.

He clasped her shoulder, stopping her from leaving the car. "Just do what the others do. It's a small group of my closest friends. You'll be fine. This is such a rush. You'll see what I mean tonight."

Peering at him, she fortified herself with the knowledge he'd told her he loved her last week. All the kids were doing this. What harm could a few prescription drugs really do? They were all prescribed for someone to take. Her mom took several every day. It wasn't the same as taking illegal drugs like meth or crack. Those could seriously mess with her mind.

As they walked toward the back entrance to the warehouse, hidden from the street, Jared grasped her hand, brought it to his lips, and kissed her knuckles. "Stay close and I'll take care of you."

His gaze connected with hers. Her stomach flip-flopped. He could always do that—make her feel so special. She certainly didn't get any affirmation from her mother, or her father, who lived in Chicago and couldn't be bothered with her.

Before going in, Jared tipped her face up and kissed her, then pushed the door open.

The beat of the music pulsated in the air. Four teens sat or stood around the huge cavernous warehouse—bare of any items as far as Kelly could see, except for a few crates used for the party. Beyond the pool of light, darkness lingered as though a black curtain encircled a small part of the building, cordoned off for the pill party.

Jared retrieved two beers from a cooler and passed one to Kelly. She hated the taste but noticed all the other kids had one. She'd pretend she liked it.

"Let's put our drugs in the bowl. When everyone arrives, we'll grab a handful and take them with the beer." Jared pulled a wad of pills from his pocket.

"Then what?"

"We drink, dance, and wait. For some nothing much happens. Dud pills. Others get a rush, feel euphoric. Either way, we'll forget our problems and have fun." He released his pills to fall into a large plastic bowl where there were a lot of drugs in various colors and sizes.

Kelly uncurled her hand, and the ones she brought tumbled on top of the others, then she took a swig of beer, suppressing her gag reflex.

Jared tapped his can against hers and then lifted his drink, downing probably half of it. "C'mon. We need to catch up with everyone. We'll be floating in no time. Not a care in the world, especially the English test you have on Monday."

While she tilted the can to her lips, he slung his arm over her shoulder and cradled her against him. His sweet action reinforced why she was here in the first place.

Jared loves me and won't let anything bad happen to me.

Her throat parched, Kelly swayed in the middle of the lit area with several teens slumped on the concrete floor. The light and dark swirled before her. She searched for Jared and found him where he'd been before she'd gone to see if there was something to drink. The coolers had been empty. To ease her dryness, she'd considered cupping her hands into the melted ice, but she didn't.

Kalvin Majors stumbled and fell into a stand with a light. It crashed to the floor and shattered. He continued wandering around in a circle, shouting every once in a while, "Go Eagles."

Kelly returned to the darker area because the room didn't seem to spin as much. She plopped down and crumpled back against a post. Jared lay not far away, and no matter how much she'd tried earlier to get him up, she couldn't. He'd just batted at her as if she were an annoying fly pestering him.

Another girl, Zoe, was stretched out on the floor moaning, while Luke, who was in several of her classes, vomited. The stench assailed her nostrils, and she almost hurled. She cupped her hand over her mouth and closed her eyes.

This isn't fun. I want to go home.

She crawled toward Jared, afraid to try standing. When she reached him, she shook his shoulder hard. Nothing. At least before, he would mumble or groan, but this time he didn't do anything. Cradling his face between her hands, she intended to yell at him until he woke up.

His skin felt cold, but it was hot in here. How could he be so cold? Her mind fumbled around trying to grasp onto something she should realize. Did she stick her hands into the ice water after all?

"Jared! Wake up!"

Someone—Brendan maybe—said, "Pipe down."

She didn't care. Increasing her volume, she shouted his name over and over.

Kelly lifted his arm to pull him up and get him outside into the fresh air. His limp arm was dead weight, making it hard to budge him at all. Finally, the effort zapped all her energy, her world spinning faster than before. She collapsed on top of Jared. A black veil descended . . .

Someone jostled Kelly, pushing her off her comfortable pillow. She blinked, a harsh light glaring in her eyes.

"He's dead," a frantic female voice shrieked, piercing through Kelly's dazed mind.

Dead? Kelly struggled to focus on the two blurs standing over another blur.

"We've got to get him out of here. This is my dad's warehouse."

"And do what?" the girl screamed.

"Don't know. Can't leave him in here."

Kelly curled up into a ball, the cold concrete against her cheek. She wanted to open her eyes again. To see what was happening but the darkness beckoned. If she slept a little longer, she would be okay.

A scraping sound penetrated the haze in her mind, but she kept moving toward the black.

Slam.

She jerked, then folded in on herself even more. Now running toward the dark void where she could escape . . .

Kelly rolled unto her back, the cold hardness beneath her demanding she wake up. She tried forcing her eyelids up but only managed to open them a slit. Through her narrow vision a face loomed close. The darkness surrounding her made it hard to see who it was. Blue eyes? Jared?

But no matter how much she tried, she couldn't keep her eyes from shutting again. Her mind in a fog, she allowed it to swallow her up.

∼⟨∂⟩∽

"Really, Mom, I don't feel well. I think it's something I ate last night." Lexie Alexander drew the cover over her head and hoped her mother would just leave her alone.

Her mom threw back the coverlet and felt her forehead. "You don't feel hot. I hate going to church by myself."

"I thought Uncle Ethan was going."

"He got a call. Some hikers found a dead body."

Lexie's stomach roiled, bile rising up. She jumped from bed and raced for her bathroom before she got sick all over the carpet. Barely making it, she heaved into the toilet.

Her mom handed her a cold washcloth. "Guess you really are sick. I thought you were trying to get out of going to church."

As Lexie hung over the rim, she shook her head.

Her mom filled a cup with water and gave it to her.

Lexie swished the cool liquid around in her mouth then spit it into the toilet. "I really did eat some spicy food that didn't agree with me. I had the Cantina deliver last night while you were out on your date with Cord."

"I'll stay home, in case you need me."

Lexie handed the cup to her mother. "I don't think there's anything else in my stomach. I'll be fine with some rest. I was up a good part of the night."

"You should have come and gotten me."

Lexie rose, glimpsing her wild short hair and pale face. "I know you're a nurse, but what would you have been able to do? Hold my hand while I puked? I know I'm not eating at the Cantina ever again."

Her mother lingered in the doorway into the bathroom. "On the way home from church, I'll stop and get some ginger ale and saltine crackers, in case you want something later."

Lexie waved her away then cupped some cold water and splashed her face. The awful taste in her mouth reminded her of that spicy food that probably was the culprit behind her getting sick. As she heard the bedroom door click shut, she put a glob of mint-flavored toothpaste on her toothbrush and scrubbed her teeth, hoping to get the nasty taste out of her mouth.

She trudged back to bed and fell across the messed-up covers. Her mind started surrendering to sleep . . .

The song "Because of You" blasted the air, startling her wide-awake. She fumbled for her cell phone on her nightstand and brought it to her ear. She didn't feel like talking—even to her best friend.

"Hello." Her answer came out long and drawn out.

"Lexie, I need your help."

"Kelly?" She pushed to her elbows. "Why are you whispering?"

"I'm at a warehouse across town. I need a ride home and bring me that blouse you borrowed last week. Mom has to think I've been up and out with you this morning."

"Where have you been?"

"At a party—all night. I'm scared. Come get me."

Lexie looked around and saw her car keys on the desk by her purse. "Where's the warehouse?"

"At the corner of Sixth Street and Bluebonnet Road."

"That's clear across town in the bad part of town."

"I know. That's why I'm not walking home. I need your help, Lex." Fear laced each word Kelly spoke in a shaky whisper.

Lexie swung her legs off the bed. "I'll be there as soon as I can."

"Pull up in back of the warehouse. I'll be watching. I don't want to leave until you come."

"Okay." Lexie hung up and snatched her jeans and T-shirt off the floor nearby. She stood to put her clothes on, but the room tilted. Plopping down on the bed, she dressed. Remembering the fear she'd heard in Kelly's voice prodded her to move as fast as her shaky body would allow.

⋘⋙

"Thanks for coming out on a Sunday morning," the police chief of Summerton said to Texas Ranger Ethan Stone.

"Cord, what happened here?" Ethan stood just outside the cordoned-off area with yellow crime scene tape.

"Two hikers found a car in Summerton Lake with a dead body in it—Jared Montgomery."

Ethan whistled. "Have you told his parents yet?"

Cord Thompson shook his head. "I can't call and tell them over the phone. I need to make sure the crime scene is processed by the book first."

Ethan removed his tan cowboy hat and raked his fingers through his hair. "Agreed." Bradley Montgomery owned the largest ranch in this area of northeastern Texas, and Jared was his only child. "Did the hikers recognize Jared?"

"They are with an officer giving their statements. One of them dove under to see if someone was trapped in the car. He saw Jared and tried to get the door open. He couldn't, but he could see Jared was dead. He hightailed it out of the water to call 911. Hopefully, since only those hikers know about Jared's death, this gives us a little time before the news gets out. I can't mess up this investigation, or I'll be looking for another job."

"What do you want me to do? You know I'm always here to help."

"Considering the potential of this case to be high profile, I'm glad you're the Texas Ranger assigned to this area." Cord rubbed his nape. "I've got a feeling this case will come back to bite me. I don't want Bradley Montgomery to find out from someone else besides the police, but as I mentioned, I need to stay here. Sending a street officer would say to the man his son wasn't important enough to our police department to have someone higher up inform him of Jared's death. Bradley is one of the people whose taxes probably pay a good part of our salaries. He goes to your church. You know him. Would you inform him of his son's death and that you'll be working with us on this case?"

"You and I go to the same church."

"I know, but you two were better friends in high school." A grin skittered across the police chief's face, but only for a second.

"So you're officially asking me to participate in the investigation?"

"Yes."

"Since when have we stood on protocol? We've known each other since childhood, and you know the Texas Rangers are here to help with local cases when needed."

"As I said, we can't make any mistakes with this case. I can already imagine Bradley breathing down my neck, and I won't blame the man when he does. I don't have children, but if something happened to my niece or nephew, I'd be all over it."

"I haven't been here long. What kind of kid was Jared? Like his father?"

"Yes. Jared is a popular guy and well-liked from what I've heard. He's on the football team as the quarterback. This will be a blow to the whole team and school."

Ethan walked to the red Porsche, still dripping water, and studied the boy, his body leaning back, held in place by his seatbelt, his head bent to the right. "Are there signs of foul play?"

"Not that I can see, but the Medical Examiner is on the way. I didn't want to move him from the car until he got here. I'll push to have the autopsy done immediately."

"Suicide?"

Cord frowned. "It doesn't feel right. He has everything going for him. That's why I want to be here when the ME arrives. Nothing about this scene looks like a suicide."

"What are you afraid of? That this is drug or alcohol-related, and Bradley's active campaign against drugs is known all over these parts?"

Cord nodded. "Why here? Yes, I suppose he could have driven into the lake because of the boat ramp here," he pointed at the pavement ending in the water, "but it's set out of the way from the parking lot where the road forks."

"Which brings us back to suicide. He could have purposely driven it into the lake. Or someone else did. So who would have it in for Jared if he's so popular?"

"You see how many questions there are. Bradley will want them all answered and then some. He'll be looking for someone other than his son to put the blame on." Cord removed his trademark toothpick from his front shirt pocket and stuck it into his mouth. According to him, chewing on it helped him think since he'd stopped smoking.

"I'll be back after I notify Bradley. I want to look at his room and check for a suicide note. It's early, he won't have left for church yet. In this region, there have been several deaths in the past couple of months from prescription medications not belonging to the deceased person. But no foul play has been determined in those cases."

"Appreciate the help. See you in a while." Cord gestured toward an arriving black van. "Ah, the ME is finally here. I woke him up this morning."

"He got to sleep in. My dog had me up at the crack of dawn to let him out."

"Get a doggie door."

"Can't. That creates a hole in my perimeter in which someone could enter my house. Not comfortable with that."

Cord chuckled. "Ain't police work grand? It makes all of us paranoid."

Ethan began walking toward his blue SUV. "I'd much rather think of it as making us alert and prepared for anything."

Cord's laughter increased. "You keep thinking that."

Ethan climbed into his car and backed away from the scene until he could turn his SUV around and head toward the highway leading to Bradley's ranch. Usually he didn't notify the next of kin about a death, at least not since he'd been a Texas Highway Patrol Officer. That was one duty he didn't miss.

Lexie's wheels squealed as she turned onto Bluebonnet Road, her stomach tight with tension. She prayed she wouldn't throw up again. Kelly needed her, and she wanted to be there for her best friend, even if lately they had drifted apart since Kelly began dating Jared Montgomery.

Passing Fifth Street, she began looking for the sign for Sixth. The area around here was creepy, buildings abandoned with several vandalized. Scanning one after another sent a shudder down her length. She hoped Kelly was watching, and she didn't have to get out of her car. Even though her Ford was over eight years old, someone around here might want to steal it, leaving her and Kelly to walk home.

That thought panicked her, and she nearly missed Sixth Street. Lexie slammed on the brakes, and her tires screeched. She fishtailed. Great. If that didn't call attention to her, she didn't know what would short of laying on her horn. She quickly moved her hands away from the horn and turned the steering wheel toward the way she needed to go.

A minute later, she pulled up at the back of a brown warehouse that at one time must have been white. Patches of the color peeked out every once and a while. For a second she contemplated honking, but she took a quick glance around and decided against it. The parking lot was as deserted as these buildings appeared, but beyond them a large, low-income apartment complex backed up to the area.

She'd call Kelly to come outside, but when she rummaged for her cell phone in her purse, she couldn't find it. She'd left it on her bed. Well then, she would give Kelly a few minutes to come outside.

Lexie tapped her hand against the steering wheel, trying to keep rhythm to an imaginary song running through her mind. A beat-up car drove down Sixth Street. Lexie held her breath. Her pulse coursed through her at a maddeningly fast rate. If Uncle Ethan knew what she was doing, he would go through with his teasing threat and really have her frozen until she was twenty-one.

❧

"Mom! A man is here to see you," Sadie Thompson's son, Steven, yelled from the entry hall.

She cringed and wondered how many people in the neighborhood heard that announcement. A man at the door for Sadie Thompson. No doubt one of them would immediately run to her parents and tell them their daughter was seeing a man. She laughed out loud. That was the farthest thing from the truth. After Harris walked out on their short-lived marriage, she hadn't had time for anything but raising her children and trying to make a living.

She finished running a brush through her hair, slipped on some sandals and hurried from her bedroom. When she emerged from the hallway and saw the man standing in her home for the first time in ten years, she stopped, placing her hand on the wall to keep her balance.

Harris Blackburn. What was he doing here? What did he want from her? The last time she'd seen him he'd had the nerve to ask her for money—money she didn't have. He'd left then, like he had right after the twins were born, three years before that, and to her relief she hadn't once seen him.

Until now.

Steven eyed the man who was his father, but she doubted her son recognized him. He then turned to go to the den where he played his video games every waking moment she would let him sit in front of the screen. She gritted her teeth to keep from saying anything to Harris until she heard the door to the den close.

"What do you want?" she asked in a surprisingly civil tone although her first urge was anything but civil.

"To see my kids. I heard you came back to Summerton."

"Who told you that?"

"A friend in town."

"You still have friends?"

He winced. "Yes. In fact, I returned last week. I have a job here. I'm staying for a while so I thought it was a good time to get to know my son and daughter."

She'd so desperately wanted to hear those words from Harris in the past. Now she dreaded them the most. "No."

"Did I tell you one of those friends is a lawyer?"

"Jeffrey Livingston."

"Yes, you remember what good friends we were back in the day."

"You can have visitation rights when you pay me for all those years of back child support. The amount is over a hundred thousand dollars. Come back then and we'll talk." Harris could never keep money for long, so the thought he had that kind of cash was ludicrous.

He stuffed his hand into his jacket pocket, withdrew a wad of money, and tossed it to her. "That's five thousand. The courts will look at it as an attempt. All I want is to see them and get to know them. You can be there."

She unrolled the money, all hundred-dollar bills, and examined them. They looked real, but she couldn't believe it. "What bank did you rob?"

"I've changed over the past few years. I've got a steady job as a private investigator, and I'm good at my job. Been at it for three years. I've settled down. My kids have a right to know their dad."

"Do you even know their names?" Derision dripped off each word. *Lord, I'm trying not to lose it. But it isn't easy.*

"Steven."

"And?"

"I don't know my daughter's name. You know how I am with people's names."

"These *people* are your kids. You call yourself a private investigator? You could have at least found out before showing up here." As much as she could use the money, she put the rubber band back around the wad and threw it at her ex-husband. "I don't want your money. Get out. If you don't leave, I'll call my brother. Just in case you haven't heard, he's the police chief of Summerton."

"I've heard." He snatched up the money and returned it to his pocket. "This doesn't change anything. You'll be hearing from me soon." Stepping back, he rotated toward the door and left, the slamming sound echoing through the house.

Shaking, Sadie finally collapsed back against the wall and slid down. She drew her legs to her and dropped her head on her knees.

She'd never thought Harris would come back to Summerton. While growing up here, he'd loathed the town and couldn't wait to get away.

Being a teacher, she still had most of the school year to finish out. She was tired of doing everything alone. She needed her family around her, but she couldn't have Harris in her children's lives.

Can I wait until next May to leave again?

❧

"Is Mr. Montgomery here?" Ethan asked the man who wasn't technically the butler because Bradley would scoff at that term. But the guy was always there to answer the door and bar anyone from seeing Bradley if he thought his employer didn't want to see the visitor.

"He's getting ready for church and—"

"This is official police business." Ethan showed him his badge, staring down the large employee with beefy arms and bowed legs.

"He hates to be disturbed at this time."

"He'll want to talk to me. It's important." Ethan stressed the last word, narrowing his eyes on the gatekeeper as though Ethan could will him to move.

"Very well. I'll ask Mr. Montgomery, but don't be surprised if he tells you to come back another time."

The man escorted Ethan to the formal living room, sterile and stuffy, containing expensive pictures with a western theme on the walls and bronze Remington statues on the tables. There was a time when Bradley would have opened his own door to Ethan. Millions of dollars later his friend kept barriers between him and the townspeople. He missed the days when Bradley and he had ridden a bit recklessly across his family ranch, much smaller in those days.

"Ethan, it's great to see you." Bradley offered him his hand.

He shook it. "I wasn't sure I would get through your man at the door."

Bradley grinned. "I pay him well to keep the riffraff out, but I'll have a word with him about you. I'll let him know you're a longtime friend, even though we've lost touch lately. What brings you here that couldn't wait until church in half an hour?" He waved his hand toward a chair while he fit his long, lean length in one across from where Ethan stood.

"I won't be at church today, and this is something I must tell you in person as soon as possible."

Bradley sat forward, his shoulders thrust back. "What's happened?"

There was never an easy way to inform a parent their child was dead. "Jared was found this morning by hikers in Red River City Park. He's dead."

The color drained from his friend's face. He gripped the arms of the chair and leaned so far forward that Ethan was afraid Bradley would topple from his seat. "No, this has to be a mistake. My son is . . ." His mouth moved up and down, but no words came out.

"I'm sorry, but it's Jared. I saw the body. The police chief ID'd your son. Of course, you'll be asked to make a formal ID."

"How could it be Jared? He should be upstairs." Bradley shot to his feet and strode from the room. "He refuses to go to church, so I haven't seen him yet today, but I'm sure I'll find him sleeping in."

Ethan followed Bradley to his son's bedroom. For Bradley's sake, he hoped Cord was wrong, but the car's registration was to Jared Montgomery.

When the man thrust the door open and stepped inside, he came to an abrupt halt. His hands balled. "No. No. Not Jared. It can't be."

Ethan guided Bradley to the neatly made bed. "Sit. Is Annabelle home?"

"No, she's in Dallas. I'll have to call her." Bradley sank onto the mattress, but he didn't move to get in touch with his wife. "How did this happen? Why Jared?"

"We don't have the answers yet on those questions. Cord stayed to make sure we processed the scene quickly. He knew you would want to know what occurred as soon as possible."

"Was—was he . . ." Bradley brought up a shaky hand and wiped the sweat from his forehead with his palm.

"We don't know the cause of death yet. He was found in his car in the Summerton Lake by the boat ramp." He decided not to mention suicide. Bradley had enough to process at the moment.

"An accident? Why in the world was Jared at Red River City Park? That isn't his normal hangout. And how did he end up in the water? We keep a boat at Monarch Lake."

"Good questions. Ones we will get answers for. Did you see him last night?" Ethan made a visual sweep of the tidy room—nothing like what he'd had when he was growing up.

"Yeah, right before he went out on a date."

"With who?"

"This girl he's been dating for a couple of months. I don't think he was serious about her, but she is beautiful and Jared is always . . ." Tears glistened in Bradley's gray eyes, making them shine like polished silver. He dropped his head. "I don't think I can get used to saying was. He's all I have." Bradley fell silent for a long moment, then he lifted his head and directed his intense, cold gaze to Ethan. "I want you on this case. Actually, I want you to be in charge of the case. If I have to, I'll call the governor. I need to know what happened. Who's responsible?"

"Cord already asked me to assist him."

"No. I want you running it. I want the state lab to run all the tests. I need to know." The urgency and fierceness in Bradley's tone heightened the tension already gripping his friend.

"I'll take care of it. I'm sure Cord will be fine with that." Ethan captured Bradley's full attention. "Understand I will dig until I discover what happened, but I won't put up with you dogging my every step about the case." He knew if his friend called the governor he would have to oversee the case, and he really wouldn't have a say on how Bradley conducted himself. Like Cord, he suspected this was the tip of something big going down in his hometown.

"Fine, but I ask you to keep me informed of any progress."

"I will, but I can't have you hampering my case." *Because you might not like what I find.*

"I understand."

Ethan didn't think Bradley really did. What if it were suicide? Or murder? Either situation brought a whole slew of questions that were hard on a family. "I have a few questions for you before I go back to the scene. Did you see your son return after his date?"

"No. He'll be—would have been eighteen in six months. He didn't have a curfew, but he was always home at a reasonable hour."

"But you don't know if he returned last night and went out this morning or if he was out all night?"

Bradley scowled. "No. He never gave me a reason to question his judgment. What are you saying?"

"Nothing. I need to figure out what he was doing last night. What's the name of the girl he was dating?"

"Kelly Winston." Bradley bit out the words, a nerve in his cheek twitching.

Ah, Bradley had dated Kelly's mom in high school, nothing too serious, but he imagined it didn't set well with Bradley since Mary Lou and he didn't end on a good note. Wasn't Lexie friends with Kelly? He'd seen the girl over at his niece's house a few times in the past month since he'd returned to Summerton.

Bradley pushed to his feet, his gaze fixing on a photo on his son's desk of a younger version of Bradley with someone who looked like Mary Lou. Kelly, the girl he'd seen his niece with. "I didn't want Jared dating her, but I was afraid he would go behind my back if I told him not to."

Like Bradley had with Mary Lou. "So you tolerated him seeing her."

"Barely. Do you think she had something to do with this? Her mother certainly could mess with a guy's mind. I should have listened to my gut and put my foot down concerning Kelly." Bradley began to pace.

Ethan walked to the desk. "Teenagers love to oppose what you think is good for them. Sometimes we have to let them make their own mistakes. You did what you thought was right."

Bradley swung around, his strong jaw line hard. "But Jared is dead."

"Kelly might have nothing to do with this. We don't even know if she was really with Jared last night. Let me do some investigating. Let me do my job."

"My son didn't lie to me. If he said he was going out with Kelly, then he was. Talk to her."

"May I take a look at his computer and this room? See if I can find anything to help me reconstruct his whereabouts last night." A suicide note or an indication someone was mad at Jared.

"Sure, but I can't stay in here. I'm going to call Annabelle." Bradley crossed to the exit, an ashen tint to his tan features. "Keep me informed."

When Bradley left, Ethan began his search of Jared's bedroom. Apprehension nipped at Ethan. Since he'd returned home, he'd only had routine investigations, but he was afraid all of that was going to change with this case.

Lexie eased open the back door of the warehouse, its creaking noise clamoring through her head and the vast building. The sound announced to anyone around that someone was coming in. As Lexie squeezed through the opening, sunlight poured into the place, mingling with the cloudy streams coming in through the dirt-crusted windows scattered along the walls on both sides of her. The stench of stale beer, urine, and vomit permeated the air, nearly gagging her.

Find Kelly and get out of here.

Her eyes quickly adjusted to the dimness while she started to the left, searching for her friend. The beer bottles and cans littered the concrete floor—lots of them. What went on here? The question kept running through Lexie's mind as she moved further into the warehouse.

Then she spied Kelly, or at least it looked like her, curled into a fetal position on the dirty floor, her back to Lexie. Not moving.

2

*B*eth Alexander drove halfway to church and made a U-turn to head home. Lexie was rarely sick. Maybe it was more serious than something she ate last night. But even if it was, as a nurse, Beth knew about food poisoning and how some people died from it. She'd feel better if she were home, in case there were complications.

She pulled into the driveway, punching the button on the garage door opener. Slowly the door rose to reveal two empty parking spaces. Had Lexie become sicker and driven herself to the hospital?

After pulling into the garage, she checked her cell phone to make sure she hadn't missed a call from her daughter. Nothing. Maybe she left her a note. Lexie was always good about doing that.

Rushing into the house, Beth went straight for the whiteboard in the kitchen where they both posted messages to each other. Blank. As she flew through the two-story house, looking for any kind of note or indication where her daughter was, Beth placed a call to Lexie's cell phone. It went to voicemail. The hospital. She punched in the numbers, praying one of the nurses she used to work with would answer.

When she connected with the nurses' station in the emergency room, she identified herself then said in a voice she hoped didn't sound as frantic as she felt, "Has my daughter Lexie come into the ER?"

"No. Is something wrong with her?" A fellow nurse she had once worked with on the surgery floor asked.

"She was throwing up this morning, but thought she was getting better. She probably went to a friend's." Beth hung up, embarrassed she'd panicked so fast. Lexie just forgot to write a note, telling her where she was going. Knowing Lexie, she was over at Kelly's house. She placed a call to check with Kelly.

"Hello," Mary Lou said in a slow, drawn out voice.

"Did I wake you up?"

"Beth?"

"Yes. Is Lexie over there?" Anxiety still cloaked her. Why did she have the feeling something wasn't right? Though Lexie would be seventeen in a month, she never gave her any trouble and disappearing without leaving word where she would be was so out of character for Lexie.

A long pause, then Mary Lou responded, "I don't think so, but I've been asleep."

"Would you please go and check with Kelly and see if she has heard from her?"

"Is something wrong?"

"She was sick earlier this morning and now she's gone. Just being a worrywart."

"Sure. I'm walking to Kelly's room right now. She's like me. Hates to get up early if she doesn't have to."

"Sorry to disturb your sleep." Beth heard Mary Lou knock on her daughter's bedroom door. She smiled. Both girls wanted their privacy. That started about the time they turned eleven.

Sounds of the door opening drifted to Beth, then Mary Lou muttering some unladylike words. When she came back on the phone, anger infused her voice. "It doesn't look like she came home last night from her date. Her bed hasn't been slept in. Let me check the rest of the house, and I'll call you back."

Mary Lou hung up before Beth could say another word. She again trekked through the house, searching for anything to tell her Lexie's location. She made another call to Lexie's phone, but all she got was her daughter's voicemail. Again. She even texted Lexie who always responded almost immediately when she did.

When Beth's phone chimed, she answered so fast she didn't even see who was calling.

"Kelly isn't here. I don't know where she is. You think she's with Lexie?"

"I don't know."

"I looked for the outfit Kelly wore last night. I couldn't find it on the floor with all her other clothes. I tried Jared and Kelly's cell phones. Nothing."

"Me, too. Lexie isn't answering. I don't like this." The nagging feeling persisted. "If you hear from either one, please let me know, and I'll do the same."

Maybe Lexie didn't have anything to do with what was going on with Kelly. She'd try some of her other friends and see if anyone had heard from her daughter.

❧

Ethan approached Cord who was tagging a set of footprints near the boat ramp. "I see the ME's van has left with Jared's remains. Did he have anything to say about the cause and time of death?"

"He thinks between midnight and five this morning. He might be able to narrow it down more after the autopsy. On his cursory look, he couldn't find any evidence of murder. No obvious signs at least. That doesn't rule out drugs, though. He'll check and see if he has water in his lungs or if he was dead before he hit the lake."

"What else have you found?"

"Several sets of footprints. However, they may be from the hikers. This one looks like tennis shoes. Another over there—boots." Cord pointed to a marker he'd left by the evidence. "We did have to cut Jared out of his seatbelt so I'll have that looked at."

"It can jam in wrecks."

"I'll give the ME a few hours, then pay him a visit. Want to come?"

"Yes."

"How did the notification go?" Cord looked directly at Ethan. "About the way I thought?"

"Yep. In fact, Bradley insists I take the lead on the case. He threatened to call the governor if he had to."

Cord shook his head. "Bradley hasn't changed since high school. He always did like to bulldoze his way through things."

"Made a great tackler for the football team, but could make it hard to take as a friend."

"But you stuck by him better than I did, so I can see why he wants you on the case. There are no hard feelings here. In fact, it takes the pressure off me and my office."

"And puts it on my shoulders."

Cord patted Ethan's back. "You've got big shoulders. Better you than me. You can take it."

Ethan sighed. No wonder he didn't have a life outside of his work and his extended family. "I have a feeling I'm going to need a month-long vacation after this is over, and you should pay for it."

"Yeah, sure, on my pay you can spend a month in the woods living in a tent. I'll supply the woods and the tent. If you want to eat, you'll have to bring your own food."

Ethan's cell phone played "The Eyes of Texas." His sister. "Ethan here."

"Lexie is missing. Something is wrong. I just know it. You've got to come over here. I don't know what to do."

"How long has she been missing?"

"A few hours."

"She's a teenager, Beth. She probably went somewhere—"

"Kelly is missing, too. Her mother is also worried about her."

Kelly. The one who had a date with Jared Montgomery last night. "I'll be there right away."

After pocketing his phone, he faced Cord. "My sister needs me."

Cord perked up, the furrows in his forehead smoothing out. "What's going on? I couldn't help overhearing your conversation. Something about Lexie?"

"She's missing. Which on its own, I wouldn't get too concerned about. I seem to remember several times she lost track of time and forgot to let Beth know. But my sister tends to forget those times."

"Then why are you leaving the scene?"

"First, I know you're a good cop, and you'll make sure everything is processed correctly. But mostly, Kelly is missing, too."

"They're best friends. No telling what they're doing. Girl stuff."

"I didn't get a chance to tell you that Bradley told me Jared had a date with Kelly last night. I don't believe in coincidences. Why is she missing when Jared turns up dead?"

"I'm coming with you. This scene is basically finished. Not much other than the footprints and a lighter on the boat ramp a few yards back."

"Lighter?" Ethan strode toward his SUV.

"Yeah, I'll have latent prints run on it. I doubt it's anything connected to this scene. I didn't think Jared smoked since he's on the football team. If coach ever found out, he would have been running laps until he collapsed and not have a breath left to smoke." Cord opened the door to his truck. "I'll follow you."

"Just like the old days. Should I be concerned you're after my sister again?"

"That was ages ago. She married the other guy." Cord gave him an innocent look.

"And is now a widow. Is that why I've seen you two together a couple of times in town?"

"We're friends. We like spending time together. That's all."

"You never married."

"Good observation." Cord cocked a grin. "You haven't married either. Let's go."

For the second time that day, Ethan left the scene. He agreed with Cord. Several officers had combed over it looking for any clues and evidence. He hoped Jared's body told the ME more than his location did, and maybe the car would tell them something, too. Bradley would demand answers and wouldn't tolerate delays in getting them.

"Mom, what a surprise. You didn't tell me you were coming by today." Sadie shut the front door after her mother stormed into the foyer and swept around to face Sadie.

Her mom planted her hand with her purse clutched in it on her waist. "I saw Harris Blackburn today at Cattlemen's Grill. What's he doing back? Why didn't you tell me?"

Sadie glanced toward the stairs that led to the second floor where her two children were. She still hadn't talked with them about their dad wanting to be in their life because she didn't know what to say. But she didn't want them finding out by overhearing their grandmother talking about Harris. "Let's go outside on the patio. Steven and Ashley don't know."

Her mother's mouth pinched into a frown. "I told you he was a big mistake."

Sadie started for the back of her house. "I know." Whether she liked it or not she was tied to Harris because of the children. Changing her last name back to Thompson hadn't changed that fact. She had to deal with it—somehow.

Out on the patio, Sadie breathed in the fall air and relished its crispness with a hint of burning wood. She didn't want to have this conversation with her mother. She would only hear about how she'd messed up her life getting involved with Harris in high school. "How's Dad?"

"Furious when he saw Harris. I was afraid he'd go over and have words with him. Instead, we cut our lunch short and left."

"Does Dad know you came over?"

"It was his suggestion. He wants the man gone from Summerton."

But her dad wouldn't come see her himself. He hadn't spoken to her other than a few civil words in the company of others since she'd left fourteen years ago with Harris. Her father saw his grandchildren, especially Steven, but when he did, it was away from her and her house. "I do, too, but from what Harris said to me earlier, that isn't going to happen anytime soon. He wants to be in Steven and Ashley's life."

"No, he can't!"

"Please, Mom, I don't want the neighbors to overhear our conversation." Nor her children. She peered up at Ashley's window above the patio. Maybe this wasn't the best place to talk with her mother about her ex-husband. "Let's walk." Her house backed up to the woods. She strolled that way, hoping her mother would follow.

She did, even in her high heels that sank into the soft ground. "What are you going to do?"

"Fight Harris on seeing the kids."

"That'll work. I doubt he cares anyway. He abandoned you and them when they were three months old. What kind of man does that when you were trying to raise twins?"

"He's working for Jeffrey Livingston. He told me he'd use his employer's services if he had to."

"Jeffrey is an excellent attorney. That's not good. Why now? It's been years since Harris left."

Thirteen, long, difficult years. Sadie stopped at the edge of the woods. "I don't know. But I don't have a good feeling about it. Harris is a schemer. He says he's changed, but I don't think that's possible."

"You changed."

"Mom! How can you say that? I was never like Harris."

One of her perfectly shaped eyebrows rose. "You weren't? From my perspective, you were wild and loved going against your father and me. But I've forgiven you. Your father hasn't. You were his little girl. He hasn't been able to get over his disappointment."

Wild? Because she thought she loved a guy who her parents didn't approve of. They hadn't even given him a chance. She'd seen Harris struggle against people's perception of his father. Having a dad in prison had made it tough on him. She'd thought she could keep him on the right track. Everything was fine until she discovered she was pregnant and eighteen with a husband who didn't want children. Ever.

"Give your father time now that you're back in Summerton. Remember he's the one who suggested I speak with you about

Harris being in town. That's a start, hon." Her mom patted Sadie's arm as if she were a young girl again. "So what are you going to do about Harris?"

"I don't know. I guess I need to consult an attorney." Where she'd get the money was a whole other question.

"I would have said talk to Jeffrey Livingston, but since Harris works for him that's out. Too bad. He's a cutthroat."

"I know. The best in town."

"There's a new lawyer that moved to Summerton about six months ago. She brought her dog to the clinic a couple of times. I've heard good things about her."

"Who?"

"Colleen Stover."

"She goes to my church."

"Then you know her."

"No, but I'll make an appointment to see her."

Her mother's dark eyes brightened. "Maybe you can get a restraining order against Harris."

"I doubt it. He hasn't done anything wrong."

"Yet." Her mother crossed the backyard toward the patio. "Tell your kids today. Otherwise, they'll find out some other way, and that won't be good."

"I know. I will when you leave. Give Dad my love."

Her mom looked sideways at her, stopped, and embraced her. "Oh, baby, I'm sorry he's so stubborn." She stepped back and framed Sadie's face. "You're a good child, honey. He'll realize that sooner or later."

"When, Mom? I've been back for over a year." Her throat thickened, but she refused to shed any tears over what happened in the past. She'd spent too many nights crying herself to sleep. She wouldn't now.

"Dad invited Steven to go hunting in November. You know how particular he can be about who goes along with him on his 'yearly trek into the wilderness'."

"I never could understand a vet hunting deer. Just doesn't seem right."

"Your father is a man of contradictions." She kissed Sadie's cheek then strolled toward the side of the house. "Go tell Steven and Ashley. I'll call you later."

She waited until her mother disappeared from view then opened the back door and went into the kitchen.

Steven stood in the middle of the room with a glare on his face. "Tell me what?"

◦◦◦

Lexie clamped her hand over her mouth to keep her scream inside. She'd talked with Kelly twenty minutes ago. Her gaze panning the warehouse, she hastened to her friend and knelt behind her. With a quaking hand, she rolled her over, jostling her. When she did, Kelly's eyes popped open.

Lexie squealed. "I thought you were dead."

Tears crowded Kelly's gaze. "He's dead, I think." She struggled to sit up.

Lexie helped her friend. "Who?"

"Jared. I can't find him anywhere."

"That doesn't mean he's dead. Kelly, what happened last night? You're acting weird."

"Jared brought me to a party."

"Here in a warehouse?" Lexie's stomach churned, not like earlier but from all the nauseating smells bombarding her from every direction. "What kind of party?" Her gaze latched onto vomit a few yards away. She quickly averted her eyes before she tried to empty her already empty stomach.

Kelly dropped her head into her hands.

Silence reigned—except for the sound of dripping water somewhere at the other end of the warehouse. Plop. Plop. The noise nipped at Lexie's frayed nerves.

"Kelly, what have you done?" A chill sent goose bumps down her body. More than anything Lexie wanted to run.

Sobs shook Kelly's shoulders.

Lexie clasped her friend. "You're worrying me."

Kelly lifted her head, tears streaking down her pale face. "I only wanted him to like me."

"Jared? But he does. Didn't he tell you last week he loved you? Why did he leave you?"

"I told you. I think he's dead."

"Why do you think that?"

"I don't know." Kelly kneaded her fingers into her forehead. "Did I dream that? I can't remember." She slapped her head.

Lexie restrained her friend's hand. "Calm down. That won't help you remember."

"I've got to! I know it's important."

"You don't remember anything about last night? What did you drink? Take?"

"I don't know." Her high-pitched voice held a note of hysteria.

Scared at what her best friend was saying, Lexie reached for her cell phone in her pocket but remembered she didn't have it with her.

Kelly swiped at her tears, only to have more fall. "When I looked outside. I didn't see Jared's car. No one's."

She's only confused. Good. "That doesn't mean he's dead. You can call him when you get home and ask him what happened. Why he left you here. Come on. I'll help you up." Lexie scanned the dark shadows around her, her gaze coming to rest on the only bowl around. What had been in it? Chips? But there was no indication there had been dip to go with them. Then she noted the coolers with water in them. Must be where the beer had been. "This place is creepy and smells awful. Let's get out of here. Everything will be better once you're home."

Kelly went even paler. "Can you take me to your house? I'll call Mom and tell her I came to see how you were doing. I don't want to go home alone. I don't want her to see me like this. I need a shower. Maybe borrow some clothes to wear."

Lexie's stomach gurgled, reminding her of her sleepless night battling nausea. "Sure. Mom went to church. She shouldn't be home for another hour." Grunting, she tugged on Kelly's hand. She rose a few inches then sank down on the cement floor. Exhausted from being sick, Lexie wrapped her arms around Kelly, and with what strength she had, she dragged her to her feet. Between them, neither had much energy.

Finally standing, Kelly swayed into Lexie who went down on one knee. She put her hand out to steady herself and encountered a puddle. She sniffed and jerked back. *Urine.* Bile rose into her throat.

Lexie scrambled to her feet and pulled a wobbly Kelly toward the exit. At the door, she paused, steadying Kelly. A chill ran up and down Lexie's spine. She glanced over her shoulder and for a second wondered if they had been alone. She pushed Kelly through the threshold out into the bright daylight.

At her car, Lexie dug into her purse, produced some hand sanitizer, and coated her hands with it. Jared might not be dead, but something bad went down here last night.

⤷❦⤶

"You need to put a BOLO out on Lexie," Beth said the minute Ethan stepped into his sister's house. She held up a cell phone. "I found this under her bed covers. It's Lexie's. So we can't track her by her GPS."

"Calm down, Beth." Ethan moved her toward the living room while Cord shut the front door after he entered. "It's only been an hour or so. You're overreacting."

"How can you say that when . . ." Beth swallowed hard, "not after what happened to Emma?"

Ethan guided his sister to the couch and settled next to her. "Emma and Lexie are different."

Her eyes simmering, Beth looked at him then Cord. "Lexie is underage. I won't allow her to run away like Emma. I can't lose her, too."

"You didn't allow Emma to run away. She just did it without your okay." Ethan took her hand and waited until he had his sister's full attention. "You haven't lost Emma. You know where she is now and that she's doing okay."

"Only because you found her. What if Lexie has done the same thing as her big sister?"

"First, I'll say it again. Lexie is completely different from Emma. She's never given you a reason to be concerned. Second, you said Kelly is missing, too. They're probably together somewhere."

Beth glanced at Cord. "Do you think I'm overreacting?"

Cord's eyes softened as he took in Beth. "I can only tell you from experience that if you smother your child, they often rebel in ways you don't want. Remember what happened with Sadie."

"Everything turned out for your sister in the end."

Cord grasped the brim of his cowboy hat and moved it around in a circle over and over. "Sadie left with Harris Blackburn when she was seventeen, but they had to wait to marry until she turned eighteen a month later. She hadn't even graduated from high school. She was determined to prove to Mom and Dad she could be her own person. At the time, they didn't know she was pregnant, but if they had, it would only have driven her further away. They would have whisked her away so far from Harris and insisted she give the babies up for adoption. I'm sure that's why she did it."

Beth's gaze fastened on Cord's face. "But look at her now. Last year, she returned and is now teaching high school English. Lexie loves her as a teacher. She's learned so much."

Cord had insisted earlier that Ethan's sister was just a friend, but their body language—a blush on Beth's cheeks, a gleam in Cord's eyes—spoke of more. And Ethan had been oblivious to it while busy settling down in Summerton after being gone for seventeen years.

"It hasn't been easy without our family's support. Dad still hasn't accepted Sadie back into the family. Harris married her, then left her almost immediately. He didn't want children and having twins right off the bat sent him packing. Sadie struggled to finish high school and go to college while raising Steven and Ashley. I helped where I could. I even tried to talk her into coming home sooner. She wouldn't until last year. It's a delicate balance for a parent when a child becomes a teenager."

Beth frowned. "What you and Ethan are saying is that I'm not balancing it well. This from two men who aren't parents. I am not smothering Lexie. I learned with Emma."

With his forehead creased, Cord shook his head. "I didn't say that. You asked my opinion. I'll always give you the truth even if you don't want to hear it. Officially we can't do anything unless we suspect foul play. Is there anything pointing to that?"

Beth shot to her feet, her hands balled at her sides. "Officially. This from my brother and—a friend. I expected y'all to do more than that."

The conversation with his sister was going downhill fast, especially for Cord. Beth sent the man stabbing looks. Ethan tugged her back onto the couch and took both of her hands so she would shift toward him. "Beth, I'll go over and talk with Mary Lou after I take a look at Lexie's room, while Cord," Ethan glanced at his friend, "will quietly have his men look for Lexie's car. When they find it, they'll let you and me know rather than approach her. She'll never know. Okay?"

Beth released a long breath. "I guess so. I just can't shake this feeling something isn't right. I got this when Emma ran away, and I was correct then."

Ethan rose. "You'll know when we do. If she comes home, call me. I'm going to Mary Lou's. Remember, Lexie is a good kid. She's never given you a reason to worry."

"Sure and Sadie never did until she ran away with Harris." Her gaze on Cord, Beth didn't get up from the couch as Ethan and Cord made their way toward the foyer.

"I didn't score any points with your sister today," Cord murmured, plopping his hat on his head.

"Welcome to my world. Things have been a mess ever since Emma ran away two years ago. Now that Emma is an adult, there is little Beth can do about it. Emma doesn't want to have anything to do with Beth. Since Zed died in a factory accident, she's clung to her kids a little too much, and Emma was Daddy's little girl. She was devastated by Zed's death."

"Is this why we never married? Families are complicated." Cord reached for the door handle.

Ethan chuckled. "That's a nice way of putting it."

&

"Time for your meds, Lucy," Patti Shea said as she entered the patient's room at Greenbrier Nursing Home.

Lying in her bed, Lucy rolled her head toward Patti, the eighty year old's eyes trying to focus on her nurse. Lucy blinked several times. "Where have you been, Anna?"

She was used to Lucy calling her by her daughter's name. Patti smiled as she slipped the woman's hydrocodone into her pocket and replaced it with an over-the-counter pain reliever she dropped into the little paper cup. "Working, but I'm here now to give you your medication. Ready?"

"How's Wally?" Lucy struggled to get up.

Patti helped her. "Daddy is fine. He sends his love. He'll be here later."

When her patient sat up, Patti presented the paper cup. Lucy took it with a glass of water Patti handed her. "Did you swallow it?"

Lucy nodded. "You're a good daughter." She stroked Patti's arm.

Patti's cell phone vibrated in her pocket. "I need to go, Mama."

Lucy stared at her. "Who are you?"

"Patti, your nurse. Rest now," she said as she headed toward the hallway, removing her phone, noting the number and quickly answering the call from her husband.

"I found someone else who can buy some pills from you. He'll be a steady client."

"I don't know if I can do it. I'm taking what I can from the patients who don't know what day it is."

"Find others. You're creative. You can come up with ways. Remember the money you get helps with the bills we have to pay."

"Yes, I'll do what I can." Patti punched the off button. How could she forget the bills she was trying to pay off? She was drowning in debt and didn't know what else to do. With her husband out of work and unable to find a job, there was little recourse for her to get any extra money.

Patti went to the medicine cart and unlocked it to retrieve the next patient's medication. This one in the room next to Lucy's missed her pill yesterday. Could she risk two days in a row? Maybe she would try it and see what happened. Betty took only tranquilizers. She'd give her another herbal supplement. Then, if it worked, she could adjust her schedule of taking pills to two days off and one day with their real medicine. She had to do something. She needed the painkillers for herself, and the other medication helped pay the bills.

❦

Sadie stared at the open window over the sink then at Steven. How much did he overhear?

"Ashley," Steven yelled. "Come down here. Mom has to tell us something."

The whole neighborhood probably heard him. Sadie stalked to the sink and stood on tiptoes to close the window. She had a feeling this wouldn't be a pleasant little conversation with her thirteen-year-old twins.

When Ashley trudged into the kitchen, she reminded Sadie of herself at that age. Her daughter's long, white blond hair tumbled down her back in curls. She had the part near her face clipped back, emphasizing her large brown eyes, dark like hers whereas Steven had hazel eyes with curly, sandy-colored hair. A person could tell they were brother and sister, but not fraternal twins, and they worked hard at making it stay that way.

"Couldn't this wait until I finished studying for my algebra test for tomorrow? I don't understand why teachers have tests on Monday." Ashley leaned against the counter just inside the doorway.

"To ruin your weekend by making you study." Steven went to the fridge and got a Coke. "There's nothing in the house to snack on."

"I'm going to the grocery store tomorrow after school. If you'd ration the chips and protein bars through the week, this wouldn't be a problem."

"Mom, what do you need to tell us? Remember, algebra test."

"Let's sit at the table."

Ashley rolled her eyes. "Oh, no. It's one of those conversations where you talk, we listen."

"No. I have to tell you two something, and then you can ask questions." Sadie took her usual chair at the table and waited until they sat across from her. How did she start? Her kids had stopped asking about their father years ago probably because she made it clear the subject of him was off limits.

"This is about your father." Sadie inhaled a deep breath, her mind racing with possible ways to continue.

"What's there to talk about. Isn't he dead?" Steven asked.

Sadie dropped her gaze to a burnt spot in the tabletop where her daughter had placed a skillet without a hot pad down. When their father had never come around to see them like their friends whose parents were divorced, they started thinking he was dead. She'd never corrected them in that assumption.

"Not exactly." She peered first at Steven then Ashley. Confusion dominated their expression. "He divorced me when you two were babies and left. He didn't want to have anything to do with us. The last time I saw him was ten years ago when he came by for some money."

"The man who came to see you earlier?" Steven's quiet voice held too much control.

Sadie nodded.

Ashley looked at her brother. "You met our dad today?"

"I guess so, but she didn't say anything to me about it. How come, Mom?"

Both her children stared at her. Waiting for an answer she didn't really have. She'd never told them the reason Harris walked out on their marriage was because of them. She'd always let them think they had fought and he'd left. That had satisfied them when they were young. From their frowns, it wouldn't now.

"He took me by surprise. I didn't realize he was in town."

"More like speechless or you could have introduced us. It's obvious Grandma knew he was here. Who else? Everyone but your own children?" Steven sat back, his arms rigid at his sides, the biceps bunching as if he were clutching the seat.

"No. Grandma saw your dad today for the first time. She came over to tell me since she didn't think I was aware of it. I hadn't known until about an hour before she saw him." Sadie slid her gaze to Ashley who hadn't said much since Sadie had made the announcement. Her daughter sat with arms crossed over her chest, looking away.

"So what are we supposed to do? Welcome him with open arms?" Steven rose so quickly the chair fell backwards. He glanced at it, murmured, "Why didn't you tell us he was still alive and could do this?" then stormed from the kitchen.

Ashley remained, her shoulders hunched over, her head down.

"Ashley?"

She lifted her chin and pierced Sadie with a narrow-eyed look. "I've always told my friends my dad died. You knew that. Why didn't you stop me?"

Because it was easier to believe he was dead than alive and coming back into our lives. "I don't have a good answer other than I thought I would never see him again, so in a way, he was dead to us. I really didn't know otherwise." Which was a cop-out and Sadie knew it.

Ashley pushed to her feet, leaning into the table. "I want to meet him."

"No."

"Why not? He's my father. I think I have a right to finally meet my own dad."

Words tumbled through Sadie's mind, but nothing stayed long enough to form a coherent sentence. Her daughter glared at her for a long moment, then hurried from the kitchen. A minute later, she flinched at the sound of the front door slamming.

Today had started out as an ordinary one, but everything fell apart when she came home from church. Now she wished she'd taken the five thousand dollars from Harris so she could pay for an attorney. But there wasn't any way she would take his money. No telling where it came from—through legal or illegal means. During the nine months they had been married, he'd moved from one job to the next, never staying long, and when he did have money, it was often because of playing poker with his friends.

Please, Lord, let him move on. Get tired of playing the father role and leave Summerton. Finally, I was piecing my life together and now this. Why?

◈

As Lexie turned onto her street, Kelly grabbed her arm and said in a panic-filled voice, "Look. The police are there at your house!"

Kelly caused Lexie's arm to jerk to the right. She fought to keep her car going straight. "Kelly, let go." She stomped on the brake several houses from hers then twisted toward her friend. "We almost had a wreck."

"What's a cop doing at your house?"

Lexie checked out the two cars in front of her home. "The one in the driveway is Uncle Ethan's new SUV. The other is the police chief's. I can tell by the sticker on the bumper. Ethan and he are friends, and Cord has been dating Mom this past month."

"Why are they at your house? We can't go there." Kelly made a frantic gesture at her dirty, crumpled clothes that highlighted she'd slept in them on a concrete floor.

The scent emanating from Kelly reminded Lexie of a few unpleasant ones from the warehouse. "Yeah, I guess they might ask questions."

"You think? I know they would."

"Then where do you want to go?"

"Home. I'll sneak into my house. Mom's probably still sleeping. She always does on the weekend." Kelly's nose wrinkled. "I have to take a shower and get rid of this smell. It's making me sick to my stomach."

Instead of driving by her house, Lexie backed up into a neighbor's driveway and turned in the opposite direction.

"Listen, Lex. I don't want you to say anything to anyone about picking me up or about the warehouse. Promise me. Please."

Lexie chewed on her lower lip. She didn't keep secrets from her mother. Ever since Lexie's dad died three years ago, her family had fallen apart. When her older sister left after the holidays her senior year, Mom had been scared she would lose her, too. She'd cried all the time and even stopped going to work at Greenbrier. She'd taken a leave from work, and Lexie hadn't thought she would ever go back to the nursing home. Finally, she did, but it had taken a long time for her mother to begin to live again.

"I will if you'll promise me you won't do anything like last night again. You don't even remember what happened to you. That means one of two things. You drank too much, or you took something." *Or both.* As she recalled the bowl at the warehouse, Lexie wondered if pills had been in it. She'd heard about some kids at school going to pill parties. Did Kelly go last night? Lexie parked a few houses from Kelly's. "Are you sure you don't remember anything?"

"Just a few things—a big bowl on a crate. Someone gave me a beer. Jared on the floor by me."

"What was in the bowl?"

Kelly shrugged, sweat popping out on her forehead. "Don't know exactly."

"Were there pills in it?"

Kelly nodded.

"Who was there besides you and Jared?"

Kelly covered her eyes with her hand, slowly shaking her head. "Friends of his. It's all a blur."

"Are you gonna promise me you won't do this again? You know how dangerous this sounds."

"Yes. I don't think it makes any difference. Jared left me there. He must have decided to dump me."

"Good. You don't need someone who would leave you in a place like that. I won't say anything, but you should talk to someone about this."

"No way! And you better not either, or I'll never talk to you again. Remember you promised." Kelly shoved open the door and scrambled from the car.

Lexie watched Kelly sneak toward her house and go around to the back. They had been friends forever, but ever since Jared started paying attention to Kelly, she had changed. Maybe last night was a wake-up call. She prayed it was.

෫ඁ

Kelly sighed when she saw the closed blinds along the back of the house. Mom must still be asleep. Kelly hoisted herself into an elm tree that butted up against the back porch. After she crawled along a thick branch, she hopped to the roof and pulled herself up to the ledge near her window. Leaning over, she pushed it up and swung toward it, going headfirst into her room at the same time the doorbell rang.

Her right shoulder cushioned the impact with the floor, but one of her legs kicked out and struck the side of a small table. It teetered and crashed to the floor. The sound thundered through her head, aggravating the throbbing pain behind her eyes.

3

Sadie approached Ashley's favorite place in the woods behind their home, an abandoned tree house she and her brother had fixed up not long after they moved to Summerton. It was where they retreated when they were troubled or lonely, especially the first few months in town. "May I come up?"

"What's the difference? You will anyway." Ashley's voice sounded heavy with tears.

"I'll leave if you want."

A long silence met Sadie's statement. She turned to trek back to the house and wait for Ashley to return.

"Fine," Ashley said, barely audible.

Sadie climbed up the boards nailed to the oak tree until she reached the six-by-six platform about twenty feet off the ground. Settling next to Ashley, Sadie surveyed the forest from that vantage point. This was the first time she'd been up in the tree house. She hadn't wanted to invade their privacy until now.

"Ashley, I handled this all wrong."

"Why did you let us believe our dad was dead?"

"It was easier to let you think that than for you to think your father didn't want to have anything to do with you two. He left me when you all were born." Sadie looked at Ashley, but she couldn't see her daughter's face. Her long blond hair hung down, veiling her expression.

"He's been alive all these years," Ashley mumbled, her clasped hands twisting.

"When you were three and started to ask questions, he had come back to see me. Not because he wanted to be in your lives, but for money. Money I didn't have. I could barely feed and clothe you all. When he heard I couldn't help him, he left. I was so angry." She thought back to that time and felt all over again how devastated she was when he'd walked out a second time. Then the rage came. It consumed her, festering in her heart until she'd done something she shouldn't have. She'd let her kids think their father was dead. And now, she had to deal with the consequences.

Sadie placed her arm around her daughter, hoping she wouldn't reject the gesture. "At that moment, I gave up hope he would ever want to be in your lives, and I cut him from mine. As far as I was concerned, he was dead to me. I lied to you. I shouldn't have and regretted it afterwards, but I didn't know what to do so I let it stand. I truly never saw your dad coming back into our lives."

"But he has. What do I do?"

The hurt and pain in Ashley's question tore at the wall Sadie kept around her own feelings. If only she could redo her life. It would be different. She wouldn't have fallen in love with Harris. She wouldn't . . .

She wouldn't have her two children if she hadn't been with Harris. That thought sobered her. She loved them and couldn't imagine life without them. "Honey, you need to search your heart and make that decision. But I'll tell you this, I won't let your father come into our lives and disrupt them. He doesn't get to after thirteen years of silence."

"But he's my father. I've always wanted to know him. All my friends talk about their dads, and I've envied them." Ashley lifted her tear-filled eyes to her. "Don't get me wrong. I love you, Mom. I always will, but what if he's been missing us and wants to make it up to us? You've always taught us to forgive when we get mad at a friend. Isn't that what God wants us to do?"

But this is different, isn't it? Her daughter was always rooting for the underdog. Ashley had such a big heart. And now Sadie had to face Ashley and tell her she was wrong when she wasn't. That her dad was an exception to the forgiveness rule, when God didn't feel that way. She swallowed those words and instead wrapped both arms around Ashley.

"Steven's and your welfare will always come first with me. That's what a parent has to do." Even if she could bring herself to forgive Harris, she would *not* let his reentry into her children's lives harm them.

❧

Kelly's bedroom door flew open, and her mom stood in the entrance with the angriest look she'd ever seen on her Botox-treated face. Her mother's fists settled on her waist with her feet planted apart. Still not as clearheaded as she should be, Kelly struggled to stand, clasping the edge of the dresser nearby.

Her mother's mouth contorted into an expression that produced the wrinkles she'd constantly fought to keep at bay. "Where have you been? Out all night with that boy?"

The screech of her mom's voice pierced Kelly's fuzzy mind like a needle plunged in it over and over. "No."

All of a sudden, her mother stood in front of her, her face so close she could smell her morning breath. "Don't lie to me. You're still dressed in the clothes you wore last night and you stink." Her nose wrinkled.

"Right. I need a shower."

"You're just getting home from your—date." Her mom moved forward, crowding Kelly.

She stepped back until she bumped against her dresser. "I don't know where Jared is. I haven't seen him since last night."

"He'll use you until he gets what he wants, then drop you." Her mom snapped her fingers in Kelly's face. "He's just like his dad."

"I was with Lexie this morning. You can call her."

"Then why are you sneaking into the house?"

Kelly's mind went blank. She didn't have an answer for her mother.

"That's what I thought. You're lying. Right now you need to come downstairs and talk to Ethan Stone. He came to talk to you."

"To me? Why?"

"That's a good question. What have you done wrong that a Texas Ranger and the police chief would come to our house on a Sunday? If you bring shame . . ." Her mother's chest rose and fell as she drew in a deep breath. "When they leave, we'll continue this little chat. I won't have my daughter shame our family."

Kelly nearly laughed at that statement. Her mother did a great job of doing that. "I need to go to the bathroom. I'll be downstairs in a minute."

Her mother backed away, her gaze raking Kelly's length. "Change while you're at it. You look and smell like you've been on a bender."

You should know. Kelly bit her lower lip to keep those words inside. *Why couldn't I have a mother like Lexie's?*

When her mom left her bedroom, Kelly waited half a minute, her heart racing as though it were going to come out of her chest. As she made her way toward the bathroom down the hall, a change of clothing in her hand, everything around her felt surreal. Her heart continued to throb at a rapid rate.

Inside the bathroom, she locked the door then leaned against the counter, looking at herself in the mirror. Her mascara ran in dark rivulets down her cheeks as though she'd been crying black tears. Her long blond hair laid in a wild tangle about her face. She was glad Jared hadn't seen her like this. Maybe it was a good thing he left the warehouse.

A flash—blurred—flickered onto the screen of her mind. Jared sprawled on the warehouse floor. Still as death. She shuddered. No—a hallucination from the pills she took last night. She'd see him later today or tomorrow, and he'd have an explanation for why he left. Then everything would be like before.

She wiggled out of her jean skirt and dropped it to the floor. Two pills rolled out of a pocket. She bent and picked them up, no idea what kind of medicine they were. Maybe they would help her feel better, get through the meeting with the cops.

She stared at them in her palm, one white, the other pink. Then she remembered the bizarre night before. Before she changed her mind, she tossed them in the toilet and flushed it.

She'd promised Lex she wouldn't do anything stupid again—like last night.

Somehow, she would get through the interview on her own.

◁◞

Ethan walked into the foyer at Mary Lou's to answer his cell phone. "Have you heard from Lexie?" he asked his sister.

"Yes, she came home a few minutes ago. She'd thought going for a drive might help her feel better. She didn't leave a message because she knew she was going to be home before I returned from church. You were right. I overreacted."

The relief he heard in Beth's voice eased some of his tension. At least his family was all right. "Great. Kelly's back, too. Was she with Lexie?"

"She didn't say anything about Kelly. I'll ask her later. She went upstairs to lie down. The drive didn't do what she wanted. She looked even more exhausted and pale than when I left for church. Come by for dinner soon. My thanks for putting up with your hysterical sister."

"Sure. See you later."

When he hung up, he peered at the staircase and Kelly slowly descending, her hand gripping the banister. She looked like what Beth said about Lexie.

Ethan waited for her at the bottom of the steps. "Are you feeling okay?"

"I think I've picked up what Lexie has."

"You were with her this morning?"

"Yeah, trying to cheer her up."

As the teen walked past him, a strong flowery scent engulfed him. He almost choked on the fragrance she wore. Instead, he sneezed.

In the living room, Mary Lou frowned when her daughter entered. Kelly sat across from her mother while Cord occupied the other chair, leaving Ethan to stand or take the seat next to Mary Lou. He preferred mother and daughter beside each other, but now it was more a fact-finding mission, since technically no crime had been committed—until they heard back from the ME. He didn't have a good feeling about this, though.

"I have a few questions for you, Kelly." Ethan took out his pad. "Did you go out on a date with Jared Montgomery last night?"

"Yes."

"Did he bring you back home?"

Her eyes dilated, she nodded.

"What time?"

Kelly glanced at her mother. "I don't know exactly."

"Can you give me a guess?"

"Why? What's this about?" Kelly's brow creased.

"I'm trying to establish Jared's movements last night. What time do you think?"

"After midnight. Maybe one. I went up to my room and fell asleep."

"Were you two drinking?" As she'd come down the stairs, she'd seemed unsteady on her feet.

"No, I don't drink," Kelly answered too quickly. "I've seen what drinking can do to a person." As she lifted her shaky hand to her wet hair and flipped it behind her shoulder, she glanced toward her mother.

Mary Lou gasped and twisted toward her daughter.

Before Mary Lou opened her mouth to say something, Ethan asked, "Where was Jared going after he dropped you off?"

She shrugged and wiped her hand across her mouth. "I guess home."

"How did he seem to you?"

"Fine."

"Did you two have a fight?" Cord asked, swinging Kelly's attention toward him.

"No, he kissed me good night, and I came inside," she mumbled, her voice so low Ethan leaned forward to hear her.

"Did you see anyone else last night?" Cord continued the questioning, giving Ethan a chance to watch Kelly's micro expressions and mannerisms.

"No. We were alone." One of Kelly's eyes twitched.

"I thought you were going to a movie. What were you two doing alone? You'd better not have done anything to embarrass me." Mary Lou tilted up her chin and combed her fingers through her bottle-blonde hair.

"Kelly, where did you and Jared go?" Ethan cut in before Mary Lou made this conversation about her.

"Some place in Lone Star Park."

"Not Red River City Park?"

"No." The creases between Kelly's eyebrows deepened.

"What part of Lone Star Park? It's a big park."

Kelly looked left and up at the ceiling. "It was dark. I don't know exactly. What's this all about?"

Her body language shouted that she was hiding something. "Why did you go to Lone Star Park? It's closed after eleven."

"You're scaring me. Why all the questions?" Tears welled in Kelly's eyes. She lowered her head until he couldn't see her expression, her hands twisting in her lap. "Is Jared missing?"

Ethan sat on the edge of the couch. "Why do you say that?"

When Kelly reestablished eye contact, a look of fear dominated her face. "Because of your questions. If you need to know his whereabouts, ask him." She stared right at him. "I was with him a few hours last night. That's all."

"Jared was found dead in his car in Summerton Lake this morning by some hikers. That's on the other side of town from the Lone Star Park."

With each word he said, Kelly's pupils got bigger, and her face grew even paler. Her eyes fluttered. She swayed, then collapsed back on the couch. "He can't be. He was all right when I last saw him." Her thready voice wavered more with each word she spoke.

"When was that?"

She didn't say anything for a moment.

"When he brought you home?"

"Yes," Kelly said, jumping on that answer and lying. Sweat coated her forehead.

"Did he say he was going somewhere after he left you?" Ethan asked again, an interrogating technique to see if the answer would change.

"He didn't say. I didn't ask."

Kelly omitted saying Jared had gone home as she had before. Another hint she wasn't telling the truth.

Tears shone in her eyes. "He can't be dead. He . . ." She buried her head in her hands and sobbed.

Mary Lou hurried to Kelly and cradled her daughter against her. "She can't answer any more questions. She's distraught."

"I have one more question. Maybe you can answer it. Where was she this morning when you went to check on her?"

"With Lexie. Talk to your niece. They were together."

Ethan rose with Cord following suit. "I will." Then to Kelly he said, "If you remember anything about where Jared might have gone after dropping you off, please let me know. I'm leaving my card with my number on it."

❧

Sadie opened the door to Cord and went into his arms. "I'm glad you could come. I didn't know who to turn to."

"What's going on?" Cord moved into her house bumping the door closed with his foot. "I'm working a case, but you sounded upset on the phone."

She glanced over her shoulder then tugged him toward the living room. "Ashley went to a friend's house, but I don't want Steven to overhear." She lowered her voice. "Harris is back in town." She pictured her ex-husband with his good looks, a charming smile he used when he wanted something, and a heart of stone. She never wanted to see him again.

"When did he return?"

"Recently. He didn't tell me when. He did tell me he wanted to see his children after thirteen years. When I last saw him ten years ago, he still didn't want to have anything to do with them. He just wanted money."

"Is that what he's after?"

"I wish that were it. I could deal with that, especially since I don't have any. He wants to be part of Steven's and Ashley's lives now."

"Oh, great. Not a card from him in thirteen years, and he waltzes right in and wants to play daddy. Why?"

"I don't know, but it can't be for a good reason. He has an ulterior motive for everything he does. He's bad news, and I don't want my kids near him."

A tic jerked in the hard lines of Cord's jaw. "I'll ask around and find out where he's staying, then I'll pay him a friendly little visit and tell him he's not welcome in this town."

"That might not be as easy as you think. He's working for Jeffery Livingston."

"Bradley Montgomery's lawyer?"

"Exactly. If he's working for the Montgomery family . . ." Whether her brother liked it or not, they ran Summerton. If they wanted someone to stay in town, that person would stay.

"Listen, Sadie, I have something to tell you," Cord said, pulling her toward the couch. "You'd better sit." After she did, Cord stepped back. "I know you have Jared Montgomery in class and—"

Her cell phone rang. "Just a minute. It might be Ashley, wanting to come home." When she saw the number, she knew it wasn't her daughter. It was Maxwell Howard, the assistant principal at Summerton High School. "Hello."

"I'm calling all of Jared Montgomery's teachers first."

Sadie fixed her gaze on her brother hovering nearby while her hand tightened about the phone. "What's going on?"

"Jared Montgomery was found dead this morning. I received a call from his father. He knew it wouldn't be long before the rumors would be flying around town. We'll have a faculty meeting tomorrow before school to discuss how to handle this crisis. Be at the school an hour early."

Sadie listened to Maxwell's talk, but the words barely registered. *Jared's dead.* She'd never had one of her students die. "What happened to him?"

"Don't know the details. Bradley will let me know when he hears from the police."

"He wasn't found at home?"

Cord scowled.

"No, at Summerton Lake. That's all I know, and I don't want to be responsible for spreading unfounded rumors. Just as I know my staff doesn't."

"Yes, you're right." When Sadie hung up, she tossed her cell phone on a cushion. "That's what you were going to tell me. Jared was found dead this morning."

Cord nodded, the scowl deepening. "It hasn't been long, but I shouldn't be surprised. In a few hours, the whole town will know."

"I wouldn't even give it that long."

"Yeah. I need to get to the station. I'm sure I'll get all kinds of calls about it."

"What do you know?"

"Not much. Not even the cause of death at the moment."

"The scene wasn't clear?"

"Nope." Cord started for the front door, stopped, and turned back. "I'll pay Harris a call. I don't care who he works for. He needs to know to leave you alone. I wish I had done something about him fourteen years ago."

"There wouldn't have been much you could do. I thought I was in love." She rose. "How wrong I was. My kids weren't too happy to hear about their dad."

"Where have they thought he was all this time?"

"I let them believe he was dead."

Cord sucked in a deep breath.

"I know. I was wrong to do that, but it stopped them from asking a lot of questions I didn't want to answer."

"You married him. There had to be some good times."

"Don't remind me. I have to live with that mistake, but I don't want my kids to."

"They may have another idea about that. It'll be hard to keep them apart if they want to get to know him. I've seen him turn on the charm when he wants something." Cord strode into the foyer.

That's what I'm afraid of. Sadie heard the front door shut. She cherished the silence, knowing it wouldn't last. It didn't. A minute later, she received a call—the first in a string of them, all focused on the tragedy of losing such a wonderful young man.

As soon as Kelly hung up from talking with Lexie, her cell phone rang. Lying on her bed, she rolled over to face the ceiling while she answered. Kids had been calling and texting nonstop since this afternoon. "Hello."

"If you know what's good for you, you'll keep your mouth shut about last night," a male with a raspy voice, as if he were disguising it, spoke low into the phone.

"Who is this?"

"Not a word to anyone, or you'll pay for your sins." He clicked off.

Kelly stared at her cell to see the number the person called from. It was listed unknown. She quickly turned her phone off and put it in a drawer. His last sentence kept playing through her mind: Not a word to anyone, or you'll pay for your sins.

Kelly sat in the middle of her bed and wrapped her arms around her legs, hugging them close to her chest. Trembling started in her hands and quickly spread to her whole body.

What if he finds out I spoke to Lexie?

First thing Monday morning, Sadie filed into the auditorium with her friend and fellow English teacher, Robin David. "I'm not looking forward to this week. This is going to hit the students hard. Jared was so popular."

Robin leaned toward Sadie. "I've heard it could be murder. Jared? Can you believe that?"

"Murder? I thought it was accidental."

"Driving into Summerton Lake? Someone would have to do that on purpose. And he had so much going for him. I can't see suicide. Besides, I heard there wasn't a note."

Cynthia Proctor, the school nurse, came up on Sadie's other side. "I heard drugs were involved. That would be awful for the Montgomery family, big supporters of the school's anti-drug campaign."

Though her brother was the chief of police, Sadie felt out of the loop. "Where did you hear that, Cynthia?"

"Around. A parent called me first thing this morning and wanted to know what we're going to do about it."

"Are you going to do something about it?" Robin asked as she sat in a chair.

"I'm meeting with Maxwell after he talks to the faculty to discuss a plan of action before the whole crisis team gets together. We want to be ready for the students when we open the doors in an hour."

After most of the faculty was seated, except for a few stragglers, Maxwell Howard, also the head of the Crisis Team, stood at the front of the auditorium with the head principal next to him. "Everyone hurry in. This meeting won't take long. I'll give you the latest I've heard from Chief Thompson fifteen minutes ago. We need to stop the rumors from flying around."

The audience quieted while the principal said a prayer for the Montgomery family and Jared's friends, then he turned the meeting over to Maxwell.

"The findings of the autopsy haven't been released yet, but will be in the next day or two. So at the moment nothing has been ruled out. However, the police don't feel it's a suicide."

Sadie heaved a sigh while others whispered to the person next to them. Then she thought if it wasn't suicide, which probably meant it was murder. A chill flashed through her body.

"Please encourage any student needing to see a counselor to come to the office," Maxwell continued, bolstering the volume of his voice over the murmurs. "We'll have extra crisis counselors here for the next few days to talk with anyone who needs to. Try to keep your routine the same as much as you can. All teachers need to be in the halls between classes. If you see a student breaking down, escort him to the office where he can get help. The funeral will be Wednesday afternoon at three. We'll end school a little early that day to accommodate the students and staff who want to go to the funeral. Any questions?"

A teacher in front raised her hand. While she asked about what the school could do for the family, Robin whispered, "You know it most likely means murder, because as I said, I can't see Jared driving himself accidentally into the lake. The parking lot and boating ramp are separated."

Cynthia bent forward. "We can't let the students hear us speculating about Jared's death. Let's wait until the autopsy is released to the public before saying what it is."

At the end of the meeting, Maxwell finished with, "Texas Ranger Stone will be here to interview various members of the staff. If Jared's teachers would stay behind, he'll see you all first."

Robin stood. "I get to escape. See you later, Sadie."

As her friend hurried toward the exit, Sadie caught sight of Ethan Stone coming into the auditorium. His long strides and confident bearing gave the impression of a take-charge kind of man. From what Cord had said about Ethan, that was exactly what he'd done. He'd developed quite a reputation in the San Antonio area. Watching him highlighted all the reasons she used to have a crush on him as a teen. Commanding. Calm in the midst of chaos. Dedicated to what he did.

For a second, her heart fluttered. Then she remembered Harris and all feelings shut down.

Ethan strode toward the front of the auditorium, threading his way through the exiting crowd. He spied Sadie Thompson in the seven people remaining. Since he'd been home, he'd seen Cord's little sister a few times from a distance. She'd grown up nicely. He could remember when she used to bug him and Cord, following them around, trying to find out what they were doing so she could tattle on Cord. He smiled at the thought and faced Jared's teachers and the football coach.

"I'll be interviewing each of you today. I would like you all to think about Jared's friends, have you ever suspected drug or alcohol use with Jared, and has he had a problem with anyone?"

"Then this is murder?" Sadie asked, remembering what Robin had said to her during the short faculty meeting.

"I haven't said it is, and I don't want you to leave thinking it has been ruled a murder. We don't have the autopsy yet. We need to know what Jared was doing the last hours of his life. That will help us."

The football coach shot to his feet. "Jared was a leader. He wouldn't use drugs. Football was everything to him. He knew if I discovered it, he would have been out the door."

Ethan came around the front of the podium, resting his elbow on its top. "The question still has to be asked, or I wouldn't be doing my job. Think back to last week with any of your interactions with Jared. Maybe you overheard him say something to someone who could help us reconstruct his whereabouts Saturday night."

"Talk to his girlfriend. She should know. When I saw them in the hall on Friday, they were tight. I mean I had to break them apart and tell them to move on," a lady he didn't know said from the first row.

"I'm aware of his girlfriend and have already spoken to Kelly Winston. Also, as you listen to the students talk over the next week or so, if you hear anything you think would help, please contact me. When I meet with you, I'll give you my card with my cell phone number. The Montgomery family is devastated and wants answers to what happened to Jared. Thank you for staying. I know how hard today will be."

As everyone rose, Ethan approached Sadie. "I understand you have first hour planning period."

She paused at the end of the row, stepped out of the way for the football coach to get around her, then said, "Yes. Where do you want to talk?"

"Mr. Howard gave me an office to use. I want to find out all I can about Jared. Was he involved in something that got him killed?"

"You think he was murdered?"

"He's dead, and most likely he didn't accidentally end up in Summerton Lake, plus everyone says Jared had no reason to kill himself." Ethan studied Cord's little sister with her platinum blond hair pulled back in a ponytail, her warm brown eyes full of concern and her full lips set in a straight line—not a smile or a frown. "The few kids I've talked with haven't been as forthcoming as they could be. It wasn't that long ago I went to this high school. I haven't forgotten what it's like to be a teenager." He started toward the exit with Sadie next to him. "Cord said you have twins—a boy and a girl, thirteen."

"Yes. They're beginning the challenging years."

"That's one way to put it." "The Eyes of Texas" sounded, and he unclipped his cell phone from his belt. "It's the office next to Mr. Howard's." He noticed the number was Cord's. "I've got to take this, so I'll be along in a minute."

As Sadie left, he answered, "Has the autopsy come back?"

"No, hi, good morning?" Cord asked on the other end of the phone.

"I think we're past that. Has it?"

"Yes, and it's not good."

4

$\mathcal{H}$e was murdered?" Ethan clamped his fingers so tightly about his cell his hand ached.

"The evidence isn't conclusive, but he wasn't dead when he hit the water. Drowning is the cause of death. The ME says the abrasions on his body indicate he tried to get out but couldn't. The seatbelt was jammed and wouldn't open. I'm having a mechanic we trust and use all the time look at it and tell me what happened."

"Had he been drinking or using drugs?" Ethan glanced around to make sure no one else was in the auditorium.

"The tox screen will be back later. That'll give us a better picture of what went down. But I'm leaning toward murder."

"I agree. This is going to cause far reaching ripples."

"Where are you?"

"The high school auditorium. I'm going to interview his teachers today and other staff members who had contact with Jared." Ethan began to walk toward the double doors at the back. "I'm talking with Sadie first, then I'll go see Bradley about the autopsy. Let me know when the tox screen comes back. I'll try to wait for that and work my interviews here around informing Bradley. He needs to know right away."

"Has it only been twenty-four hours since Jared was discovered? Seems longer. When you finish at the school, come by the station."

"Will do." Ethan started to hang up when Cord stopped him.

"Be gentle with my sister. Her ex has shown up in town and is giving her a hard time. After thirteen years of absence, he finally decided he wants to get to know his kids."

"I was thinking of giving her the third degree for the times she spied on us as kids," Ethan said in a mockingly serious voice.

Cord laughed. "She *was* a nuisance. I'd forgotten about that."

He hadn't. He remembered a cute girl with pigtails and freckles who made life difficult for Cord and him. A chuckle bubbled to the surface and escaped as Ethan pushed the door to the hallway open.

Teenagers poured into the building from each end of the corridor. Instead of the noise level rising, it was subdued. Too quiet. Glimpses of the kids' faces showed sadness and disbelief. The ones talking did so in whispers. Two girls hugged each other and burst out crying.

Sadie hurried to the pair and ushered them toward the counseling office around the corner. He waited by the auditorium for her and studied the students as they filed by him, some scrutinizing him as they passed. Groups of teens headed straight for the counseling office. Another teacher escorted four students past him, two openly weeping while the others' eyes shone with unshed tears.

Sadie came back in the hallway, and he strode toward her. "Ready?"

She looked around at the scene in the commons. "As much as I can be. It's going to be a long day. A long week. Jared was well-liked, and these students don't understand how he was fine one day and gone the next. It makes them realize they aren't immortal."

But was Jared *really* well-liked? Did someone kill him? Or help it along somehow? Ethan pointed toward the office he'd been assigned. "I won't keep you long. I can see you'll be needed out here."

She smiled, a light in her eyes completely wiped the picture of a cute little girl from his mind. Sadie Thompson was a grown woman who dealt with serious issues, especially if Harris Blackburn returned to town. He was a people user—taking what he could from a person, especially emotionally. He'd been a few years younger than Ethan, but he'd seen how the guy had operated in high school. When he'd heard from Cord that Sadie ran off with Harris, he'd prayed things would work out for her, but in his heart he'd known they wouldn't.

In the office, Ethan waited until Sadie took a chair then he sat across from her. "I noticed Jared's grades last year were good, but how was he doing so far this year?"

"Without looking at my grade book, I can't say exactly, but he did what was expected of him—barely. I had him right before football. Maybe his mind wasn't on English."

"Was he in jeopardy of not being able to play?"

"No, but I know he has—had a lot of potential, but I didn't see him working as hard as he's capable of this year. I even talked with some of his other teachers recently about it, and they said the same thing."

"Could it be because he was having problems with someone?"

"Like girlfriend problems?"

"That or with someone else."

"He was usually surrounded by a ton of kids, vying for his attention. I've seen him and Kelly in the hall, and it appeared he was really into her and she was into him. What did she say?"

"Do you have her in class?"

She smiled. "When Cord doesn't want to answer a question, he throws out another question. I get it. This is an investigation, and I'm not part of the team." A twinkle glinted in her eyes. "No, Kelly isn't in any of my classes. I do have your niece, though. She and Kelly are really good friends."

"I've talked with Lexie."

"And you won't tell me what she said," she murmured with a laugh.

"I always knew you were sharp."

She leaned forward. "Then can I tell you something that has been bothering me?"

The space shrank between them. He noticed she only had a few freckles now on her nose. "Anytime."

"This may not have anything to do with your case, but last Friday as class was dismissed for the day, Luke Adams passed Jared a note as Luke walked by his desk. Jared read the paper, balled it up, and threw it away. When the room was cleared, I picked it up."

"Why?"

Deep lines grooved her forehead. "I can't honestly say. Maybe a look that passed over Jared's face—relief."

"What did the note say?"

"She's been approved. Bring her."

"Nothing else?"

"No."

"Who do you think Luke was talking about? Kelly?"

"Probably, but it's a guess. And before you ask, I have no idea what the female was approved for. But the note bothered me. Since I heard he died, I've been wondering if there's a connection."

"Do you still have the note?"

"Yes, upstairs."

"Good. If you can get it for me by the end of the day, I'd appreciate it." He rose, allowing himself to relax completely for a few seconds while he shook her hand, the feel of hers, warm and soft. His pulse quickened. "If you hear anything else strange, please let me know even if you don't think it's important. I could use someone here informing me about what's going on. What are the kids talking about? I can remember rumors flying around school when I was here. The thing is, some of them were true."

"It hasn't changed."

"It does seem strange that Luke wrote him a note and didn't text Jared instead."

"Not really. First, if I hadn't been looking at them the second he gave Jared the note, I wouldn't have seen it. Fast and sly. Second, the administration banned cell phones during school hours, and I know the football staff doesn't want them anywhere near the locker room. Coach wants his players' undivided attention." Sadie placed her hand on the doorknob. "I figure you're going to the funeral Wednesday."

"Yes, I'll see you there."

Ethan followed Sadie out into the corridor. He watched her walk away, speaking to some of the students congregated in small groups.

He saw his niece nod at Sadie, then head toward the counseling office, Lexie's eyes red, her mascara running down her face. He took a step toward her, but she'd already disappeared inside, the place crammed with kids. He'd check with Lexie later, but right now, she would get some of the help she needed for her grief. He wasn't too good dealing with feelings like that.

He checked his watch and let the secretary in the principal's office know he was leaving for an hour and would be back to talk to the next teacher. Then he drove toward Bradley's home. Halfway there, he received a call from Cord.

"What did the tox screen say?" Ethan asked, pulling over to the side of the highway so he could jot down any notes he needed.

"Not good. Jared was full of a mixture of prescription drugs." Cord rattled out the names of a painkiller, a sleeping pill, a high blood pressure med, and a tranquilizer. "The ME said no doctor should prescribe that mix of drugs. A lethal combination, especially when combined with alcohol."

"So he was drinking, too?"

"Yes."

"Could some or all of those drugs be in his drink?"

"I suppose they could, but not likely. I would say he knowingly took some of them. The amount he took was more than the usual for the tranquilizer and blood pressure."

"But he was alive when he hit the water, so they didn't really kill him. He died from drowning."

"He'd be out cold with that mix—not able to drive."

"Thanks. Now I get to tell Bradley what killed his son. He's going to want to know who killed his son because that's where the evidence is pointing. Murder." Ethan finished writing the list of drugs on his pad, then started the engine, and pulled out into the light traffic.

"I'd help you, but I'm going back to where Jared was found. I'm going to have some of the officers scour the area for anything unusual."

"Like?"

"Maybe some kids drinking and partying at the park. If that's the case, they might have left some evidence behind, and it might mean it was an accident if he was trying to go home from the park and got turned around with his senses so impaired. I'll have one of my guys check some of the traffic cameras around the park, but some of the ways into it aren't covered by any."

"I hope that's the case rather than someone murdering him. I wish it were an accident, but my gut says it isn't. I'll talk to you later."

As he turned into the Montgomery ranch, his hands clutched the steering wheel tighter. He let out a long sigh. *Lord, give me the right words to tell Bradley these most recent findings concerning Jared. Losing a child has to be the worst nightmare for a parent, but then to find he could have been murdered just adds to the anguish.*

Ethan tried to put himself in Bradley's shoes but couldn't. He'd withdrawn from close relationships because of all the evil he'd seen in his work, which left him feeling vulnerable. Protecting himself from feeling was about the only way he knew to keep working and functioning as a law enforcement officer.

A few minutes later, Ethan entered Bradley's home office. His friend stood at the window overlooking a pasture with horses, his hands stuffed into his jean pockets. Even when Ethan shut the door, Bradley remained staring out the window.

Ethan cleared his throat. "Bradley?"

When he rotated toward Ethan, Bradley looked like a man who hadn't slept since he found out his only child had died. "I was just wondering why this was happening . . ." Closing his eyes, he shook his head. When his gaze reconnected with Ethan's, a haunted look dulled his eyes even more. "Never mind. Wondering doesn't change what has happened."

"I wanted to let you know what we have discovered so far. I told you I would keep you informed. I know how important that can be to a loved one."

Bradley gestured toward some chairs nearby then sat in one. "I appreciate it."

Ethan took the seat across from his friend, dreading the next few minutes. "Jared's tox screen indicated he had a combination of drugs in his system--a painkiller, blood pressure pills, tranquilizers, and a sleeping pill. The amounts in his system indicated more than one blood pressure pill and tranquilizer."

Bradley paled. "Was he drinking?"

"Yes. He would have been out cold with what he took." *And without medical intervention, he probably would have died.*

"Was there evidence in his car he'd been drinking and taking pills in it?"

"No."

"Then how did he get to the park if what he took would have put him out?"

"With help." Ethan hated this part of his job. He took a deep breath and continued. "He wasn't dead when he went into the water. The cause of death is drowning. From his abrasions, it appears he tried to get out of his seatbelt, but it was stuck."

Bradley's eyes glistened. He buried his face in his trembling hands. Finally he shot to his feet and returned to the window, his back to Ethan. "Then it was murder?" His voice cracked, and he leaned against the sill.

"The evidence is pointing to murder. We're having a mechanic look at the seatbelt to find out why it didn't unbuckle."

Bradley hung his head, raking his fingers through his hair. When he pivoted toward Ethan, a sheen in his eyes, Bradley dropped his arms to his sides, his hands still shaking. "I want this person found. I'll offer whatever reward I need to for information leading to an arrest."

⤳✤⤳

Mrs. Adams let Ethan into her house late Monday afternoon. "Luke is upstairs."

"He wasn't at school today. Is he all right?"

Mrs. Adams forehead wrinkled. "All right? One of his best friends died. He's been too upset to go to school. What's this visit about?"

"I need to talk with him. We can do it here or down at the station."

Her eyes grew big. "Does he need a lawyer?"

Interesting question. "Only if he's done something wrong. I'm talking with all of Jared's friends to track his whereabouts before he died. This is not unusual in this type of death."

"What type? I've heard all kinds of rumors."

"Murder." After the police searched the park and viewed the cameras in the area, he and Cord decided they had to treat Jared's death as a murder.

"Were drugs involved?" She folded her arms against her chest and backed away from the front door to allow him inside.

"Why would you ask that?"

Her body went rigid. "Rumors. I heard one of the parents at the country club say there was talk about drugs and drinking. Luke assures me nothing like that was going on."

I'm sure he did. What kid wouldn't? When he'd talked to Bradley this morning he'd asked him to keep the findings quiet until the police released the information. Nothing had been said yet officially, although he knew Cord was going to some time Tuesday morning when all the forensic reports were in. "Who told you that at the country club?"

"Mrs. Livingston. She heard from her husband who talked with Bradley, so it's really more than a rumor." Her eyebrows dipped down. "Besides, if a weapon had been used, it would have been obvious from the beginning. You wouldn't have had to wait on the autopsy to declare it was a murder."

"I can't comment at this time since it's an ongoing investigation." He'd much rather confirm it was murder when Luke was in the room and see his reaction. "May I talk with your son now? You may stay, since he isn't eighteen yet."

"Please go in there while I get him." Mrs. Adams waved her hand toward the left.

When Ethan moved into the living room, the first thing he noticed was a picture of the football team. Kneeling in the middle of the front row was Jared with Luke next to him. According to Bradley, Luke was Jared's best friend. Jared had been the quarterback on the football team while Luke was the wide receiver. They had been a good pair, leading the Eagles to a winning season last year and were four-zero so far this one.

Luke, his face pale, slinked into the room with his mother following him. The unkempt look to his hair coupled with his haggard expression spoke of the depth of the friendship he must have had with Jared. He stood at the end of the couch.

"Have a seat. I've got a few questions about Jared." Ethan waited to sit until Luke and his mother had. "What happened to Jared is a tragedy. This town will miss him." He studied the effect his words had on the teen.

Luke looked down, clenching his hands into fists. When he finally raised his head, his eyes glistened. "He was the best friend a guy could have." His voice, raw and raspy, sounded barely above a whisper.

That was the way Cord and he had been in high school. It was hard for him to imagine losing a close friend like that. "I heard you gave him a note Friday about someone being approved and to bring her. Who were you talking about? Where was Jared supposed to bring her?"

Luke dropped his gaze again, his hands opening and closing at his sides. "I don't know what you mean," he said, with manufactured confusion on his face when he reestablished eye contact.

"Someone saw you give the note to Jared who read it and threw it away."

"Who?"

"Not important."

"Someone put it on my desk. I saw it was for Jared and gave it to him."

"How did you know it was for Jared?"

Luke shrugged, rubbing his nose. "His name was on the front of the note."

"Who put it on your desk?"

Luke ran his palm down his jaw. "Don't know. I was gathering my books, and when I turned to leave, I saw it there."

He was lying. Written on his face and in his gestures. Ethan straightened. "Who sat in front of you?"

"Don't remember. We don't have assigned seats so it's different each day."

In Ethan's experience, most people gravitate to the same seat each day. It was certainly the case at the church he attended. So why was Luke continuing to lie? "Okay. So what do you think the note meant to Jared?"

Luke snapped his fingers. "I bet it was about his new hunting dog, Candy."

"Why do you say that?"

"When hunting season opens, there's a group of us . . ." Luke swallowed hard, balled his hands, and continued in a stronger voice. "We're going hunting. A new dog could mess up the dynamics of a group."

"Who else in your fifth-hour class is in the group?"

"Brendan Livingston and Kalvin Majors."

"Thanks. I don't have anything to write that down on. Could you get a piece of paper and write their names down for me?"

"Sure," Luke said, drawing the word out, then rose and went to a desk at the other end of the large formal living room.

"What does hunting have to do with Jared's death?" Mrs. Adams asked, watching her son as he came back and gave the sheet to Ethan.

"Yeah, the season doesn't open for a couple of weeks yet." Luke remained standing.

"Just tracing Jared's steps through Friday and Saturday, looking into everything." Ethan fixed his gaze on Luke. "Tell me about Jared and Kelly."

"You need to ask Kelly about that."

"But you two were best friends. He never talked about her?"

"Sure. He liked her. She's hot."

"Nothing else?"

Luke shook his head, his jaw clamped in a tight line.

"I find even the little things can be important. Thank you for your help." Ethan rose. "I'm sure I'll see you at the funeral." He started to leave, stopped, and swiveled around. "Oh, I almost forgot. When I saw the note you gave Jared, I didn't see his name on the outside of it."

Luke's face blanched.

"So did you give it to him because it was from you or someone else you're protecting?"

Mrs. Adams stood, rigid. "This conversation is over. Luke may be a little confused because of all that has happened. Quit harassing him. The next time we talk it will be with our lawyer in attendance."

"You can bet we'll talk again. Someone murdered Jared, and I intend to find out who." Ethan studied Luke as he said that last sentence. Surprise flashed into his eyes, his mouth dropping open. "He was alive when his Porsche hit the water. Someone jammed his seatbelt so he couldn't get out of the car."

Quickly, Luke snapped his jaws closed, and fear invaded his expression. He lowered his head, hiding his face from Ethan.

As he left the house, he examined the names on the paper. Luke's handwriting appeared to be the same as on the note to Jared that Sadie had given Ethan, but he would have an expert look at it to make sure. So why did Luke lie to him, and was the female referred to in the note Kelly? Why the fear—because he killed his friend or because he knew something?

When Ethan pulled up to the curb in front of Kelly's house, he studied it for a long moment. She was the key to this. He would keep talking to her until she admitted what she and Jared had really done Saturday night. With long strides, he hastened to the front porch and rang the bell. After a minute, he pressed it again. Five minutes later, after peering into a couple of the windows, he returned to his car to wait until someone came home.

An hour later, Mary Lou drove into her driveway and parked at the side of the house. Ethan hurried toward her. She climbed from her car and stared at him as he cut the distance between them.

"I need to speak to Kelly."

"Why? She doesn't have anything else to tell you. She has told you that she went to Lone Star Park with Jared. That she didn't know where he was going after he dropped her at home not long after midnight."

"I showed Kelly and Jared's photos to the people who run the rides and the food vendors. No one saw them there."

Mary Lou planted her hand on her waist. "I work at Greenbrier. Visitors come and go there, and I don't remember everyone I see. That isn't that unusual."

"No, especially if they never went." Cord and he had checked the area around the amusement park where people picnicked, walked, and rode bikes. That part closed at nine while the ride section stays open to eleven. "Lone Star Park shuts down completely at eleven. What did they do for over an hour after that?"

Mary Lou howled with laughter. "Are you that old you can't figure it out? Lone Star has some great places to go—and make out. Kelly is gorgeous and any guy would be lucky to have her as a girl-friend. You just wait. She'll find someone even better than Jared."

"What happened to you, Mary Lou?"

"Life. My husband two-timed me then walked out. Of course, that was after Bradley dumped me. Not good enough for him." She thrust back her shoulders to emphasize her attributes. "I was at one time."

"I'm surprised you let Kelly date Jared after how Bradley dropped you our senior year."

"I was rooting for my little girl. I saw how Jared looked at her when he was with her. He worshiped her. I wanted her to have what I didn't." She lifted her shoulder. "Oh, well, there'll be someone richer and more handsome for my Kelly. You just wait."

"I need to see Kelly now."

"Fine. But there isn't anything else she can tell you. You're wasting your time." Mary Lou stuck her key in the lock and opened the door. "Come in. Make yourself at home. I'll go get her. There's something to drink on the bar. It's five. Fix yourself something."

"That's okay." After he worked so many accidents as a Highway Patrol Officer where alcohol was involved, he'd lost all desire to drink.

While he waited, he examined the much smaller living room than the Adams's, remembering when Mary Lou hadn't been so hard—and unhappy. He'd seen that tigress in her eyes as she checked him out.

Finally, ten minutes later, Mary Lou returned with a quizzical expression on her face. "She isn't here. I told her to get out of the house. Staying in her room all the time wasn't good for her. I guess for once she listened to me. But I called her half an hour ago, and she was here. You just missed her."

"I've been sitting out in front of your house for an hour. Are you sure she was here?"

Her eyebrows scrunched together. "Yes. Maybe she's in the backyard." She headed for the kitchen.

Ethan followed.

After they searched the outside and the downstairs, Mary Lou stood in the foyer. "She hasn't wanted to see anyone, not me or Lexie. Maybe after the funeral, she'll be ready to face the fact Jared is dead. The funeral ought to give her some closure."

As he left, he wondered if Kelly was hiding somewhere in her house and Mary Lou knew, or if her daughter had snuck out when he came. Either way, he wanted to know why the teen didn't want to talk with him. Could she have murdered Jared because he was going to reject her like his father had her mother?

～❧～

With her nerves stretched taut, Kelly squatted behind some bushes in her neighbor's yard and watched Lexie's uncle leave her house. Even when he drove away, she stayed hidden, afraid he would come right back and catch her.

She didn't have anything to do with what happened to Jared, and yet guilt swamped her. She didn't even know what really happened.

Because I was out cold. Blissfully ignorant of what was going on around me.

She wanted that now.

Her mom had some sleeping pills. She'd take a couple so she could at least get a good night's rest before going to school tomorrow—and the funeral the following day. How was she going to get through that? She stared down at her hands, shaking like a leaf in a tornado. Clasping them together, she squeezed tight to stop the trembling. Instead, the rumbling swept through her body.

Maybe Carrie or Missy had something to help her get through the funeral. She had to go. Her mom was making her go to school tomorrow, too.

And see everyone—Lexie. No more hiding.

5

$\mathcal{A}$t the end of the day, exhausted physically and mentally from working the Montgomery case, Ethan left the police station after talking with Cord about their next move. They had found nothing at Red River City Park, but Jared's seatbelt was deliberately jammed with a strong glue so he couldn't release it. Tuesday they needed to find the primary scene where Jared drank and took the prescription drugs. No sign of drugs or alcohol in the Porsche. If not at the park, then who brought him there and rigged the seatbelt to keep it from opening, before pushing the car into the water?

As he slipped into his SUV, he saw a text from his mother on his cell. *Don't forget your visit with Nana at Greenbrier.*

Fifteen minutes later, he entered the nursing home and waved to an older gentleman who always sat on the couch in the area near the door, dressed as though someone was going to pick him up to go to a fancy restaurant.

"Are you here for me?" the man asked Ethan every time he passed him on his way to his grandmother's room at the end of the first hall.

"No, Mr. Nelson. How are you doing today?"

"Fair to middling. Do you know when they will come for me?"

"Hopefully soon."

"Oh, all right." Then Mr. Nelson turned and stared at the front door.

The first time it happened and he found Mr. Nelson still sitting in the same place when he left, he asked one of the staff about him. The man's family was all gone. At ninety, he'd outlived all his children, and the grandchildren weren't in Summerton. After that, he made a point of talking with the man when he could.

When Ethan entered his grandmother's room, she was up and roaming about, twisting her hands together. He looked at his mother and said in a low voice, "What's going on?"

"Lucy, the lady next door has been groaning and crying out since I first came in. These walls are so thin it's like we're in the same room. Thankfully, they gave her some pain meds, and she has settled down, but Mom is agitated. I can't seem to calm her down. The nurse is bringing her a tranquilizer. Normally she's calm, but when I came, she was upset even before the lady started screaming. I'm going to talk to the doctor. I don't think what she's taking is working like it used to. I'm also going to talk with Beth and make sure she visits Mom more often, especially since she works here."

Ethan knew medication was needed for certain patients, but after hearing about all the meds Jared had taken, he thought about how easy it was to get prescription drugs. In San Antonio, he'd arrested a man who had gone from one doctor to another to get the painkillers he became addicted to after he'd had knee surgery. Finally, he had resorted to stealing to keep himself supplied with his medication.

"What's wrong with the lady next door?"

"The poor dear is in the end stage of cancer." His mother glanced toward the door, then back to Nana. "See if you can get her to lie down. With her osteoporosis, she needs to be careful walking. She won't listen to me."

After removing his cowboy hat and putting it on a table, Ethan approached his grandmother. He smiled, although the sight of the woman he'd known all his life, hunched over, her once sparkling brown eyes dull with lack of recognition, broke his heart. "Hi, Nana. How have you been?" He put his arm around her frail body to give her support.

She tilted her head toward him. Her gaze narrowed. "Who are—" A light dawned in her eyes. "Oh, my, you've finally come, Walt. I've been waiting for you. Did you ask Father for my hand?"

"Yes, and he was happy to give us his blessing to get married. Let's sit and talk about our future." This wasn't the first time his grandmother had mistaken him for her deceased husband. When he saw a picture of his grandfather, he could understand why she did. He looked a lot like him.

After he guided her to a small couch, he took the seat next to her, holding her hand. "You look lovely as usual."

She gripped him with strength that surprised him and leaned close, her gaze clear and direct. "Something is wrong here."

He stiffened at the urgency in her voice. "What do you mean?"

She blinked. "Mean what, Walt? What are you talking about?"

He relaxed as his grandmother did, squashing his first instinct to think something bad and instead enjoyed Nana's company. "Oh, nothing. Tell me what you did today."

When she launched into a description of a day she would have had as a young girl, a prickling at his nape persisted. One of the reasons he'd come back to Summerton when an opening occurred was because he was getting so cynical and mistrusting in San Antonio. He needed his family and old friends around him to remind him not all people were bad. As he peered at the trusting look on his grandmother's face, he remembered all the wonderful times he had at her house as a kid. He needed that reminder, especially after the past couple of days.

Tuesday outside in the courtyard area at school, Lexie found Kelly eating by herself. "I've been looking for you. What's up? We always eat lunch together. I tried calling you the last few days, especially when you didn't come to school yesterday. I must have left a dozen voicemails and texts. I know you're upset about Jared. I am, too."

"Shh." Kelly tugged her down next to her on the grass. "Don't say anything about him or what happened on the weekend."

"My uncle came to talk to me Sunday night about being with you that morning. He came back last night to have dinner with us, and he kept asking about you."

"What did you say to him?"

"Nothing other than we were together on Sunday."

"Good." Kelly tossed most of her sandwich into a sack and scrunched it up into a tight ball.

"I promised you I wouldn't, but Kelly that was before I knew Jared was dead. Murdered! What happened Saturday night? I heard he died from drowning in the lake, trapped in his car, the seatbelt jammed. I've heard nothing else, and I haven't been able to talk to you. Do you know what happened?"

Kelly shoved to her feet. "If you're my friend, you won't say a word."

Rising, Lexie grabbed Kelly's arm before she walked off. "We need to talk about this."

Kelly glanced around. "Not here. We'll meet later."

"When?"

"I'll call you."

"Promise? I'm going to have to talk to Uncle Ethan."

Kelly jerked free of Lexie's clasp and thrust her face into Lexie's. "Don't you dare!" Kelly stabbed her forefinger into Lexie's chest. "I couldn't harm Jared. I loved him. You don't know what's going on here."

"Do you?"

With a glare, Kelly strode to the trashcan and threw away her sack, then hurried into the building. Lexie saw a couple of kids, friends of Jared's, follow Kelly. Lexie headed after her friend.

Oliver Wright pushed off the post near the entrance. "Are you all right, Lexie?"

She paused when she heard her name and glanced to the left at Ms. Thompson's student aide in Lexie's English class. "Yes. As much as any of us could be with what happened to Jared."

"Yeah, I know what you mean. I saw you and Kelly arguing. Is she okay?"

"No. She probably shouldn't have come to school today."

"Everyone's nerves are on edge. See you sixth hour." Oliver walked away, leaving Lexie to continue her trek into the building to find Kelly.

At the end of the hall, Lexie saw her friend at her locker surrounded by several of Jared's friends. Lexie started toward them. Kelly locked gazes with her and said something to the teens. By the time Lexie stopped in front of Kelly, everyone had left. One girl Lexie knew from several classes looked straight at her, but her expression held nothing friendly in it.

Lexie shivered. "What's going on?"

Kelly averted her gaze and busied herself opening her locker. "Nothing. They're just sad about Jared and wanted to know how I was doing, especially in light of the fact he was murdered. We still can't believe that. He was fine the last time I saw him." Kelly's hand quivered as she lifted her history book and stuffed it in her backpack.

Scared for her friend, Lexie moved close to Kelly, blocking her path. "Meet me after school outside Ms. Thompson's room. I'll give you a ride home. We can talk then. Maybe go by Sonic and get something to drink."

The first bell rang, indicating lunch was over. Kelly slammed her locker and started down the hallway. "Sure. I've got to get to history early to borrow notes from yesterday."

"See you," Lexie said to her friend's quickly retreating back.

Lexie hardly listened to her fourth-, fifth-, or sixth-hour teachers. She couldn't shake the feeling something was very wrong with Kelly—even beyond Jared's murder. Why would someone kill Jared at the lake? If he had drugs in his system, when did he take them? With Kelly at the party? Afterwards? Did he meet his killer at the lake? What did Kelly take? Question after question inundated Lexie until her head pounded with tension.

Suddenly, she remembered the empty bowl she'd seen at the warehouse when she'd come to take Kelly home on Sunday morning.

From what she'd heard about pill parties, often the kids would put all their medication together in a bowl and grab a handful. Was that what happened at the warehouse? According to Kelly, she'd passed out part of the night. What happened when she did? She needed to have it out with Kelly, then talk to her uncle.

Five minutes before her last hour class was over, Ms. Thompson asked her a question. Lexie didn't even realize it until she discovered everyone in class was staring at her. When she spied Oliver sitting at the small desk near Ms. Thompson's, grading papers as her student aide, a sympathetic look stared back at her, but still embarrassment colored her cheeks. "Sorry, Ms. Thompson. I don't know." She wasn't even sure what she didn't know.

Her teacher gave her a quizzical look then asked the boy in front of Lexie, "When is the test I was going to give yesterday postponed to?"

"Thursday," he answered.

Lexie would have known the answer if she'd been listening. At least Ms. Thompson didn't make a big deal out of the fact she wasn't paying attention. Ms. Thompson wanted to give everyone time to grieve and study. Lexie appreciated it because another teacher went ahead and had a test earlier today. She doubted she did very well. How could she when her best friend was hurting? Possibly in trouble? She knew Kelly wasn't the murderer, and as her friend, she wanted to protect Kelly as much as possible.

When the bell signaled the end of school, Lexie's classmates filed out of the room while Ms. Thompson said, "Lexie, please stay for a moment."

"Ms. Thompson, I finished grading the quizzes," Oliver said and placed the papers on Ms. Thompson's desk, smiled at Lexie, then left the room.

She knew it would take Kelly a few minutes to come to Ms. Thompson's classroom, so she planted herself near the door to keep an eye out for Kelly. "I'm sorry I didn't know the answer earlier."

"I'd suggest you ask a friend for a copy of her notes. I don't think you heard a word I said today. I didn't realize you were good friends with Jared."

"My best friend Kelly was dating him. Just concerned about her."

"I know how hard this can be, especially when his death was murder. When I was a sophomore here at Summerton High School, we had one of our classmates shot in the middle of a robbery at a store. It really hit the student body hard. I can imagine what everyone is going through. Do you want me to talk to Kelly?"

"I'll see. I'm meeting her in a minute."

"Well, let her know I'm a good listener. I don't have her in English, so she might not be comfortable talking to me."

That wouldn't be it. More because Ms. Thompson was the police chief's sister. "I'll let her know." For a few seconds, she thought of telling Ms. Thompson what she knew occurred on Saturday and see what she thought concerning Kelly. But she couldn't. Not until she talked with Kelly. Her friend had always been there for her, and this was when she needed Lexie the most.

She swung her backpack over one shoulder and hurried from the room, glancing up and down the corridor. Not many students were in the hallway. She checked the clock on the wall. It hadn't been long. Kelly would be here soon. Lexie lounged back against a set of lockers and waited.

Fifteen minutes passed and still no Kelly. She had chemistry as her last class, so Lexie headed for the science hall to see if someone had delayed Kelly, like Ms. Thompson had her. Other than two boys at the far end of the hall, no one else was around. Lexie stuck her head in Kelly's chemistry class and found it deserted except for her teacher.

"When did Kelly leave?"

"She was the first one out the door."

Was her best friend avoiding her? She headed for her car in the junior parking lot. Maybe Kelly misunderstood where to meet her, and she was there waiting for her. As she crossed the street, she glanced across the near empty lot. Still no Kelly. Worry grew as Lexie drove away from the school. When she swung by Kelly's house and went to the door, she rang the doorbell several times, but no one answered it.

They shared everything—even what happened Saturday night. Or had they? Had Kelly remembered something and didn't want to tell her? As she drove away from Kelly's, Lexie's fingers strengthened about the steering wheel. She would catch her after the funeral and make it impossible for Kelly to evade her.

❧

The next day Ethan stayed at the back of the crowd that squeezed into the church for Jared's funeral. Watching. They were looking into Jared's death as a murder. Where did the myriad of drugs in his system come from? Did he know he was taking all those combinations? Or were some slipped to him without his knowledge? Had he passed out and someone put him in the lake? There was no evidence found in his car of any medication or alcohol. So where was he before his death? A party? Not according to Kelly, but she was lying about something. Had she given Jared the drugs? The key was Kelly.

Whatever went down, it didn't change the fact Jared had fought to get out of the car. He hadn't driven himself into the water. He hadn't wanted to die. Until Ethan could answer those nagging questions, he wouldn't rest.

What led teens to take drugs not prescribed for them? Or for that matter, anyone. It wasn't just teenagers. Only a month ago, a man had overdosed on some antidepressants, which he hadn't had a prescription for. He'd self-diagnosed and acquired some from a source they couldn't track down. His family was still reeling from his death.

Just as Bradley and his wife, Annabelle, were. The staunch expression on Bradley's face masked a deep sadness. He knew from having been at Bradley's house when his friend fell apart at the news of the ME's findings. At first, Bradley had no idea where his son got the blood pressure and sleeping pills, antidepressants, and painkillers that were in his system. But Annabelle had checked their medication and was sure a few of her painkillers were gone from her plastic surgery a few months before, and Bradley thought he had more of his blood pressure pills left than were in the bottle. The idea their son took their medication only added to their grief. But that still left where the antidepressants and sleeping pills came from? What role, if any, had they played in Jared's death?

He was going to have a talk with Kelly after the funeral. She had avoided him a couple of times since he talked with her Sunday, and he got the feeling that Mary Lou had helped her. But he knew where Kelly was now. Two rows behind Bradley's family, weeping with her mother on one side and his niece on the other.

As the funeral ended and mourners began exiting, Cord came to stand next to him, folding his arms over his chest. "This has hit the town hard."

"Yeah, Jared was the sole heir apparent to Bradley's ranching empire. His death has left a hole in the family, but also the student body at Summerton High School."

"Sadie told me she hasn't done much this week. Her class Jared was in has all but shut down since his death. Actually most of her classes. A lot of students were absent the first couple of days."

"Can't blame them. It makes them realize their mortality. That can be sobering." Standing taller than a lot of the people in the crowd, Ethan watched some teens join Kelly, a couple of the girls taking over comforting her from Mary Lou. His niece backed away from the group, looked around, and saw Cord's sister nearby. When Lexie approached Sadie, Ethan shifted his attention back to Cord.

"I know how you think," Cord said, one corner of his mouth quirking. "What are you looking for at this funeral? A suspect attending the funeral of a person he killed?"

"It's possible. He might have gotten the painkillers from his mother's bottle and the blood pressure from his father's medication, but not the others in his system. So where did he get them and who gave him the other drugs? How did he get the alcohol?"

"You're thinking pill party?"

Nodding, Ethan straightened away from the wall as Sadie, who was talking with Lexie, made her way toward the double doors next to Cord. "Which means either Jared attended Saturday night with Kelly or went afterwards."

"So Kelly is lying."

Ethan recalled her odd behavior Sunday when he interviewed her. "It won't be the first time a teen has lied to us."

"Have you talked with your niece?" Cord clamped a toothpick between his teeth.

"Yes, briefly. She confirms she was with Kelly Sunday morning. Lexie was sick Saturday so she may not know anything. I'll talk to her again after I chat with Kelly. I want to hear what Kelly has to say first when I confront her with what we know now. What if Kelly didn't come home Saturday night like she said? That was the impression Mary Lou got when she first discovered her daughter gone on Sunday morning."

"Maybe Lexie knows something about where Kelly was Saturday night. You know how kids talk, and they are best friends," Cord murmured, then turned toward his sister and smiled then hugged her. "I know how hard this is for you. You care so much for your students."

"This has been a difficult week. But we're going to get through it, aren't we, Lexie?" Sadie squeezed the teen's hand before shifting her attention to Ethan. "It's nice seeing you again."

"I wish we were meeting under more pleasant circum-stances." Ethan was still amazed how much Sadie had changed from when she was a teenager, trying to make her older brother's life miserable. When she'd eloped with Harris Blackburn, it had devastated Cord. At the time, he wouldn't talk about it to anyone—even him.

"Are you going to the Montgomery house?" Sadie asked.

"Yes." Ethan spied the Montgomery family shaking friends' hands as they filed by and offered their condolences. "Right now they have enough people wanting their attention. I'll catch Bradley and Annabelle later." When the sight of the casket wasn't fresh in their minds.

"Uncle Ethan, can you give me a ride to their house? Mom isn't going, and I want to be there for Kelly."

"She's going?"

"Well, yes. She was his girlfriend," Lexie said.

Ethan scanned the people still in the sanctuary, but she'd disappeared. "Where did she go?"

"She was leaving out the side door with her mother, at least that was the plan before Carrie and Missy joined her."

He recognized disapproval in his niece's voice. Interesting. Why? Jealousy or was there something else going on? "Sure, I'll take you. I probably won't stay real long. I just want the family to know how I feel about what has happened." And he wanted to talk to Kelly even if he had to bring her down to the police station from the reception at the Montgomery's house.

"Lexie, if you want to stay longer, I'll take you home."

"Thanks, Ms. Thompson. I'm only going to stay as long as Kelly does, in case she needs me. She's taken this very hard."

Ethan looked around the sanctuary again, in case he'd missed Kelly earlier. Still no sign of her or the two girls his niece mentioned joining Kelly. But he did find Mary Lou waiting to talk with Bradley and Annabelle. Something didn't feel right about all of this.

❧

"I'd rather not go to the Montgomery Ranch. I can't act like you want." *Dumb and innocent.* None of them were. Kelly rubbed her fingertips into her chest over her heart as though that would stop the racing of her heartbeat. She inhaled one deep breath after another, but it became more difficult the nearer Carrie drove to Jared's home.

Missy shot her a narrow-eyed look. "You need to act like you're grieving Jared's death as his girlfriend. If you don't show up, people will wonder why, what you're hiding."

"His parents don't want me there."

"Why wouldn't they?"

"They wouldn't even acknowledge me at the funeral."

"Well, duh. They're mourning their son. That doesn't mean you don't act as you should. To the world you were the last person to see Jared alive when he dropped you off at home."

"That's a lie. I can't do it anymore. I wasn't the last person who saw him alive."

"Then who was?"

"I don't know." The thump-thump of her heart sounded in Kelly's ears like the one from Edgar Allen Poe's *The Telltale Heart.* "All I remember is he was passed out on the floor near me. When I woke up, he was gone. Did you all do something?"

Missy sent her a glare. "No way. Jared was a good friend to all of us. To tell you the truth I got sick and left early. You and Jared were still there."

Panic gripped Kelly. "I didn't do anything to him. I didn't wake up until morning." Tears blurred her eyes. "I can't say anything to his parents. I . . ."

Carrie pulled over to the side of the road and twisted toward Kelly sitting in the back by herself. "They'll want to talk with you, and you'll say what we rehearsed. Do you want to take the blame for Jared's death? The group is prepared to put the blame on you. Remember there are six of us to your one. Who do you think they're gonna believe? Us or you? We're prepared to say we left you two at the warehouse and the next thing we hear is that Jared is dead at the lake."

The sneer that curled Carrie's lip flash-froze Kelly. Swiping her tears away, she dragged her gaze from the pair in the front seat while she continued to try and calm herself enough to breathe decently. But her chest hurt, and her heart wouldn't stop racing. "But he wasn't there. He was gone. I was alone." A hazy figure leaning over her flickered into her mind. Blue eyes like Jared. Did he wake up, get in his car, and drive away from the warehouse, leaving her alone there? How could he? He had been out cold.

"No one murdered Jared. They'll find out Jared was disoriented and drove into the water." Carrie glanced at Missy, then retrieved her purse and rummaged in it until she found a bottle. She shook two pills into her palm. "Take these. They'll calm you down. You look like you could use them."

"No." The sleeping pills last night she'd taken from her mother's stash had left her so groggy she'd stayed home from school like she had on Monday.

"That wasn't a request. Take these tranquilizers. You need them." The steel in Carrie's voice drilled through her.

Kelly swung her attention to Missy, hoping to find an ally but the teen's harsh expression only confirmed she'd better take the tranquilizer or else . . . "I don't have anything to take them with."

Missy passed her the bottle of water she'd been drinking.

Both girls watched Kelly as she popped the pills into her mouth and washed them down with warm water.

"Wise decision." Missy took the bottle back.

Carrie put the car into drive and again headed toward the ranch. "So now you know what you'd better do. It was an unfortunate accident and no good would come from you telling the world what Jared was doing his last moments alive. It would hurt his reputation, and it won't bring him back. The police will discover he wasn't murdered. It was some kind of unfortunate accident."

"What about the glued seatbelt—"

Missy turned back toward Kelly interrupting her with, "Jared's reputation doesn't need to be damaged any more than it is already. You can't do that to his parents."

More likely to y'all. Do you even care for anyone but yourselves? Kelly wanted to scream that at them. Why did she ever think she wanted to be part of their crowd? For friendship? Status? None of those things were important now. She hated how she'd felt ever since taking a bunch of unknown drugs—some could have even been illegal ones like druggies took. It had been four days, and she still didn't feel right, but she couldn't even say anything to anyone—not her mom or Lexie. In fact, if they knew Lexie had picked her up at the warehouse, no telling what they would do. Harass her, too? That was why she had been staying away from her best friend when she needed her the most.

"I won't," Kelly murmured to her lap, not wanting to look at two of the most popular girls at school.

Everything she did made her stomach roil. She'd seen them out of control, yelling and fighting at the party. What had they taken to make them that way, or was it the way they were when their inhibitions weren't masked? Could one of them have killed Jared? None of them had been in their right mind. Kelly couldn't shake the blurry person with blue eyes hovering over her. Who else in the group had blue eyes? She pictured each one: Brendan, Carrie, Missy, Luke, Zoe and Kalvin. Luke's eyes were hazel and Carrie's gray while the others were brown.

Kelly tried to remember anything else besides blue eyes, but the more she tried the tenser she became until her head began to throb like a bass drum against her skull. When was the tranquilizer going to take effect? When would she forget Saturday night?

"We'll be close by. If you have a problem, we'll be there to help you."

Kelly hated the nasal quality of Missy's voice. Was she the one who called her every night—the number never the same? When she saw a number on the second prank call, she'd hit the return button to phone the person back. It had been a payphone. The same with the other couple of calls she'd gotten—the voice always the raspy, almost mechanical sounding one from Sunday night. She'd thought it had been a guy, but now she wasn't sure—of anything.

By the time they arrived, Carrie parked at the end of the long road that led to the main house. Kelly limped toward the mansion in high heels that were killing her feet. Today was only the second time she'd worn them, and she already had several blisters.

She'd dated Jared for two months and had never been to his home. How odd that her first time was because he had died. Falling into step with Carrie and Missy, Kelly resisted the urge to flee—run away before going inside. If she was truthful, she had been relieved when Jared's parents hadn't said anything to her at the church. What if they did now? How could she look at them, knowing what their son had been doing the final hours of his life? What happened at the party that might have caused Jared's death? Little by little, she was remembering the night and none of it was good.

Carrie clasped her arm right above her elbow—in a grip that sent a clear warning through Kelly. Behave or else.

Inside the large foyer—the size of her living room at home—people, some Kelly knew, milled about, looking as if they didn't know quite what to do. She definitely didn't and glanced back at the door, thinking about leaving. Escaping. *Why aren't the tranquilizers working?* She felt as though she were crawling out of her skin.

The marble-floored foyer—straight out of a design magazine—shouted elegance and wealth from the crystal vase with fresh-cut flowers to the rich-looking pieces of furniture with gold inlay.

The butler opened the intricately carved wooden door again, and Lexie entered with her uncle. He'd been trying to talk with her, and she'd avoided him. She didn't know how long she could lie to the man about that night.

"Let's go in the other room," Kelly whispered in Missy's ear, her body trembling so badly it was obvious to anyone who looked at her.

Missy peered behind Kelly, then tugged her toward the dining room on the left, equally luxurious. This was what Jared had grown up with while she and her mom had struggled. Why had Jared dated her? Doubts seeped into her mind like fog slithering over the ground.

Kelly quickly managed to disappear into the crowd. She wouldn't be able to avoid the Texas Ranger for long. Lexie talked about her uncle Ethan and his work. She'd once said he was like a bloodhound on a trail. He never gave up until he found what he was searching for. In this case, he thought she had some answers. And she did. But she could never tell him. Missy and Carrie made that clear today. What if "the group" put the blame for the murder on her and tell the police they left Jared and her at the warehouse, making her the last person to be with Jared. Except the killer. Six to one. She didn't have a leg to stand on. She was alone in this. Not even Lexie could help her.

In the back den, Missy and Carrie stopped moving, standing back and facing the door with the third girl from the party, Zoe Sanders. The pounding rapidity of Kelly's heartbeat made her lightheaded.

She plopped in the nearest chair, trying to catch her breath. She shouldn't have taken the tranquilizers. What if they weren't what Carrie said they were?

"What's *he* doing here?" Carrie asked Missy and Zoe.

Kelly followed the direction the girls were staring. Ranger Stone threaded his way through the mass of people in the den toward her. Panic seized her again, even worse than in Carrie's car, and she clutched the arm of the chair, looking for a way out.

Trapped. With Carrie, Missy, and Zoe as an audience.

Kelly's lungs burned. She couldn't draw in enough oxygen-rich air. The room spun before her. She closed her eyes, but her mind was still swirling. Suffocating. Dizzy. Coming out of her skin.

"Kelly?"

Lexie's worried voice came to her. Kelly opened her eyes slowly. The room still twirled like on the Tilt-a-Whirl at the county fair.

"Kelly, you don't look well." Lexie's face loomed before her, but the words sounded strange—alternately loud and soft.

"I'm not."

Carrie stepped up on one side while Missy and Zoe took the other. "We'll take you home. This was too much for you after the funeral."

They started helping her to her feet when Lexie's uncle said in a forceful tone, "Girls, I'll take care of her and get her home."

"But we brought her . . ." Carrie's voice faded at the intense look on Ethan Stone's face.

"She may need to go to the hospital. I'll take her. Go join your friends over there." He tossed his head toward a group of teens watching them.

Kelly's gaze flitted from one person to the next in the group. Carrie's diamond hard gaze bored into Kelly. She resisted Lexie and her uncle helping her and dropped back onto the chair. "I'm fine. I haven't eaten today. I'm just a little lightheaded. Everybody give me some space." She glared at Lexie, hoping she did as Kelly said.

Her best friend scanned the people in the room, all focused on the drama with Kelly.

Their stares, especially Brendan and Luke's, urged Kelly to leave before she totally blew it. "On second thought, Carrie, can you give me a ride home?"

Her "chaperone" quickly said, "Yes," and moved in between Kelly and Lexie.

Both Carrie and Missy flanked her as the crowd parted to let them through. Zoe stayed back. While Brendan and another friend hemmed Ranger Stone in on the right side with Zoe on the left. At the doorway into the den, Kelly glanced back at Lexie and her uncle, hoping they didn't follow. Luke stepped into Lexie's uncle's path, sticking his hand out to shake. Kelly hurried her pace. Her last look at the crowd in the den showed them surrounding Lexie's uncle. The suffocating panic crowded in as the people did.

Outside, the fall air did nothing to cool Kelly's heated face. She increased her strides, going ahead of Carrie and Missy. She didn't know if she would ever go back to school. All she'd wanted was to fit in and now her life was a total mess. Her heartbeat picked up speed as she almost ran the rest of the way. Gasping, she latched onto her goal, Carrie's car.

❧

When Ethan emerged outside the Montgomery home after practically fighting his way through a crowd of Jared's friends, Carrie's car was leaving. If he had any doubts that Kelly was hiding something, he didn't now.

When Lexie came up behind him, Ethan said. "I have to go. I need to talk with Kelly. I'll drop you off at your house unless you want to stay. Ms. Thompson said she could give you a ride home."

"No. I only came for Kelly."

Ethan strode to his SUV, determined to see Kelly one way or another today. Something was really wrong. For a few seconds, he'd considered calling 911 in the den. She'd gone pasty white, her breathing labored. A panic attack? On some kind of drug? Guilt?

Then, when the teens swarmed him, he thought of bees protecting their queen. Short of causing a scene at Bradley's house, he was stuck with a crowd of teenagers between him and Kelly. With all that the Montgomery family was going through, he wouldn't do that to them, but he would get some answers. Today.

As he drove toward his sister's to let Lexie off, he tapped his fingers against the steering wheel. Was his niece involved somehow in whatever was going on? "You didn't go out at all on Saturday night?"

"I was sick. I went to bed early. Didn't sleep, though." Her hands clasped together in her lap, she kneaded her thumb into her palm.

"I know you told me you and Kelly were together Sunday morning. Why? You always go with your mom to church."

He'd seen her nervous habit with her thumb. Was she lying, too? Or upset with what happened in the den?

"I was still sick to my stomach when Mom left. I didn't want to throw up in church."

"But you went out with Kelly. Why? Weren't you afraid you'd throw up in your car?"

A long moment passed. Ethan pulled into the subdivision where Lexie lived. He threw a glance toward his niece. "What are you hiding, Lexie? I'm here to help. To get answers."

"I'm not hiding anything. I haven't done anything wrong." She looked out the side window.

When he stopped, she jumped from the car and strode toward her house. He thought about following her and demanding answers, because his niece just lied to him. He didn't have to be astute to know Lexie lied. He was thankful she didn't have that skill down pat.

He'd come back and talk to her after he saw Kelly. He was more concerned about getting the truth from Kelly. As he pulled up to her house, the two teenage girls who had brought her to the Montgomery ranch were getting into a car. He parked on the street right behind the Ford Mustang that belonged to one of Kelly's "guardians" and jotted down the license plate number.

As he walked toward Kelly's house, they didn't leave. They sat in the car. He could feel the drill of their gazes. He would find out who they were. The driver was Carrie, but he didn't know her last name or the other girl's. Besides those two females, Brendan Livingston and his cousin Luke Adams were in the group. Who else? Other football players? The third girl at the Montgomery house? Before this investigation was over, he intended to discover everything he could about these four and anyone else he thought might know anything about what Jared was doing Saturday night after midnight.

When he rang the bell, Mary Lou answered the front door. As she sighed and leaned against the wooden frame, clutching it as if it was the only reason she was upright, he smelled liquor on her breath.

"What do you want, Ethan?"

"To talk to Kelly."

"She ran upstairs crying. This has been a hard day for her. She lost her boyfriend. You probably don't know what it means to lose someone you care about. It isn't easy." Her words slurred together.

Had she come home from the funeral and started drinking? "I need to talk with her. We can do it here or down at the police station."

Mary Lou's eyes widened. "My baby at the police station? She didn't do anything wrong." She lost her grip on the doorframe and nearly fell.

Ethan caught and steadied her. "There are questions that have to be answered. You may sit in on the conversation, but I need to have it."

"You're just being mean because I chose Bradley over you in high school."

"Are you able to go upstairs and get Kelly, or do I need to?"

She straightened herself, lifted her chin, and turned slowly. "I am very capable of getting my daughter."

Ethan stayed in the foyer at the bottom of the staircase, concerned that Mary Lou might not make it back down without falling. He'd heard rumors she drank a lot but hadn't seen it until now. Having only been reassigned to the Summerton area recently, he hadn't gotten a chance to get reacquainted with everyone from the old days yet. Coming home had been more difficult than he'd thought. Cord Thompson had made it easier. But when he had known them as a child, it was harder to hold himself apart from others.

A pale Kelly descended the stairs next to her mom with her arm around Mary Lou as though the girl was used to helping her mother cope when she drank too much. At the bottom, Mary Lou waved her hand toward the living room and charged across the foyer ahead of him and Kelly. The teen kept her gaze lowered and trailed after her mother.

Ethan sat across from Kelly and Mary Lou, relaxing against the back cushion of the chair. He hoped his relaxed stance would calm the frightened look in Kelly's eyes when she glanced up for a second. "Are you feeling any better? I think everyone in town was at the Montgomery ranch. That can be a bit overwhelming."

Eyes dilated, Kelly nodded, but her hands shook. She clenched them into fists and hid them at her side—not quite sitting on them, but close.

"That's why I decided not to go." Mary Lou collapsed back against the couch and slid her eyes closed.

"Kelly, I need to go over Saturday night again. When I talked with you before, I didn't have the autopsy report yet. Did he tell you he was going to the Red River City Park?"

She shook her head. "I didn't even know he was going out after dropping me off. He didn't say anything to me."

"What did he say to you when he dropped you off?"

She shrugged. "The usual. Good night. See you tomorrow."

"So he wasn't mad at anyone? No one was upset with him?"

"Not that I know." Her eyelids drooped closed, then snapped open.

"No one saw you at Lone Star Park at the amusement area. You weren't there, were you?"

A sheen in her eyes, she whispered, "No."

"Why did you lie about going to the park? What are you hiding? Where were you really?"

Kelly blinked rapidly, pressing herself into the couch as though trying to disappear.

Mary Lou perked up. "Kelly, where were you?"

"On a date," Kelly said slowly as though trying to figure out what to say.

"Then tell him where so he'll leave. I'm getting a killer headache." Mary Lou massaged her temples.

"Kelly, we can talk down at the police station if you want."

Her eyes huge, Kelly bit into her lower lip and slid a glance toward her mother. "We wanted to be by ourselves. We loved each other." She emphasized that last sentence as if she was convincing herself as well as him.

"Where?"

"At Lone Star Park in the recreation part. After it closes, the guards don't come around until after the amusement rides close down later."

Everything about her posture, slouched over, now sitting on her hands, screamed the teen was still lying. He leaned forward, propping his elbows on his thighs and loosely clasping his hands. "If you loved Jared as you said, then I know you want to help me figure out how he ended up in his car in the lake across town from where you two went that evening. If it hadn't caught on an underwater boulder, it would have disappeared completely, and we might not have found it for a long time. We wouldn't have known about Jared's death. His parents and friends would be in limbo with no closure."

Finally Kelly looked at him. "You think he was murdered? He couldn't . . ." Her voice faded into the silence.

"Yes, we're looking at it as a murder until we discover otherwise. He had a lot of drugs in his system, ones he wasn't prescribed. Do you know where he got them? Was he aware of taking them? Did he take them with you? Why did he take them? Did you take some with him?"

Kelly bolted to her feet. "I can't help you. Don't ya think I would if I could? I loved Jared, and he's gone. What am I going to do with him gone? I was here after midnight Saturday." Sobs tore from her.

The sound of her crying rallied her mother who pushed to her feet, glaring at Ethan. "She's told you what she knows. Nothing. She was here Saturday night when Jared died. I can vouch for that."

"But you told my sister she hadn't come home." Ethan rose.

"That was Sunday morning. At the time I was surprised she wasn't in her room Sunday morning. I'd forgotten about her coming in earlier. I may have drunk some after that and your sister woke me up. I'm not a morning person, and it takes me a long time to get up and function fully."

"Then she could have gone back out after midnight, and you wouldn't know it."

"But I didn't." Kelly locked gazes with him. "Not until Lexie came and picked me up Sunday morning." Her carefully applied makeup ran down her face in streaks.

"Where did you and Lexie go?"

Her face bleached of all color, Kelly swallowed hard. "Riding around."

"Why?"

"We were just talking. The usual." She collapsed back onto the couch.

"What?"

"School, teachers, clothes."

"No boyfriends?"

Kelly shook her head.

Ethan studied Kelly for a long moment. The girl squirmed on the couch and covered her eyes. "I'm not feeling well."

"I'll be back tomorrow. This won't go away, Kelly."

"Don't you understand? I've told you what I can."

Her shout blasted him. In the middle of the interview, there had been a few truths. That last sentence Kelly said was one of them. He started for the front door, turned back, and asked, "What were the names of the two girls who brought you home from the Montgomery ranch?"

"Why?"

"One was Carrie. What is her last name?"

"Bannister," Kelly said with a glare, all tears gone.

"And the other one?"

"Missy Collins."

"Does her daddy own the bank on Sage Avenue?"

"Yes."

"Interesting."

"What do you mean by that?"

He continued his trek toward the door. "They just don't seem your type."

                    ⟱

Kelly left her mother in the living room and ran upstairs, slamming her door so hard a picture of a horse on her wall shifted, hanging at an angle. She paced from her bed to her closet, her heart racing, her chest hurting as she tried to drag in enough air.

When her cell sounded again, she didn't even look at it. The ring tone was Lexie's. She couldn't talk to her. Her uncle knew she was lying. He would come back until he got the truth. What was she going to do?

Something hit her window. She stared at it. Again, a pebble dinged against the glass. What if it was Lexie? She wished she'd never called her Sunday morning. She knew part of the truth. What if she told her uncle, even though she'd promised her she wouldn't say anything to anyone?

Her phone rang, but this time it wasn't Lexie's special ring tone. She crossed to her dresser and looked at the screen. Carrie. If she didn't answer, Carrie would think she had something to hide. Slowly, not really wanting to talk to Carrie either, Kelly reached for her cell, her hands shaking so badly she nearly let it slip from her fingers as she brought it to her ear.

"Yes."

"What did you tell him?" a male voice—Brendan's—demanded.

"Nothing. I promise."

"Come to the window."

She walked to it and peered into her backyard, the dim light of dusk throwing two figures in the shadows, but Kelly could tell it was Carrie and Brendan.

"We're going out with some of the group to mourn Jared's death in our own way. We want you to come with us."

"I'm not—"

"It's not a request."

6

Why had Luke lied to him? Ethan drove to Luke's house after leaving Kelly's. What did Luke have to hide? He intended to bring the young man down to the police station for questioning. The analysis of the handwriting on the note passed to Jared indicated Luke wrote it.

If he had to rattle all Jared's friends to get to the truth, he would.

When he rang the doorbell, Luke's dad, a high-powered Realtor in the area, answered it almost right away. "I need to speak with Luke."

"He isn't here." Mr. Adams filled the doorway as though to block Ethan from entering.

"I want him brought down to the police station at eight tomorrow morning. If he isn't there, two officers will be dispatched to bring him in."

"Why? What's this all about?"

"When I talked with him last, he lied to me. I want to know why." Ethan tipped his hat, then swung around and stalked from the front porch.

Not long after that, Ethan pulled up to his sister's house and noticed the blazing lights. The way this investigation was going, he'd half-expected Beth and Lexie to be gone. When Beth opened the door, he entered. "I need to see Lexie."

"She went to the library to study. It seems two big tests were postponed and now she has to take both tomorrow."

"The city or the school library?"

"The one at the high school."

He turned to leave.

Beth caught his arm and stopped him. "Why do you want to see her? What's going on? When she came back from the funeral, she was so upset. She went to her room and only came out when she told me she needed to study at the library."

"Does she usually study there?"

"Sometimes. She says there aren't any distractions like her computer or TV."

"Then I'll talk with her there."

His sister frowned. "Why?"

"She lied to me, and I intend to find out the truth." Anger festered in the pit of his stomach. He should be used to people lying to him, but his own family?

"What?"

"She's protecting Kelly. Her friend knows something about Jared's death."

"If you see her, bring her home. If you don't see her, let me know."

"Will do." He strode to his SUV and headed for the high school. Halfway there, his cell phone rang. "Stone here."

"Ethan, this is Sadie. Lexie is here and wants you to come over to my house. She has something to tell you."

"Why is she there? She's supposed to be at the library."

"She needed some advice."

"Be there in ten minutes." Ethan clicked off and tossed his phone onto the passenger seat, the anger still churning his gut.

❧

Lexie paced about Sadie's kitchen, rubbing her thumb into her palm. "Uncle Ethan is gonna be so mad at me. But something is wrong, and I won't let Kelly get hurt. She's acting so funny. I think she took something today and Saturday night."

Sadie's nerves tautened. It wasn't too many more years before her two kids would be in high school. She couldn't be more thankful they were upstairs studying and not out getting into trouble like Lexie told her about Kelly. "If she is, she'll get the help she needs. The point is these pill parties need to be stopped. They're like playing Russian roulette with a loaded gun. Someone is going to overdose and die."

"I should have said something from the beginning. I was trying to protect my friend. I do know Kelly didn't have anything to do with Jared's death. She was bad off and was left alone at that warehouse, passed out. She's jumped into the deep end and doesn't know how to swim with the big fish."

"The kids Jared hung out with?"

"Yes, Carrie, Missy, Brendan, and Luke. There are a few others, but those four are the core group. Carrie is a junior, and the other three are seniors. I'm sure they're involved somehow."

"Do you have any evidence?"

"Only what Kelly has told me."

"We need Kelly to tell Mr. Howard what happened. Those two boys, at least, should be kicked off the football team. They signed a contract about drugs at the beginning of the season."

When the doorbell chimed, Lexie gasped. "He's here." She clutched her stomach. "I'm gonna be sick."

"I'll bring him in here while you compose yourself in the bathroom." She pointed in its direction. "Remember I'm here to help. You're doing the right thing by saying something. Kelly will thank you later."

Sadie hurried to the front door and let Ethan in. His scowl carved deep lines into his face. "Please go easy on Lexie. She came to see me because she didn't know what to do, but she didn't like what she saw this afternoon with Kelly at the Montgomery's."

"Her friend's on something, or lying? There seems to be a lot of that going around lately. Kelly. Lexie. Luke."

"About the note?"

"Luke denied he wrote it, but it was his handwriting. If he was innocent, why would he lie to me?" Frustration poured from Ethan. "Now I know why I'm not married with children. They can drive you crazy."

"But they can bring joy, too." *Unless they're demanding to see their father when you don't want them to.*

"I'm not sure what my sister is going to do. First, Emma gave her problems, and now it seems Lexie is, too."

"I'm sorry, Uncle Ethan."

He swiveled around to stare at Lexie in the hallway. "What do you have to tell me?"

Sadie glanced up the stairs where her children were doing their homework. "Let's go into the kitchen. It's more private in there."

Lexie whirled around and hastened down the short hall into the kitchen with Sadie and Ethan trailing behind her. She stood in the middle of the spacious room, cradling a hand while her thumb kneaded its palm so hard her skin turned red.

Sadie passed her. "Let's all sit at the table. This can be worked out."

Ethan sent his niece a piercing look while Lexie trudged to the chair and eased onto it, staring at her lap.

Sadie sat at the head of the table with Ethan to her right and Lexie on her left. "Lexie went to the library but couldn't study because Kelly has her worried."

"She should be. Kelly is in a lot of trouble. Withholding information from the police in an investigation is serious."

"Ethan, if this is going to work, you'll have to give her a chance to tell her story." She fixed her teacher's stare on him that conveyed he'd better behave. When the hard lines of his face evened out some, she continued. "Lexie, tell your uncle what happened Sunday morning."

"After throwing up again, I told Mom to go to church. I was going to try and get some sleep since I hadn't the night before. I wasn't feeling great, and when the phone rang, I wasn't going to answer it until I saw it was Kelly. I know she'd been nervous about going out with Jared and his friends to some party, so I answered it.

She was frantic. She'd passed out at the party she attended Saturday night and woke up alone Sunday morning. She needed a ride home. No one else was there."

"Where?" Ethan interrupted.

"Give her a chance," Sadie said, half expecting him to glare at her.

Instead, his stiff posture relaxed some, and he leaned back, resting his clasped hands on the table.

"A warehouse on Sixth Street. Abandoned and creepy."

"You went there—"

Sadie placed her hand over his but didn't say anything.

"Kelly sounded in bad shape. She was scared and upset. I did what any friend would do. I went to pick her up. When I walked into the place, it was clear something went on there. Beer bottles and cans were everywhere. An empty plastic green bowl sat on a crate off to the side. A couple of ice chests were nearby. The smells were awful—vomit and other things." Lexie shuddered and hugged herself. "All I wanted to do was get her and get out of there. I saw her curled up on the floor. At first I thought she was—" she dropped her arms to her side and mumbled "—dead."

After half a minute of silence, Ethan bent forward, threw a glance at Sadie, then said, "But she wasn't. Did she take something?"

Lexie lifted her head, with tears streaking down her cheeks, and nodded. "And she didn't know what she took. She promised me she wouldn't do it again, if I didn't tell anyone. I told her yes. I didn't know about Jared then. She thought he'd left her and was upset about that, but . . ." She stared off into space, her brow furrowed.

"What?" Sadie asked because Lexie hadn't told her this part.

"She said something about Jared being dead, but when I asked her about that, she couldn't remember anything about that night after the pills she took. She said it was a blur. I thought he had probably passed out like she had. I was mad at him for leaving her. Now I realize that doesn't sound like Jared. He was good to Kelly."

"Yeah, so good he took her to a pill party. That kind of loving a gal can do without." Ethan unclasped his hands and stood.

Lexie directed her full attention at her uncle. "Kelly did not kill Jared. I know that."

"Kelly knows more than she's saying. I need you to show me where this warehouse is."

Lexie scrubbed the tears from her cheeks. "It's nighttime. That part of town isn't the best . . ." She looked at her uncle, cleared her throat, and pushed to her feet. "O—kay."

"You need to call your mother and let her know what you're doing and where you've been." Ethan gave his niece his phone.

"Can't I wait until I get home?"

"No."

Considering what Lexie had held back, Ethan was in control, restrained. He used to be a hothead, taking on the world when he felt he needed to. She'd really liked Ethan back then. Sadie liked this version even more.

Lexie placed a call to her mother and walked toward the foyer while talking to Beth. Ethan started to follow his niece.

Sadie stopped him by moving into his path. "Give her some alone time to tell her mother what's going on."

"Why didn't she come to me about this?"

The anger he'd held in check poured out in that question. Only a couple of feet from him, Sadie saw the tic in his jaw line and the tenseness in his neck as though he were clenching his teeth. But she also glimpsed the hurt in his eyes before he masked it.

"Lexie is a kid. They don't always make the best decisions." She smiled, a fleeting one. "Neither do adults. Giving her word not to tell meant something to Lexie, and she didn't want Kelly to start taking drugs—even the prescription kind."

"Prescription kinds kill just as easily as illegal ones, if not taken the way they're intended. People can become addicted to prescription ones as well. She should have trusted me enough to come to me."

"She planned to, but first she wanted to talk to someone about it. I think she just needed me to give her the courage to face you after she'd lied. I was her softball coach last year, and we became close.

I was thrilled when I got her as a student this year, and she hasn't disappointed me."

"What changed her mind about saying something?"

"As I mentioned earlier, Kelly's behavior today at the Montgomerys, but also your talk with her on the way home from there. She hated lying to you. She couldn't study tonight. She couldn't do anything but think about how disappointed you would be in her if you knew she kept something from you. She doesn't want to be a snitch, but she saw how important the truth was, especially with what happened to Jared. But she kept stressing to me Kelly couldn't have killed him. She can't see anyone doing it. She still thinks it must be some kind of accident, in spite of what you have said."

"I may go gentle on her, but my sister will go ballistic."

"She realizes that. Will you let me know what happens?"

His gaze connected with hers, and he stepped closer. "Yes, and thank you for calling me. This party may be the key to what happened to Jared."

His look roped her to him, and she couldn't move. "I'm concerned about what's happening to some of my students. If this trend keeps up, more of them are going to die. Are they getting their prescription drugs from their parents' medicine cabinets?"

"Some, but there are also people out there who sell them. All we can do is educate parents and students about what's going on. Parents need to dispose of prescriptions they're no longer taking and to keep track of the ones they still are."

"Where are these prescription drugs coming from?"

"There are various sources. People who aren't taking their prescriptions, but selling them. People who have access to these drugs siphon them off to sell. Where there is money to be made, they find a way, and then something like what happened to Jared occurs. What if Jared left to get more drugs and something went wrong? He was killed instead. If he'd been taking drugs, he probably wasn't in any condition to defend himself. Or the type he took made him go off on the wrong person. No telling what drugs were taken. I doubt any of the kids knew."

Sadie never wanted to let her children leave her house again. How could she protect them from something like what had occurred Saturday night? She'd start with educating herself and have a long talk with Cynthia at school.

"What I'm really concerned about is if there's an organized network forming in Summerton to supply these drugs to people—adults and children."

"Children, as in my twins?"

"Yes. I've seen it in middle school, too."

Her fear multiplied. She felt as though she were at the top of a roller coaster and it suddenly plunged down a hundred feet in a couple of seconds—leaving her stomach at the top. "What can I do as a parent, teacher?"

"Be aware of what's going on around you. If there has been one pill party, there have been others. As I said, keep count of any medication you have."

"Uncle Ethan, Mom wants to talk to you," Lexie shouted from the foyer.

"I'd better go. It's a school night, and I need to find this warehouse."

Sadie paused in the kitchen to give him some time to talk to Beth. It was a family issue. Goodness, she had enough going on in her own life that she didn't want zipping around the gossip grapevine. Seeing Ethan again only made her realize what a mess everything was with Harris back in town. Ashley had informed her this morning she wanted to meet her father while Steven had told his sister she was crazy. That had triggered an argument between the two that was still unsettled tonight.

When she entered the foyer, Ethan, with a frown on his face, said good-bye to his sister and put his cell phone away.

"She's gonna ground me for the rest of the month," Lexie muttered.

"I'm surprised it's not the rest of the year. She was mad. Ready to go?" Ethan glanced over his shoulder at Sadie. "Thanks. I'll call you later."

After she closed the door on the pair, Sadie looked around her house. Pulling her life together after Harris walked out on her with two three-month-old babies had been rough, but she'd made it on her own with no help. The Lord and her hard work got her here, and it would get her through this latest crisis with her ex-husband.

With a sigh, she made her way toward the living room. Her cell rang. Ethan. She answered it, a smile coming from deep inside her. "Did you forget something?"

"No, but I wanted to tell you I saw Harris getting out of a car at your house as I rounded the corner. Do you want me to come back?"

The thought that Ethan would do that for her in the middle of tracking down the scene of the party where Jared had probably gotten the drugs infused her with a warmth she hadn't experienced in a long time. "No, but thanks for offering." The doorbell chimed. "He's here. Gotta go."

Sadie hated disconnecting with Ethan, but it couldn't be helped. She strode to the door. With a deep, fortifying breath she opened it. Harris stood there with his arms crossed, a smug look on his face.

Sadie penned him with a penetrating glare. "You aren't welcome here. Don't come by, especially unannounced."

"You might not welcome me, but my daughter called and asked me to come. She wanted to meet me."

⚬⚬⚬

Blindfolded, Kelly stood between two males who gripped her arms. Her heart pounded erratically, skipping a beat, then racing. Her mind, still fuzzy from whatever Carrie had given her earlier, couldn't focus on anything but the feeling of being trapped and a group surrounding her. She heard them whispering, making small noises. Someone giggled. Another snorted.

So scared. What are they gonna do?

All energy in her legs gave way, and she sank toward the floor. Halfway down, the two people who held her jerked her back up on her feet. Only by their strength did she remain upright. Her body quaked, her lungs burned from trying to breathe. She did manage to inhale short gasps every once in a while. Sweat coated her face and shirt, dripping off her.

A door opened and footsteps approached.

"We've been waiting for you," Brendan said in a gruff voice that only added to her fear.

Someone from behind her yanked off her blindfold, and she blinked at the light shining in her eyes. She stood in what looked like a cabin. She couldn't tell for sure. The brightness nearly blinded her.

Luke Adams moved in front of Kelly, blocking the light. "Sorry I'm late. Dad got a call from the police. They have a warrant to search the warehouse on Sixth Street where our last party was." He glared at Kelly. "The Texas Ranger came by earlier to talk with me when I wasn't there. Now I have to go down to the station tomorrow at eight. Dad wants me home immediately."

Suddenly Luke stepped even closer and thrust his face into hers. Rat-a-tat. Rat-a-tat. Faster and faster the staccato of her heartbeat thundered through her dazed mind. Was one of them a murderer? That question froze Kelly in place even though her mind yelled to run.

"Are you the reason the Texas Ranger wants to see me? Did you snitch? That's unacceptable once you're part of this group. You've broken the cardinal rule."

Bursts of his breath, with drops of spit, splattered her face. All she could focus on was the anger in his eyes. The trembling in her body increased. "I didn't tell him anything. I swear I didn't."

One of the teens behind her scooted a hardback chair up against her knees. Brendan and Kalvin forced her to sit.

Then Brendan, along with the other two boys, hovered around her and said, "It could only be one of us who was there. And no one else has. That leaves you."

Three girls—Missy, Carrie, and Zoe—crowded in around the chair, too. As the others taunted and shouted at her, anger blasted her from all sides. Fear as she'd never experienced deluged her. She needed to think, to find a way out of this. *Why can't I?*

Did one of them kill Jared?

"I didn't say anything to anyone but . . ." She snapped her mouth closed.

Brendan's large, rough hands squeezed her face as he filled her vision. "But who? Who did you tell?"

"Lexie," she spat out. "You all left me at the warehouse. She came and picked me up. I didn't know about Jared then, I swear."

"Why didn't you tell us that?" Carrie moved in front of the guys. "We're your friends now. We'll take care of you. Lexie isn't one of us. You are."

As Carrie spoke, in a soft voice that chilled Kelly more than a loud one, Brendan, Luke, and Kalvin backed away. Carrie and Missy dominated Kelly's view, everyone else fading into the background. Her muscles ached from holding them so taut.

Zoe joined the other two girls, a smile on her face. "We didn't mean to scare you. We wanted you to tell us the truth. Don't you feel better now?"

Mouth dry, Kelly nodded.

"We thought we would celebrate Jared's life. Pay tribute to him. He wouldn't want us to be sad, but happy," Missy said, helping Kelly to her feet.

"I wish I could stay. Gotta go. Celebrate for me, too." Luke gave Missy a quick kiss then left the cabin.

Now that Kelly wasn't so scared, she tried to relax but couldn't. Adrenaline pumped through her body. She wanted to ask about what had happened after she'd passed out, but she wouldn't. If she acted like she knew nothing, which was true, they might leave her alone.

"You did good. Remember when you want to talk, come to us. Lexie betrayed you today, and we have a way for you to get back at her." Missy guided Kelly to the couch at the other end of the cabin.

Yeah, why did Lexie do that? She promised me. Anger began to replace her fear. Anger at Lexie. Anger at Jared for dying.

Sadie faced her ex-husband, blocking him from coming into her house. "No, you don't get to decide when you can come over to see my children. You lost that when you walked away from your children."

"Mom, I called him and asked him to come over. I want to hear what he wants to say."

Sadie glanced over her shoulder, her body still perched in the doorway as if that would stop Harris from coming inside. Ashley stood on the staircase, gripping the banister, her expression neutral.

"I'm thirteen and want to know about my father. I think I have a right to, especially since you didn't tell us much of anything."

"Then I'll tell you and Steven without him here." Sadie turned toward Ashley, whose gaze had locked onto her dad.

"No, I want to hear from *my* father."

Harris leaned toward Sadie and whispered, "What are you afraid of? That she'll love me more than you? If your bond is strong, then you have nothing to fear."

Sadie stiffened and moved away from Harris. Her few steps into the house allowed him to enter.

Harris cocked a grin. "We can do this the easy way or the hard way. I'll take you to court if I have to."

"Mom, please. You can stay."

Sadie looked from Harris's smug expression to Ashley's pleading one. "Fine. This is a school night, so this will be a brief meeting." She fixed her gaze on Harris, challenging him to protest.

His smile grew. "That's all I ask. It's a start."

"Let's go into the living room then." Sadie waited until Ashley and Harris made their move before closing the front door. *Lord, what do I do? I can't let him in my daughter's life. He uses people. He'll chew her up and spit her out—just like he did me.*

Ashley sat on the couch while Harris took a chair across from his daughter. Surprised he didn't take the seat next to Ashley, Sadie did.

She checked her watch. "It's eight, so no more than fifteen or twenty minutes."

Her daughter pulled out a sheet of paper from her pocket. "Why did you come back to Summerton?" Ashley asked in a matter-of-fact voice.

"I was offered a job with Mr. Livingston. I did some work for him in Dallas. He liked it. When I heard you all were here, I decided it was a sign to come back."

"Why?"

"Because I've regretted not being involved in your life. When I left, I was just a kid who didn't know what he wanted. Frankly, I was immature and searching for thrills and fun. I've grown up since then."

It took a great effort for Sadie to keep her mouth from dropping open. The Harris she'd known would never have admitted that. For a second, she wondered if maybe he had changed, but quickly shut down that train of thought. Not possible. Her teeth clamped together to keep from laughing at his remark.

Ashley looked at her sheet. "Why haven't you contacted us before this?"

"Because your mother and I didn't end on a good note. I didn't do right by her, and I felt guilty. I shouldn't have let that affect my decision to stay away, but I did. You and your brother are old enough now to make up your own minds."

No. No, you can't come in here and be reasonable. Tomorrow after work, she would go see Colleen Stover. She needed advice from a lawyer.

"How do you want to be a part of my life?" her daughter asked another well thought out question, which made Sadie realize she was serious about getting to know her father.

"I'd like to spend time with you. Do things with you. For us to get to know each other. I have thirteen years to make up in child support," Harris threw Sadie a look full of appeal, "and being here for all of you."

Glancing at her watch, Sadie bolted to her feet. "It's time for Ashley to finish her homework. Remember school is tomorrow."

Ashley rose. "I have just one more question. When can you come back?"

Harris pinned his attention on her. "Sadie, when?"

She couldn't think of anything to say but, "I don't know. I'll have to think about it. I'll call you."

"Mom?"

"Really. A lot has happened lately, with one of my students dying. I attended his funeral today." She leveled a searing gaze at Harris, daring him to make her look bad in Ashley's eyes.

He bowed his head. "I look forward to hearing from you." His charming smile that melted Sadie's heart in the past, graced his mouth when he turned to Ashley. "Thanks for calling." Sadie followed him and Ashley to the front door. He laid his hand on her daughter's shoulder and told her goodnight.

After her father left, Ashley rotated toward Sadie. "Thanks, Mom. Everyone deserves a second chance."

As her daughter ran up the stairs, beaming with a smile, Sadie wilted into the nearest chair, burying her face in her hands to keep her scream inside. *Harris doesn't deserve a second chance.*

Massaging her fingertips into her forehead, she pulled herself together. She needed to talk with Steven. As she stood, she glimpsed an envelope on the table in the foyer. She snatched it up and opened it. Inside was a check from Harris for a thousand dollars marked for child support.

～❧～

After processing the scene at the warehouse, Ethan stood with Cord by the back door where Lexie had said she'd come into the abandoned building. He'd taken his niece home to an angry Beth after the teenager had described what she had seen. None of the debris was evident. Clean—too clean for an unused warehouse.

Ethan folded his arms across his chest, trying to picture the pill party. "I'm not surprised it's been cleared of any evidence. So all we have is Lexie's statement about what she saw Sunday morning after the fact."

Cord removed his toothpick from his mouth. "We need to talk to Kelly again. I think we can break her."

"I agree. Let's pick her up first thing tomorrow morning before school. Take her to the station. Interview her first, then Luke. His father owns this warehouse. Maybe he'll put some pressure on Luke to tell the truth."

"We can only hope, but we don't have much physical evidence to go on. Jared's dad wants to know exactly what happened to his son. He's offered a reward for any information that leads to the killer."

"Let's keep this scene sealed. I want to come back in the daylight and have another look around. Another perspective might help. Also, have your officers search the dumpsters in the area."

Cord started for the door. "It's been a long day, and it doesn't look like tomorrow will be any better. I'm bushed."

Ethan left the warehouse and decided to swing by Sadie's house and make sure Harris's car was gone. He was going to ask around about the man. He didn't like how he had strolled back into Sadie's life, using the children against her.

He turned onto her street. Good. The car was gone. As he drove by her house, he glanced at the dashboard clock. Almost ten and he needed to go home and hit the sack. He slowed his SUV. The lights were on downstairs. Before he realized it, he parked in her driveway and headed for her porch.

"How did it go with Harris?" he asked when she opened the front door.

"Not good, but I appreciated the heads up. I should be getting ready for bed, but I can't sleep. All I can think about is his conversation with Ashley. She invited him here to talk to her."

"How did she get his number?"

"I asked her that a little while ago. Information. My resourceful daughter." She attempted a smile that didn't stay on her face.

"Do you want to talk about it? I can't sleep either. The warehouse was empty. Nothing to even indicate there had been a party."

"You believe Lexie, don't you?"

"Yes, the place was spotless. The people who cleaned up should have thrown around some dirt and dust. Added a few cobwebs."

She stepped to the side. "Come in. I was heading to the kitchen to get some hot chamomile tea. My mother says it works to help you sleep. I hope she's right."

"How are your parents getting along?"

"Mom is fine. My dad—I don't know."

"So he's still not talking to you?"

"I've never met a man so stubborn. I have to admit the men in my life haven't been too supportive, except for Cord." Sadie put a kettle of water on the stove. "I can fix you a cup, too."

"Think I'll pass just in case your mother is right and it works. I have to drive home. I wouldn't want to fall asleep on the way."

She laughed. "We can't have that happening. Too much is going on in town. I know Cord appreciates your help."

Ethan removed his cowboy hat and set it on the counter, then plowed a hand through his hair. "I haven't been back long, but there's a definite feel that's different. We did some stupid things growing up, but pill parties are over the top on any list. When I talked with Bradley, he was clueless Jared was taking prescription drugs. I get the same thing from Mary Lou."

"Kelly's mom has her own problems. I doubt she spends much time thinking about her daughter. Sad. As a parent of two kids coming into their teenage years, I'm concerned. You think you're doing the right thing and something happens to shoot that out of the water. Rock your world."

"Like Harris coming back?"

"Partly, but if good kids like Jared are taking drugs, it makes you wonder about everyone, even my own. I know you have to keep the communication between you and your kids open, and I thought I was until Harris showed up. I never imagined Ashley would go behind my back and contact him. Actually, if I had to choose which of my children would want to know their dad, it would have been Steven." The kettle whistled, and Sadie poured the hot water into a mug and dunked her tea bag into it.

"Why Steven and not Ashley?" Ethan lounged against the counter across from Sadie. The tired lines about her eyes tugged at him. The worry in her gaze drew him to her. He could remember once when he was eighteen having to rescue her from a rattlesnake, then consoling her. She'd cried against him until he'd thought she had nothing left inside her. Her tears had shaken him, and all he could do was hold her until she'd calmed down.

Sadie cupped her mug between her hands and took a sip. "I've worried about Steven not having a male figure in his life. I came back to Summerton for several reasons. One being that my son needed a good male influence in his life. Cord has been great and even my dad. He may not have anything to do with me, but he is establishing a relationship with my children."

"A lot has happened to us in the eighteen years since we last saw each other."

"Yeah, I got married, had two children, and became a teacher."

"I remember when you used to play teacher as a little girl. It was kind of cute seeing you try to get your dolls to do their schoolwork."

A flush infused her cheeks. She studied the contents of her mug, releasing a long sigh. "Ah, the good ole days with no worries. It wasn't easy going to college with two small children, but I love teaching."

"What's your opinion about certain students that go to Summerton High School?"

"Who?"

"Jared Montgomery. He was considered one of those good kids with a bright future. From your earlier comment you're surprised he'd taken so many different drugs."

"Yes, I guess I am. He had everything going for him. He was part of the popular group at school. On the football team, charming, actually a nice kid, but teenagers take risks. They don't think the rules apply to them. I didn't growing up. I'm still paying for the stupid choice I made eloping with Harris Blackburn." Her full lips tinged with a hint of pink lipstick formed a frown. Tiny lines made grooves between her eyebrows.

He didn't want to talk about Harris. The guy was a fool to have left her. He hadn't run into him yet, and maybe that was a good thing or he might have given him a piece of his mind for what he'd done to Sadie. "Were you surprised Jared was dating Kelly? She's not from the rich crowd."

"She's stunning and what guy doesn't like a pretty girl? But yes, to a certain extent I was. Kelly didn't run around with his group of friends until she started dating Jared."

"Brendan Livingston."

"He's a senior, and I'm sure you know, co-captain of the football team with Jared. He's dating Carrie. I often see them with Luke Adams and Missy Collins. If I had to pick the leaders of the popular kids it would be Brendan and Carrie."

"Have you heard any kids talking about pill parties?"

"No, but I've heard about them taking place in certain parts of the country. You think we've got that kind of problem at Summerton High School, or is this what happens when some rich kids get bored and look for a thrill?" She took a long sip of her drink then placed her mug on the counter next to her.

"I don't know how deep this goes or exactly what went down in the warehouse and later at the lake, but I intend to find out. I don't want anything to happen to my niece."

"Lexie is a wonderful kid to have in class. She's one of the students I don't have to worry about. Good head on her shoulders. Mature beyond her age."

"She lied to me."

"Not for long, because even though she'd promised Kelly, she knew she had to break that promise. That isn't easy for a person like Lexie. Her word is important to her."

"You seem to know my niece better than me."

"When I coached her in softball, I got to know her well. She's a leader. She'll go far." She smiled, dark brown eyes shining, as if only for him. "Give her time. You just returned to Summerton not long ago."

"I know. But I didn't realize how much I have missed in her life. I never had kids, and I think of her as one of mine, especially since her dad died a few years ago."

"And why didn't you marry?"

Surprised by the question, he chuckled. "Always straightforward. I'd forgotten that about you. It's one of the things I liked about you."

"You did?"

"I remember the time when I was going on a date and you told me I looked like a dork. You were twelve and I was sure you didn't know what you were talking about. I only had one date with the girl."

"Ah, yes. That was when you were wearing your hair a bit wild like you'd just gotten out of bed. You always looked best in jeans, cowboy boots and a hat with a solid-colored shirt. Dress pants didn't fit you, especially with bed head."

He grinned. "As much as I would like to continue down memory lane, I'd better go home and try to catch some sleep." He shoved away from the counter, picked up his tan cowboy hat and set it on his head.

Sadie walked with him to the front door and opened it. Her faint scent of vanilla teased his senses. He liked her clean, fresh smell. He liked her—a lot. That thought caused him to pause for a few seconds. She turned to him, a question in her eyes.

She was a friend, one he had known for a long time. Nothing more. He passed her and swung around. "Goodnight. If you ever want to talk, you know how to get in touch with me."

"Information?" she said with a twinkle in her eyes.

He chuckled.

"You know I've been thinking—why don't you come to dinner Friday night? Over the years, I've developed into a pretty good cook. If you're anything like my brother, your eating habits are horrible."

"Guilty, and yes to Friday night. I get one home-cooked meal a week from Beth and another from my mom, but otherwise I'm on my own and it isn't a pretty picture."

Laughter bubbled from her, a sweet sound after all that had gone on lately. "I've been to Cord's house. It could be declared a disaster zone."

"Mine's not that bad. My house is neat, and so is the kitchen because I have little in it. I usually eat out."

"I'll have to add my house as one of your stops during the week."

He snared her gaze, pleased by the offer but—

A loud crash sounded from above. Sadie glanced back then faced him. "I'd better go see what one of my kids broke this time. It's probably Steven. He's growing so fast he can't control his limbs sometimes."

"Mom, come here," Ashley shouted.

"Gotta go." Sadie shut the door.

Ethan made his way to his SUV. He'd never answered her about why he hadn't married. He'd come close a couple of times, but something always stopped him. Something had been missing. Maybe he felt he couldn't totally commit to another person. He'd seen so many of his colleagues over the years struggle in a marriage that ended with a divorce. Any woman he dated had to understand the kind of job he had and that wasn't always easy to find. What he dealt with in his work left its mark on him.

❧

"Mom, Steven fell and hit his head. It's bleeding," Ashley shouted as Sadie ran up the stairs and toward her son's bedroom.

When she entered the room, Steven sat on the floor, his eyes dazed. Ashley held a dirty T-shirt against his head, but blood quickly saturated the cloth. Beside her son laid a bottle of cough syrup.

Sadie knelt next to Steven. "We need to get you to the hospital. Go get a clean towel, Ashley." She eased the T-shirt off the wound to see how bad it was. A gash a couple of inches long graced the hairline at his left temple. "What happened?" she asked to see how coherent her son was.

He blinked. "I tripped over my guitar." He slurred his words, his tongue tripping over them.

Ashley rushed into the room with a towel.

Sadie took it and pressed it against his injury. "Maybe you should keep your room cleaner. This might not happen then." She glanced at Ashley. "Get my purse and meet me in the kitchen. I'm walking Steven down the stairs."

Her son batted at her hand holding the towel. "I can walk by myself."

"Are you sure?"

Instead of answering her, he struggled to his feet, swayed and fell back on the bed.

7

"I got here as soon as I could. What happened to Steven?" Cord asked the second he appeared in the waiting room.

Sadie had debated whether to try getting Ethan back to help with her son or calling an ambulance. She was so used to doing everything herself that she chose the latter. "I called an ambulance when I couldn't get him down the stairs after he fell and hit his head on the bedpost. The doctor is with him now."

"Where's Ashley?"

"Mom came and got her. I promised them I would call when I heard anything. I could be here for a while, especially if they keep him overnight." The image of the cough syrup on the floor intruded into her mind. She wanted to shove it away, to deny what it might mean.

"If it's a concussion, they probably will."

"That's what I was thinking. Mom is staying with Ashley at home and will make sure she gets to school." She twisted her hands together over and over.

"How did he fall?"

"Over his guitar. Actually he stepped on it. It's busted."

"Stepped on it? That's pretty hard to miss."

"I think—"

The doctor's appearance in the waiting room cut off Sadie's next words. The solemn expression on his face told her that what she suspected was right.

"We checked and yes, Ms. Thompson, your son ingested a large amount of cough syrup with codeine in it. We gave him activated charcoal and pumped his stomach."

Sadie closed her eyes and sucked in a deep breath. "That's what I thought when I saw the bottle on the floor. The last time I took the cough syrup, I opened a new bottle, and I only had a couple of doses. But now the bottle is empty, and I didn't see much spilled on the carpet."

"Sadly, this is something we see with kids. They think it's a cheap, safe high for them because it's just cough syrup. We had some teens come in who are high from taking the over-the-counter cough syrup with dextromethorphan, also known as DXM."

Cord put his arm around Sadie. She leaned against her brother, glad he was here, but wishing Ethan was, too. Her world was collapsing around her. First, Harris, and now this.

"Are you keeping him overnight?"

"Yes, for observation. Then I would recommend counseling and intervention for your son. This can become quite a problem. A form of escape, if allowed to continue. An escape that can lead to overdosing and death. An opiate like codeine can suppress the respiratory system."

A knifelike pain sliced through her chest. She couldn't get enough air. She leaned even more against Cord. Not her baby. What was Steven thinking? Until recently he usually told her everything.

"We're transferring him to room 215. I imagine you'll want to stay the night."

Sadie nodded, her throat jammed with emotions she couldn't express.

"Give them a few minutes to get him upstairs, then you can see him. He's pretty out of it. I gave him something for the pain."

"Not a narcotic one, I hope." Thinking about Jared sent a bolt of panic through Sadie. That would be all she needed, her son becoming addicted to painkillers.

"No, especially in light of what he was doing. But he's going to have one nasty hangover when he wakes up."

After the doctor left, Sadie finally released the tears cramming her throat. They ran down her face. "What have I done wrong, Cord?"

"Nothing. You're a great mother. But I'll tell you I don't like what has been going on in this town lately. I know we've had drug issues in the past, but it seems worse now. Like someone has moved in and is behind this rise in use."

Could it be Harris? That made her even more determined not to let him alone with her kids. She could see Harris doing something like selling prescription drugs to make money. Having a wad of cash had always been so important to him. She worshiped the Lord. Harris worshiped money.

༺৯

"What can I say? Lexie is lying. She's upset with me because I've made new friends." With her eyes puffy and a pallor to her cheeks, Kelly sat next to her mother in an interview room at the police station. "I know she's your niece, but she isn't who you think she is."

Ethan gripped his pen so tight he was afraid it would snap in two. "Who is she then?"

"Jealous. Envious of others, especially the kids I'm friends with. She wants what they have. We were together on Sunday morning. That much is true, but only because she came by my house to talk. We went driving. She ranted the whole time about how Jared wasn't good for me, and then she had the nerve to go to his funeral like she cared about him."

"So you know nothing about the warehouse? Or a pill party?"

"Why in the world would anyone do something that dumb?" Kelly's gaze darted to Mary Lou.

"I don't know. That's a good question. Why?"

Kelly shrugged, but the gesture wasn't as casual as she probably wanted to convey. There was a stiffness to her movement, betraying her inner turmoil.

Mary Lou rose slowly, putting her hand at the small of her back. "Next time, let's chat at a decent hour. My daughter has told you everything she knows. None of my medicine is missing, so if she had gone to this so-called pill party, what did she take?"

"We're not through here." Ethan said, grinding his teeth to keep from saying something he would regret.

"Yes, we are. We have cooperated. I even allowed Kelly's fingerprints to be taken because she is *innocent*. Unless you're gonna charge Kelly, I'm taking her to school. Late, by the way because you insisted on talking to her this morning. C'mon, honey. Let's go."

Kelly pushed to her feet.

Standing, Ethan caught her gaze. "I will find out the truth. I won't give up until I do."

"All you have is Lexie's word against Kelly's. My daughter has a group of the top students in school ready to support what she said. Do you want your niece's name dragged through the mud?" Mary Lou's voice increased several decibels as she tossed out her threat.

"Remember how I was in high school, Mary Lou? I never gave up until I succeeded. I still have that same determination. Actually, even more so because what I do is important. I catch criminals who think they can get away with breaking the law."

The color washed from Mary Lou's face as she stared at Ethan for a long moment before averting her gaze. She slung her arm around her daughter and tilted up her chin, returning her glance to his face. "Good. You might want to look close to home."

He watched the two leave, Kelly leaning into her mother who kept her posture straight, shoulders back. What happened to Mary Lou? She used to be a friend in high school. She'd cared about others back then, but now he didn't know what she cared about other than drinking. He recalled once when they had been talking, how she'd cried about a boy in one of her classes who was being bullied. She'd begged him to step in and help her classmate. He did and became friends with Jeffrey Livingston.

Cord paused in the doorway. "I just got here. I caught most of the interview. I never thought I would hear Kelly say something like that about Lexie. They've been friends since grade school."

"Yeah, I know." Ethan half sat, half lounged against the table. "I don't like what's happening on so many levels. I meant every word to Mary Lou. I'm going to find out what's going on in Summerton." He studied Cord who appeared to have combed his hair with his fingers. "What delayed you this morning? Your officer only told me you would be late because of a family problem."

A scowl darkened his friend's face. "Sadie had to call an ambulance last night. Steven fell and put a big gash in his head. She couldn't get him down the stairs to take him to the hospital."

"I'd just left there. If only I'd known, I could have helped." Why hadn't she called him? He would have turned around and gone back to her house.

"Steven drank almost a whole bottle of cough syrup, the kind with codeine. I went by the hospital this morning to make sure everything was all right. I knew you could handle picking up Kelly and Mary Lou."

"Has Steven said anything about why he did it?" Sadie must be devastated. He wished he could have been there for her.

"No, he's sleeping, but you better believe I'll be asking that question. What was the boy thinking?"

The urge to make sure Sadie was all right hit him, demanding he forget his job for the time being. But he couldn't. Kids were being hurt. He tamped down the impulse and said, "I'm going to stop by the hospital after I talk with Luke. Then I'm going back to the warehouse." A compromise he could live with.

"I'll meet you there. Call me when you head for the warehouse. I have another case I have to look into. A couple called in a while ago about someone breaking into their cabin on the lake. I need to check that out."

"Is Luke here?"

Cord pulled a toothpick out of his pocket and rolled it between his thumb and forefinger. "Yep. And not too happy. Jeffrey is here representing him."

"Is his dad here?"

"Nope."

"Interesting. I would have thought he would be."

"Mr. Adams, like Bradley, leaves legal issues to Jeffrey."

"When did the Adams family move here?"

One of Cord's eyebrows arched. "What are you thinking?"

"Nothing. Just curious."

"Four years ago. He started buying up a lot of property. He came in spending money right and left. Definitely a shark. He didn't have to pay full price for most of the property he purchased. It was when the market was so depressed. He was like a chocoholic in a chocolate store told to take whatever he could grab."

Ethan laughed. "Nice visual. I can relate to that." He made his way into the hallway. "You're welcome to join me."

"I'll let you have the fun. A warning, though, Jeffrey isn't the puny guy you knew in high school. He's ruthless and will go in for the kill when he sees a weak spot."

"That's what I've heard. He certainly looks different from back then." Something else not the same as when he'd grown up in Summerton. Why couldn't people and places stay the same?

"I understand he swims every morning no matter what the weather is."

"Even in the winter? I know they are usually mild here, but not that mild."

"Yep. I've seen him." Cord went into the room next to the one Ethan would be using to listen in on the conversation.

Ethan strode toward the front of the station to escort Luke and Jeffrey back to the interview room. He shook Jeffrey's hand. "It's good to see you again. I wish it was under different circumstances, though."

"So do I." Jeffrey's large frame filled out his expensive suit nicely. Tanned, not a hair out of place, the person Ethan had known eighteen years ago had completely changed—not necessarily a bad thing.

The day he'd first met Jeffrey flashed into his mind. A group of boys were stuffing Jeffrey into his locker. Ethan broke the group up and told them if they ever laid a hand on Jeffrey again they would have to answer to him. At that time, Ethan had grown within a couple of inches of his height today—six feet four. But he'd also been weightlifting to beef up for the football team. Jeffrey had cowered behind Ethan that day, shaking. The lawyer's bearing now wasn't anything like that frightened kid. Just another reminder nothing stayed the same.

Jeffrey set his briefcase on the table as though setting up a barrier between them. "I have a full day. Let's get this done so I can go to the office and Luke can go to school. You have nothing on Luke. He is here out of a courtesy to you. We want this to end today."

"So do I, but for that to occur certain questions need to be answered satisfactorily. I'm sure you want to clear up what happened to Jared. Answer his parents' questions concerning their son's death." He met Jeffrey's gaze head on, sizing up the new man. Then Ethan turned his attention to Luke. "You lied to me. You did write that note passed to Jared. Why didn't you tell me the truth? Are you hiding something?"

Luke glanced at Jeffrey. His lawyer nodded. "I didn't think it was important. We were planning to go camping one weekend, and our girlfriends were going to meet us. Jared wanted to bring Kelly. We don't bring anyone on those weekend trips without getting everybody's okay. We're a close group, and one person can ruin it if we aren't careful."

The teen spoke as if he had recited his spiel in front of a mirror until it flowed naturally from him. But it was too practiced. "Do your parents know about these—little outings?"

"We've been doing it for a while, but only recently have we taken along our girlfriends. Their parents don't know, so you can see why I wanted to keep it quiet." His cheeks reddened, a nice touch to emphasize his embarrassment. "It had nothing to do with what happened to Jared, so I saw no harm in saying what I did."

Ethan didn't believe him. Small tells gave Luke away—his eyes twitching, his finger rubbing the skin above his mouth. "When was the last time you went?"

"The weekend before school started."

"Where did you go?"

"Why?"

"Because I'm going to check out your story." Ethan wanted to expose Luke's lies, force him to tell the truth.

"What's this got to do with what happened to Jared?" Jeffrey asked.

"I'm not sure yet, but Luke lied to me because of the weekend outings. I want to make sure he's telling me the truth this time."

"I am." Luke raised his voice several levels and clenched his hands.

"Then you have nothing to worry about. Where did you go before school started? Who went with you?"

Luke's face reddened even more, his knuckles taut and white.

Jeffrey placed his hand on the boy's arm. "Give him what he wants, then we're leaving. We will *not* participate in a fishing expedition."

Luke inhaled then exhaled a large breath. "Jared, Kalvin, Brendan, and me. The only girls were Carrie and Missy. Kalvin's girlfriend, Zoe, couldn't get away, and Jared hadn't been dating Kelly long. We camped on the north side of the lake in the woods."

Jeffrey rose. "I can tell you my son did go on a camping trip right before school with them. If you have more questions for Luke, contact me." He indicated to the teen to stand.

Luke immediately complied, keeping his gaze averted.

Cord entered the interview room twenty seconds after the pair left. The police chief shook his head. "I'll have one of my detectives check into this—story."

"I think there'll be truth to at least the camping trip in August. But he rehearsed what he was going to say, because what he said about the last trip that was planned was a lie. When you are planning a lie ground it in as much truth as you can."

"So what do you want to do about this?"

"Have the detective verify the one in August. I'll be contacting the parents of the girls about the one supposedly planned for now. It'll be interesting to see what they say. I know the kids are acting as one, but are the adults, especially Bradley and Annabelle? I might even call them all down here together. Have the other parents in the same room as Bradley and Annabelle. Will they keep the pretense up when faced with Jared's parents?"

"You know, I think you're a good match for Jeffrey. You can be ruthless and merciless." Cord grinned.

"I don't want to see other teens die like Jared."

"I have a call into Maxwell Howard about doing a program at the high school concerning prescription drug abuse. He usually schedules the assemblies."

"Good. I want to be included in that one. Sadie told me that Cynthia Proctor counsels students concerning drugs at the high school. She might want to participate in the assembly." Ethan picked up his hat he'd placed on a chair against the wall. "I'm going to the hospital. I'll call you when I head to the warehouse."

Twenty minutes later, Ethan poked his head into Steven's room. Sadie looked up and smiled, motioning for him to come inside. As he passed the bed, Steven lay asleep in a darkened room with streams of light leaking through the blinds—enough that he could read the exhaustion and worry on Sadie's face. He took the seat next to her on the small couch.

"How's he doing?"

"Finally sleeping peacefully. For part of the night, his stomach was upset. When I helped him into the bathroom, he was wobbly on his feet. "

"That's the cough syrup. It can make a person sick when they take so much."

"Serves him right. I hope he remembers that."

"What are you going to do?" Angling toward her, Ethan settled his arm along the back of the couch.

"Find out why he did it. Get him some help. And keep a close eye on him. I'm going to find out what's happening to the kids in Summerton."

He took her hand. "That's my job."

"No, it's every parent's job, too. I know some of the teachers at the middle school. I want to get their take on this, and I'll be talking with our nurse. Cynthia might be able to help me deal with this, because right now I'd like to ground him until I'm no longer responsible for him."

"Would that change anything? Do you think once he turns eighteen you'll turn off being his mother?"

Sadie's shoulder sagged. "No, it's a lifetime job. Why can't they behave like I want them to? Then there would be no problems."

Ethan chuckled. "If only that were true."

"Cord said you were interviewing Kelly and Luke this morning. Did you discover anything that will help your case?"

"Kelly is getting more sure of herself when she lies, and Luke has his story down pat. Next time I'm going to have Cord talk with Kelly since my niece is involved."

"What did Kelly say?"

He told her. "The thing is she's backpedaling from what she said on Sunday when I talked with her. And why would Lexie make up a story? What does she gain by doing that?"

"I know Lexie. What she told me last night was the truth. She gained nothing by telling me, then you, about the warehouse." Sadie put her hand over her mouth to stifle a yawn.

He assessed her, noting the dark circles under her tired eyes. "Did you get any sleep?"

"Are you kidding? No, I heard every sound last night."

He placed his arm around her and tugged her back against him. "Rest. I'll be here if Steven needs something."

"Maybe I will for a short time." She yawned. "I know you have better things to do than baby-sit me."

"Nope, it can wait. Friends help friends. You need your rest if you're going to handle Steven when he wakes up." He wanted to be here for her.

She snuggled against him, laying her head against his shoulder. Her eyelids drifted closed, and the tension he felt in her body gradually eased. For a long time, he watched her sleep, taking in the soft curve of her jaw line, her pert nose, the long, dark lashes dusting the tops of her cheeks.

When she murmured something and shifted in his embrace, her long blond hair fell forward, hiding her from his view. He smoothed the errant strands behind her ear and continued his perusal. Delicate. Pleasing to the eye.

How could Harris walk out on their marriage, leaving her with two babies?

Although layers of grime covered the windows in the warehouse, the lighting was brighter than the night before, making it easier for Ethan to search all the nooks and crannies. As he completed checking the perimeter and began to move closer in, Cord came into the building.

He started in the center and worked out toward Ethan. "Sorry I'm late. I stayed at the station thinking you'd be calling half an hour or so after you left. When you didn't, I went to see about the cabin someone broke into."

"Sadie was upset. Steven had a restless night. She didn't sleep at all. I decided to stay and give her a chance to rest. I told her I would let her know if Steven needed her."

Surprise flitted across Cord's face. "She didn't say anything to me when I was there earlier. What's going on with you two?"

Ethan paused in his trek. "Nothing. We're friends."

"Since when?"

"Since we were young," Ethan said and tried to ignore Cord's snort. "Okay, we weren't exactly friends then because of the age gap, but I've known Sadie for years."

"Do I need to ask your intentions toward my sister? She's vulnerable right now."

"I know. Harris isn't making life easier. But we're just friends. With all that's going on when would we have time for anything else?" Ethan caught a glimpse of something shiny out of the corner of his eye and squatted to examine a hidey-hole in the wall that he hadn't seen before.

"You want there to be something else?"

"I could ask you the same thing concerning Beth. I'm not blind. I've seen the looks you two exchange."

"I asked first."

Ethan pulled out his flashlight to inspect the place and used a pen to poke into it. "Quit being a big brother and put on your cop hat. Come over here. Look at what I found."

After donning latex gloves, Ethan withdrew a silver chain with a heart dangling from it with the letters KAW engraved on it. He opened the locket to see a picture of Jared in it. "Bingo. I'd like to see Kelly explain this to me after her earlier statement. But before we present her with the evidence of her presence here, I want to check for latent prints. Good thing I took her fingerprints to rule out she was at the warehouse since she insisted Lexie was lying." He gave the evidence bag to Cord. "I'll let you handle its transport."

"Maybe we'll find something else."

"We can only hope." Ethan resumed his search of the warehouse. "Did you discover anything at the cabin?"

"Definitely someone used the place without permission but nothing was stolen. A few things were moved around, but the owners met me at the cabin and couldn't find anything gone."

"Was there anything worthwhile to take?"

"TV and a sound system. Some small appliances in the kitchen."

"So someone used the cabin for what?"

"Partying probably," Cord said with a frown. "We dusted for latent prints, but it was pretty clean, especially if a party took place there."

"Like someone had wiped it down?"

"That or wore gloves. They're putting in a silent alarm, in case the person or persons come back."

"Is the cabin isolated?"

"Yes. Woods all around. They routinely check on the place twice a month. Guess when?"

"The first and the fifteen?"

"The fifth and the twentieth of the month."

Having completed the search, Ethan met Cord at the door. "If anyone knew the owners' routine, they would know when the cabin would be empty."

"That's my thinking. I told them to keep it quiet about the silent alarm."

"So you're thinking what I'm thinking. It's kids, maybe even the group who threw the pill party here."

"Last Saturday was the fifth."

"Who is the couple?"

Cord grinned. "The Collins."

"As in Missy's parents."

"Grandparents."

Ethan chuckled. "I hope they keep it from their family. If so, we might actually catch these kids in the act."

"That is, if they do it again. After what happened to Jared if they're smart, they won't."

"Who said they're smart? They're kids. Invincible. They think bad things won't happen to them. Remember when we felt that way?"

Cord nodded and left through the warehouse's back entrance. "I wish I could protest that statement, but sadly they might not for a while, and I bet they'll eventually do it again."

Ethan slapped his friend on the back. "That's why we're here. To stop them before they do it again. And pray to the Lord that we'll break this wide open before another kid falls victim."

❧

On Friday, Lexie stood at the door of the cafeteria, tray in hand, surveying the room. Just one quiet spot in this entire place, was that too much to ask? She shook her head. There was nothing quiet about the large room at lunchtime. But at least she found a table to sit at with only one girl. If it weren't raining, she'd go outside where she could be by herself in an isolated place on campus.

"Hi, I'm Susie," the teenager across from Lexie said.

"I want to be left alone," she wanted to shout at the girl who she was sure was a freshman by the books stacked on the table. Instead, she smiled but didn't reply. She didn't want to carry on a conversation when her whole world was falling apart around her.

The teen looked at Lexie for a few seconds, then stuffed the rest of the sandwich in her mouth, gathered her backpack and textbooks, and left.

Lexie kept her gaze down until the girl was gone. She didn't even care that she'd made a student mad at her. If the girl knew who she was, she wouldn't have stayed anyway. With all the rumors about her being a liar flying around the school, Lexie Alexander was a pariah. The memory of the looks she'd received all morning knotted her muscles. Few people had acknowledged she was even at school. It was like she was invisible. She peered at her pizza, but her stomach churned as the odor of congealing cheese hit her.

A nearby table full of juniors stared at her. Other students leaned close and whispered to each other, then fixed their gazes on her.

All because she'd finally told her uncle the truth. She should have sooner, but she'd let the years she and Kelly had been best friends sway her to go against what she knew was right.

She gave up trying to eat, stood, and shoved her chair back. After gathering her food, she headed for the large trashcans near the double doors. She rounded the corner and ran into Kelly, Lexie's drink splashing onto both her and Kelly. Her paper cup flew out of her hand.

Lexie didn't care that she was wet or her Coke was all over the floor. Her attention riveted on Kelly, who she'd tried to find all morning ever since she heard the first rumor about the warehouse.

"I didn't mean to get you in trouble," Lexie blurted out before Kelly's surprised expression changed to anger.

Eyes wide, her friend glanced down at her drenched blouse then at Lexie's equally wet shirt and burst out laughing. "You'd think we had been outside standing in the rain."

"You aren't mad?"

"You mean about being dragged down to the police station yesterday morning?"

Lexie nodded, waiting for her anger to erupt. "I didn't lie to my uncle about what happened."

Kelly pulled her away from some teens. "I know. I had to say that. My mother made me. She was scared I'd get into trouble."

"How did people find out about your interview?"

Kelly shrugged. "My mom loves to talk. She went to get her hair cut yesterday. I'm sure she said something about it. She was furious about me being treated like a criminal. I'm sorry about all the talk. If they see we're still friends, people will quit saying things." She started for the food line. "Get some paper towels while I get both of us a drink and we'll talk."

Confused, Lexie watched Kelly walk away. Did she hear the conversation right? Kelly wasn't mad at her. They had been through a lot together. Maybe that counted for something. She hurried to the restroom to get some paper towels to help dry them off.

As she returned to the hallway, Kelly was there waiting. She handed her a Coke then pulled her toward a set of stairs at the far end of the corridor away from the crowd of teens.

"Tell me about the science test. I haven't studied like I should. I think I'm gonna flunk it. How can any of us concentrate with all that has been going on this week?" Kelly took a seat on the second step.

Lexie glanced up toward the top of the stairs and spied several kids talking, but otherwise it was quiet. Much better than the lunchroom, especially with her best friend speaking to her. She'd called and texted Kelly last night, but she hadn't acknowledged them. Lexie knew how intense her uncle could be when working on a case.

She dug into her backpack and pulled out her notes. "I can tell you what will be covered on the test. That might help."

Kelly smiled. "Oh, good. I thought you'd be mad at me because of the rumor. Your uncle didn't believe me, so at least you won't be in trouble." She raised her drink. "Here's to friendship."

She'd started to ask Kelly why she didn't return her calls last night but decided it wasn't important. She was talking to her now at last, and people were seeing there were no hard feelings between them. Relieved that something was going right at last today, Lexie clicked her Coke against Kelly's. "We've both made mistakes, but that can't stand in the way of us being friends."

"No, I like knowing who my friends are."

As Lexie took a long swig of her drink, laughter from the group above filled the stairwell. She looked up to find Missy had joined them. The teen glared at Lexie. "Maybe we should go somewhere else."

"No, don't let them bother you. Let me see what I need to look over next hour." Kelly took a drink from her cup.

With another sip, Lexie opened her notes. "You'll need to know the periodic table forward and backwards."

Kelly groaned and bent over the page.

⁓𝕰⁓

Since the past week, Sadie made sure she was outside her room as the students passed to their next class. Although exhausted from the ordeal with Steven Wednesday night and Thursday, she still dragged herself out into the hall, vigilant. She wasn't going to let her son go down the path Jared, a good kid, took. Nor was she going to let these students if she could do anything about it.

Through the throng of teens, pressing their way through the crowd, she watched for any signs something wasn't right. She'd been reading about prescription drug abuse, and it made her sick how prevalent it was. She should have been more aware. She'd become complacent, and now she had a son who thought he could take cough syrup anytime things weren't going the way he wanted, believing that drugs would make things all better.

If they only knew, it made the situation much worse.

Lexie passed her to go into the room. She appeared the way Sadie felt, tired, going through the motions of the day with as little effort as she could get away with. Lexie didn't even say hi as she usually did when she saw her. It had been a hard week for her, too, and today she'd heard rumors flying through the student body about how Lexie had lied to the police concerning Kelly.

As time neared the start of class, the hallway began to thin out. Sadie made a final visual sweep. Her gaze fell on a student in a black hoodie at the end of the corridor bump into another teen, slid his hand out of his pocket and pass something to the boy who gave him something, too. Their gazes connected for a brief moment, then both hurried away—one rounding a corner, leaving the corridor. The other in the hoodie went into a classroom at the far end of the hallway. She spied the face of the boy rounding the corner. It was one of her students: Kalvin Majors. Normally she wouldn't have thought much of it, but now she couldn't shake her doubt. What if it was drugs? Wasn't Kalvin part of Jared's group?

The bell rang, and she headed into her class. She hated this. Seeing every action as a possible drug deal going down. Kalvin was from a good family. Why would he need money selling drugs, even prescription ones? She was overreacting to what happened to Jared.

After taking roll, Sadie started her presentation about the new novel her students would be studying. Twenty minutes later, she finished with her PowerPoint on the Smart Board and turned around to take in the whole class. "I want you to research the culture of China at the time *The Good Earth* was written. Let me know on Monday what aspect of the culture you want to write a three-page paper on. The assignment is due next Friday." Her gaze swept over the five rows of students to assure herself they had heard. Come Monday she would have some declare they hadn't known anything about the assignment.

Her glance landed on Lexie with her head down on the desk, eyes closed. As she walked toward the teen, she said, "You can have thirty minutes on the Internet to start researching China in the early twentieth century for use as possible topics for your paper. Sign out the computer you're going to use."

At Lexie's desk, Sadie shook the girl's shoulder, trying to wake her up. Nothing. She jostled her more and raised her voice loud enough to be heard over the noisy students. "Lexie, wake up."

Still no response.

Sadie glanced at her student aide. "Oliver, go next door and get Mrs. Baker."

Everyone in class swiveled around and stared.

"Lexie, wake up," Sadie yelled near Lexie and tried lifting her up, but she was dead weight.

Her heartbeat galloping like a runaway horse, Sadie straightened and started for the phone as Mrs. Baker came in. "Can you take my students to your class?" She gestured toward Lexie, still out cold.

Mrs. Baker hustled the kids out of the room while Sadie called for the nurse. Then she went back and felt for a pulse, nearly wilting with relief when she found one. She tried again to stir Lexie and met with no response. If she hadn't felt the girl's life forces beating beneath her fingertips, Sadie would think Lexie was dead. Which could still happen. The thought sent Sadie's pulse racing even more through her body, and perspiration covered her forehead.

Robin David, her friend down the hall, came in to help, but nothing she did roused Lexie either. Sadie kept looking at the clock. It had only been a few minutes since she'd called Cynthia, but it seemed an eternity until the nurse hurried into the classroom.

"I can't get her up. We've," Sadie indicated herself and Robin, "tried everything."

Cynthia checked Lexie's pulse, frowned then examined her further. "Call 911."

8

$\mathcal{F}$riday afternoon, Ethan stuck his head into Cord's office on his way to see his grandma at the nursing home. "The latent prints on the locket match Kelly's, and I found a picture of Kelly on Facebook wearing the same locket with Jared's arm around her. I'm going to call Mary Lou to bring her back in. I'm on my way to meet up with Mom at the nursing home. She's upset about something. I'll be back to speak with Kelly."

"I'll let them stew in the interview room until you're back."

"Good. It might accomplish something. You should see the comments left on Kelly's Facebook about how lucky she is not to be friends with Lexie anymore. They're even saying my niece was a traitor. My blood boiled as I read them. When I went to Lexie's Facebook page, I nearly tossed the computer against the wall. This all in the past twenty-four hours."

"I'll take a look. Cyber-bullying can be bad news. How did everyone find out about what Lexie told you?"

"It wasn't us, so that leaves Mary Lou and/or Kelly. Something is going down, and my niece is caught in the middle. I don't have a good feeling about this. I'll need to go see her this evening."

Cord rose from behind his desk. "I'll take care of Mary Lou bringing Kelly in. Family is one of the reasons you came back home."

"And one of the reasons you stay. It seems we've both had a lot of family obligations lately."

"Yeah, I'm paying Steven a visit again later. Last night he wasn't communicating to anyone. All he did was sit in his room and basically pout. Something is festering in him."

Ethan leaned his shoulder against the doorjamb. "Could it have to do with his father showing up?"

Cord released a slow breath. "Possibly. Or something going on at school. Thirteen can be a difficult year in a kid's life."

"Is that coming from experience?" Ethan's mouth tilted up in a grin.

"What do you think? We went through it together," Cord said with a laugh. "I still remember some of the trouble we got into. That's why Sadie asked me to try and talk to Steven."

"A good male role model is what Steven needs." He knew firsthand. His father died when he was ten. If it hadn't been for Cord's dad, he wouldn't have had one. At home, there had only been females—his older sister, Mom, and his grandmother. He shivered when he remembered all the estrogen flowing around the house when he was a teen. "I can't tell you how much I appreciated your dad helping me and listening when I needed a male's perspective."

"I keep hoping Dad will come see Steven at the house. I've never seen him hold onto his anger so long against Sadie. He does things with Steven but hasn't stepped foot in Sadie's home."

"Have you talked with him about it?"

"Tried to. He cut me off and left the room. He can be one stubborn ole coot."

Ethan chuckled. Some of the tension from reading the scathing comments about Lexie dissolved. "Don't let him hear you say that."

"Are you kidding—no way."

Ethan's cell phone played "The Eyes of Texas." He glanced at it. Beth. He wasn't surprised to hear from her. She kept an eye on Lexie's Facebook page, and no doubt she'd seen it. "What's up?"

"She's been taken to the hospital," his sister said, sobs wrapped up in each word.

"Who? Lexie?"

"Yes. The school just called. I'm heading to the emergency room now. Please meet me there."

"Yes." Before he could say he would come pick her up, his sister disconnected. He looked at his friend. "Hold off bringing Kelly in. Lexie has been taken to the hospital from school." Ethan started to turn away.

"I can take care of Kelly and question her."

Ethan froze and clutched the doorframe. "*No.* I want to be there when she's interviewed again. I have a bad feeling about this."

Cord nodded. "I understand. Please let me know what's going on. Tell your sister if she needs me, I'll be there."

Ethan left Cord's office. One of the main reasons he'd come back to Summerton was to be closer for his family, especially as his mother got older and Nana had to be put into a nursing home. But when you care about another, you become vulnerable. You no longer have control over your own emotions. First, Sadie with her son, and now Beth, with his niece. Tightness in his chest made each breath labored. He'd worked so hard to close himself off from others in order to do his job. But at the moment, he felt gutted.

Lord, what's going on? What do I do?

⁂

The second Beth saw Ethan come into the ER waiting room, tears welled to the surface and flowed down her cheeks. She hurried to him and clasped him, needing to feel his arms around her. She felt so alone.

"She was unresponsive. She could die," Beth cried against her brother's chest.

Ethan rubbed his hand up and down Beth's back. "What happened?"

His calm voice filtered through the frantic sensations—heart hammering, pulse racing, breath panting—bombarding Beth from every side. She closed her eyes and tried to visualize her sweet baby when she'd left for school that morning. She couldn't. All she could see was her lying in the cubicle in the emergency room, out cold while the doctor and nurse worked on her.

Trying to save her life.

What if they didn't?

"Beth? What happened to Lexie?"

Focus on Ethan. Answer his question. Don't think about what ifs.

The advice came out of nowhere, but she latched onto it. "She was in Sadie's class when it happened. Sadie found Lexie with her head on her desk. Totally out. They couldn't wake her. The paramedics couldn't. What if she doesn't ever wake up?"

Ethan's arms tensed around her, but his voice held the same soothing tone as he said, "She will. She's where she needs to be with the doctors working on her. I called Mom, and she's on her way here. Cord will be here soon, too."

"I ran out of the nursing home and didn't even think to tell Mom. Nana is being difficult today. Agitated. We may have to up her tranquilizer. I had a call into the doctor about it. This is the third day she's been like this."

"C'mon. Let's sit down." He tugged her toward a corner with several chairs. "Tell me how Lexie was before leaving for school. Upset? Sad?"

"Both. This thing with Kelly has really gotten to her. She tried to call Kelly several times yesterday, but she couldn't reach her. She's sure Kelly is mad at her. I told her she should be mad at Kelly for putting her in a situation where she had to lie to us. When I grounded Lexie and took her car away, she didn't even protest it like she usually does."

"This can be hard on everyone. There are a lot of questions and few answers."

The ER doctor appeared in the entrance of the waiting room. His brows were drawn, and his lips pressed in a thin line. Her heart sank. She gripped Ethan's hand while the doctor made his way to her.

"We've done all we can. She's stabilized but is still unresponsive."

"What happened to cause this?"

"Don't know. Any history of seizures, allergic reactions—anything like this before?"

"No. Lexie has always been very healthy."

"I've drawn blood, and we're running some tests. Is she on any medication?"

"No, what do you suspect?" Beth stiffened, her fingernails digging into Ethan's skin. He winced, and she loosened her grasp but needed the physical connection with her brother. She wished Cord were here, too.

I'm not alone. I'm not alone.

"An overdose. I should get the results back on a tox screen soon. I've asked the lab to rush it. I'll let you know when I hear something."

"Can I stay with her?"

"Yes."

Beth stood, her legs so weak she swayed into Ethan. He clasped his arm around her.

He helped her to the room, then paused at the bed, taking Lexie's hand in his. "Lex, I'll get to the bottom of this whole mess. That's a promise. Don't you worry. Just wake up." His voice roughened, thick with emotions her brother usually kept locked away.

Beth touched his arm. "I'm so glad you're here in Summerton."

Without looking at her, he headed toward the hallway. "I'm going outside to wait for Mom, so she'll know what's happening. She should be here soon." At the entrance, he glanced back at Beth, his eyes watery.

"Thanks. I appreciate that. She's probably freaking out with all that has gone on."

"I'll calm her down before I bring her in here."

When Ethan left, Beth sagged against the back of the padded chair. Her hands trembling, she fit them together as though she was praying. But no words came to her mind. No matter how much she told herself she wasn't alone, a deep sense of isolation and loneliness blanketed her.

Even when Ethan returned with their mother, and she had her family around her as they waited, she watched her daughter lie in the bed hooked up to an IV and felt her life spiraling out of control.

Tox screen? Overdose? Not Lexie.

Lexie's eyes fluttered open. Beth jumped to her feet and hurried to the side of the bed. "Get the doctor. Baby, I'm here."

Ethan hurried from the room while Beth's mother stood next to her. Lexie licked her lips and tilted her head slightly toward Beth.

Lexie's eyelids slid closed halfway. "Mom—where—am I?" she asked in a groggy voice.

"The hospital. Ms. Thompson couldn't wake you up at school." Beth held her daughter's hand. "You're gonna be all right, baby."

"What happen . . ." Her daughter ran her tongue over her lips again.

"I was hoping you'd tell us."

Ethan and the doctor came into the cubicle. She glanced back at them. "She's awake."

"Good," the ER doctor said and crossed to the bed to check Lexie out. "Did you take any medication today?"

"No."

"What did you have at lunch?"

"Nothing. Not—hungry." Lexie closed her eyes for a few seconds.

"Anything to drink?"

"Coke." Lexie pressed her mouth together. "Water. Thirsty."

The doctor nodded.

As Beth poured a cup and helped Lexie to take a sip, she asked the man, "What's going on?"

"Let's have a word out in the hall," the doctor said in a solemn voice.

"Mom, can you help Lexie with the water?"

"Sure." Her mother took the cup from Beth.

She strode out into the corridor with Ethan right behind her. "Is she going to be all right?"

"Yes, with time. In fact, we won't keep her overnight."

"But you don't know what caused this."

The doctor frowned. "Mrs. Alexander, I got the tox screen back. Your daughter took a large dose of tranquilizers."

That evening Ethan answered his sister's front door to find Sadie standing on her porch with Lexie's backpack. "I could have come and gotten it. I know you've had your hands full with Steven."

"Mom came over so I could see how Lexie is. When I called the hospital and they said she had been discharged, I figured it was a good sign. How is she?"

He opened the door wider for her to enter the house. "She's sleeping now."

"What happened? I was so worried."

"Come in. Beth's upstairs sitting with her while our mother went home to get a nightgown and change of clothes. She's going to stay here tonight to help Beth." He dragged his fingers through his hair, rolling his head around to loosen his taut neck muscles. "It's been a long day."

"I can imagine. Do they know what's wrong?"

"Yes, she took too many tranquilizers."

"She's on medication?"

"No, and she doesn't have any idea how she took them. The only things she had since breakfast were the water in her bottle she carries and a Coke at lunch."

"Do you believe her?" Sadie sank down on the couch.

Her question ignited the anger simmering in his gut. "A few days ago I would have said yes without any hesitation, but since she didn't tell me what really happened with Kelly until much later, I don't know for sure." He sat next to her. "I know what drugs can do to people. It changes them."

She took his hand on the couch between them. "It's hard when you begin to doubt someone you thought you knew."

"I figured you would understand." The touch of her palm against his skin sent warmth up his arm. A light vanilla fragrance surrounded him and unraveled some knots in his stomach.

"For what it's worth, I don't see Lexie taking a bunch of tranquilizers."

"Not even after what went on at school today? She said most of the students ostracized her because she told on Kelly. There were a lot of nasty comments left on Lexie's Facebook page."

Her forehead crinkled, her eyebrows dipping down. "After school I heard some kids saying they weren't surprised she turned on her friend, since her uncle was a Texas Ranger. A couple of students stood up for Lexie. When I stopped to ask what was going on, they all hurried away." Sadie angled around to face him squarely. "No, I still think Lexie wouldn't do it. She was too concerned with what Kelly did on Saturday night. She was worried her best friend was in trouble."

"Let's agree that Lexie didn't take tranquilizers knowingly. That leaves taking them unknowingly."

Sadie's eyes widened. "You mean someone slipped them in something like her Coke or water bottle."

"It had to be at school because she crashed in your class after lunch. It wouldn't take long for those tranquilizers to take effect with the amount in her system, especially if she hadn't eaten anything."

"Come to think about it when she walked into my classroom, she was moving slow. She looked tired. Since I was aware of what had been going on with her and Kelly, I chalked it up to not sleeping last night. It's not easy to break a promise to a friend and not fret over it. At least for Lexie."

"She should never have promised her in the first place."

"I agree, but we're talking about kids. They don't always make wise decisions."

"We do? I've made my share of mistakes."

"Me, too."

His gaze locked with hers, and in that moment a connection sprang up between them he couldn't deny, no matter how vulnerable he felt laying his emotions on the line. "Have you heard from Harris lately?"

She crossed her arms and rubbed her hands up and down them. "No, but then I'm not surprised."

"Does he know what Steven did the other night?"

She lifted her shoulder in a shrug. "I don't know. It's not my place to inform him. He lost that right when he walked out. I know I should forgive him, but I can't. All I can remember was how hard it was to raise Ashley and Steven alone, holding down a job and going to school."

"You should have come back to Summerton. Your mother and brother would have helped."

"Cord probably would, but Mom wouldn't have. At first she was so angry with me like Dad still is. She came around eventually because of the kids."

The sound of the front door opening and closing brought Ethan to his feet. "Mom?"

"Yes."

"Good, I'm glad you're staying tonight at Beth's," he said as his mother appeared in the entrance to the living room.

"It's nice to see you, Sadie. I heard what happened to Steven. You would think there's something in the water making these kids do crazy things."

"Or someone," Ethan said under his breath.

His mother's eyes popped wide open. "Like a drug ring?"

"Usually where drugs are involved, there are pushers and suppliers also. Money is to be had with the sale of prescription drugs. Millions of dollars. Even though they aren't what people think of as illegal ones like heroin or cocaine, they can do as much damage and become addictive."

Sadie frowned. "Look at what happened to Jared."

His mother's face blanched. "And my poor darling, Lexie. If she'd taken just a little more, the doctor said she would have died. Someone tried to kill her."

"So you don't think she took them?" Sadie asked.

"No way. She doesn't even like taking an aspirin for a headache."

"You're right, Mom. I'd forgotten about that."

"Well, I'm going upstairs to relieve Beth. She needs some rest."

Sadie drew in a deep breath and let it go slowly. "Who would spike Lexie's drink?"

"Someone who wants to make a point. Someone who wants to keep her quiet." *Or dead.*

"Discrediting her is a good way to make what she told you unreliable."

"I'm talking with Kelly again tomorrow. I intend to find out what contact she had with Lexie today, then I'll check with my niece to see if the stories match."

"So you're thinking this is Kelly's doing?"

"I don't know, but the way Kelly has been acting it could be." Ethan remembered Kelly's interview yesterday and her declaring Lexie lied. "I want the drugs fully out of her system and my niece alert. Right now she is still groggy and not herself. I want to lay a trap for Kelly. The more lies she tells the easier it will be to catch her."

Sadie shook her head. "They have been friends for years. Close like sisters."

"That obviously doesn't mean anything to Kelly."

"What's this about Kelly?" Beth asked as she came into the room, her eyes red and puffy.

Ethan hadn't had a chance to talk to Beth yet about Lexie's Facebook page, but she needed to know. She would find out anyway, but he hated telling her right now. "There are students at school who think Lexie is lying about Sunday morning with Kelly because Kelly said it when I interviewed her Thursday morning."

Beth curled her hands into fists. "Why didn't you tell me this before? Now people are going to say that's the reason Lexie took the tranquilizers. I don't have any here at the house. How could Lexie get hold of them?"

"It's a strong possibility students at school are selling prescription drugs, especially in light of all that has been happening. Sadie and I have been talking about someone putting it in her drink today."

"Kelly?" Beth covered the distance between them and sat in the chair across from the couch.

"Maybe. There was a group of kids at the pill party where Jared died. Anyone of them might have done it. It's not just Kelly who is involved."

Sadie cocked her head to the side. "The kids leave their water bottles unattended all the time. They might bring their stuff into the room and put it in their chair then go back out to talk to friends or use the restroom. And with me being in the hallway between classes, I won't see anything."

"I need to find out what classes Lexie has with the clique. I'll ask her tomorrow." Ethan swung his attention to his sister. "Leave the questions to me."

Beth nodded, her eyes drooping with exhaustion.

"I brought her backpack, but I didn't see her water bottle." Sadie rose, went to where she'd placed it on the floor, and rummaged in the bag. When she looked up, her forehead creased. "It's not here."

Beth sat up straight. "Someone took it."

"I guess, but I'll look around my classroom to make sure."

The hairs on his nape tingled. "Can you do it tomorrow?"

"Sure. The building is open on Saturday morning for various student activities. What's it look like?"

"It's the one the school sells in the school colors. She wrote her name on the side of it, and I washed it last night so any fingerprints would be from today."

"Good, since half the kids use that type of water bottle." Sadie grabbed her purse. "I'll call you tomorrow after I go to my classroom. With being gone part of this week, I could use time in my room doing some work for next week. I'm determined to get my classes back on track."

Ethan walked with Sadie to the front door, opened it and stepped out onto the porch with her. "Thank you for making a special trip to the school. If you find the bottle, call me. I'll come pick it up to have the container tested and dusted for latent prints. It could be a great way to shake some kids up and maybe someone will talk."

"I'll do anything I can to help Lexie. She's a good student."

He moved closer, his hands tingling from wanting to hold her. He stared at her full lips with a hint of pink lipstick still on them. What would it be like to kiss them? Her chest rose and fell with a deep inhalation. Her eyes glinted in the glow from the security light nearby.

He shortened the distance between them even more and took both of her hands in his, tugging her the remaining foot. He dipped his head toward hers and murmured close to her, "If you need help with Steven, I'm here."

Her mouth curved into a smile that penetrated through his heart, warning him this lady would never settle for casual. He should back away. But for the life of him his feet wouldn't move. Instead, he bent further toward her until his lips settled over hers, and he tasted her sweetness.

He framed her face, deepening the kiss that felt so right. As her arms wound around him, she pressed herself against him, meeting his passion with her own. He didn't know if he would have pulled back if the front door hadn't opened, the wash of light from the house encircling them.

He stepped away as he stared at his sister in the entrance who was trembling. She started to say something, then snapped her mouth closed.

"What's wrong?" he asked Beth.

"I got a call from the assistant principal at the high school. Mr. Howard wants me to come to his office with Lexie first thing Monday morning to discuss her suspension for using drugs at school."

9

"I wondered if Mr. Maxwell would pursue a suspension for Lexie," Sadie said and turned to Beth. "I can speak on her behalf to Mr. Howard. That might help."

"I'll go with you." Ethan touched Sadie's hand briefly, then headed toward his sister. "I need to talk to him in light of what I'm finding out."

"Don't worry about it. I might find the water bottle tomorrow. That could support that Lexie was drugged by someone else."

Beth twisted her hands together. "Even if you found some tranquilizers in the water, they could claim Lexie put them there."

"Maybe, but it could put some doubt in Mr. Howard's mind. Lexie has a great record and hasn't been in trouble." Sadie noticed the time and realized she'd been longer than she had intended. "I have to go, but Ethan, I'll call you tomorrow one way or another about the water bottle."

As she drove into her driveway ten minutes later, she spied two cars parked in front—her mother *and* her father's. Her stomach plummeted. Dad must really be angry if he'd gone inside. When he came to pick up the kids, he stayed on the porch. Somehow, it would be her fault Steven drank the cough syrup, and he'd tie it back to her marrying Harris.

Sadie trudged into her home, trying to prepare for the confrontation. She could remember a time when she could do no wrong in his eyes. She'd been his little princess who was going to conquer the world.

Voices came from the living room, and she headed that way, pausing before she entered. Her heart thumped against her chest. Boom—boom sounded in her ears.

"Sadie, is that you?"

"Yes, Mom." She stepped into the room, relieved to see her daughter sitting there. Her dad probably wouldn't say much with Ashley present.

"How's Lexie?" her mother asked, grasping her father's hand on the couch next to her.

Although she couldn't tell, she imagined her mom squeezing his fingers tightly to remind him to behave. "She's better."

"First that Jared kid, then my grandson, and now Lexie, a student in your class. What's happening in Summerton?" Her father's gruff voice filled the whole room, reminding her of her booming heartbeats.

"I don't know. That's what Ethan and Cord are trying to figure out." Too on edge to take a seat, Sadie leaned into the back of the chair where Ashley sat. "It's nice to see you here, Dad."

"I came to have a talk with my grandson."

"How did that go?"

"Not well. He acted like he was listening to me, but I don't know how much he really heard. He remained silent almost the whole time except a few one-word answers to questions. I have a mind to cancel our hunting trip coming up in a couple of weeks."

"Dad, don't do that. It'll be good for him to be with you. You know, male bonding."

"If you had listened to me and married someone—" Her father winced and pulled his hand from her mother's grasp.

She rolled to her feet. "Now that Sadie is home, it's time for us to go. Honey, if you need help this weekend, give me a call."

"Will you come over tomorrow morning for a few hours while I go to school to catch up on some work?"

"Of course. I can be here at nine."

Her father slowly rose, his gaze penetratingly intense. "Why don't you just bring your work home instead of doing it at school?"

"Normally I do, but . . ." She couldn't tell her father she would be searching for Lexie's water bottle. He wouldn't want her to get involved, but she had to do something. "I have work I can only do there."

He harrumphed. "You should be here getting through your son's head what a stupid thing he did."

"I'm doing the best I can."

This time he snorted. "If only you had listened to me."

Sadie came around the chair and glanced at her daughter. Ashley clutched the arms of the chair, her lips flattened as she stared at a spot in the carpet. She placed a hand on Ashley's shoulder. "I hope you'll come again, Dad."

"Let's go, Ruth. It's getting late."

As they headed toward the foyer, the doorbell echoed through the house. Now who? Cord? Sadie hurried to open the door, not even sure she wanted to talk to her brother after the day she'd had.

In the entrance stood Harris, and it took all her willpower to swallow her moan. If he had to come to the house, why couldn't he wait five minutes until her parents left? "This isn't a good time."

Her father stopped next to Sadie, his body so tense she could feel the anger pouring off him. "What are you doing here?" He drew himself up as tall as possible, as though he would fight Harris if he came inside.

"I want to see my son. I just got Ashley's message about what happened yesterday. I've been out of town the past two days."

Why didn't you stay gone? was on the tip of Sadie's tongue, but instead she clamped her teeth together until pain streaked down her neck.

Her father moved in front of Sadie. "You're thirteen years too late."

Harris's look shifted from her dad to her. "Ashley asked me to come."

She needed to set some ground rules with her daughter. No inviting people over without talking it over with her. It had never been a problem until now. "Dad, I'll take care of this. Thank you for coming." She gave him a quick peck on his cheek, much to his surprise and hers.

Her mom took his arm and dragged him out of the house. Harris sidestepped to allow the pair by. As her father left, he glared at Harris.

Harris snorted. "I see his opinion of me hasn't changed any."

"Do you blame him?"

He peered at her for a long moment. "No, I don't. I was wrong."

"Dad, I'm glad you came," Ashley said behind Sadie. "Come in."

"No." Sadie blocked him from entering. "It's been a long, tiring day, and we all need to get a good night's sleep."

"Don't force me to hire a lawyer. I don't want to do that. We're two adults and can come up with a compromise."

"Mom, please. I would like to talk to Dad."

"Five minutes? On the porch?" Harris asked, a plea in his words.

Surprised at the sound of his voice, Sadie murmured, "That's all. It's late."

"It's not even nine yet." Ashley rolled her eyes and stepped out onto the porch.

"I'm aware of the time." *Why is Ashley doing this? Why am I not enough for my daughter?*

As Ashley and Harris sat on the swing, Sadie propped herself against the wall near the slightly opened window and listened. It was her duty as Ashley's mother to eavesdrop on their conversation.

"Is Steven okay?" Harris asked.

"No. He's furious at me for inviting you over."

"He won't talk to me then?"

"No, but I still want to see you. Steven is gonna have to learn to deal with it instead of pulling a stunt like the cough syrup."

"Maybe it's a call for help. He may not want to talk to me, but you need to be there for him as his sister."

Sadie's mouth fell open. Harris wasn't capable of sensible advice. *He can't come in now and try to be a parent. His appearance most likely drove Steven to his desperate cry for help. Lord, how do I get rid of Harris before he hurts my kids anymore?*

❧

"This time we brought our attorney. I'm tired of my daughter being harassed by the police." Mary Lou plunked her big purse on the table in the interview room.

Ethan settled against the wall while Cord sat at the table with Kelly sandwiched between Jeffrey Livingston and Mary Lou. Fear marked Kelly's beautiful features, nothing left of the indignant young woman from a couple of days ago. He wanted nothing more than to interview Kelly again, but what happened with Lexie yesterday reinforced the need for Cord to take the lead with the teen.

Cord shuffled a stack of papers, prolonging the start of the interview. "New evidence has come to light. Kelly, you said that you weren't at the warehouse. That Lexie lied. Correct?"

Staring at the table, Kelly nodded.

Ethan shifted, clenching his teeth to keep his mouth shut. *Kelly is the weak link, the one we can get the information we need from.*

"What new evidence do you have?" Jeffrey asked as Mary Lou was opening her mouth.

Cord withdrew a couple of photos from a folder. "We have verified Jared Montgomery gave this locket to Kelly a few weeks ago for her birthday. We have a photo of her wearing it. We found it at the warehouse."

"She lost it. It had to be planted there," Mary Lou said immediately, while Kelly stared at the picture, tears in her eyes. "Probably by Lexie to support her lies."

"Did you lose it, Kelly?"

The girl nodded.

"Where and when?"

"That Friday before Jared died. At school, so anyone could have picked it up," Mary Lou again answered for her daughter.

Cord swiveled his head toward Mary Lou. "Kelly is to answer." Then he turned back to the teen and asked again in a softer voice, "Where and when did you lose the locket?"

"Like Mom said, at school last Friday," Kelly mumbled to her chest.

Kelly's mom hadn't said that exactly. Ethan pushed away from the wall, wanting to intervene and take over the questioning.

"Kelly, if you're lying to us about this crime, it'll make this situation a lot worse for you." Cord took another picture and slid it across to the girl. "This is where it was found. Any idea how it would have gotten there? The warehouse isn't in a nice part of town. Not somewhere a young girl should be, especially at night."

"Chief Thompson, what crime are you investigating?" Jeffrey asked.

"This is all tied to the murder of Jared, but also to taking prescription drugs illegally—possibly distributing them."

"My client has answered your question. Badgering her will not be tolerated. We're leaving unless you want to charge Kelly with something. Do you have evidence my client took drugs and distributed them? I'm not even addressing the murder charge, because that's ridiculous."

Mary Lou grunted. Kelly hunched her shoulders.

Cord fixed his stare on the young girl. "Kelly, if you lost this locket somewhere, then why are your fingerprints the only ones on it?"

She burst out crying. "I haven't done anything wrong. You're doing this to me because he," Kelly stabbed Ethan with a hard look, "is trying to protect his niece. I'm mourning my boyfriend's death, and all I've been doing is answering question after question. Leave me alone." She bolted to her feet and raced for the door.

When Cord started to stand, Ethan came toward the table, saying, "Let her go, Chief Thompson. Mary Lou, contrary to what you may think, I'm concerned for Kelly. We think a group of Jared's friends had a pill party, and somehow Jared ended up dead. We believe someone orchestrated his death. With what drugs were in his system, I'm surprised he didn't die from an overdose. He was alive when his car hit the water. He couldn't get out of his seatbelt. Trapped, he drowned. Something is very wrong here. This will not go away. More kids will die if what we think happened continues."

With her head held high, Mary Lou rose and picked up her purse. Then she ruined the effect she wanted to convey by clutching the bag to her chest. "Kelly is a good girl who was in love with Jared. His death was an accident and a tragedy. That is all." She flounced out of the interview room.

His lips compressed, Jeffrey followed his client's mother.

"I thought we would get another lecture on harassing Kelly." Cord gathered up his stack of pictures and sheets of paper.

Ethan stared at the doorway. "Yeah, I thought so, too. If Mary Lou would listen, I'd suggest she get another lawyer. There may be a conflict of interest here since Brendan Livingston is one of Jared's good friends."

"I wonder what Bradley thinks about this. Jeffrey is his lawyer."

"I want to give Bradley an update. He's been surprisingly quiet lately. I'll pay him a visit after I talk with my niece. I need to figure out how someone slipped her the tranquilizers."

"So you believe her?"

"Yes. Sadie was right last night. Lexie doesn't even like taking medication when she should. She definitely wouldn't knowingly take tranquilizers."

Cord's eyebrow arched. "Sadie? Last night?"

"She came by to check on Lexie. My niece was in her classroom when she lost consciousness."

"You know she used to have a crush on you."

"She did?"

Cord's laughter rang in the quiet. "Did you really think she followed us around because she wanted to be with her big brother? For a Texas Ranger you sure can be clueless at times, Stone."

Ethan sent him a look that should have made Cord stop laughing. Instead it only increased his merriment. Ethan left before the whole police department heard their chief.

But as Ethan strode toward his SUV, he thought back to when he was a teenager and the times Sadie tagged along with them. Nah, there was no way she'd had a crush on him. And yet the kiss they had shared had been special—one that had kept him up for hours the night before.

❦

"Honey, your uncle is here to see you," Lexie's mother said from the doorway.

With her head buried under the covers, Lexie wanted to stay in bed forever. Never leave her room. She could just hear the rumors flying around after what happened Friday on top of the ones about her lying to the police.

"Lexie?" Her mom shook her shoulder. "You need to get up. You can't stay in bed all day."

"Yes, I can." She sat up straight, letting the covers fall to her waist. "How could someone put tranquilizers in my drink? I was so upset at what was going on at school I didn't even pay attention to what I was drinking." Her eyes blurry with unshed tears, she stared at her mother. "I could have died."

Her mom sat on the bed. "I know. The doctor said you were lucky. Much more and . . ." She cleared her throat. "I can't believe anyone would do that either, but that's what your uncle needs to talk to you about. Whoever did needs to be caught before they do it to someone else. Prank or not, it could have ended deadly."

Lexie ran her index finger up and down her thumb. "It wasn't a prank."

"Yeah, I know. That makes it even more serious and important your uncle finds out who is after you."

Kelly. Lexie couldn't rid her thoughts of her best friend turning on her, telling the police Lexie had lied. Did Kelly put something in her drink? Then what was yesterday at lunch about?

"Mom, I don't want to go to school Monday."

"You have to. Mr. Howard wants to see you. I'm not going to let him suspend you for something someone else did. Ethan is coming to the school then, too."

"No. I love my uncle, but he needs to stay out of this." *I have to do this myself. Just as I have to see Kelly. I'm not giving up on her.*

"He's not going to, and I don't want him to stay away. A crime has been committed. Come on." Her mother pulled back the covers. "He's waiting. You haven't done anything wrong. Don't hide like you're guilty."

That was easy for Mom to say. She didn't have to deal with the kids at school.

Her mother waited at the doorway for Lexie to follow her. Slowly, as though the various parts of her body had trouble working together, she scooted to the side of the bed and rose.

As she walked down the hall, her mother slung her arm over Lexie's shoulders. "I know this is hard, but you're not alone. We're here for you."

"Why is this happening? All I was trying to do is help a friend."

"Kelly may be hurting and scared right now, but I'm not going to let her take you down to protect herself. I don't want you to have anything to do with her."

"But, Mom—"

"No buts, Lexie. You're in trouble. I have to look out for you."

"Who's going to look out for Kelly?"

"That's *her* mom's job."

Lexie halted and faced her mother at the end of the hall. "She's in more trouble than Kelly. Someone needs to reach out and help them."

Her mother smoothed Lexie's hair back. "Oh, baby. I wish the world were full of people like you. But it isn't. Aren't you angry with Kelly?"

"I was. God wants us to forgive her. What kind of friend would I be if I didn't? Besides, I don't like feeling angry."

Her mom drew Lexie against her. "You're right, but you still have to take care of yourself, too. I'm not saying stay away from her forever, just until your uncle and Cord figure this out."

I can't, Mom. I can't. But Lexie couldn't voice that out loud. "Let's get this over with. I'm still tired and want to sleep."

Uncle Ethan sat at the kitchen table, drinking a cup of coffee. He looked up when she entered, assessing her with that sharp gaze.

"I've been worried about you, Kiddo. How are you doing?" Her uncle lifted his mug and took a long swig.

"Like I've been trampled by a herd of cattle."

"I imagine. I'm sure your mom told you I needed to talk about yesterday."

She shuffled to the table and sank into a seat across from him. "Then you do believe me that I wouldn't take tranquilizers? Take it from me, this feeling isn't something I want to experience again. I don't know why people take them."

"Prescription drugs are beneficial if used correctly. The problem comes in when they aren't, and that's what's happening in Summerton. Actually, from what I've been reading all over the country."

"And Kelly is mixed up in it?"

"I think so. Who had access to your water bottle yesterday?"

"In second hour, I forgot something in my locker, so I left my backpack with the water bottle in the side pouch on my desk and ran to my locker before the bell rang. Also, I went to the restroom during fourth hour and left it back in the room."

"What was going on in your class when you left?"

Lexie centered her thoughts on yesterday. The closer to her English class the fuzzier her memory became. "There was a sub in fourth hour, so it was pretty hectic. It was toward the end and most of the kids were talking—except me. That's why I asked the sub if I could go to the restroom."

"Any other times?" Uncle Ethan asked.

Lexie looked toward the counter, at her mother fixing another pot of coffee. Her movements were sluggish, and her eyes drooped. This situation had caused that. She hated that.

"Lexie, how about lunch?"

Her uncle's question drew her back. "I sat by myself, but couldn't eat. When I left the cafeteria, I ran into Kelly—literally. Her drink and mine went everywhere."

"How was she?"

"Almost her old self. She asked if I could help her with a test she would be taking later. We found a place in the stairwell and went over the material."

"Did she have access to your water bottle?"

"No, it was right there." *But what about the Coke she brought me? No way. Why would she? She may have changed, but not that much.*

"Anything else you remember."

"No, a lot is still hazy."

"Are any of these kids in your second- or fourth-hour classes? Brendan Livingston. Luke Adams. Missy Collins. Carrie Bannister. Kalvin Majors. Zoe Sanders."

"Zoe, Missy, and Kalvin are in my second-hour, and Carrie and Luke in my fourth-hour."

"When I come to school on Monday, I'll be talking with at least your second hour teacher and then finding out who the sub was in your fourth hour. When did you drink from your water bottle?"

"A little in each hour. It was pretty hot that day, and the air conditioning in some rooms wasn't working well. By afternoon, I drank more. In fact, I only had a little left by the end of fifth hour. I started to refill it, then remembered that I hadn't finished my Coke from lunch. I had put it in my locker. Between fifth and sixth, I finished it off."

"Coke? I thought your drink went everywhere when Kelly and you ran into each other."

"I got another one."

"Does anyone else have access to your locker?"

"No, but I've heard of some kids getting things stolen even when they were locked."

"Okay. This gives me something to work on."

"Just let it go, Uncle Ethan."

"No," her mother said and joined them at the table. "You could have died. The person who did this might have wanted you dead. What if that person killed Jared? We don't know what is going on."

"But . . ." Lexie's voice sputtered to a stop. Had that been the intent? Would they try again?

"Baby," her mother patted her arm, "maybe it's a good thing if you stay home from school until Uncle Ethan finds who did this."

"You want them to suspend me?" Her life kept swirling out of control. *Why would someone want to kill me? Kill Jared? There is no connection between us.*

Yes, there is. Kelly.

"No, that's why we'll go to school on Monday, and if Mr. Howard suspends you, I'll fight it. I don't want it on your record. If he doesn't, I'm informing him you'll be staying home until the person responsible is found. You aren't safe at school right now."

The trembling started in Lexie's hands and snaked through her body. She clasped her arms and hugged herself as if it would warm her. Ice zipped through her veins to every part of her. "Fine," she mumbled and pushed herself to her feet but gripped the side of the tabletop until she felt steady enough to walk.

Ethan rose. "Walk me to the door, Lex." He slung his arm over her shoulders and started toward the front of the house. "I'm not going to let anything happen to you. That's a promise, hon."

"I know. I'm glad you're here. If anyone can get to the bottom of what's going on, it's you."

At the front door, he opened it and stepped outside. "It's a beautiful day. Go out in the backyard and enjoy the sun. It'll make you feel better."

She couldn't do that. All she wanted to do was escape to her room and hide under her covers. "How am I going to face the kids at school, especially with all the rumors about me lying?"

"You know the truth. That's the most important thing right now. I'll get to the truth in this, and then everyone will know it." He tweaked her nose. "I love you," he said with a smile and turned to leave. His gaze caught on something on the porch. His forehead wrinkled as he bent over and picked up a vase of flowers. "This is for you." He plucked the card out of the middle of the bouquet and handed it to Lexie.

She stared at the array of different blooms from roses to carnations to daisies. The glass container overflowed with them in a riot of colors. "Who would send them? Did you?"

"No, but I wish I had thought of it. Open the card."

She tore into the envelope and pulled the white sheet out. "I hope this brightens your day. I know you're innocent." She glanced at her uncle. "It wasn't signed."

"You've got a secret admirer, and he believes in you."

"He?"

"It's a guy thing, but I guess it could be a girlfriend." He kissed her cheek. "Remember your family is behind you and at least whoever sent you the flowers."

When she closed the door, she leaned back against it, hugging the bouquet to her, the floral aroma swirling around her. Someone believed she was innocent. That thought penetrated the self-pity she'd been wallowing in and lifted her spirits.

✑

Sadie strode toward her classroom on Saturday and looked for her wastebasket by the door. It wasn't there. Then she remembered in her haste to leave Friday after what had happened with Lexie, she hadn't put it out in the hall for the janitor. And as upset as Oliver was, she doubted he had either, although as her student aide he often did. But in this case, it was good news. The water bottle was most likely still in her classroom.

She unlocked her door and found her wastebasket across the room by her desk. But when she searched it, she didn't find Lexie's water bottle. Who could have taken it?

In case the bottle had been stashed somewhere in the room, she checked every place it could be—even in her cabinets. When she didn't find it, a mantle of disappointment cloaked her. She walked into the hall, locked her classroom, then scanned the area. Someone's locker? Maybe. Then she noticed the large trashcan at the end of the corridor. She hastened to it and breathed a sigh because the janitor hadn't gotten to it yet today.

She knocked it over and rummaged in the scattered trash on the floor, using a pencil to move it around so she didn't have to touch it. The smell of old socks and something rotten blasted her. She gagged.

Then she saw it—a bottle with Lexie's name on the side. She called Ethan.

"I found Lexie's water bottle in the trashcan in the hall."

"I'll be right there."

"What about the trash I dumped on the floor? The janitor should be here soon to empty it."

"Leave everything where it is, and don't touch anything. If he says anything, tell him I'm on my way and it's evidence."

As she stood guard over the strewn trash, a couple of kids passed her and gave her strange looks. One said, "Dumpster diving is more fun."

She was sure come Monday morning the news that Ms. Thompson liked to go through the trash would be all over the school.

⋙⋘

Lexie parked around the corner from Kelly's house and snuck into the backyard. Kelly was home. She'd seen her through the kitchen window. Her mother's car was in the driveway. If she was going to speak to Kelly, she had to now and then get back home before Mom returned from the grocery store.

One way or another, I'm getting to the bottom of this.

Keeping an eye on the back, she crept closer to the house and the tree she'd have to climb to get to Kelly's bedroom window. She wasn't going to ring the doorbell and have Kelly's mom send her home. Her friend—and she still thought of her that way—rarely locked her window so Lexie could climb inside and wait for Kelly to come upstairs.

Breathing hard, Lexie reached the limb where she could shimmy out to where it brushed up against the roof of the back porch. She knew Kelly got in and out of her house this way, but she'd never done it. Looking down at the yard twenty or thirty feet below scared

Lexie. She didn't like heights. The ground swayed or she did. Either way, she clutched the branch and clung to it.

Maybe if she inched along like a worm, she could make the five or six feet to the porch. She tried but scraped her knee on a broken twig.

Not far. Keep going. I didn't come all this way for nothing. I want answers. I want my friend back.

When she reached the thirty degree slanted roof, she dug her fingernails into the wood and swung carefully around to drop a couple of feet onto the shingles. Her heartbeat thundered in her ears like cymbals clashing against her skull. Her legs dangled in the air for a moment before she scooched farther down and let go. She landed in a crouch to balance herself, hoping the neighbors weren't looking or the sound of her setting down wasn't too loud.

How in the world did Kelly do this all the time?

Creeping toward the house, Lexie scanned the area. She reached Kelly's bedroom and peered through the glass pane. Empty. Lexie tried the window. Unlocked. With a deep inhalation, she eased it up, then crawled inside.

Her pulse still speeding, she knew she would have to rethink how she was going to leave. She couldn't climb back down the elm. Maybe Kelly would help her sneak out of the house.

She crossed to the door then cracked it open slightly and listened. Silence. She glanced back at the bed and decided to sit and wait. Kelly preferred hanging out in her room. She'd come upstairs soon.

Lexie took a seat, leaning against the headboard and stretching out her legs.

⁓❧⁓

"Mom, we don't have any food in the house," Kelly said as she came into her mother's bedroom where she'd been since they arrived home from the police station.

When Kelly saw her mother lying face down on top of the covers, she looked at the nightstand. The bottles of sleeping pills and tranquilizers were there as they usually were after a rough situation or day. Kelly rushed to the bed and felt her mom's pulse. It beat beneath her fingertips. But her relief was brief. Anger swamped her as she sat next to her mother and tried to wake her up.

She moaned and batted Kelly's hands away. "Leave me—alone." Her mother rolled to her side and curled into a ball.

Kelly checked the bottle and counted them as she did every day now. She took one sleeping pill and two tranquilizers. She bent over her mother to smell her breath. No alcohol.

Good. At least she wouldn't have to call 911. But one day she would.

What would it feel like to escape like Mom?

Kelly snatched up the bottles, gripping one in each hand. The anger surged, and she squeezed hard on the plastic containers until one cracked. Her heart raced as it had all week. She released her tight grasp and plodded toward the bathroom to put the pills up.

If Mom wanted any more, she would have to get out of bed.

After putting them in the cabinet, Kelly continued to her bedroom. She didn't know what to do. She was in a big mess and digging the hole even deeper. Lexie could have died yesterday. Who gave the tranquilizers to her? How did they? It had to be one of Jared's friends. They were scared. They wanted to make sure she wouldn't talk.

They weren't just afraid of the police, though. They didn't say anything to her when she was with them, but she'd seen the fear in their eyes, especially Wednesday night. What had happened after she'd passed out at the warehouse? That was the key. For a few seconds blue eyes wavered in her mind taunting her. Jared's?

If only I hadn't involved Lexie. At least she wouldn't be caught up in this mess. But what can I do now? They're keeping something from me.

As she entered her room, she chewed on her thumbnail, nothing coming to mind. She hadn't felt like herself since that night with Jared. If she could do it over, she would. She was afraid of Jared's friends, but she didn't want anything to happen . . .

Her thoughts came to halt when she caught sight of Lexie on her bed asleep. At least that was what she hoped. She hastened to Lexie, picking up her left arm to feel for a pulse—just as she'd done with her mom a few minutes ago. She was getting good at this.

Lexie jerked away, her eyes snapping open, then growing huge. "Kelly, when did you come in?"

"This is my bedroom. When did *you* come in? How?"

Lexie's cheeks flamed. "A while ago. By climbing your elm."

"Why are you here? Why not ring the doorbell?"

"I didn't want anyone to know. My mom doesn't even know I'm gone."

"Are you grounded—for—what happened yesterday?" Kelly sank down on her bed and sat cross-legged, facing Lexie.

"No. My mother and uncle believe someone slipped me the tranquilizers. At least someone believes me. The whole school might not, but my family does." Lexie raised her chin, her mouth pinched in a frown. "How about you?"

"You need to leave. If Mom found you here, she would go ballistic." Kelly didn't know what to do about Lexie, how to make what happened to her better. She nibbled on her other thumbnail.

Lexie scooted off the bed and stood over her. "Did you give me the pills?"

Kelly bit off a chunk of her nail. "No."

"So you didn't put something in my Coke?"

Kelly shook her head. "Is that how you got it?"

Lexie shrugged. "Don't know. Trying to figure out how someone almost killed me. Do *you* know?"

Kelly dropped her gaze.

Lexie moved into her personal space. "Do you know?" Her voice rose several decibels.

"Shh. You don't want my mother in here."

"I almost *died*. Tell me who did it?"

10

 don't know. Honest," Kelly shouted, scrambling from the bed and rounding on Lexie.

"Why did you tell the police I lied?" The anger she'd been suppressing since she'd discovered the lie Kelly told Uncle Ethan exploded.

"Because you promised not to tell anyone. You broke your promise. Why did you? I could have gotten in trouble."

"And you don't think your behavior will get you in trouble? Look what happened to you at the warehouse. You don't even know what you took." Lexie gulped in big breaths to try and fill her lungs. Her chest burned.

"I know, and there were a few times afterwards I thought something bad was happening to me."

"You never told me that. What happened?"

"My heart raced. I got feverish. Then my heart skipped some beats. I felt like I was coming out of my skin."

"Why didn't you tell me?" Lexie's anger receded as she looked at the girl who'd been her best friend since they were six.

"I didn't think you'd understand, and I knew I had already disappointed you. I was acting like my mother," Kelly lifted tear-drenched eyes to Lexie, "and I never wanted to be like her. She won't hear us because she's passed out on her bed—oblivious to the world and certainly her own daughter."

"Drinking?"

"I wish that was all. No, she's been taking sleeping pills and tranquilizers to numb herself—at least that's what she told me one day as I was helping her to the bathroom."

Lexie's anger deflated like a popped balloon. She hugged her friend. "I'm sorry. My mother may be overprotective, but I do know she cares and will take care of me."

"I wish I had your mother." Kelly collapsed onto her bed.

"I wish I had a sister." Lexie sat next to her.

"You do—Emma."

"Not the same thing. She's gone, and when she was here, she didn't have time for me." Lexie blew out a long breath. "What a pair we make."

"Yeah. I'm gonna make this right. I didn't know my mother was going to tell her hairdresser and from there it flew around town. What a mess I've made. I was doing what Carrie and Missy told me to do Wednesday night. I was too scared not to."

Lexie settled her arm on Kelly's shoulder. "I couldn't keep lying to Uncle Ethan and my mother about what happened Sunday morning. I'm sorry."

Tears leaked from Kelly's eyes. "I don't know the truth about what happened to Jared like your uncle thinks I do. I even thought sometime late Saturday night Jared was hovering over me, but then I passed out again. What if he was trying to get me up and I wouldn't move, then he left by himself and someone killed him. That part of town is scary."

"You think that's what happened?"

"I don't know. No. Maybe. There was even a time I woke up for a minute and thought he was dead. I thought someone had said that, but your uncle says he died from drowning so that memory can't be right." Kelly scrubbed her hands down her face. "Now you see why I'm so confused and afraid."

"We're in this together. That's what a friend is for."

Kelly brushed a wet track from her cheek. "Somehow, Lexie, the truth will come out. I'll figure out a way."

❧

In spite of the heavy dose of deodorant Kelly had put on before coming to see Carrie, sweat drenched her blouse, especially under her arms. Kelly stopped on the porch at her classmate's house and lifted her finger toward the doorbell. Her hand trembled so much she squeezed it into a tight fist and used a knuckle to press the button. With each second that passed, her heart thudded against her ribcage—faster and faster.

She started to leave, flutters of relief washing over her, when the door swung open. Carrie stood in the open doorway with Missy next to her. The impulse to flee propelled her to back away.

"What's wrong, Kelly? Why are you here?" One of Carrie's hands settled on her waist.

"I—I . . ." Kelly took another pace toward the steps.

Missy came outside and clasped Kelly's arm. "C'mon in. We heard you went to the police station this morning. Tell us what happened."

Her firm tone coupled with her firm grasp on Kelly dared her to flee. She dragged her feet but moved forward with Missy.

I can't do this. What do I say? Did you give Lexie the tranquilizers?

Before Kelly realized it, she was upstairs for the first time in Carrie's bedroom—all pink with frills everywhere. She felt as though she'd jumped into a big batch of cotton candy. Sugary sweet, but bad for you.

"I can just imagine how scared you were being interviewed again, but at least you had Brendan's dad with you. He's the best. Brendan asked him to help you. He was worried about you." Carrie sat on her bed.

Probably afraid I would tell what really happened last Saturday or at least what I know. "Yes, me and Mom appreciated it."

"Good. Now tell us how it went. Why did they want to see you again?" Missy took the place next to Carrie.

Leaving Kelly standing in front of them like a criminal in front of a judge. Her anxiety tripled. "They found my necklace at the warehouse—the one Jared gave me for my birthday. They wanted to know how it could have gotten there, if as I said, I was never there."

Missy's eyebrows hiked up. "What did you say? You didn't admit to being at the warehouse, did you?"

Kelly shook her head. "I told them someone must have planted it there. That I lost it a week ago Friday. The cops had a picture of me on my Facebook page the day before with it on. I had to think fast."

"So what do you think?" Carrie grasped the edge of the bed.

"I don't know. I lost it at the end. I cried telling them I'm mourning the loss of Jared then ran out of the interview room. No one came after me. I waited for Mom by the car. She thought it was okay. If they'd had real hard evidence, they would have come after me. Maybe arrested me."

Carrie's mouth twisted into a frown. "For what? Jared's death was an accident. I don't care what anyone said. He overdosed on drugs. He probably woke up, got disoriented, and drove himself into the lake."

After Lexie had left Kelly's house earlier, she'd gone over and over that evening Jared had died until her head ached. "Yeah, well, I've been thinking about that night the past few hours. I thought I heard someone scream he's dead. Then someone, I guess Luke, said they had to get the body out of the warehouse because his dad owned it." Tired of standing, Kelly searched for somewhere to sit. The only chair in the room had clothes piled on it. She remained on her feet.

"So? How do we explain our presence at the warehouse, what we were doing? They would have arrested us for illegally using drugs." Carrie tapped the side of her head. "Duh, what century were you born into?"

"I personally would look hideous in an orange jumpsuit I see the prisoners wearing on TV." Missy flipped her ash blond hair behind her shoulders, then giggled.

Anger bubbled in Kelly's stomach. "Jared is dead, and you're laughing about orange jumpsuits?"

Carrie and Missy glanced at each other, then Carrie asked, "What do you want us to do? Wear black like they used to for a year?" Laughter burst from her.

"I want you to take this seriously. I can't keep lying," Kelly shouted, losing any control she had left. "Have you two been sending me threatening emails?"

Carrie exchanged a puzzled look with Missy. "No. If I want to threaten you, I'll do it to your face."

"Who drugged Lexie?" Kelly opened and closed her hands, the urge to hit both girls so strong she was afraid she would.

All merriment died in the two teens on the bed. A deadly serious expression descended.

Missy rose, her shoulders thrust back. "We didn't, and I'm offended if you think one of us did."

"I didn't say that. Someone did, though, and she almost died."

Carrie hopped to her feet. "The rumor is she did it to herself. Case closed. Lexie is not your friend. We are. You need to remember that."

"Did you all put Jared in his car at the park and drive him in the lake?"

Carrie slapped Kelly. "How dare you think that?"

At that moment, Kelly did lose it. She curled her hand into a fist and struck Carrie in the jaw, then whirled and raced out of the room, the air vibrating with Missy's screams of outrage.

Outside Kelly dug into her pocket for her cell and called Lexie. It went to voicemail. "I did it. I'm through with them." A lightness of spirit lifted Kelly for the first time in days.

⟡

Sadie knocked on her son's door, waited half a minute then entered. As she expected, he was sleeping or faking he was. He had stayed in here since he came home from the hospital a couple of days ago. He was grounded, but not confined to his room.

Crossing to the bed, she dodged some dirty clothes and school-books. "Wake up. You've been sleeping enough," she said, shaking his shoulder.

Steven moaned. "I'm tired."

"No, you're hiding in here. It's time to rejoin the family."

He pushed himself to a sitting position, his hair flopping over into his eyes. "What family? It's just you and Ashley."

"It may be only three people, but that's our family."

"Why do I have to get up? I can't watch TV, use the computer, call or text my friends, so there's nothing to do but sleep."

He started to draw the covers up around him, but Sadie stopped him by pulling them out of his hands. "Mr. Stone is coming to dinner tonight. I want you to join us."

"What about Ashley?"

"She is, too."

"Half the family should be enough." He plopped onto the bedding and turned his back on her.

I don't know what to do, Lord. How do I reach someone who won't talk to me? Why is he so angry? Why is he doing this?

Sadie fell back on a technique she used when she felt over-whelmed. She pictured Jesus in a meadow, the breeze blowing multicolored wildflowers that laid a floral carpet before her. She walked toward Him, keeping Him in her vision. He exuded peace, love, and strength. When she paused near Him, He wrapped His arms around her. Everything would be all right. Somehow. She had to believe that.

"Steven, I know you're having a hard time right now, but things will get better. I'm here for you. Dinner will be ready in fifteen minutes. I hope you'll come down to eat with us."

Her son didn't say anything. Sadie left, remembering that image of the Lord in the meadow. So often it was what got her through those tough, lonely times when she was raising her twins with no support and little money.

When she reentered the kitchen, the sight of Ethan at the stove stirring her spaghetti sauce caused flutters in her stomach. Such a domestic picture. She was tired of being alone—being both mother and father to her kids. Right now, she had a son angry with her and not talking and a daughter who wanted to get to know her deadbeat father.

Ethan glanced at Sadie. A slow smile tugged at the corners of his mouth. By the time his dimple appeared, his cinnamon brown eyes warmed on her, melting her anxiety the more she looked at him. She moved further into the room.

"I put the spaghetti in the boiling water and the bread into the oven like you told me." He took a deep whiff of the sauce. "This smells delicious. Is Steven coming down?"

"I don't know. Probably not. I'm at a loss what to do with him. We had problems before Harris came to town, but now they're a lot worse."

"Maybe he's upset about Harris suddenly reappearing in your life. You said he doesn't want to have anything to do with his father."

"Whereas Ashley is hounding me to invite her father to dinner and is mad that I'm having you here instead."

He set the wooden spoon on the counter and turned toward her. "I'm sorry. You should have said something to me. I can leave." His eyes brightened. "And maybe send me home with a helping of this spaghetti."

"No, you're staying. Ashley has to learn I'm not having Harris over for dinner. I don't want to have anything to do with him. What you said about Steven might be what's bothering him. He's always been the man around the house, my protector. I've been so wrapped up with everything happening at school, I haven't addressed it with him."

"Sometimes it takes an outsider to point out the obvious."

"Do you really think that may be Steven's problem? Then why did he take the cough syrup?"

"Could be a cry for help."

"Maybe I can get him to talk to me about taking the cough syrup if I approach him about his father's return."

"What does your son like to do?"

Sadie went to the cabinet and removed the dishes to set the table for four. She hoped both her children came down. "Steven loves basketball, and the way he's growing he might have the height for it."

"I noticed you have a hoop attached to your garage. I haven't gotten to play like I used to, but possibly Steven and I could shoot baskets some time. Would that be okay with you?"

"I'd love it. Cord sometimes does. Steven enjoys it or at least he did. Lately he hasn't been doing anything but moping in his room." Sadie finished putting the silverware by the plates. "After I went to school today—"

"Thanks again for finding Lexie's water bottle. We're running the latent prints on it as well as testing the little water left inside."

"Good," Sadie said with a nod. "I want answers."

"Lexie told me there was about fourth of a bottle left, but when you gave it to me there was only a few drops."

"Someone emptied it?"

"Since the lid was still on it, yes, someone must have."

"I know Lexie didn't put the bottle in the trashcan outside my room. Someone else did and believe me, my students in class don't pick up each other's trash and throw it away."

"I'm sorry. I interrupted you. What did you do after you went to school?"

Sadie opened the oven and a rush of heat flushed her face as she took out the French bread with garlic butter. While she put it in a basket, she continued. "I met with Colleen Stover today. She thinks we have a chance to stop Harris from being in my children's lives. After all, he didn't support them for thirteen years and only saw them once. Just long enough for me to tell him I didn't have any money he could borrow."

Sadie looked at Ethan who stared at the doorway behind her. She swung around to discover Ashley standing there. Fury grooved her daughter's forehead and darkened her eyes.

"You really are going to try and stop Dad from seeing us— me." Ashley thumped her chest, the sound resonating through the kitchen. "He's my father. I have a right to see him. Why are you doing this? Because Grandpa won't have anything to do with you?

That isn't a reason to deny me seeing my father." She whirled around and stormed down the hall and up the stairs.

A few seconds later, a door slamming shook the house. Sadie winced. "My timing could definitely improve. I don't know if I should leave her alone to calm down some before going to talk to her or go right now."

"If she's not calm enough, she won't hear what you have to say. Sometimes waiting is a good thing."

"Are you sure you aren't a parent?"

"Yes, I'm sure. But I'm world worn. I've seen and dealt with a lot of situations with children and their parents, often during tense times." He quirked a grin. "Also, that's what my mom used to do all the time, and it worked with Beth and me."

"Let's eat before my masterpiece becomes overcooked." Sadie dished the spaghetti and sauce into bowls, brought the garden salad from the refrigerator, and put all the food on the table along with a pitcher of sweetened iced tea and the bread.

Ethan came around to help her into her chair, which threw her. She hadn't dated much since Harris, and Harris certainly never pulled her seat out for her. "Thank you."

"What can I say? My mama taught me manners."

As he took the chair next to her, the sound of footsteps pounding down the stairs alerted her to the possibly her daughter would leave out the front door. She started to get up to go after her when her son appeared in the entrance.

Steven sat, his mouth not technically set in a frown but close. "I smelled the bread and realized I'm hungry."

"I'm glad you came down. Steven, you know Mr. Stone. He and your uncle were best friends for years while they were growing up."

"Your mom was telling me you like to play basketball. Cord and I were on the basketball team in high school, but what we loved to do was play a pickup game. I hear you're good. If I got a few guys together, would you like to play some with us? You and my cousin who is fifteen probably can dribble circles around us old men."

That last sentence coaxed a brief smile from Steven. "Yeah, Uncle Cord has mentioned doing something like that, but he never has."

"I hate to say it, but your uncle is not the most organized man. He tends to forget things like that. Once he had me waiting at the court for half an hour, then he comes moseying up as though he were early for our one-on-one."

"Why did you stay around? I'd have left." Steven reached for the basket of bread.

"I was practicing to beat the pants off Cord, and I did that day."

Steven chuckled and dug into the spaghetti.

The sound of her son's laughter lifted Sadie and gave her hope things would work out between Steven and her. He was at least having dinner with her and Ethan. "Let's say a prayer so we can eat."

She clasped Steven's hand then Ethan's. Bowing her head, she said, "Heavenly Father, thank You for being here for us. Please protect our children and help Ethan and Cord find out what's going on in Summerton. Bless this food. Amen."

Halfway through the meal, most of the conversation between Ethan and Steven about sports, Sadie stood. They stopped and looked at her. "Keep talking. I'm going to see if I can get Ashley to come down for dinner."

"You lasted longer than I thought you would," Ethan said with a wink.

"What does that mean?" Sadie clasped the back of the padded chair.

"I thought you'd leave to see Ashley before we sat down."

Sadie hurried up the stairs to Ashley's bedroom, knocked then when she didn't say, "come in," Sadie opened the door. To find her daughter was gone.

⟨❧⟩

While Cord and Ethan stood watching Sadie, she paced from one end of the living room to the other. "You two need to do something. Ashley is gone. I've checked the whole house. We had a fight right before we were to eat. I went to her favorite place she goes to when she's mad. She wasn't there. I called her friends. They don't know where she is."

Cord, dressed in casual jeans and a light blue shirt, hooked his thumbs in his brown belt that boasted a big silver buckle. "I've alerted my officers. They all know what Ashley looks like. They'll find her."

"So where do we go look for her? I can't sit here and wait." Sadie rubbed her thumb into her palm.

Ethan glanced at Cord then said, "But that might be the best place for you. You've done what you can. Let Cord and his men search Summerton. She probably has a new place she goes to."

Sadie stopped and snapped her fingers. "What if Harris took her? I wouldn't put it past him to." She snatched up her purse and started for the door.

"Where are you going?" Ethan fell in step with her.

"To see Harris."

"I'll come with you."

"Fine. I could use your help, Ethan." Because if Ashley was with Harris, no telling what she would do. Sadie glanced at her brother. "Can you stay with Steven or take him with you?"

"Don't worry about him," Cord said.

"We'll call you one way or another after I check with Harris." The word we flowed so easily from her. The feeling she wouldn't be alone when she confronted her ex-husband soothed her anger a little. She was almost positive he had something to do with Ashley being gone. Her life had been uneventful until he'd come to town. Actually, not much that was eventful happened before he came. Had he brought trouble to Summerton?

"If we find her, I'll let you know. I'll go by all her favorite places to hang out, then go by her friends' houses." Cord stepped out onto the porch with Sadie and Ethan.

"I'll drive." Ethan withdrew his keys and strode toward his SUV.

"A wise decision. I'd probably crash." Fear and fury rampaged through her. What if Ashley wasn't at Harris's place? What if she ran away? What if . . . She had to stop that train of thought.

Lord, I need You. Help.

"Where does he live?" Ethan pulled away from the curb.

"The Sagebrush Apartments on Tenth Street."

"Not too bad."

"Yeah, I know. Whenever I knew him, he always had money problems. So where is his money coming from now?"

"You said he was a private detective."

"So he says. I don't believe anything he tells me. I learned the hard way not to."

Ethan stopped at a red light, looking over at her. "People do change when given a good enough reason."

"In all your years working as a law enforcement officer, how many people who operated in the gray areas changed?"

"Are you saying Harris is a criminal?"

"When we were married, I had my suspicions where his money came from, but I had no evidence of it."

"I'll check around or has Cord already done so?"

"I didn't ask him. Whether Harris is or was doesn't change what he did years ago. But if you find out he is, it'll help my case against giving him visitation rights to see the kids. Today my lawyer asked me to document everything between Harris and me."

When her cell phone blared she quickly answered it, hoping it was news of Ashley. "Sadie here."

"Ashley arrived at my apartment five minutes ago."

When she heard her ex-husband's voice, Sadie sat forward, her grip on the cell so tight she thought she could crush it. "I'm almost at your place. Both of you stay put. I can't believe you did this to me." The volume of her voice rose with each word she spoke in the last sentence. Now that she knew Ashley was all right, anger took hold and shook her to her core. She clicked off before she totally lost it.

"Ashley is with Harris?"

"Yes. I told you he was behind her leaving. This will prove to the courts he's an unfit father. Somehow, my thirteen-year-old daughter went four miles to his apartment. How? What if something had happened to her en route? It's getting late."

"I know you may not want to hear this, but you need to calm down. If you go in with both guns blazing, you'll only make the situation worse with Ashley. You'll push her toward her father. If Ashley is anything like you, she gravitates toward the underdog. You always did."

She tried to relax the stiffness in her body, but she couldn't calm her rapid heartbeat or breathing. "I'm locking both my kids in the house and never letting them go anywhere."

Ethan pulled over to the side of a residential street, a glow from a streetlamp bathing the inside of the SUV. He turned toward her. "I've never seen you like this. What exactly did Harris do to you all those years ago?"

"He left me with no word. One moment he was there. The next gone and I didn't hear from him for forty-eight hours. Then when I did, it was a call to tell me our marriage was over. He couldn't be the father and husband I wanted. Then he hung up. He didn't give me a chance to talk to him. Ashley and Steven started crying. They were three months old. I was eighteen and didn't know what to do. I called my parents. My dad hung up on me." Tears flowed down her cheeks as all those memories deluged her. The loneliness and helplessness overpowered her again as though it were yesterday. She shivered in spite of the warmth in the car.

Although a console was between them, Ethan put his hand on her shoulder, massaging her taut muscles. "Let it go. This anger toward Harris is harming you. Whether you like it or not, he's the twins' father, and it looks like Ashley wants to get to know him. I don't want you to be the bad guy in all of this."

She wrenched away from his touch. "I'm her mother. I know best. If you don't start this car, I'll get out and walk the rest of the way."

"Sadie, I'm here to help—"

"Then let's go. What if he's taking her away as we speak? He'd do it just to hurt me."

"Really, do you think that? He called you about Ashley being at his apartment."

His calm, even tone penetrated her panicky feeling, enticing her to relax, to listen to what Ethan was saying. Again, he placed his hand on her shoulder and kneaded the tightness beneath his fingers. "You don't know how this went down. Find out first. Later, you'll appreciate the advice."

She forced herself to take deep breaths to ease the ache in her chest. "What a time to come back into my life—when it's falling apart."

"Actually I don't think it's bad timing. You needed someone. I sure don't mind obliging you on that score. What are friends for? Here, turn and face the window. Let me get your other shoulder. You're wound tighter than a ball of barbwire."

"I feel like that, too. Since coming back to Summerton, I'd finally begun to feel my life was falling into a good routine. My dad is even melting toward me, and my mom and I have a good relationship. I needed that. Why did this have to happen?"

"Hey, where is it written our lives would be easy? If you've seen it, then that person doesn't know what he's talking about. I've seen people's lives at the worst possible moment. It's very sobering. What's the Lord telling you?"

"To forgive Harris."

"Then you know what to do."

The strength in his hands worked magic on her as though he could melt her tension away—at least for a few moments. "I've known for quite a while what God expects of me, but I don't know if I'll ever be able to do that. Remember when we found that dog that had been abused by its owner."

"You were ten and ready to take the man on. Cord and I had to hold you back."

"I haven't forgiven that man for what he did to an animal in his care."

"And what's it done to you? Has it really made you feel better to hold onto that anger?"

She swiveled around. "Okay. You've made your point."

"Good. Start with the dog owner and work your way up from there. I have a feeling it isn't only Harris you need to come to terms with."

"What do you mean?"

"Your dad. Every time you mention him, your voice tightens and you pull yourself up a little. He hurt you, too."

"Let's go. I'm as ready as I'm going to be. I just want my daughter back." She wasn't going to address her father and his issues—not on top of dealing with Harris. It was too much.

"Think of that when you confront Harris. What you really want is your relationship with Ashley to stay strong."

"Do you think I'm afraid I'll lose my daughter to Harris?" The question came out without her really thinking about what she was saying until she proposed it to Ethan.

"I think you need to look deeply within yourself to answer that question."

Did she? She would have said no when she first saw Harris again, but lately she didn't know. There were times when both of her children had missed out on not having a father—like when Ashley's classmates a few years back had "a take your dad to school" afternoon. Or the time when Steven was in scouts, and he had to settle on her helping him with his woodcraft projects. Poor kid. She was out of her element with tools.

As Ethan continued toward Harris's apartment, Sadie placed a call to Cord to let him know Ashley was at Harris's place so he could call off the search for her daughter.

When Ethan parked in front of the Sagebrush Apartments, he asked, "Ready?" as she pushed the passenger door open and hopped to the pavement.

When she strode toward the building, she began with an easy pace for about two seconds before she quickened her step. She wouldn't feel better until she saw Ashley with her own eyes.

On the second floor, Sadie found his apartment number and pounded on the door, which flew open almost immediately. She tried to charge inside, but Harris blocked her path. "Back off. You remember Ethan Stone. He's a Texas Ranger and here to help me."

Harris nodded toward Ethan, then said to Sadie, "Ashley is upset about what she overheard tonight. She doesn't want us to fight over her."

"Good. I don't either. Leave us alone, and I won't pursue taking you to court."

"I don't have a problem with going to court and letting a judge decide. I'm just telling you what Ashley feels, before you barge inside and demand she leave. I think you need to listen to her first."

Sadie set her fists on her waist. "Who are you to tell me what to do? You lost that right thirteen years ago."

"It doesn't erase the fact I'm their father, and I'm trying to pay you child support now."

"Thirteen years too late." She started to shove past Harris when she felt Ethan's light touch at the small of her back. She hadn't been ready to have this conversation with Ashley or Harris. But she was here, and she needed to get through it somehow. "Fine. I'll behave," she said between clenched teeth.

When she entered his place, Sadie wasn't prepared for what she saw—an apartment with personal touches. She never imagined Harris would have books out on his coffee table. He'd hated to read in high school. Nor the photos of his family—even one of Ashley, her most recent school picture. The biggest surprise was there was no TV in the living room. He'd used to watch it from the moment he came home from work to when he went to bed—usually while drinking beer. It had been the center of his home life while they'd been married.

Ashley sat in a lounge chair, her chin practically resting on her chest.

"Ashley?" Sadie said in a quiet voice, afraid to say too much more. The surprise of seeing Harris's home was still reeling through her.

Her daughter didn't glance up.

"Ashley, we need to go home."

That was when she lifted her head. A look Sadie was hard-pressed to describe—maybe like the one her daughter had when she'd brought a baby bird home for her to nurse back to health—

reflected a deep sadness. "Dad was telling me how you two met, what happened when he left."

"I bet he was." Sadie tossed a narrowed gaze at Harris.

"No, you don't get it, Mom. He put the blame for the divorce totally on him."

"Please have a seat, Sadie. Ethan. I was just now explaining why she can't come over here without your knowledge. No matter how much I want to see her, that's wrong."

Am I hearing him right? What kind of game is he playing? Sadie pivoted toward Harris. "What have you done?"

"I don't want there to be an ugly fight over Steven and Ashley. I just want to be part of their lives from time to time—if they want it. I respect how Steven feels right now. I don't blame him. Give me a chance to prove I'm different from the boy you used to know. Give me a chance to have at least a relationship with my daughter."

Sadie opened her mouth to say no, but Ashley's words cut through the silence. "Mom, I didn't want him to call you. He insisted."

Yeah, only because he knew I would check to see if you were here. After years of not trusting Harris, she couldn't do it now. Until Ashley and Steven were born, he used to charm her into almost anything. Then he changed after their birth; she changed, too. Her priorities shifted.

"I've talked with Jeffrey, and he says I have a good chance for at least visitation rights. I don't want to fight about this in court, especially if Ashley would like to see me. Can't we work this out?"

"Mom?"

Ashley's pleading expression solidified Sadie's stomach into a rock. Somehow in a short time he'd turned her daughter against her. Behind her she felt Ethan's support through the light touch of his hands on her upper arms. She drew strength from his presence. He said she wasn't alone in this, and she wasn't—not like when Harris had walked out on their marriage.

"It's your call, Sadie. I'm willing to take it slow and one step at a time. I'm not going anywhere this time." Harris leaned forward and clasped his hands, his gaze glued to her.

A scream of frustration welled up in her, but she couldn't release it. No matter how much she wanted to. "All I can say is that I'll talk with my lawyer and decide the best way to go for *my* children."

Relief washed over Ashley's face. "Thanks, Mom. I know you'll do what's right."

Sadie crossed her arms over her chest. "This doesn't get you off, young lady, for leaving the house at night without telling me where you were going. That's unacceptable. We're going home. Now."

Ashley glanced at Harris.

"She's right. Parents worry if they don't know where their children are." Harris rose.

Oh, he's good. How in the world does he know what parents feel? Sadie's fingernails dug into her upper arms in stark contrast to Ethan's gentle touch only inches from her fingers.

As they headed toward the door, Ethan took her hand. That simple gesture meant so much to her. A physical connection that underscored he was there for her.

Ashley turned before leaving and said, "Dad, I'll talk to you tomorrow at church."

Harris smiled at her daughter. "See you then."

Sadie bit into her lower lip to keep from laughing hysterically or shrieking at the top of her lungs. She wasn't sure which one. Church? Since when had Harris started going to church? He'd teased her about attending when she went as a teenager to the point she'd stopped going after they'd run away together.

When Sadie settled in Ethan's SUV, she wanted to have it out with Ashley right then and there, but knew in the end it would only make things worse. She needed to cool down before they talked about what Ashley did tonight and its consequences.

Silence dominated the ride to her house, and the second Ethan parked his car, Ashley opened the door and hurried to the porch.

"Do you want me to come in?" Ethan asked in the darkness.

From the sound of his question Sadie knew he would and stay as long as she needed him, but it had been a long day for both of them. All she wanted to do was fall into bed and sleep for twenty-four hours. "This past week has been rough on our families with what has happened in Summerton. How's Lexie holding up?"

"Okay. She's understandably upset, but also worried."

"That someone will try something again?"

"Maybe, but I don't think that's it. I think she's worried about Kelly even after all that girl has done to her."

"If she stays home, I'll do what I can as far as her English class or any of the other ones. Have you got any results on the water bottle?"

"Probably not until Monday. If there are two sets of latent prints on the bottle, I can rule out Lexie's, but I probably won't know who the other prints belong to unless they're Kelly's, Luke's, or someone in the system."

"How did you get Luke's?"

"From the paper you gave me and the one he gave me when I interviewed him."

"Most of the other kids' fingerprints in Jared's group aren't in any system?"

"No, and the ones I want probably wouldn't agree to be finger-printed. The only reason I think Kelly did is she wanted to prove she didn't lie about being at the warehouse. At this time I can't get a warrant for them, so we may not know much other than someone else touched the bottle. But we'll know if the water was tampered with."

"But not in time for the meeting with Mr. Howard."

"Beth is calling him to meet with him after school Monday rather than before. I should know by then."

She pushed her door open. "I'd better go. Thanks for everything."

As she rounded the front of the car, Ethan climbed down from the driver's seat. "I'll walk you to the door."

Suddenly, Sadie felt thrust back to when she'd been dating in high school and a boy would do that at the end of a date. Often it led to a kiss. Heat from a blush scored her cheeks. When she'd had a crush on Ethan, she'd dreamed of him kissing her, but with five years between them back then it had been a hopeless dream. But his kiss the other night took over her thoughts as she made her way to her house. Sizzling. Full of promise.

On the front porch, she turned to say goodnight, only to find he was nearer than she realized. Only a foot away. She could touch him. She could close the distance between them with a small step. But awkwardness held her rooted where she was.

He smiled. The security lamp nearby cocooned them in a circle of light.

Trapped by the intensity in his eyes, she forgot to breathe for a long moment until her body protested. Her chest rose with a deep inhalation. Her throat swelled with needs she hadn't realized she had. For years, she'd been determined to make it on her own. Not to depend on a soul. But tonight, she'd liked having Ethan go with her to confront Harris. Although he said little, she sensed his support the whole time.

"I guess we should say goodnight," she finally said in a raspy voice as though she wasn't used to talking.

"Probably."

"Yeah." But she didn't. Couldn't. Transfixed by him, she could have stayed on the porch all night.

Kiss me, screamed through her mind.

"Goodnight." He rotated toward the steps. "See you tomorrow at church."

No, don't go yet. She took a pace toward him.

He stopped and swung back toward her, grasping her upper arms and dragging her against him.

11

*E*than's hands cradled her face as he dipped down and brushed his lips across hers. Sadie wrapped her arms around him, wanting him closer. As he deepened the kiss, she surrendered to him and poured all her pent-up emotions into it. She needed to feel cherished, feminine. And Ethan did that.

When he pulled back, still only inches from her, his gaze glittered as it moved over her features, slowly, as if savoring the sight of each one. His shallow breathing matched hers.

Words escaped her mind. All she could do was stare at him staring at her.

He grinned. "We need to do this again."

"Kissing or dinner?"

His eyes twinkled. "How about both?"

"Sounds good to me."

She stood on tiptoes and settled her mouth on his, clasping his shoulders to keep herself upright. The touch of his lips siphoned all her willpower, all her strength. She was like a piece of clay, ready for him to sculpt. His arms wound around her and pressed her against him as he trailed whispery kisses across her cheek and nipped her earlobe. She melted even more into him.

"I'd better leave, or I won't want to."

"Yes. You better," she managed to say through the haze of her spinning emotions. "My kids will wonder if I decided to run away."

He clasped her arms and placed her a foot from him then backed away. "I'll call you about dinner. This time, my treat."

"Sounds good. See you tomorrow."

As he walked toward his car, he glanced back and waved at her. She sighed. She'd dated so rarely through the years, she wondered if she'd done the right thing by kissing him back. Stopping halfway to his SUV, he swung around, strode to the porch and planted a hard, brief kiss before leaving again. Without a word. But he took her heart with him.

He started his engine, but didn't pull away from the curb. Then she realized he was waiting for her to go into her house. She did and heard his car drive away.

She headed for the kitchen to clean up the dishes, hoping Steven had done them after Cord dropped him off. But as usual, the plates and pans were stacked in the sink. She laughed. Now this was her reality.

She didn't care. Kissing Ethan was a wonderful way to end an evening that had been difficult at best. For a while, she was going to forget about Harris and focus on Ethan. So different from her ex-husband, and even as a young girl she'd known that when she pined for Ethan as a thirteen-year-old.

While she rinsed off the silverware, loud voices from above disturbed her peace. She dried her hands and rushed up the stairs to the second floor, listening to Ashley and Steven in the hallway, yelling at each other.

"Why can't you give him a chance?" Ashley screamed at her brother.

"He doesn't deserve it. I've been doing his job just fine."

"What job? You're a kid," Ashley retorted. "An immature one at that. What stupid kid drinks cough syrup?"

Before Sadie could get to the end of the hall, Steven shoved his sister and shouted, "I hate you," then stomped off, slamming into his room.

Ashley caught herself before falling, saw Sadie, and stormed into her room, the door banging close.

Yes, this was her reality, especially of late.

⌘

A ringing sound pierced through Mary Lou's cloudy mind. Over and over. She twisted around in bed to bat at the annoyance. Finally, it stopped, but then a voice blared into the silence.

"Mrs. Winston, this is Summerton High School. We're calling because Kelly didn't show up at school, and no one called in about her being gone. We need you to call to let us know about Kelly's absence."

The words echoed through Mary Lou's mind. One by one, finally their meaning registered with her. She fumbled for the phone on the bedside table.

What day is it? Monday? Must be if the school is calling.

She struggled to sit up and looked at the clock. 10:20. As the lady was leaving the school number, Mary Lou snatched up the receiver. "This is Mrs. Winston."

"Oh, good. Is Kelly sick today?"

Is she? No telling with what has been going on lately. She hadn't seen her since yesterday afternoon when she stomped up to her room, all upset by a phone call.

"She isn't feeling well. This has been a rough ten days."

"I understand. I'll mark down that she's ill. Don't forget to call in tomorrow if she stays home another day."

"Yes," Mary Lou mumbled and hung up, then sat on the side of the bed, staring at the floor.

I need to do something. What?

Mary Lou fell back on the bed and curled up her legs. Maybe a little more sleep would . . .

⌘

As Sadie left her classroom for lunch, her cell phone vibrated on silence. Seeing that it was Ethan, she stepped back into her room and answered it. "Hi, how are you doing?" she asked, leaning back against the wall by the door. Memories of yesterday at church with Ethan sitting by her and her children flickered in and out of her mind, goose bumps rising on her arms.

"Doing okay. I wanted you to know what I found out about the water bottle. I wouldn't have it without you dumpster diving."

"I'll have you know it wasn't a dumpster, just a large trashcan. I already heard one of my students talking about it. Zoe Sanders wanted to know what was so interesting in the trash that I would dump it out on the floor."

"Did you tell her?"

"No way. I told her to sit down, that class was starting. Were there more than Lexie's fingerprints on it?"

"Yes, one clear set other than Lexie's. I checked with Lexie to see if anyone touched her bottle beside herself. As far as she knew, no one else did unless they did it without her knowledge. Also, the tranquilizers were given to her through her water. Since her bottle is blue, she didn't see the liquid content so I think someone took the bottle and poured crushed-up pills into her water."

"What I don't understand is why someone would deliberately do it."

"She may have made someone mad. I would say Kelly except the other latent prints we found weren't hers, but we don't have anything to match them against in our database."

"So they aren't Luke's?"

"No. I checked that right away. There were a few smudged ones so that could be someone besides Lexie or whoever else held the bottle."

"A third person? So you can't totally rule Luke or Kelly out?"

"No, although Lexie is positive it isn't Kelly who drugged her."

Sadie's gaze fixed on Lexie's usual desk, and flashes of Friday brought her panic back to the surface. "First the rumors, then the spiked water bottle. I think it's a good thing to keep Lexie home for a while."

"I agree and so does Beth. I'll stop by your room at the end of the day and let you know how our meeting with Mr. Howard goes."

"I'm certainly going to talk with the other teachers about what's going on with prescription drugs. Maybe we can do some things as a school. If nothing else, I'm going to be more alert to what's going on in the hallway and my classroom." She remembered the incident on Friday involving Kalvin and the kid with the hoodie. She thought about saying something to Ethan about it, but she really had no idea what the two boys exchanged. Although she hated hanging up, she still needed to eat lunch. "I've got to go. See you then."

As she left her classroom for the second time, Luke and some boy she didn't know were talking near her door. After the chat with Ethan and what had happened, she wondered if either one overheard any of her conversation. She stared at them, and they both turned and walked away. Who was that kid with Luke? She'd look at a yearbook and see if she could find him. She didn't like the fact they were outside her room. Although her door was partially closed, it was cracked open enough they could have been eavesdropping.

She shook her head. *I shouldn't have to suspect everyone around me. But I do.* Which students were abusing prescription drugs and not thinking anything was wrong because they were prescribed for people to use?

In the cafeteria, she kept an eye on the kids as she moved through to the teacher's lunchroom. What in the world was the attraction to taking a bunch of unknown prescription drugs? Even with her son, all she got from him was that he didn't know why he did it. She hoped the counselor he was seeing would get something more out of him.

After she grabbed some food, she sat at a table with Cynthia Proctor, Robin David, and Jack Hughes, another English teacher down the hall from her. Right after she sat down, Maxwell Howard took the chair across from her.

"There isn't nearly enough time to eat lunch. Maxwell, can't you do something about the lunch schedule?" Jack said as the assistant principal picked up his fork and speared his bite-sized piece of meatloaf.

"Above my pay grade. What about me? I have to grab something between hall and lunch duty."

Sadie finished chewing some of her turkey sandwich and washed it down with sweetened tea. "Personally, I think we need to be doing more hall and lunch duty."

Robin gasped. "Hush. Not with Maxwell here."

"I hope it doesn't involve dumpster diving." Jack winked at Sadie.

Everyone chuckled, glancing at Sadie.

Maxwell pinned her with a quizzical look. "Why, Sadie, do you think the staff needs to be doing more? Like what? We might have a teacher uprising."

A blush still heating her cheeks from Jack's reference to Saturday, Sadie answered, "I think things are going on around us that we need to be more vigilant about. Look what happened to Lexie Alexander."

A frown darkened Maxwell's blue eyes. "She took drugs and passed out at school. That would be hard to stop."

Sadie returned Maxwell's stare. "No, she didn't. Someone here at school slipped them into her water."

"What?" Cynthia said, her voice sounding over the din of voices at nearby tables. "How do you know that?"

"I know Lexie. She doesn't even like taking aspirin when she has a headache."

Maxwell scooped up his peas. "People can change. Right now the evidence points to her."

Sadie started to tell them otherwise, but that needed to come from Ethan or Cord. "The truth will come out. Cynthia, what can we do here at school?"

"One is a zero-tolerance policy toward any kind of drug. The students have to come through me, even to take an aspirin. If you see someone not doing so, the person needs to be reported. After what happened to Jared and Lexie whether she did it intentionally or not, we can't ignore there's a problem with some of our students. I agree with Sadie. We need to be trained for signs to look for."

"We were last year," Jack said, rising with his tray.

"But we have new teachers every year and what's popular to take changes, too." Cynthia glanced at Sadie. "Cough syrup, in liquid and pill form, has been a problem at the middle school. Easy to get. Over the counter."

"Like people who sniff glue. If they want to get high, they seem to find a way." Jack left to throw his trash away and take his tray to the cart.

Were Steven's friends and classmates buying cough syrup? Sadie needed to have a discussion with her son until she got to the bottom of what was going on. "I don't think it's just the teachers that need educating. Also the parents. Prescription drugs need to be disposed of properly. Not left half-used in the medicine cabinet."

"They shouldn't be flushed down the toilet. We don't need them going through our water system," Cynthia added.

"I'm guilty of leaving unused medicines in my drawer, but then I don't have kids." Robin checked the wall clock. "I can't believe the bell is going to ring in a few minutes."

"I agree with Sadie about having a presentation about drugs for the staff," Maxwell said and finished the rest of his meatloaf.

"Let me see what I can pull together. And we should consider doing something for the students, too." Cynthia gathered up her lunch sack and stood.

When everyone left but Sadie and Maxwell, she said to him, "Lexie is a victim and could have died. Our children should be safe when they come to school. You need to look into it."

"It happened in your class. Did you see anything?"

"I think it happened before she came into my class. It takes a while for the pills to take effect."

"When I have evidence to pursue, believe me I will, but I have to have something to go on."

"Who are the students who have taken drugs? Start with them."

"Jared, as far as I knew never had, but then I guess because of what happened last week I'm wrong about that. Some kids are quite good at hiding what they do. I can't accuse the ones who have in the past without evidence."

Her assistant principal headed for the cart, leaving her alone for a moment. She had a good relationship with a lot of her students.

Maybe some of them would be willing to talk to her. It wouldn't hurt for her to try.

❧

Ethan was running a little late, but he hit the reception area as his sister and niece went into Maxwell Howard's office. In "uniform"— tan pants, white long sleeve shirt, boots, tie, cowboy hat, and his Texas Ranger silver star over his heart—he didn't stop to explain his presence to the secretary, but quickened his pace and stepped into the entrance before the assistant principal closed the door.

The man's eyes widened slightly before he smoothed out his expression into a neutral one. "You're joining us, too?"

"Yes." Ethan entered the office and took a seat at the round table next to his niece, covering her hand on the arm of her chair. "I have information important to this meeting."

Howard settled himself at the table. "Unless you can erase the fact Lexie took tranquilizers that led to her being taken to the hospital from her sixth-hour class, I don't see the need for you to be here. Your position as a law enforcement officer must make it clear to you the school has to have a tough policy in place concerning taking any kind of drugs at school, over-the-counter, prescription, or illegal ones. Then we have to enforce it. If we didn't do that consistently and without any exceptions, we would have a worse problem than we have."

"So you acknowledge there's a drug problem at school?" Ethan relaxed back against his chair, feeling as though he were going into battle.

"Why are you here, Ranger Stone?" A tic jerked in the assistant principal's face, emphasizing the man's tension.

"To tell you about a piece of evidence we recovered—Lexie's water bottle."

"Where?"

"From the trashcan in the hallway up by Ms. Thompson's room on Saturday. She didn't throw it away. Lexie kept it in the side pocket of her backpack. When Ms. Thompson brought it by my sister's house Friday night, there was no water bottle in it."

"So you came up to the school and searched for this bottle?"

"No, Ms. Thompson was coming to school as she often does on Saturday and said she would look to see if it was in her classroom."

"But it wasn't. Is that why she dumped the trash on the floor?"

Ethan grinned. "Yes."

"So how in the world do you know what she found was Lexie's?"

"I have my name on my water bottle because so many kids have the one that is blue and yellow with the school emblem on it." His niece's hand gripping the arm of the chair tightened beneath Ethan's palm.

Howard's gaze swung from Lexie to Ethan. "So what kind of evidence did you find in it?"

"The bottle had been cleaned in the dishwasher the night before. Lexie filled it Friday morning and put it in her backpack. Her fingerprints are on it, but so are one set that is clearly not Lexie's and another smudged set that the lab can't match."

"Well, that can be explained. Someone must have thrown it away."

"Exactly. Why would anyone take it out of the side pocket of her backpack? Unless they wanted to cover up the fact the water in the bottle was spiked with tranquilizers. We tested the small amount left in it, and it was spiked."

Howard released a long swoosh of air. "How does that exonerate *your niece*?"

Ethan didn't miss the emphasis the assistant principal put on the fact he was related to Lexie. "Why would she crush tranquilizers, which by the way she doesn't have access to, into her water? It's much easier to swallow them and could be done without anyone seeing her if she wanted them so bad to take them at school."

"How do you know she doesn't have access? I'm sure Mr. Montgomery would say the same about Jared, and yet somehow he took a combination of different prescription drugs. I also understand that Lexie was having a difficult day because of some rumors going around about her lying to the police."

"Okay this is enough," Beth said, scooting to the edge of her chair. "My brother will be investigating this as an attempted murder because my daughter almost died from the tranquilizers someone else gave her."

Howard leaned forward. "He can do what he thinks is best, but I also have to. Lexie will be suspended for four weeks and will have to meet with our school nurse, Ms. Proctor, concerning the use of drugs before she is allowed back into school."

Beth bolted to her feet. "I'll appeal this to the school board."

"That is your right."

"Lexie was going to be staying home until Ethan found the person responsible, but I'll not have a suspension for drug use on her permanent record. She's innocent."

"I'm sorry to say this, but many kids caught doing something like that plead the same thing. However, in my experience they aren't innocent." Howard rose, facing Beth across the table.

The color washed from Lexie's face. Ethan squeezed her hand gently, conveying his support. He might be as jaded as the assistant principal, but Sadie and Beth were right. Lexie wouldn't have taken the tranquilizers knowingly.

Ethan stood at the same time as Lexie. "I want a list of students in every class that Lexie has."

"If you wait a few minutes, I'll have the secretary run the class lists for you."

"I would also like to know if anyone in those classes has been in trouble concerning drugs of any kind. I'll have a court order to you later today."

"I'll glance at them and see if any students stand out, but I don't see why a person would give Lexie a drug when pills can bring money on the street. I strongly recommend you and your sister get Lexie the help she needs. That would be the best use of your time."

Ethan ground his teeth together until his jaw hurt rather than tell the man he was wrong. The assistant principal had made up his mind Lexie was guilty and wasn't willing to listen to reason. Ethan intended to prove him wrong.

Ethan escorted his sister and niece outside to Beth's car while the secretary pulled up the student names he required. He wanted Beth and Lexie away from the school before the final bell rang for the day.

The second Beth left the building, she rounded on Ethan and exploded in anger. "When this is all over, I'm going to complain to the superintendent and the Board of Education about Mr. Howard. I'm not without some pull. I went to school with two members sitting on the board."

"Beth," Ethan waited until she looked at him before continuing, "Mr. Howard is doing his job. Discipline isn't an easy job. Most of the problem students go through his office."

"All the more reason he should realize Lexie isn't one of them. He's never seen her in the couple of years she's been in high school. That ought to give him some pause."

"I doubt he ever saw Jared either except to congratulate him on how well the football team was doing. I didn't like how the meeting went either, but he has a tough job. I'll get to the bottom of what's happening. Don't worry. This'll work out."

"How, Uncle Ethan?"

"For one, I want you to go home and think about your moves through the whole day on Friday until sixth hour. Who did you run into? Who could have had access to your water bottle? How were you feeling each hour? I know we talked a couple of days ago, but we need to again. I'll be over later this evening. As something comes to you, write it down. Okay?"

Lexie nodded, her eyes glistening.

He ran his index finger along her jaw and tapped her chin. "I know this is hard, but you've got me, your mom, and Ms. Thompson on your side. We believe in you."

She attempted a smile that didn't stay long on her face. "You forgot the Lord. He knows I didn't do anything wrong."

Ethan continued their trek to Beth's car. "Well, then that's all you need."

"But it would be nice if everyone else believed what was true." Beth went around to the driver's side.

Before Lexie climbed into the vehicle, she twisted toward Ethan. "Are you going to interview Kelly again?"

"Yes. She knows something she isn't telling me."

"She didn't have anything to do with drugging me."

"How do you know?"

Lexie's gaze latched onto his. "She told me, and I believe her. If you do, please do me a favor. Go easy on Kelly. She's vulnerable and fragile right now. I'm worried about her."

"I am, too. When I've seen Mary Lou, she isn't the same person I knew in high school. Has Kelly ever said anything about her mother drinking or something like that?"

"Yes. I've seen her drinking when I've been at the house."

It may be more than that. "Don't you worry about Kelly. I'll take good care of her, as if she were my niece."

Lexie stood on her tiptoes and kissed his cheek. "You're a great uncle."

"And Kelly has a good friend in you. I hope she appreciates it."

"She does."

Ethan moved back and watched them drive from the parking lot before he traipsed back into the building to get the class lists. He'd stop by Kelly's house on his way to see Lexie later.

Sadie input the finishing touches to the instructions for the essay about addiction she would have her classes write this week. She would tie it into literature by having them read an approved novel with a character that was addicted and analyze how the author dealt with the problem and portrayed it in the story. Cynthia, as not only the nurse, but also the drug counselor at the high school, agreed to talk to her classes tomorrow to kick off the unit.

Satisfied with her start on educating the students about the dangers in taking prescription drugs, Sadie relaxed in her chair, set her head on the backrest and closed her eyes. Slowly, the awareness of someone else in the room with her seeped into her mind. Tension whipped through her.

When she sat forward, she stared at Ethan in front of her desk. "Sneaking up on me is not allowed. What are you doing here?"

"Lexie's meeting with Mr. Howard."

"Ah, I forgot it had been changed to this afternoon. I let him know how I felt earlier today. How did it go?"

"The evidence with the water bottle didn't impress him. He suspended Lexie."

"I guess I can't blame him. All day he deals with the problem kids at school."

"Sorta like I deal with criminals all the time in my job?"

"Yeah, you're looking for reasons a person is guilty—not innocent. I think that is how Maxwell sees his job."

"He's wrong in this case, so now I just have to prove it. I don't want this affecting Lexie's future in any way." He placed some sheets on her desk. "Will you take a look at these class lists and let me know if there's anyone on there I should look into? I know that Lexie really likes you and often talks to you. Anyone she's mentioned that has bothered her. I'll be asking her but would appreciate your thoughts, too. You may see something she doesn't."

"There are a few of Jared's friends on this—Brendan, Missy, Carrie, Luke, Kalvin. She has a class with all of them. But really no one else stands out. Kelly doesn't even have a class with Lexie. The ones in the morning you can probably rule out. I'd take a look at fourth- and fifth-hours. Maybe lunch. What does Lexie say?"

"I'm going tonight to talk to her again. I need to recreate her day. Who she saw? Where she went? When her backpack was left alone? We've discussed this before, but that was not long after the incident. I'm hoping time will help her remember more."

Sadie unlocked her desk drawer, withdrew her purse, then grabbed her tote bag. "I need to leave to pick up Steven. He's going to his first counseling session. I may have to drag him kicking and screaming, but I'm praying in the end this will help him."

"I'll walk you out. I'm going by Kelly's house. Lexie thinks she'll be willing to talk to me now."

"It sounds like they made up. Good." Sadie locked her classroom door then strolled next to Ethan toward the parking lot. "Robin, Kelly's English teacher, told me that Kelly wasn't at school today when I mentioned I didn't see her going into her room earlier."

"Kelly was absent? Then maybe she's home now."

At her car, she waved good-bye to Ethan, then slid behind the steering wheel and started the engine. Ten minutes later, she picked up Steven and Ashley at the middle school. After dropping her daughter at home, Sadie drove Steven to his therapist, Dr. Morgan, a man in his forties with wire-rimmed glasses. For the first meeting, he wanted to talk to Steven alone.

Sadie pulled out some papers to grade while waiting. But she couldn't keep her mind on her work. What if she did a little investigating of Jared's friends? Talk to the teachers and counselors. Someone knew what was going on. If she got a lead, she'd give it to Ethan. It would be easier for her to talk to the kids rather than Ethan.

When her cell phone sounded, she hurriedly answered it, glad the reception area was empty except the lady behind the glass partition. "Ashley, what's wrong?" Sadie asked in a low voice.

"Mom, you were upset last time I asked Dad to come to see me. I've done the little homework I had and want him to come tonight. This'll give you a chance to see how he has changed."

"How would you know? You didn't know him until last week."

"The man I'm getting to know regrets walking out on us. That must mean he's changed. Remember what our pastor said yesterday about how the Lord gives us second chances all the time."

Sadie swallowed the moan that welled up in her. "Fine, but it's a school night. He can't stay long."

"Thanks, Mom."

Fifteen minutes later, Steven came out of his therapist's office with Dr. Morgan right behind him. Her son kept walking toward the door into the hallway.

Sadie approached Dr. Morgan. "How did it go?"

"About how I expected for our first session. He didn't say a whole lot. He did share his father is in town. That he hadn't ever seen him until a week ago Sunday."

"Yes, and he won't have anything to do with Harris. My daughter wants her father in her life. The tension at home has been thick between them as well as with me."

"I think the next session I would like you to attend part of it."

"So you think it's his father showing up that set this all off?"

"Could be. I did ask if his friends had done anything like what he did. He didn't answer me."

"Thanks, Dr. Morgan. We'll see you next week."

When Sadie reached the car, Steven stood by the passenger door, avoiding eye contact with her. "How did it go?" She pulled out of the parking lot into rush-hour traffic.

"I'm sure he gave you the rundown."

"Actually he didn't really other than to tell me you mentioned your father being in town. Is that what's bothering you?"

"Why should that bother me? I haven't had a father for thirteen years. I don't need one now, so as long as he stays away from me, I'm fine."

She turned down their street, her fingers locked about the steering wheel. "He's coming over this evening to see Ashley."

Silence greeted that announcement.

She drove into the garage and peered at Steven. The expression on his face shouted fury. She started to say something, but Steven escaped from the car and hastened into the house. After she pried her hands loose, she opened and closed them to relieve the ache caused by her tight grip.

When she entered the house a moment later, Steven wasn't in the kitchen where he usually stopped after he came home from school to grab something to snack on until dinner. The aroma of chocolate chip cookies, the twins' favorite, saturated the room with a mouth-watering smell. Her daughter was at the sink, cleaning up.

"Dad called and said he was going to bring over a couple of large pizzas, so you don't have to worry about making dinner."

So, now it would be dinner, too. "That's considerate of him." Even Sadie winced at the sarcastic bite to those words.

Ashley ignored them and continued. "I made cookies for when Dad comes. He mentioned he liked chocolate, so I'm sure he'll love these."

Since when had her daughter begun baking? This was a first. She'd tried to get her to, but Ashley had always found a reason not to. "I'm sure he will. Where did Steven go?"

"I guess his room. He glared at me and stomped through the kitchen." Ashley wiped down the counter by the sink. "He did say he wasn't going to be around when Dad came. I assumed you told him about tonight."

"I had to. This is his house, too, and you know how Steven feels about Har—your father. I have to respect those feelings."

"Why, because they're what you feel?"

"No. I've not kept it a secret how I've felt from the beginning."

"Then all I ask you to do is respect my feelings. I have a chance to establish a relationship with my dad."

"Why do you want one after all—"

Ashley rotated toward Sadie, the look in her eyes full of disbelief. "I know if Grandpa forgave you, you'd welcome him into your life even though he pretty much disowned you when you ran away and married Dad. Why aren't you angry with your father? Why do you want a relationship with Grandpa? He abandoned you—us when we needed him. I've heard you and Nana talking about it."

Good question. Why was she so eager to forgive her father and not Harris? "It's not the same thing."

Ashley set her fist on her hip. "Yes, it is. Both are about being rejected and not forgiving."

She studied her daughter for a moment, seeing a maturity in her that she didn't have at that age. "Maybe I have something to learn from you."

"Mom, are you okay?"

Before she could answer her daughter, the phone cut into the quiet. The sound surprised Sadie, and she jumped. She hurried to pick up the receiver. "Hello."

"Do you know where your son is?" someone said in a deep, gruff voice as if through a cloth. The next thing Sadie heard was the dial tone, taunting her with the prank call. Or was it a prank?

12

$\mathcal{M}$ary Lou's eyes blinked open, sunlight leaking through the slats on her blinds over her west window. What time was it? The clock on her radio read 4:45 p.m. She closed her eyes, feeling the lure of sleep. Then she remembered work. She needed to get to Greenbrier by 5:45 p.m. for her twelve-hour shift that started at six.

She rose—too fast. The room swirled. She sank back onto the bed and laid her arm over her eyes to still the movement.

She couldn't call in sick, not after taking a couple of days off last week. But it felt as though someone was tap dancing in her head to the beat of a bass drum. Being the office supervisor on duty at Greenbrier Nursing Home at night gave her perks other jobs wouldn't. Not many people were around to supervise her activities. She liked that. She couldn't jeopardize it.

This time she pushed herself up slowly and took her time making her way to the bathroom where she intended to have an extra-long shower. After she dressed for work, she headed to Kelly's room to see why she didn't go to school today. No doubt, she was still having a hard time over Jared. She couldn't blame her daughter with the police hounding her as if she knew something about her boyfriend's death. Kelly made the same mistake she had—falling for a Montgomery. They married their own kind, not people like them.

When she opened the door to Kelly's bedroom, her daughter wasn't in there. Her backpack sat by her desk where she put it when she came home from school. Her bedcovers looked like a wrestling match occurred last night. Before she left the house, she walked through it, checking to see if Kelly was anywhere else, then she called her daughter's cell and had to leave a message for her to call.

In the kitchen, she grabbed a bottle of water, went to her stash of pills, and downed some hydrocodone. She could no longer keep them in the medicine cabinet. She couldn't afford to have her daughter take any of her *medication*. By the time she got to work, she would be better—capable of handling the job. And maybe Kelly would call her by then. She was probably with Missy and Carrie.

<hr />

Sadie raced out of the kitchen and took the stairs two at a time. The pounding of her steps as she ran down the hallway matched the frantic beating of her heart. She barged into her son's room and came to an abrupt halt a few feet inside. Steven sat on his bed cross-legged with his earphones on, listening to his music.

"I'm not coming down if that man is here, no matter what you say," he shouted over the noise no doubt inundating his eardrums.

She walked over to him and removed the headset. "I can't carry on a conversation with you listening to your songs."

He frowned. "Ashley invited him. Not me. I'm staying up here until he leaves. Let me know."

"He's not here, but he's bringing pizza for dinner tonight. It's your favorite food."

"I don't care. I can eat it cold after he leaves. So now, you're having him here for dinner, and you had to barge into my room to tell me. I thought you didn't like him."

"Is that why you don't want to have anything to do with him?"

He opened his mouth, then snapped it closed. "No."

"Then why?"

He scowled and put his headphones back on. "Isn't it obvious? He had a chance to be the man of the house, to be our father. He didn't. We don't need him. We've done just fine without him." Then he went back to listening to his music, using two sticks to tap against his bed.

She turned off his iPod. "Is your father showing up in Summerton the reason you drank the cough syrup?" She stared at him for a long moment, not sure what was going through her son's mind.

The door chimes resonated through the house.

"Is it the reason?"

His eyes became slits. "All the kids are doing it. I wanted to see why." He turned his iPod back on and lowered his head.

She needed to talk with Steven about what he said, but his body language proclaimed it was useless right now. She'd chaperone Ashley and her dad, then return to find out what Steven meant by all the kids were doing it.

The sound of voices came from the kitchen. Sadie headed that way but paused before entering. *What do You want me to do? Forgive him? What's happening now can't continue. My family is in turmoil. How do I make this better?*

But no answer came to her mind.

When she finally strolled into the room, Ashley had set the pizza boxes on the table, poured four glasses of tea, and put the plate of chocolate chip cookies within easy reach. Her daughter beamed as she sat across from Harris.

"I made the cookies for you. I hope you like them." Ashley's cheeks flushed.

"For me? That's the sweetest thing I've had anyone do for me in a long time." Harris twisted toward the counter and grabbed a cookie, then took a bite. For a fleeting second, his eyes grew round, but he maintained his smile and popped the rest of the sweet into his mouth. When he was through, he gulped his drink until it was half-gone. "I will cherish these."

Keeping her lips pressed together, Sadie approached the table, stealing a cookie as she squeezed through the space behind Harris. She nibbled on it as she eased into her chair. Its salty flavor overpowered the chocolate. Her eyes watered, and she quickly swallowed some tea.

When she looked up, she caught Harris's gaze on her. In that moment, she realized he wanted to make this work with Ashley. What was she afraid of? That he would come in and take the kids away from her? That they would stop loving her and love him? Or was it built-up anger because he left her and she never really dealt with it?

Ashley shifted her attention from Harris to her. "Is something wrong with the cookies? I haven't had a chance to have one yet."

"This was a good first attempt, but they're a bit salty," Sadie said before Harris felt he had to reply.

Ashley rose and plucked one off the plate. When she took the first bite, she went to the trash and spit it out, then glanced at her father. "You ate this? How? It's awful."

"But you made it for me. That means the world to me."

Ashley marched to the counter, seized the product of her efforts, and tossed them in the garbage can. When she turned toward them, a huge smile plastered Ashley's face. "I'll do it again for you with Mom's help. And I promise I'll test them first."

He winked at Ashley. "I look forward to the next batch."

As her daughter retook her seat, Sadie decided what she needed to do.

Mary Lou hurried to catch up with the elderly gentleman before he left the nursing home. "Dr. Wells, may I have a word with you?"

The thin, gray-haired man, who had been practicing medicine for forty years, turned toward her. His immediate grin and the twinkle in his blue eyes reassured her she would get what she wanted. He hadn't let her down yet. "Yes, my dear. Are you still having trouble with your neck after the wreck?"

Mary Lou massaged her nape. "Yes. I thought I would be so much better after that little fender bender, but I woke up today with a pain shooting down my spine. I should have stayed home, but Greenbrier is already shorthanded. I don't want to put a burden on the rest of the staff, especially after staying home a couple of days last week because of my daughter. She's distraught."

"Ah, I heard about that boy dying. Did Kelly know him?"

"They were dating seriously. It hit her really hard."

Dr. Wells, who was semiretired but still saw a few patients usually at the nursing home, sighed. "Young love."

Before he started talking about the good old days, Mary Lou inched closer, turning on her smile. "I'm almost out of the painkillers you prescribed for me."

"You are? Didn't I refill it recently?"

"Three weeks ago. The pain is getting worse. I doubled up a couple of times." She fudged a week and hope he didn't remember the exact date the last time she'd seen him at the nursing home. If she went through his office, his staff kept records of the dates. When she caught him at Greenbrier, he usually forgot to mark it down or just gave her the samples he had on hand. Lately, she'd needed more and more, and what he prescribed for the month wasn't working anymore.

He wagged his finger at her. "You can't take too much of it. I suggest instead you go to my young partner, get another MRI, try physical therapy again. Your neck should be better by now. We need to determine why you're still in so much pain."

"But—"

"Call my office tomorrow. I'll make sure you get in right away."

"Can you help my daughter? She is anxious and depressed because of everything happening. I'm worried about her."

"Bring her in with you when you come. See you soon, my dear," Dr. Wells said then walked toward the double doors.

No. No. In the past, Dr. Wells accommodated her with no questions asked. Why wasn't he now? Kelly had taken some of her tranquilizers and painkillers, which had depleted her supply even more. She *needed* her medication.

She paced the foyer, rubbing her hands up and down her arms. Did he know what she was doing? Was that why he wasn't refilling the prescription? If she got another MRI, it would show her neck was fine. She couldn't do that.

What am I going to do?

There were meds everywhere around here, and most of these old geezers didn't need them like she did. She had to figure out how to get them without anyone seeing her. Late at night would be the best time. Having viewed some lock-picking videos on the Internet, she thought she could do it, and she wouldn't be blamed, because she wasn't a nurse. She didn't have a key to the medicine cabinet.

Pumping her arm into the air, she said, "Yes!"

A young nurse's aide stared at her from behind the counter nearby.

Heat suffused Mary Lou's cheeks. She nodded at the aide and hurried to her office to look again at the videos and find what she needed to use as a pick.

She'd practice tonight and then come back tomorrow night when she wasn't on duty. She could get into the nursing home through the kitchen area without anyone seeing her. She knew where the cameras were and could avoid being caught on them. The perfect crime. She would have enough pills to last her until she could come up with another source, possibly in a surrounding state.

When her cell phone rang, she thought it was Kelly and answered it quickly, "It's about time."

"Time for what?" the male voice asked.

"Who is this?" Mary Lou was pretty sure she knew, but she needed time to change gears.

"Ethan Stone. I'm calling because I went by your house earlier to talk with Kelly, but no one answered. I need to see her again at the police station. Tomorrow afternoon at one. If you need your attorney, this'll give you time to arrange it with him."

"Haven't you talked to her enough?"

"Until I solve the crime, no."

He hung up, leaving Mary Lou desperately needing a tranquilizer to calm her frazzled nerves. When was this nightmare going to end?

"I know this is a school night, so I'd better go." Harris rolled to his feet and shifted toward Ashley who rose beside him on the couch in the living room.

Ashley threw her arms around him and gave him a hug. "It was fun hearing about you and Mom in high school." She pulled back and glanced at Sadie. "Now I know where she gets her fear of mice from."

Sadie laughed. "I did learn a lesson. Never have a science fair project with mice involved, especially when they must have been clones of Houdini. I won't ever forget the one in my bed. I've never moved so fast in my life."

"Yeah, she called me and had me come over immediately and find that poor scared mouse and the other two."

"I beg your pardon." Sadie pointed at herself. "I was the one scared. I'm sure the neighbors heard my scream. My parents were gone, and I wasn't going to stay by myself in that house with a mouse."

"I guess I can't use them in a project then. Rats," Ashley said with a giggle.

"You better get ready for bed. School's tomorrow. I'll walk your father to the door."

"Sure." Ashley's forehead scrunched, her tone full of doubt.

Harris sent Sadie a similar look. "She did get your okay for me to come tonight?"

"Yes. I'd like to talk to you for a few minutes on the porch."

Harris strode to the door and moved outside with Sadie right behind him. She flipped on the light, eyeballed the swing at one end of the porch, and decided not to use it. Instead, she sat on the top step hugging the railing to give him plenty of room to sit also, but not too near her. The evening might have gone well, but she didn't want to give him any ideas.

"What's up?" Harris stretched out his long legs as he sat across from her.

"I've been thinking. I've decided not to pursue fighting you about seeing the kids. As long as they want to and I have a say in when and where, you can see them."

His eyebrows hiked up. "What changed your mind?"

"Holding a grudge only hurts me in the long run. We should never have married. Neither one of us was ready for it. Ashley is determined to have a relationship with you, and I can understand that. Since we married, mine with my dad has been nonexistent. But I would like one with him even with all that has happened between me and Dad." Harris started to say something, but she held up her hand. "But if you hurt Ashley, you'll have me to answer to. If you get tired of the father gig, you better give Ashley warning, not just disappear one day like you did with me. And as far as I'm concerned, you'll only get this one chance. Ashley thinks you have changed. I don't know if you have, but I'm going to give you the benefit of the doubt. Remember that Cord is the police chief."

Harris chuckled. "I'm aware of it. He's paid me a visit and told me I'd better treat you fair or else. And I got the point what the 'or else' would mean."

"Good. I'm not by myself this time. I have family and friends who care."

"Like the Texas Ranger?"

"Yes, he's a good friend," she said, realizing she wanted more than friendship. For the first time in thirteen years, she was ready to move on. Was Harris's appearance in Summerton what prompted this change? Maybe she'd needed to confront him with what he did and how she felt in order to move on.

"Any suggestions to get to know my son?"

"Time, I guess. Truthfully, I'm not sure what's going on. He's angry all the time."

"You think it's me, don't you?"

"Yes. Remember how angry I was at my dad when he cut me out of his life after we ran off and got married?"

He nodded.

"I think that's Steven concerning you. Dad and I are slowly working things out between us. He doesn't leave when I come over to see Mom like he did a year ago when I came back to Summerton. He even came over here the other night. That's why I say time might be your best bet."

"I don't have much of a choice. I haven't seen much of him. He's scarce when I come over."

"He's starting basketball practice soon and in November there will be games. You could go to them with Ashley and me. If he sees us together getting along all right, he might reconsider. But I can't stress it enough. The first time you aren't who you say you are now, that's it. We'll have to fight it out in court no matter what Ashley wants."

"So you've really forgiven me?"

Forgiven him? She hadn't thought of it in those terms, but she knew she couldn't keep the hostility up much longer—not with everything else happening around her. "I guess so, but I haven't forgotten what you did. It was a hard lesson to learn, but you have taught me what I want in a relationship. Good looks and charm will only get a man so far."

"Does that mean you think I'm good-looking and charming?"

"Marginally," she said in a serious voice, but her mouth cracked into a grin. "Okay, you know you are. All the girls in high school were after you. I think it was that bad rep you had."

He stood. "Thanks. I'm trying my best to change that 'bad rep.' I won't let you down this time."

She'd heard that a number of times when they had been together. She prayed he meant it this time. She might have forgiven Harris for what happened in the past, but that didn't mean she wouldn't keep an eye on him because she assumed everything was all right. Not with her children in the middle of it.

As soon as she closed the front door and locked it, she climbed the stairs to the second floor and continued to Steven's room. She hadn't forgotten what he'd said about the other kids taking cough syrup. *Please give me the right words to say, Lord. I've been naive when it comes to what's going on around me at home and work. My focus has been what it has always been, surviving one day at a time, raising my children, and making a living. It needs to be more. That's not enough with all that's occurring in the world.*

Sadie half-expected her son to ignore the knock, but seconds later he thrust open the door. "Is he gone?"

"Yes."

"Good. I'm starved." He started for the stairs.

"We need to talk."

"Now? I haven't had anything all day."

If he didn't appease his ravenous appetite, she would never get anywhere with him. "Yes, now. I'll come downstairs with you, and we can talk in the kitchen."

Five minutes later, with the box of leftover pizza in front of him at the table and a large glass of milk, Sadie asked, "What do you mean by the other kids at school are taking cough syrup?"

He scrunched his mouth into a frown. "Just that. I wouldn't have thought about it if I hadn't heard about it at school. A little of it is fine. A lot taste yucky. Made me sick to my stomach."

Good. She hoped that would at least stop him in the future. "Why did you do it?" she asked. Although after talking to the school nurse, she had a feeling why, but she wanted to hear it from her son.

Steven shrugged. "To make me feel better." He popped half a slice of pizza into his mouth, eating it, then downing several swigs of milk.

"Did it?"

"No. I told you I felt sick to my stomach."

"Then why are the kids doing it?"

"I guess not all kids feel that way. I've heard a couple of students are selling the crushed kind that doesn't do that to you. But honestly anything labeled a cough suppressant, DM, or has 'tuss' in the title will give a person a high if they take a lot of it. It's easy to get. Not expensive."

"Who's selling it?"

"Mom! I'm not a narc."

She shouldn't be having this conversation with her son. In a perfect world, this would never be an issue. *What have I done wrong as a parent?* "Do you know what can happen to a person who abuses cough syrup and remedies like it? They can become addicted to it. Taking excessive amounts can lead to death. What if when you fell and hit your head, it had killed you or put you in a coma?"

"Calm down, Mom. I'm not gonna do it. I didn't like it. Not worth a cracked head and my stomach pumped out."

Sadie closed her eyes and breathed deeply, trying to calm down. "These kids selling it at the middle school should be stopped."

Steven took the last piece of pizza and shut the empty box. "I don't know who they are. I think they're a couple of eighth graders selling various drugs."

"Various? What?"

"I don't know. Things to calm you down, perk you up."

"Are your friends buying any?"

He shook his head. "Not my close ones." His gaze slid away.

"But some of the kids you know?"

"Maybe. I don't know for sure."

"You should talk about your experience with your friends. Let them know how close you came to really hurting yourself. Let them know how it felt to have your stomach pumped out. They need to hear the other side of taking cough syrup."

Steven downed the rest of his milk and shoved to his feet.

"Was your dad's return the reason you wanted to get high?"

He blinked then looked toward the door.

"We need to talk about this. Your dad isn't going away."

"Why not? Aren't you going to fight him in court? I'll testify I don't want him around."

"Why do you feel so different from Ashley?"

He clenched his hands at his sides, his eyes becoming slits. "Because he deserted you—us. A man doesn't do that." Grandpa told me. He whirled around and hurried from the room.

Sadie rubbed her fingertips down her face. She felt in the middle of two warring factions—Ashley on one side, Steven on the other.

And in the middle of this, her eyes had been opened to what was going on around her. She'd held herself apart from others for long enough. Tomorrow she would inform the principal at the middle school what little she knew, and then in the afternoon after work, she would go see her father. The talk she'd had with Harris tonight and even Steven was the first step in righting her life.

⤷❧

Her feet dragged with fatigue as Mary Lou entered her house through the garage early Tuesday morning. She noticed the blinds over the sink were still open. Kelly usually shut all of them before she went to bed.

She went over to the counter and pulled the string to close the slats on the darkness that still blanketed the landscape at 6:10 a.m. in the morning. Mary Lou trudged up the stairs to her bathroom, exhausted from dealing with a patient's death a few hours ago and searching for the right tools to use to pick the lock on the medicine cabinet. Mary Lou withdrew the bottle of her last two painkillers from deep in the linen closet. Shaking one out into her palm, she stared at the oblong pill. This and the last one would get her through the day. Then tonight she would get a new supply to hold her for a while until she came up with another source.

Mary Lou popped the painkiller into her mouth and swished it down with a gulp of water from the faucet. She followed it with one of her tranquilizers so she could sleep. Then, as she padded to her bedroom, she thought about checking on Kelly. Nah, her daughter was asleep, and she certainly didn't need to disturb her.

But later she would have a word with her about not returning her call last night, and the fact she had to go to the police station again at one. Mary Lou would only be able to sleep a couple of hours. In her room, her bed beckoned her, and she fell face down onto the mattress, the darkness like the night blanketing her.

⤷❧

Mary Lou rolled over and fumbled for the phone. "Hello."

"Mrs. Winston, this is Summerton High School again. Kelly hasn't been at school today, and you haven't called in this morning yet."

The hazy red numbers on her digital clock read 12:30 p.m. At least she thought they did. She rubbed her eye and tried to focus better. Yeah, 12:30. Didn't she set the alarm for 7:45 a.m., so she could catch Kelly before she left for school?

"Mrs. Winston, are you there?"

"Yes. Sorry. I worked last night and came home early this morning and fell asleep. I meant to call. She's still not feeling well. I'll make sure she gets to school tomorrow."

Before the secretary could say another word, Mary Lou slammed the receiver in its cradle and pushed back the covers. She didn't even remember pulling them over her. The softness of her bed enticed her to return to sleep, but she had to make it clear to Kelly she couldn't skip school, and she had to get over Jared. But even more importantly, they only had half an hour to get to the police station. Last night she'd left a message for Jeffrey to meet them there. She hoped he would because she couldn't deal with Cord or Ethan without him.

Mary Lou shook her head. *Kids think they know what love is. They don't have any idea what it is.*

She shuffled toward Kelly's room, barely able to pick up her feet. Her muscles protested the exercise. Inside, she made a slow three-sixty. This was exactly like it was a couple of days ago. Slowly, the significance of what she was seeing seeped into her foggy brain. Her daughter was gone.

13

*T*hanks for calling me and letting me know Dad was here." Sadie entered her parents' house right after work on Tuesday. "I have to pick Steven and Ashley up at school by four."

"I'm not sure having a talk with your father will do any good. He's one stubborn man. Don't you think I've already tried?"

"I know he never liked Harris, but why?"

"You didn't ask him?"

"Yes, but all he would say was he had his reasons, then expected me not to date him."

Her mother fiddled with the pearl drop earrings she was wearing. "He never would say, but I have my suspicions."

"What?"

"Harris's mother. Your dad dated her in high school, and she dropped him for Harris's father. Then the man was caught breaking and entering homes of people he knew and stealing their valuables."

"So you think Dad was angry at Harris because his father took his girlfriend away? A man who robbed people?"

Her mom nodded. "All these years I've known I was his second choice. That Veronica was his first one, and he would have left me if she'd ever encouraged him."

"Why didn't you tell me?"

"What woman wants to admit she's the runner-up, not the winner?"

Sadie enfolded her mother into her embrace, trying to tamp down her anger. She had come to reconcile with her father, to apologize for leaving all those years ago. Now she didn't know if she could. "Where's Dad?"

"In his office."

Sadie strode toward her father's home office. At the door at the end of the hallway, she filled her lungs with as much air as she could and raised her hand to knock. She blew a long breath out and dropped her arm, turning away. She couldn't do it. Earlier, listening to the pain in her mother's voice stirred up Sadie's anger again. How could Dad do that to Mom?

The sound of the door opening startled her, and she gasped, whirling around to find her father in the entrance.

"Why are you standing there? Did you need to see me?" His brusque voice rubbed her nerves the wrong way.

All the years of tiptoeing around her father, avoiding the real subject she wanted to discuss overwhelmed her with the wasted time and the prideful bearing of not only her father but her own. Someone had to give, and looking at his proud stance as though he was readying himself to do battle made her realize it wouldn't be him.

"Mom told me about Veronica. Is she the reason you were so against Harris?"

Shock filled his eyes. "I don't owe you an explanation." He strode toward his desk.

Sadie charged into the office. "Harris wasn't his mother," she said to his back, startled she was defending her ex-husband after all he had done to her and the kids.

Her father pivoted, the sharp needles of his eyes piercing right through her. "No, he was worse. Look what he did to you. He left you with two babies."

The blast of his voice hit her with its full force. She stepped back. "Since when do you care?"

"His mother and father were no good, and neither is he. I'm glad you're going to fight him being in the children's lives."

"I'm not going to fight him. Ashley wants to get to know her dad."

"Just because your child wants it doesn't mean you should give it to her. Didn't you get it all those years ago when I forbade you seeing Harris? Look what happened to you in the end. He abandoned you at the worst possible time."

And so did you. "Oh, I got it. If I chose Harris, you would have nothing to do with me. I was only weeks away from being eighteen, and you were dictating what I was going to do. It was your way or the highway. It always was and still is." Words spilled from her bruised heart that she hadn't acknowledged in years.

"He's going to hurt you again."

"Then so be it. That isn't a reason you should turn your back on me. My wise, thirteen-year-old daughter told me a person deserves a second chance in life. That's what the Lord would want. I'm giving that to Harris. Don't you think your own daughter deserves one?"

The veins in her father's neck stood out. She could almost see them throbbing faster and faster. "I didn't want you making the same mistakes. I knew what kind of person Veronica was—a user."

"Well, you might want to talk to your wife about what she thinks. She always thought she came in second in your life to Veronica." Sadie backed away until she was in the doorway and said, "And Harris wasn't the only one who abandoned me at the worst possible time," then swept around and hurried down the hall.

I can't do it, Lord. He's too bitter and hard. He doesn't know how to give any.

"Meet me at Mary Lou's house," Cord said to Ethan over his cell phone.

"What's going on?" Ethan slowed and parked along a street while he talked with Cord. "I was headed that way now because she and

Kelly didn't show up at the station. Jeffrey didn't know what was going on. I told him I would bring them in."

"Kelly is gone. Mary Lou thinks for at least thirty-six hours, possible forty-eight."

"But she doesn't know for sure? Does she check on her daughter at all?" Ethan snapped his teeth together so hard, he hoped he didn't crack a tooth.

"I know. That's a conversation for another day. Believe me, I intend to have it out with Mary Lou, especially in light of everything going on lately. I haven't gotten to call you yet. I'll be coming from the scene of a wreck. Luke Adams ran into a tree. DOA."

Dead on arrival. Ethan closed his eyes. "What happened?"

"Don't know. I'll leave my men to process the scene. No other car was involved. It appears he lost consciousness because there are no skid marks to indicate he attempted to swerve away or put on his brakes."

"Two teens dead and one missing in less than ten days—all, we believe, at that pill party."

"It would seem. See you at Mary Lou's."

Ethan had the strong urge to call his sister and make sure Lexie was all right. Before pulling back onto the road, he punched in Beth's cell phone number. She answered on the second ring.

"Ethan, I'm glad you called. We had a patient die last night who shouldn't have."

"You're work in a nursing home with old and ailing people. Why do you feel the patient shouldn't have?"

"Lucy was in the room next to our grandmother. Remember that day she was screaming and moaning. She may have dementia and severe arthritis, but otherwise she was quite healthy. On her meds, she is harmless, docile. Last night she went berserk and ended up stabbing herself with a pair of scissors over and over."

"Where did she get the scissors?"

"From the patient across the hall who is perfectly lucid and knits a lot to keep herself active. What I don't understand is why she did it? Something doesn't feel right. I'm requesting an autopsy."

"You expect foul play?" With tension twisting the muscles in his neck, he rolled his head.

"I don't know. I can't see why. But I do have questions, and since I'm the supervising nurse at Greenbrier, I need to have answers, even if Lucy doesn't have any family. I didn't mean to lay this all on you. It's probably nothing. Why did you call?"

"Where's Lexie?" Ethan asked in the calmest voice he could. He had a bad feeling about all of this. It all seemed connected somehow. Drugs were at the center of a lot of events occurring in Summerton lately.

"Why?"

"Kelly has been missing for at least thirty-six hours. Do you think Lexie knows anything?"

"She said something to me about Kelly not being at school and that she's left several voice messages and texts on her phone. She was going by to see her this afternoon and make sure she was all right. I'm not sure when."

"Call her and ask her to stay home. I'll come by later and let you all know what's going on."

"Should I go home?"

"With all that's happening at Greenbrier, no. Bye." Ethan disconnected and put his cell phone in the cup holder then pulled onto the street and headed toward Mary Lou's.

Sitting at a stoplight, Ethan tapped his fingers against the steering wheel. He couldn't let go of the fact everything tied to prescription drugs. First Jared, then Lexie. Even what Steven told Sadie last night about some eighth graders selling drugs at the middle school. No doubt, the same was going on at the high school although he didn't have concrete proof. Kelly's behavior had been out of character lately, another indication of drug use and possibly fears. Was there a single supplier or a less coordinated network with multiple dealers?

When the light changed to green, he pressed the accelerator and five minutes later parked in front of Mary Lou's two-story home in a subdivision that had begun to decline. Walking up to the porch, he panned the house and yard. Unkempt came instantly to mind. The beds were overgrown with weeds and grass, choking out the flowers and scrubs. Patches of peeling paint and a couple of torn screens finished off the picture.

When Mary Lou opened the door to let him in, he got the same impression from her tangled hair, bloodshot eyes with dark circles around them, and sweats with stains on them. In high school, Mary Lou had been one of the best-dressed and made-up girls in their class. Then Bradley Montgomery broke up with her, and something happened to her. She changed.

"Cord just got here. We're in the living room." Mary Lou led the way, hugging herself and scratching her arms. She sat in a chair across from him and Cord. "I don't know what happened to Kelly. I've called everyone I know, and no one has seen her. Do you think she ran away? I can't blame her with all that's been going on. She really cared about Jared. His death devastated her."

Cord cut into Mary Lou's ramblings. "What's been going on lately with Kelly? Since we saw her on Saturday at the police station?"

Her long fingernails continued their trek up and down her arms, leaving red marks on her skin. "You know. Her and Lexie. It's hard losing your best friend because she lied."

Ethan sat forward. "I heard from Lexie she and Kelly made up."

Mary Lou shook her head for a good half a minute. "No. That has to be a lie, too. Kelly couldn't believe how much Lexie had changed since Kelly started dating someone so popular like Jared."

Was Mary Lou losing touch with reality? Did she even know what was going on in her daughter's life? Ethan suspected both, especially since she hadn't known she was missing until a day and a half to two days later. "Mary Lou," he waited until her gaze darted to him, "are you all right?"

She jumped to her feet and began prowling. "No. My daughter is gone." Her voice grew louder with each word. "I know you aren't a parent, but how could you ask such a question? Kelly is hurting and is out there somewhere. She could be in trouble. She is in trouble. I can feel it." Hysteria inched into her tone.

Cord rose and went to Mary Lou. "Is there anyone I can call to come over and be with you while we look for Kelly?"

Wide-eyed, Mary Lou turned toward him. For a long moment, she didn't say anything and then when she did, tears flowed down her face. "No. I have no family. No . . ."

"Who's your doctor?" Ethan stood, pulling out his cell phone.

"Why?"

"I think you need help."

"I'm fine. I'm fine." Tears continued to flood her eyes and run down her cheeks.

Cord guided her back to her chair. "Still, I think we need to call your doctor and let him help you."

She nodded again and again. "Yes. Yes, you're right. Dr. Wells. I feel like I'm falling apart. My poor baby. Please find her. She could be in trouble."

Ethan called information then Dr. Wells's office. The doctor was leaving for the day and agreed to come by and see Mary Lou. Then he punched in Beth's number and asked her to stop by and be with Mary Lou. Beth and Mary Lou had been friends because of Kelly and Lexie. Only lately, that had been strained. But Beth was a nurse and might be the best person here to help Mary Lou.

With Mary Lou's permission, Ethan went upstairs to check Kelly's room, while Cord sat with her.. When she had said Kelly could be in trouble, Ethan had a strong feeling she was right. When he first entered, his impression was how similar Kelly's bedroom was to Lexie's—messy. With all that was going on, he decided to call Sadie and ask a favor of her.

"Hello. What are you doing?" she answered.

The sound of her voice brought a smile to Ethan. "I'm over at Kelly's house. She's been missing a couple of days. Mary Lou is distraught. Her doctor is coming to see her, but I asked Beth to be here with her since they know each other because of the their daughters. But that leaves Lexie home alone. Can she come over and stay with you?"

"Sure. I'm heading home. I'll swing by and pick her up. She can stay as long as you all need her to."

"I knew I could count on you. In case you haven't heard, Luke was killed in a car wreck a couple of hours ago."

"No! Not another one of my students. What happened?"

"I don't know all the particulars. Cord is here with me at Mary Lou's. He came from the scene. It's still being processed, but the timing of it meant he left school probably after your class fifth-hour."

"This is going to rock the student body, especially if Kelly can't be found. I hope nothing is wrong with her, too."

"You think there could be?" he asked her, even though he had already come to that conclusion.

"Don't you? In less than two weeks, something has happened to four teens—all connected to each other in one way or another."

"Yeah, that's what I think. I'll stop by later. I need to talk with Lexie. Right now, I'm going through Kelly's room. Bye."

Next, he placed a call to his niece. "I need you to go stay with Ms. Thompson for a while. Your mom is coming over to be with Mary Lou. Kelly is missing."

Lexie didn't say anything.

"Lexie?"

"When did she go missing?" The roughened sound of her voice conveyed her struggle to keep her emotions together.

"Mary Lou isn't sure. Probably a day or two ago."

"Her mom wasn't aware of much that went on with Kelly. Do you think she ran away or . . .?"

"Or? What are you thinking?" His gaze flitted from one mess to another.

"She told Missy and Carrie she didn't want to have anything to do with them. She had a fight with them sometime Saturday."

"How do you know?"

"Kelly told me. I talked with her Sunday morning before going to church but couldn't get in touch with her after that."

"How did Kelly usually keep her room?"

"Sometimes neat, sometimes she would let things go."

"Right now, I'm standing in the middle of a very messy room. Is that normal?"

"She was trying to keep things in order, but with all that has been happening she might have let her room go."

"Later, I'll have you go through the room with me. See what you think." He was beginning to feel Lexie knew Kelly better than Mary Lou. He wanted to get both of their takes on how the bedroom appeared to them. "Ms. Thompson is coming by to pick you up. I'll tell your mom where you are. See you later."

After sticking his phone back in his pocket, Ethan started at the right side of the door and searched the perimeter before working his way toward the center of the room. When nothing popped out at him, he went to her desk, sat, and turned on her computer. It was wiped clean. That, and the fact her closet was still full of clothes reinforced his feeling Kelly was in trouble. Did Kelly dump her information from the computer or someone else?

Ethan took another tour around the room, looking again for the girl's cell phone. It was gone. He paused at her window and checked to see if it was locked. It wasn't, and outside, the roof of the back porch slanted slightly up toward the room. A huge elm had several big limbs hanging over the roof. Big enough to support a person's weight and elm trees were great for climbing. Someone could have sneaked in here. As clueless as Mary Lou seemed to be, she probably would never know if someone did.

Ethan returned downstairs and found Dr. Wells checking Mary Lou. As Ethan entered the living room, the doctor gave Mary Lou a shot.

"I'll call in a prescription for a tranquilizer to help you calm down." Dr. Wells glanced toward Cord. "Is there anyone going to be here with her?"

"Yes, Beth Alexander is coming."

Mary Lou lifted her head. "She is? Why? I'm fine by myself."

Dr. Wells patted her shoulder. "You shouldn't be alone right now. I gave you a sedative that will help you sleep. Since Beth is a nurse, that is even better. You need to rest and let the police look for Kelly. I'm sure they'll find her."

"How long before it takes effect?" Ethan approached Dr. Wells.

"Fifteen minutes or so."

"Mary Lou, I'll help you upstairs to your bedroom. Before you go to sleep, do you think you could take a look around Kelly's room to see if anything is gone?"

"You think she's run away?"

"I don't know. I'm trying to figure out what's going on. I'm considering all options."

What little color she had in her face vanished. "Anything to help my little girl come home safely."

Ethan assisted Mary Lou to her feet, and she leaned into him. Putting his arm around her, he crossed to the foyer and the staircase while Cord answered the doorbell. Mary Lou didn't even look around to see Beth enter, followed by two police officers. Mary Lou clung tighter to him the nearer they came to Kelly's room. Her body trembled, and Ethan wasn't even sure she would make it the fifteen minutes.

Inside the doorway, Ethan asked, "Is this the way her room was the last time she was in here?"

Mary Lou blinked. "I guess so. I remember it was messy with some clothes on the floor."

Ethan swept his arm wide. "This many. It looks like half her closet is in piles."

"I'm not sure." She massaged her fingertips into her temple.

"Does she keep her phone somewhere when she is home?"

"By her. She's always on it—texting or talking."

"What's the number? If she has it with her, we can use the GPS to track her."

Right after Mary Lou recited Kelly's phone number, she twisted out of his embrace. "I need to lie down." But when she took a step, she wobbled and began to sink to the floor.

Ethan grabbed her and held her up for a few seconds before he swung her up into his arms and headed into the hallway.

Mary Lou laid her head on his shoulder and barely pointed toward a closed door at the end of the corridor. When he laid her on her unmade bed, he covered her then hastened down the stairs. He needed to bring Lexie to see Kelly's room. Whether it was from the medication Dr. Wells had given Mary Lou or the fact she didn't often go into her daughter's bedroom, he'd gotten very little helpful information from her.

Beth stood at the front door with Dr. Wells, saying good-bye to him. When she turned back into the foyer, her gaze latched onto Ethan. "Cord said Mary Lou was beside herself."

"Yeah. I couldn't get much out of her. The medication must have kicked in faster than Dr. Wells thought. She's in bed and will probably sleep a long time."

"I called our pastor. He's organizing some ladies at the church to take shifts to be here for Mary Lou since she doesn't have any family. Also, tomorrow I can check with some of the people she works with at Greenbrier."

"Maybe we'll get lucky and find Kelly by then."

Beth frowned. "Do you think that?"

"Honestly? No. I don't have a good feeling about this. I hope I'm wrong."

"So do I. Lexie was so happy when she and Kelly made up on Saturday. That had given me hope things would work out in the long run. Now, I don't know."

"Speaking of Lexie, Sadie picked her up and took Lexie to her house. I didn't want her to be alone, especially in light of the fact someone drugged her. I need her, though, to help me check Kelly's room, so I'm going to bring her here."

"Until someone relieves me, I'd rather her not stay here. It'll just upset her. It will be bad enough her going through Kelly's possessions to see if anything is gone. Do you think Kelly ran away?"

"No. If she did, she couldn't have taken many clothes with her. They are all over the floor upstairs, and her computer has been wiped."

Cord joined them in the foyer, putting his hand at the small of Beth's back. "Thanks for taking care of Dr. Wells. I wanted to have my men search the house. Kelly's car is in the garage so I guess she walked or someone picked her up. I heard you're bringing Lexie over. While you do that, I'm paying a few kids a visit. Get their reaction to the fact Kelly is missing."

Ethan leaned in and kissed his sister's cheek. "Thanks for doing this. Mary Lou is going to need some friends. I know you two were once."

"If my daughter can forgive Kelly's lies, then I can forgive Mary Lou's behavior."

Cord took Beth's hands and squeezed it. "I'll be back later to check on Mary Lou."

Ethan opened the front door and strode out of the house first. He glanced back and spied his best friend kissing his sister—and not on her cheek. They both needed someone. He hoped it worked out for them. As he continued toward his SUV, he pictured the woman whose home he was going to. Sadie. A smile flirted with his mouth, and there was a bounce to his walk.

※

Lexie lifted up Kelly's mattress and pulled a journal from beneath it. "She used to write in this every day. We both started keeping one when we started middle school. It helps us when we get upset about something." She flipped through the pages. "But Kelly was acting so weird lately, I don't know if she kept this up." When she turned to the page where the entries ended, she noted the date of the last one: Monday after Jared died.

"Did she?" Ethan moved to her side.

"Her last entry reads: He's dead. I can't believe it. I loved him so much. We should never have gone to the party Saturday night, but Jared wanted to. His friends had accepted me into their group, and he wanted me to get to know them better. That was the biggest mistake of my life." Blotches of ink covered the page as if Kelly had been crying as she wrote the words. Lexie glanced at her uncle. "Kelly never said anything to me about this."

Ethan took the journal and continued reading. "They aren't anything like I thought they would be. Missy and Carrie are mean and would just as soon push me off a cliff as accept me. They made it clear I'd better not say a thing to anyone about the party or else. What would they do? We're all to blame that Jared is dead."

Lexie gasped.

"I just wish Saturday had never happened. I want Jared back." Ethan finished and closed the book. "This is what I need to get these kids to talk. I'll start by bringing in Missy and Carrie." He strode to the laptop on Kelly's desk and gathered it up. "I'm taking this as well. Someone may have erased what was on the computer, but there are ways to recover it. I'll have the tech guys see what they can find."

Listening to Uncle Ethan map out his plan, Lexie sank onto the bed. *We're all to blame that Jared is dead.* She couldn't rid her mind of those words. How? Why? Not Kelly. She loved him. Sadie could remember how Kelly went on and on about what a wonderful boyfriend he was. About how lucky she was and . . .

"Lexie, are you okay?"

Her uncle's question drew her back to the present. "No, my best friend just said Jared is dead because of them. I think about what she has been going through, and my problems are nothing compared to hers. You've got to find her."

"We're doing all we can. Do you see anything missing in the room? Like something she would take if she ran away."

Lexie circled the room, opening and closing drawers and standing in the closet, searching for all of Kelly's favorite outfits, shoes, accessories. When she emerged from it, her gaze zeroed in on a picture of Kelly and Jared taken a few weeks ago. "No. Everything I think she would have taken with her if she had run away is still here. The duffel and backpack she would have used is here. She doesn't have luggage."

As she stated all the items that made it clear to Lexie that Kelly didn't leave on her own accord, her heart began beating faster and faster. Her chest hurt, which reminded her of the last face-to-face conversation she'd had with Kelly. "Saturday when we talked, she described how the pills she'd taken at the party made her feel. She was still having some effects from them—racing heartbeat, feeling like she wanted to crawl out of her skin. Whatever was in that bowl they put the pills into was potent. When I saw the bowl, it was empty. What happened to all those pills? Did they take all of the drugs? If so, that's a lot to take in an evening. If not, which partygoer emptied the bowl of the remaining pills?" She shivered, recalling the scene at the warehouse—the remnants of a party that had gone wrong.

"Your questions about the pills are important ones. I want you to sit down and think back to that Sunday morning when you picked up Kelly. Any impression you had, anything you saw, heard. Maybe something else will come to mind that you've forgotten. Nothing is too small."

"I'll try, but I was so focused on getting Kelly out of there I don't know if I'll remember much more than that."

Uncle Ethan slung his arm over her shoulder. "That's all I can ask. To try. Let's go see what your mom wants to do with you."

When Lexie went into the living room with her uncle, her mother sat on the couch, drinking a cup of tea and listening to the news. She switched the TV off when she spied Lexie, but not before she glimpsed Luke's wrecked car, the front smashed into a huge oak tree to the point the car looked like a partially collapsed accordion. The sight of the crash hit Lexie with the fact she had lost another classmate. What if Kelly was dead, too? What if someone tried to finish her off?

"I'm through here for the time being. Has Mary Lou rallied any?" Ethan withdrew his car keys and jiggled them.

"No, but she shouldn't for quite some time. The lady who was going to relieve me can't until early tomorrow morning, so I'm staying, but Lexie I don't want you to. I called Sadie, and she said you're welcome to stay at her house tonight. I'll swing by and get you in the morning then you can go to work with me. I'm not leaving you alone." Beth peered at Ethan. "I figured you would be working part of the night, especially with Luke's death. Cord called and said he was pushing the ME to do an autopsy right away. In the meantime, they are processing Luke's items from the car."

"I'll take Lexie to Sadie's house, then go down to the station. If you need me, you know how to reach me."

Lexie hugged her mother before following her uncle outside to his SUV. Settled into the passenger's seat, she asked, "Wasn't Luke's death an accident?"

"Don't know. Something made him go off the road and into that tree."

"I'm scared."

He started the engine, cocking his head to look at her. "I'm not going to let anything happen to you. You'll be with someone at all times until we have this figured out. It's probably not necessary. Just something we need to do as a precaution."

"Because we don't know who spiked my drink?"

"Right, or why."

When he pulled into Ms. Thompson's driveway, he accompanied Lexie to the porch. When Ms. Thompson opened the door, Lexie thought her uncle would leave, but instead he came inside.

"You both are in time for dinner. I hope you're hungry."

Uncle Ethan glanced back at the closed door. "I can't stay too long."

Ms. Thompson slid her arm through the crook of Uncle Ethan's. "You've got to eat, then you can go to work. Cord called. He's gone to grab something for dinner, so he won't even be at the station for a while."

"Why did he call?"

"He knew I had Luke in class. Then I received another call from Maxwell Howard about Luke's death. This is going to hit the student body hard. Luke, like Jared, was on the football team and looked up to by the underclassmen. Come on. Steven and Ashley are starving. Well, Steven is. He'll be glad you all are here so we can eat."

❧

Mary Lou stumbled out of bed, her room dark except a slither of light from under her door. She walked a couple of steps and clasped the top of her dresser to steady herself. She hadn't had anything to drink, but she felt drunk.

What time is it? What day is?

Slowly memories intruded into her mind. Sitting in the living room with Dr. Wells standing over her. He gave her something. She had been upset. Why? She tried to grasp onto the reason—just out of reach.

Leaning over, she laid her head on the top of the dresser, closing her eyes. Kelly. It had something to do with her daughter.

Then she remembered why Dr. Wells was in her house earlier.

Kelly's gone.

How dare her leave me to deal with everything on my own.

Mary Lou brought the flat of her hand down on the wooden top. Pain shot up her arm, but she didn't care.

She turned back to the bed and found the nightstand. Fumbling around, she finally grasped the lamp's chain and pulled it down. Light flooded the room. She blinked, then closed her eyes to the brightness assaulting her.

She fell onto the bed, needing to sleep more. But something niggled her thoughts. She needed to do something. Rolling over, she spied the digital clock and the time. Still a few more hours of night.

Through the haze that clouded her mind a picture of the medicine cabinet at Greenbrier came into view. She struggled to sit up. The vision wavered. She squeezed her eyes closed, trying to latch onto what she needed to do. She imagined reaching out touching something through the mist. She felt something solid, smooth.

Painkillers. She only had one left. She had to get to the nursing home. Thanks to Dr. Wells, she had some tranquilizers, but she still needed to find another source for her medication.

The time was now. She staggered out of bed and toward her bathroom. For a moment, she thought about taking a shower but something kept nagging at her not to. Instead, she splashed cold water on her face. Peering into the mirror, a stranger stared back at her. A wild mass of blond strands about her gaunt face. Eyes bloodshot and sunken.

She swayed into the counter, clutching the edge with one hand while opening a drawer with the other and rummaging for a brush. After barely bringing order to her hair, she pulled out another drawer—the one that held her prescriptions. They weren't there. Panic drenched her. Sweat beaded her forehead and underarms.

No! I still have some left. Where are they?

Then she recalled she'd hidden them in the kitchen and linen closet.

Still unsteady, she practically fell against the linen closet doors. Tearing through the stacks of towels, she finally located her bottle of uppers she'd bought from one of Kelly's classmates six weeks ago for times she had to be extra alert. What was his name? She tried to remember and came up blank. She'd think of his name when she wasn't so stressed.

She needed the painkillers, and the stimulant would make her alert enough to break into the medicine cabinet and not get caught. Then she could turn all her energy to getting Kelly back safely. She dug into the bottle for one of the uppers.

Kelly, baby, doing this for you.

After swallowing the pill, Mary Lou reentered her bedroom, her steps and movements slow. She changed into black sweats and a long sleeve shirt, then sat on her bed and waited for the medication to take effect. Once she felt more stable and clear, she would leave for Greenbrier. She'd gone over how to get into the nursing home undetected. She'd practiced last night opening the lock with her homemade picks. And she knew the perfect time.

When her senses became sharper, Mary Lou made her way into the hallway and down the stairs. A lamp still on in the living room lured her to its entrance. It should be off. There on her couch lay Beth Alexander with a blanket thrown over her. Snatches of conversation that had occurred earlier in this room invaded her mind. Dr. Wells saying she shouldn't be left alone. Ethan talking about calling his sister. Why hadn't she protested more? She didn't want Lexie's mother here.

Beth moved, fighting the blanket that had ridden up on her legs. Mary Lou ducked back into the foyer, listening to the creaking of the couch as Beth settled into another position. Mary Lou rotated toward the hallway to the kitchen and garage. She needed to hurry and get back before Beth woke up and came upstairs to check on her.

When the sounds of the garage door going up and her car starting resonated through the quiet night, Mary Lou cringed, her gaze glued to the entry into her house. She'd rather not have anyone know she'd left in the middle of the night, but if she got caught, she would say she had driven around searching for Kelly. As she backed out of the driveway, leaving the garage door up for her return, her heart rate increased.

She was going to be successful. Then she could deal with Kelly missing.

14

The lack of comfort in the lumpy cushion beneath Beth demanded she give up trying to sleep. She pushed to a sitting position, her neck aching, her left arm tingling from the lack of blood flow. Shaking it, she scanned the living room, orienting herself to her surroundings—Mary Lou's house. One lamp on the table by the lounger glowed, illuminating the area in a soft, warm yellow light.

Beth checked her watch. Four in the morning. Although her stiff body didn't feel like it had gotten any sleep, she must have. She hadn't looked in on Mary Lou for several hours and decided she'd better. Over the years, she'd known the woman through Lexie's friendship with Kelly, she'd seen Mary Lou change and became more intense—desperate. They used to work the same shift at the nursing home, but a year ago, Beth received a promotion to head nurse and began working the daytime hours.

Beth plodded up the staircase to the second floor and headed toward Mary Lou's room to peek in and make sure she was all right. A slit of light from under the door indicated Mary Lou might be up. Beth stopped in front of the door and knocked. Nothing. She rapped again, a little louder. When there still wasn't a response, she turned the handle and pushed into the bedroom, worried something might have happened to the woman. She could have gotten up, and with the medication Dr. Wells had given her, she could have become disoriented and fallen.

The sight of the rumpled covers on the bed, which might have concealed Mary Lou beneath them, forced Beth to go further inside to make sure Mary Lou was all right. Beth tiptoed forward until she stared down at the bunched sheets, no Mary Lou in sight. She tossed them back then slowly made a full circle searching for the woman. When she covered the distance to the bathroom, she checked in there, too. Towels from the linen closet, still open, littered the floor.

Concern for Kelly's mother lent urgency to her step as Beth left. She went from room to room upstairs. She couldn't even explain why she felt something was wrong, but she did. She could imagine how she would be if Lexie was missing. The medication must have worn off. Mary Lou might be in a bad place mentally. Frantic. Desperate to find Kelly. She'd need a friend.

She strode toward the staircase to walk through the rest of the house. At the top, Beth's gaze fell on Mary Lou starting up the stairs, hugging a large black tote bag against her front. When Mary Lou saw Beth, the woman's eyes became so big they dominated her face.

"Are you all right? I came up to check on you, and when you weren't in your room, I got worried." Beth came down halfway.

"I'm fine. It's Kelly who isn't. I decided to drive around and see if I could find her. Go to some of her favorite places."

"In the dark?"

Tears welled into Mary Lou's eyes. "I had to do—something." Her voice choked on the last word.

Beth closed the space between them. "I can understand. I know how I'd feel if anything like that happened to Lexie. I went through it with my oldest daughter, but she turned up fine. She just didn't want to live at home. In the end, it was the hardest part to get through."

"Kelly would never do that to me. Something bad has happened to her. Those girls weren't very nice to her."

"What girls?"

"Part of Jared's crowd—Missy, Carrie, and Zoe. You know how they can be in high school. Downright mean."

"Yes, I know," Beth murmured, recalling what they did to Lexie the day someone slipped her the tranquilizers. The rumors going around the school had hurt Lexie as much as a fellow student spiking her water bottle. "I'll make some coffee, and we can talk. It's been a while since we sat and talked about our girls."

Mary Lou took a couple of steps. "Maybe later. I think the fresh air and activity has caught up with me. I'm going to lie down."

"I'm here if you decide not to. Marge Livingston from church will be relieving me in a couple of hours."

"Really, no one has to stay with me. I'm better now. Call Marge and tell her she doesn't need to come." Mary Lou continued to mount the steps.

"Are you sure? Dr. Wells—"

"No." At the top of the stairs, Mary Lou whirled around. "Dr. Wells has good intentions, but I don't need anyone. I'm sure your brother and Cord will find Kelly today."

"Okay, but if you need anything call me."

"I will. Just lock the door as you leave."

This clearly meant to Beth she was not to go home in a few hours, but now.

⊷

After dropping Lexie off at church to work in the office, Beth headed for Greenbrier and walked into the building only a few minutes late. Instead of going to her office, she decided to make her early morning rounds to check on each wing and assure herself there was adequate staff. Chaos greeted her when she arrived at her first stop, the west wing. Cord and Ethan stood in the small room to the left of the nurses' station where the medicine cabinet was located. She entered, her gaze immediately zooming in on the empty shelves usually filled with multiple bottles of various drugs.

"What happened?" Beth moved between Cord and Ethan. "Were we robbed?"

"Yep," Cord said around a toothpick clamped between his teeth. "As you can see the thief practically wiped you out."

She looked closer at the bottles left on the shelves. "The person who did this knew what he wanted. What's left are the drugs for things like blood pressure and urinary tract infections that wouldn't be popular on the streets."

Ethan frowned. "We'll need a list of what was taken and the names of all your staff as well as their shift time."

"You think it's someone who works here?"

"Possibly. There was no break-in, no entrance compromised. We'll check all the ways in and make sure, but it appears the person was either here or had a key to get in." Ethan rotated toward the doorway and stared into the hall.

Beth followed his line of vision. Staff as well as patients and visitors crowded the hallway outside the room. She walked out into the corridor. "Y'all need to get back to work. We have patients to see to." Then she pulled Patti Shea to the side and said, "I'll be reordering the medication, and as soon as the pharmacy brings it, we need to get it to the patients. Try to do what you can until then to keep our patients calm."

"I can't believe someone broke in here last night. What have the police said?" Patti peeked into the small room.

"They'll be investigating. I don't have a lot of information right now. When they're through with processing the room, you should be able to give out the medication still left."

After the nurse walked away, Beth stayed in the corridor until all the people had moved along, then she returned to tell Ethan, "I'm going to be in my office working on that list for you and what I need to reorder, but first, I want to list what is left. Is that okay?"

Positioned in front of the cabinet, Cord glanced over his shoulder at Beth. "Yes, so long as you don't touch a bottle or anything. If you need to turn a medication to see its name, let me know. I'll do it. We're going to fingerprint everything, then get fingerprints from all the staff."

"Good. This was thousands of dollars of medication."

One side of his mouth tipped up. "We'll find who did this. I hate thinking of all those drugs on the street."

The warmth from his look melted some of the tension inundating her from all sides. One good thing was going right. Cord. They had only been on a few dates, but then so much was happening in Summerton in the past couple of weeks, he was working nonstop, like her brother. Still, she felt there was something there between them.

As she walked into the hallway, Ethan followed her and pulled her over to the side away from any people. "Where's Lexie? I thought you were going to bring her to work."

"I'm glad I didn't with this happening. I'm going to meet myself coming and going. I dropped her off at the church to answer phones in the office. I think it'll be good for her. She's so upset about Kelly, and if she needs to talk with the pastor, she'll be able to."

"After we process the room, Cord and I will come to your office and talk about toughening your security, especially where the drugs are kept. It looks like there are scratches on the lock as though someone tried using a pick at some time."

"So no key?" The earlier tension came back in full force, drilling through her head and into her skull.

"Possibly. But those marks may be old. I don't want to rule anything out."

"You're going to work this case?"

"Yes. We think this could be connected to what's happening concerning the kids. Drugs are involved in both."

"A kid could have done this?"

"What if one of the staff with a key had a child who stole it so he could sell the drugs at school?"

"The key to the medicine cabinet doesn't leave the building."

"That's good to know, but that doesn't rule out a teen."

"You really are going to look at everything."

"We have to. As you said thousands of dollars are involved, but worse it's the prospects of all those drugs being on the street and used in ways not intended."

"Like what happened to Lexie?" The thundering beat of her heart clamored through her head. With little sleep last night and now this, she didn't know if she could do what she needed to do.

"Exactly. Luke's death is tied to an overdose of tranquilizers. He fell asleep at the wheel. The amount he had in his body didn't take long to go into effect."

"Suicide?"

"No indication it was. I think murder. His water bottle was laced like Lexie's with the same kind of medication."

Beth inhaled a deep breath then held it for a few seconds before slowly releasing it out through pursed lips. What if instead of falling asleep in class, she'd fallen asleep behind the wheel? She could be going through what Jared and Luke's parents were handling right now if her daughter hadn't gotten help right away. "Lexie may never return to school."

"Another thing I think you should do. Do a secondary audit on your drug inventory. Make sure on the other wings everything is where it should be. I remember you telling me about that patient who died."

"Lucy was on this wing."

"I'm asking the ME to rush that autopsy. If you think something isn't right, it might not be."

"Have you looked at the security DVRs yet?"

"No. But that's where I'm going right now while Cord and his officers finish with the room. After that, Cord and I will talk with the people who worked here last night. Maybe someone saw something."

"I hope so," Beth murmured, still thinking of what happened to Luke. So similar to Lexie but she hadn't been driving a car. *Thank You, Lord, for that.*

"Go take care of your patients' needs. See you in a while." Ethan headed down the hall in the direction of the main office where they kept the security DVRs.

Beth made her way to her office for the first time that day with her purse clutched to her side under her arm. As she crossed to her desk, something nagged at the back of her mind. What was she missing?

༼ঌ

The security guard pulled up to the back of the warehouse on Sixth Street to check it out. Paul Quinn parked by the door, grabbed his flashlight from the seat, and climbed out of his car. Maybe he would grab an early lunch since he didn't eat breakfast.

At the door, as he dug into his pant pocket for his key to the warehouse, his gaze wandered down the long length of the building. Fifteen yards away he noticed a busted window. He strode to it, hoping it was some kid using the parking lot for a field for one of their sports. Last Saturday he'd found a group of young boys from the low-income apartments playing soccer. He'd had to chase them off.

At the window about six feet off the ground, a gaping hole, large enough for a person to go through greeted his inspection. Too big probably if just a ball went through it, even a soccer ball.

Paul hurried back to the door and unlocked it. As he stepped inside, he withdrew his gun as a precaution although he doubted anyone was inside the building now. More likely, a bum broke in last night to get in out of the rain that poured for a few hours.

As he moved into the warehouse, he panned the area around him.

Until he found a body hanging from the rafters twenty feet inside to his right.

15

After leaving Greenbrier, Ethan drove toward the police station while Cord wrapped up the investigation at the nursing home. Ethan had requested Missy and Carrie be brought in. The teens and their parents should be there by now. "The Eyes of Texas" blared from his phone. He answered the call, noting it was Cord.

"I just got a call from a security company who has been checking the Adams's warehouse since the incident. This morning a guard found a young girl there, dead. From the description he gave me, I think it's Kelly. I'll meet you at the warehouse."

Ethan turned at the light and headed away from his original destination. "I'm ten minutes away." When he clicked off, he punched in the police station's number and informed the sergeant to have Missy and Carrie wait and make sure they stayed.

When he arrived at the warehouse, he saw a police cruiser parked next to a security company car near the back door. An officer stood outside with the guard, writing down something on a pad. As Ethan approached them, both of the men shifted their attention to him.

"Ranger Stone, this is Paul Quinn. He arrived to check the building this morning at ten. He found who I have ID'd as Kelly Winston hanging from a rafter not far inside this door." The young officer tossed his head toward the entrance. "He said this place is checked twice a day. At night and in the morning. Everything was fine last night at ten."

"How did someone get inside? Mr. Adams was making sure all the doors were kept locked."

The officer pointed down the back of the warehouse to a window that was broken. "I think that way. It wasn't like that yesterday according to the security guard."

"Right. It has to be the way she got in." Quinn turned to Ethan. "Can I go now? I have other places to check on my route. I've told the officer all I know."

"Have you got all the information?" Ethan asked the officer who nodded. "You can leave then, but I may be contacting you with more questions later."

After the security guard drove away, Ethan put latex gloves on and started for the door. "The police chief will be here soon. Send him in but keep everyone else out."

Inside Ethan paused by the entrance, letting his eyes adjust to the dimmer light while he took in Kelly's body. The stale air reeked of death. The ashen color of her face drew his attention first. Then he ran his gaze down her length to her swollen dark purple legs, ankles, and feet where her blood pooled in her lower extremities, which indicated she had been there a while. Below on the floor were black flats she must have kicked off or had fallen off. Near the shoes laid a chair on its side. Where had that chair come from? When he had last been here, he hadn't seen it. A few crates but no chairs.

The rope used was slung over a rafter. He could see her doing that, but was the knot one she could have tied or did someone else? Kelly's arms hung at her side, but was there evidence they were tied together recently? He moved to the girl and examined the wrists for signs of bruising, tape residue, or rope burns. Nothing. Which gave him pause. If she wasn't bound and forced to stand on the chair, could she have killed herself?

He went behind her and tried to see the knot. From this angle, he couldn't tell, and he wanted to wait until Cord and the ME showed up before moving the body and processing the crime scene. He stepped back.

His gut twisted, Ethan closed his eyes, wishing he could have found the teen alive. On the surface, it appeared a suicide, and her behavior the past couple of weeks would reinforce that verdict, but something didn't feel right to him. She'd been missing for several days. Why the warehouse? Why now?

Why would Kelly hang herself? There were other less painful ways to kill herself. Easier. Why not a drug overdose?

He took in the area around the body. The warehouse had only recently been released as a scene of a suspicious death. There was little dirt and dust to help indicate footprints and the presence of others in here.

He strode down the back wall to where the window had been broken with a big rock. Shards of glass littered the cement floor. So, someone threw the stone through the large pane, and it shattered. Ethan walked to the hole and stood on tiptoes to peer into the parking lot. A few jagged pieces of glass stood up along the bottom. He inspected them for any signs of blood. None.

Interesting. If Kelly or whoever came through this way at night, he was surprised the person hadn't been cut. And the culprit would have jumped to the floor and should have steadied his landing by putting a hand down. But no blood on the floor either.

Ethan made his way outside to check the window from there. On the asphalt were pieces of glass. There shouldn't have been that many if the pane was broken from the outside. Also, how did the person get up and through the window? There was nothing stacked under it to help someone up and into the building. If Kelly had committed suicide, how did she get into the warehouse this way without cutting herself? His doubt it was suicide grew. And if it wasn't suicide, it was murder—a third one in less than two weeks.

⁓❧⁓

Alone in her house, Mary Lou sat cross-legged in the middle of her bed and dumped the contents of her tote bag onto the blue coverlet. Bottles and bottles tumbled all over the place. She scooped a few up in her hands and looked at their names. She had enough supplies for a while. She hit the mother lode. No more begging Dr. Wells for painkillers—at least for a couple of months. By then, she'd find another doctor even if she had to go to another nearby town or across the state into Oklahoma or Arkansas. She knew someone who could fake an ID for her. He lived in Hugo, Oklahoma.

She reached for her glass of water, opened a bottle of painkillers, took one, then popped it into her mouth. She hadn't felt this good in a long time. Everything would be all right now.

Soon, Kelly would be found. Life would go back to the way it was. Those thoughts brought a smile to her face.

When the doorbell rang, she jumped, sloshing the water in her glass. She set it down on the nightstand, then hurried and gathered up the bottles. The chimes sounded again. Her gaze darted from the dresser to the closet to the bathroom trying to figure out the best place to hide her stash. She quickly stuffed them between her mattresses before rushing down the stairs.

When she opened the door, Ethan Stone, dressed in uniform, and his gun strapped to his waist, appeared every bit the lawman he was. The sight intimidated her, and she backed away a few paces. "Beth left hours ago."

"I know. I came to see you."

"Why?" They couldn't know she was the one who took the medication. She made sure anytime she was caught on camera, her face was hidden, and her clothes were baggy. She even faked a limp. Since she was a tall woman, they wouldn't be able to tell if the person was a lady or a man. No, it was probably something to do with Kelly. "Have you found where Kelly is?"

"Yes."

"Where? Why isn't she here?"

"May I come in?"

Her stomach plummeted. "She's at the hospital?" She took a step back, then another.

Ethan moved into the foyer and closed the door. He looked around. "Where's the lady from the church who was relieving Beth?"

"I don't need anyone here. I'm fine. I . . ." The look on his face told her it was worse than Kelly being hurt. Her legs gave way, and she sank toward the floor.

Ethan grabbed her and held her up. "Let's go into the living room and sit."

As he helped her onto the couch, then took the seat next to her, she shook. She needed her "happy pills." She didn't want to hear what he'd come to tell her.

He cupped her hands between his larger ones. "Kelly was found at a warehouse on Sixth Street earlier today. She'd been dead for a few hours."

No, he's lying. He has to be. "Suicide?"

"It doesn't look like she killed herself."

"Accident?"

"No, definitely not."

"Murder? How?" She lifted her eyes to his, and through the blur, she saw a flash of pain.

"She was hung."

No, I've taken too many pills. I'm having a nightmare or a hallucination. But she focused on the grim set to Ethan's expression. She felt the rough texture of his hands over hers and smelled the lime scent of his aftershave lotion. *Too real. Not a dream.*

A sound—like a moan that morphed into a shriek—came from her mouth, and she couldn't stop it. She yanked her hands free and buried her face in her palms. "No. No. This can't be true. She ran away. That's all. You've got the wrong person."

Ethan held her as she sobbed. "I can't leave you. Who do you want me to call to come over?"

Mary Lou pulled back, swiped at her tears and inhaled deeply. "No one. I don't want people around."

"I can't leave you," he repeated. "Let me at least call one of your neighbors to come over and sit with you."

She looked at the determination in his eyes and knew she had to agree for someone to come. Then once he left, she would send the person away like she did this morning. People couldn't help her.

"Fine. Nancy is home during the day. She lives to the left of me." She gave Ethan her neighbor's phone number and listened as he called her.

Upstairs under her mattress was the only thing that could help her forget.

❧

Later after Mary Lou's neighbor came over and Ethan returned to the police station, he sat across from Missy, her father, and Colleen Stover. He guessed Jeffrey couldn't represent everyone in this case—conflict of interest. He opened Kelly's journal and began reading, "They aren't anything like I thought they would be. Missy and Carrie are mean and would just as soon push me off a cliff as accept me."

"She is lying." Missy came up out of her seat, her voice high-pitched. Her father put his hand on her arm, and she took her chair again. She glanced at her dad, then her lawyer. When she finally faced Ethan, calm evened out her expression. "We're friends. We've been worried about her mental stability ever since Jared died."

Ethan bent his head over the journal and continued. "They made it clear I'd better not say a thing to anyone about the party or else. What would they do? We're all to blame that Jared is dead." His gaze bore into Missy. "Would you like to explain this, especially in light of the fact we found Kelly dead this morning?"

Missy gasped, her pupils dilating. "Dead?"

"She was hung from the rafters at the warehouse where the party didn't take place according to you. Where were you from midnight to six this morning?"

"She was home in bed," her father answered.

Ethan turned his attention to him. "And you know this how?"

"I—I . . ." He clamped his mouth closed.

"Why do you want to know where my client was?"

"That's the time that Kelly was killed."

"Killed? Murdered?" Missy's pupils took over almost all of her irises.

"We'll know for sure after the ME does an autopsy, but the scene has some inconsistencies making me question this is a suicide. So where were you?"

"In bed."

"No way to prove it?"

"No, where else was I supposed to be? It's a school night." Missy set her mouth in a tight line.

"So you never sneak out of your house?" Ethan kept his gaze trained on the teen.

"Are you charging Missy with anything?" Colleen asked.

"Should I, Missy?"

"No," she said quickly.

"Well, here's the deal." He rose. "I'm going in to interview Carrie. The first person who talks will get immunity in this case. I want to know what happened to Jared, Luke, and Kelly. We're looking at three possible murders."

"I thought it was a car accident." Missy's eyes filled with tears. "Luke murdered? Why?"

The sound of Ethan closing the journal charged the air. "That's a good question."

"I would like to confer with my client."

"Do that. I'll be talking with Carrie in the other room and giving her the same deal." Ethan gathered up the journal and started for the door.

"No, don't leave," Missy blurted out, a frantic edge to her words.

As Ethan turned back, Mr. Collins said, "We need to talk with our lawyer. My daughter didn't do anything wrong, and I don't like these tactics to get her to confess to something she didn't do."

Ethan fastened his look on Missy. "Are you so sure, Mr. Collins?"

The color leeched from the teen's face. Ethan pivoted and left the room. Outside in the hallway he met Cord. "I think she'll talk."

"I escorted Carrie, her mother, and Jeffrey Livingston into interview room two. They weren't happy campers."

"I'm not surprised. I'm about to shake up Carrie's life."

"Do you think the robbery at Greenbrier is connected somehow to what's going on with these teens? What if one of them did it? I'll be checking the staff's background for any teenage kids. Maybe one of their friends' mother works there. If they had a lot of pill parties, they might have gotten their drugs from another source. If they took too much from their parents, maybe they feared one or more might get caught."

"Yes, it could be connected. The pills these kids are taking have to come from somewhere, and although some are getting them from home, I agree maybe not all of them." Ethan strode toward the other interview room. "Hang around in case Missy and her entourage decide to slip away. I know we can't hold them, but I have a few parting words for them."

When Ethan opened the door and entered, all talking among the three stopped. He sat across from Carrie and went through the same journal entry as he had with Missy, but Carrie didn't respond. At the end, her expression was cold almost as though she'd removed herself from the room.

"Is that all?" Mrs. Bannister asked, her perfectly made-up face equally cold as her daughter's.

"Yes, that's all from the journal I care to share for now." Ethan swiveled his attention to Carrie. "But what I want to know from you is why would Kelly think you all are to blame for Jared's death?"

One of her eyebrows arched. "I don't know. Ask her. She's unstable."

"The problem is I can't ask her. She was found dead this morning at the warehouse." Ethan purposely used the warehouse, not a warehouse, to see if he could get any reaction from the girl.

She blinked several times, but otherwise her expression, as if carved from ice, remained. "Did she commit suicide?"

"No. Where were you from midnight to six this morning?"

"Home in bed. I'm worthless without at least eight hours of sleep."

"In other words, no one can verify where you were?"

Carrie lifted her chin. "I'm in the gifted program at school. If I had done something wrong, believe me, I would have had an alibi."

"There have been three murders."

"Who else?" Carrie twirled the end of her long brown hair around her finger.

"Luke."

"Luke? He was in a car wreck."

"Full of tranquilizers, his water bottle laced like Lexie's. They released the autopsy this morning. I'm going to tell you the same thing I told Missy. The first one to talk about what went on the night Jared died, as well as what has been going on recently in connection with Kelly and Luke, will get immunity in the case."

Jeffrey leaned forward to say something, but Carrie flashed her lawyer a look and said, "Then this is over with. I have nothing to tell you. And neither does Missy. I've seen this technique on TV. Divide and conquer. It won't work in this case because we're innocent. We have nothing to hide." Carrie rose, the sound of the chair scraping over the floor echoing through the room.

As Carrie and her mother filed out into the hallway, Jeffrey paused. "If you want to question Carrie, contact me. I'll arrange it. She won't be talking to you without me present."

Ethan watched Carrie stroll away. At the end of the corridor, she glanced at him, her phone in her hand, her fingers flying over the tiny keyboard. She grinned, then disappeared from view.

Ethan charged into the interview room Missy was in. The teenage girl read a message on her phone, then looked up when he closed the door. She pocketed her cell, leaned over to her lawyer, and whispered something.

Colleen stood. "My client doesn't have anything further to say. We're leaving. Good day, Ranger Stone."

As they walked out of the room, Ethan said to Missy, "Take a good hard look at your friends. Someone in your group is playing hardball. If it isn't you, are you sure you're safe? Do you know what's really going on?"

Her eyes flared before she lowered her eyelashes and turned away from him.

Missy was the weak link. He felt it deep in his gut. She was eighteen. All he needed to do was find a way to speak with her when Carrie wasn't around. That might be hard. They were always together.

Until then he would bring in Brendan, Kalvin, and Zoe to see what they had to say.

⟨⟩

The last of Sadie's students had left the classroom for lunch. She stood at her door as the teens passed her in the hallway and headed toward the cafeteria. When the corridor emptied of kids, Sadie stepped back into her room to grab her purse and make her way to the cafeteria herself. At her desk she half-sat, half-leaned against it for a moment—a moment she really didn't have if she wanted to eat and get back before the next hour class.

She didn't even think a fully-staged rock concert would engage her students' attention this morning. With Kelly now missing and two of their classmates dead, the teens were hurting. How fragile life could be hit them square in the face.

When her cell sounded, she gasped and jumped away from her desk, staring at her purse where she kept her phone. Another blare of her ring tone prodded her into action. She answered the call.

"I hope I've caught you at lunch," Ethan said, weariness coming through loud and clear.

"Yes, I was just about to leave for the cafeteria. Is something wrong?"

"Why would you ask that?"

"Oh, I don't know. You don't usually call me at school to chitchat. Call it women's intuition if you want."

"Yeah, something is wrong. This is the first chance I've had to call you. I never want to have a morning like this one again."

"You found Kelly?" Although a question, she knew the answer.

"Yes. Dead, and it isn't looking like a suicide or an accident."

Sadie sank into the nearest student desk. "Where? How?"

"At the warehouse where the pill party took place. She was hung. Staged to look like a suicide, but I have too many questions about the crime scene. We pulled latent prints from several places."

"This is going to be awful for Lexie."

"Yes. I called Beth before you, so she could let Lexie know."

Panic swamped Sadie as she pictured Kelly in her last moments. "Where is Lexie?"

"She's safe. At church, with our pastor who is an ex-Marine. Beth is letting him know what's happening probably right now." His tone softened. "I wanted you to know about Kelly because I'm sure it won't take long before the kids at school find out. This kind of news circulates quickly."

"Especially since it's lunchtime."

"I'd better let you go. Like I said, this has been a crazy morning. Besides Kelly, Greenbrier was robbed of prescription drugs. A lot has been happening."

"I thought my day was bad. Yours beats mine." She rose and snatched her purse off her desk.

"The bright spot was hearing your voice. Good-bye."

His last words soothed some of the tension zipping through her for a few seconds as she left her classroom to head for lunch. She'd cut across the auditorium to speed her trek to the cafeteria. She was sure it was open, because one of the teachers was using it today with her classes. When she slipped inside the cavernous hall, off to the side a couple of rows back from the door, she spied Kalvin with a junior she had in class. Sam Travis held some money while Kalvin held something in a plastic packet.

The door closing behind her clicked loud in the silence. They turned toward her and froze in place. Sam swung around, snatching the money back, and ran while Kalvin stuffed the packet into his pocket.

Without thinking, Sadie rushed forward and caught Kalvin's arm. "Stay put."

He glared at her.

"What do you have in your pocket?"

"None of your business."

"Show me."

"No."

His scowl cut through Sadie, and suddenly she realized where she was with a teen that was not happy with her. She fumbled in her purse and withdrew her cell phone. After placing a call to the office with her hand still on Kalvin's arm, she turned her head toward a seat nearby.

"Sit. Mr. Howard is on his way and should be here any second."

Kalvin glanced at the door in the back of the auditorium where Sam had disappeared then back at her.

"Don't think it," she said in a tough voice while inside she quaked. The teenage boy was over six feet and burly. And they were very alone with most of the building empty.

Suddenly, he shrugged and slouched into the chair. "You've made a mistake. I've done nothing wrong."

"Fine. Mr. Howard will sort it out. Keep your hands where I can see them." The sound of the door at the back opening drew Sadie's attention. Some of the tension drained from her as her assistant principal came into the auditorium.

When Mr. Howard stopped near her and peered at Kalvin, then her, Sadie began to shake. What if Kalvin had defied her and run away like Sam? What would she have done? Gone after him in high heels? If he got rid of the packet, what proof would she have something was going down in the auditorium? What she saw wasn't something innocent, especially with Sam and Kalvin's behavior afterwards.

"What happened, Ms. Thompson?"

Sadie told the assistant principal what she had seen, keeping an eye on Kalvin to make sure he didn't slip his hand into his pocket and toss the packet away.

"I'll take it from here." Mr. Howard moved closer to Kalvin. "You still have some time for lunch."

"You'll let me know what you do?"

"Of course. I'll fill out a discipline referral for Kalvin." Mr. Howard indicated for the teenage boy to stand. "We're going to my office."

Sadie watched them walk toward the set of double doors at the back. She had to tell Ethan when she got a chance. Since Kalvin attended the pill party, this might be a connection to what happened with Jared, Luke, and now Kelly. What if Kalvin was a murderer, killing people to protect his business?

❧

Mary Lou sat in the middle of Kelly's bed, tears running down her cheeks and dropping onto her lap. When she picked up the pillow nearby, she lifted it to her face and smelled of her daughter's scent—apples because of the shampoo she'd used.

No more.

Gone.

I'm alone. Totally.

She threw the pillow to the floor and stomped into her bedroom, grabbed her cell phone, then marched back to Kelly's room.

They can't get away with it.

She tore her daughter's room apart until she found her list of numbers for classmates. After finding what she wanted, she punched in the series of numbers and waited, her teeth biting into her lower lip.

It rang several times before it went to voicemail. The taste of blood only hardened her resolve to make sure they paid for killing her daughter.

"I know what you did, and you will pay for it. You killed my baby."

Sorrow pushed the need for revenge to the background. All of a sudden, her throat swelled, choking off her words, her air. Then the sobs returned. The phone slipped from her grasp and tumbled to the floor. She fell to her knees and cried.

❧

What a day! Beth pulled up to the church to pick up Lexie. All she wanted to do was sleep for the next twelve hours. Right before she'd left, she had to calm her own mother about Greenbrier. Mom didn't leave Nana's room all day. She couldn't blame her after Lucy's unexpected death and then the stolen medication. Nana hadn't gotten her pills until the afternoon. There had been a lot of agitated patients.

All of this on top of the news Kelly was found dead in a warehouse. Having to tell her daughter about her best friend's death had been the hardest thing for her, especially over the phone. She couldn't leave work, but at least their pastor had been there for Lexie.

She came out of the building, the pastor watching her from the door. When her daughter slid into the car, she immediately said, "We need to go by Kel—Mrs. Winston's house." Urgency added an edge to the atmosphere in the car.

"What's wrong?"

"I've been calling all day to make sure she was all right. Kelly's death will be hard on her, and she doesn't cope well. Kelly was always worried about her mother."

"Maybe she doesn't want to see anyone. Ethan said he made sure a neighbor came over to her house to be with her if she needed anything."

"Is the neighbor still there? Wouldn't she had answered her phone for Mrs. Winston?"

Beth pulled away from the church. "Maybe Mary Lou didn't want her to."

"Kelly didn't say much about this to even me, but I think her mom drinks too much and she's taking too much medication. She is often sleeping or just not completely there when I've been over there lately. I asked Kelly about it, and she said her mother has been worse since her car wreck. She complains about neck and back pain, but she usually moves all right, bending over and getting up from a chair." Lexie pinned Beth with a pleading look. "Please, Mom. I don't have a good feeling about this."

"We can try, but she might not answer the doorbell if she doesn't want to see us. Some people prefer mourning by themselves and don't want people around them."

"Our pastor was on the phone or seeing people all day. Parents are worried about their children."

"I can imagine. Three kids dying in such a short time is a shock for any town."

"Although nothing has been said officially yet, there's speculation Kelly was murdered."

Beth glanced at Lexie, then back at the road. A car stopped at a light, and she slammed on the brakes, barely missing the vehicle. "Ethan hasn't said anything to me, but then I've been busy, and I'm sure he is with the robbery at Greenbrier as well as Kelly's case."

"You didn't say anything to me earlier about the robbery. What was stolen?"

"Drugs." Beth turned at the corner that led to the Winston's home. "We'll try to see Mary Lou. If she doesn't answer, I'll check with the neighbor."

"Thanks. I know you were upset with her because of what happened at school with me, but you still stayed with her last night. We can't stop being there for her now more than ever."

"You aren't upset with Kelly's mom? Didn't you tell me she was the one who spread the rumors in the first place?"

"She was protecting Kelly."

Sometimes she felt her daughter was too kindhearted, but Lexie was the reason she'd agreed to stay at Mary Lou's house last night in spite of what happened between the girls. If Lexie had forgiven Kelly and even Mary Lou, then she could, too. Through all this, she was seeing Lexie as a good example of what she needed to strive for.

Beth parked on the street in front of the Winston's house. "I'm sorry I had to tell you over the phone."

Her daughter's eyes filled with tears. "I know. All I want to do is leave Summerton. I don't like what's happening to everyone around me."

Beth covered Lexie's hand on the console between them. "I wish we could. But we have to stay."

Lexie rubbed her tears away. "Let's check on Mrs. Winston."

Beth followed her daughter up to the porch. Lexie pushed in the bell, again and again. Beth walked to a window on the left side and peeked into the living room. It was vacant. She did the same to the other window on the right. The dining room and a glimpse into the kitchen was the same—empty.

Lexie walked to the garage and looked inside. "Her car is here. She must be, too."

"She obviously doesn't want to see us. I could tell this morning when I left she was relieved I did. I thought it was because of what happened between you and Kelly."

"But we worked that out. Please check with the neighbor."

"Which one?"

Lexie pointed to the left. "I don't think she knows the other one."

"Stay here. I'll be right back." As Beth crossed the yard, she remembered Mary Lou's odd behavior this morning, clutching her large tote against her, jittery. She'd chalked it up to Kelly missing, but in light of what Lexie said about Mary Lou taking too much medication, maybe it was something else.

She rang the doorbell, a tickling at the base of her neck nagging her. What if Mary Lou had . . .

Nancy, an older woman who went to the same church, opened the door. "Hi, Beth. What are you doing here?"

Beth gestured toward Mary Lou's. "My brother said you were staying with Mary Lou. Did she go somewhere?"

"No. She was adamant she was fine and wanted to be alone. I know when my husband died several years back I felt the same way. I couldn't insist I stay against her wishes. I did call our pastor. He's coming by to see her this evening."

"How was she?"

"Tired. She said she was going to bed. That she hadn't slept much the night before."

But she had because Dr. Wells had given her something. "Thanks. I was concerned since she didn't answer the doorbell."

"I'll try later. I thought I would take over some dinner."

"Good. Call if you think I should come back."

"I'll do that."

As Beth left the neighbor's house, she couldn't shake the feeling something wasn't quite right. Then she recalled Nancy interrupting her thought a few minutes ago. For a minute, she couldn't remember what she was thinking about, then it came to her. What if Mary Lou was behind the drugs being taken at Greenbrier? Although she wasn't on duty last night, she had the knowledge of the nursing home layout and access to the building. Did she have the need or desperation to steal the drugs?

As Beth mounted the steps to the porch at Mary Lou's, she panned the area. *Where's Lexie?*

A scream ripped the air—coming from the backyard.

Beth bounded down the steps and ran around the side of the house. "Lexie, where are you?" she asked when nothing else sounded. She saw the gate open and rushed through it. "Lexie?"

"Mom, up here."

Beth looked up to find her daughter at the edge of the roof over the back porch. "Get down. No, wait. I don't want you falling." Her heart doubled its beat, especially when she stared at Lexie—afraid and shaking. "What's wrong?"

"I think Mary Lou is dead or hurt."

"Why do you think that? How did you get up there? I'm calling your uncle." Words rolled one after another through her mind, gaining speed as they tumbled from her tongue. "Don't move. We don't need you falling and breaking something on top of everything that has happened."

"Mom, I'm okay. It's Mary Lou. She's on the floor in Kelly's room, face down, not moving."

Beth fumbled for her cell phone in her pocket and managed to call Ethan as she said again, "Sit down, Lexie."

The second her brother answered she told him where she was and what Lexie said.

"I'll be right there. Is Lexie up on the porch roof by Kelly's window?"

"How did you know?"

"That's the way Kelly gets in and out of her house. Lexie told me."

She heard the sound of an engine starting come through the line. "I think Mary Lou might have taken the drugs at the nursing home.

Lexie told me she believes Kelly's mom was drinking and taking a lot of medication. I need to help her."

"Be careful," was the last thing Beth heard as she switched off the phone. "Okay, Lexie. Did you use a ladder or something?"

"The elm tree. I tried to get inside to check on Kelly's mom, but the window is locked."

"Then we'll break it. If she's in trouble, time is important."

16

Ethan stood on the porch with the bottle of painkillers in an evidence bag, the medication labeled for a patient at Greenbrier. He'd found it on the floor next to Mary Lou in her daughter's bedroom. The ambulance pulled away from the house with Mary Lou, barely alive. If Beth and Lexie hadn't come over, she probably would have died. She might still.

Cord strode up the sidewalk to the porch. "I've got the warrant."

"Good. I want this by the book, even though she had medication that didn't belong to her. I told the paramedics what I found, so the doctor would have an idea of what she took."

"Are Beth and Lexie inside?"

"Beth is. Sadie came and picked up Lexie a little while ago. Beth didn't want her staying around while we searched. A lot of memories for Lexie in this house. If we find the stash of pills, Beth wants to check to see if it's all that was taken from Greenbrier or if some is missing."

"Do you think Mary Lou sold some of it?"

Ethan went inside the house. "Right now, anything is possible. Beth told me about her behavior this morning. She caught her coming back into her house around four. Mary Lou said she went looking for Kelly. She was carrying a tote as if it were her purse. I found Mary Lou's real one in the kitchen."

When Cord entered the living room, he smiled at Beth. "You keep finding trouble."

She rose and bridged the distance to Cord. "This is so overwhelming. Mary Lou and I were friends because of the girls, but I'm finding I don't know anything about her. Very sobering. Who else has fooled me?"

Cord clasped her arms. "Not me. What you see is what you get."

A grin flirted with the corners of his sister's mouth. Ethan started to leave to begin his search of the house in Mary Lou's bedroom.

Cord stopped him with, "I got Lucy's autopsy results back. There was only a slight trace of the prescription painkiller in her system. Not nearly enough if she was taking the medication as the doctor ordered."

"From what I saw today, there were no discrepancies with the medication. The patients were receiving what they should—at least on paper, but I know when you're dealing with people who have memory problems or other debilitating issues, it can be easy to switch out their drugs or just not give them their correct medication."

Ethan moved back into the room. "Who's responsible for dispensing the medications at Greenbrier?"

"A nurse in each wing, and she has to reconcile what is left with the nurse on the next shift. If medication is missing, it should be caught. It's accounted for three times a day with the personnel change each shift. It goes to the intended patient, or it's in the cabinet."

"But it can be circumvented by someone giving a patient something different or possibly nothing at all, especially for a patient who wouldn't know either way." Ethan had been involved in a case in San Antonio where that had occurred. "So first, we look at all the nurses who are responsible for giving out medication."

"I can go back to the nursing home and run some tests on different patients to see what their level of medication is in their system. If it isn't what it's supposed to be, then we may be able to pinpoint who is responsible. Or at least narrow down the suspect list. Some may not show up. If the nurse is smart, she would cut the amount down but not take it totally away so it may be harder to find the person."

Ethan frowned. "Or persons. Do it today. Make sure no one knows what's going on." Turning to Cord, he continued. "We'll finish the search here, then begin running background and financial checks on all the nurses, especially the ones who handle the medication. We may have to expand to the rest of the staff later."

"Do you think the nurse or whoever is doing it is alone? For herself, like Mary Lou?" Cord held Beth's hand as he faced Ethan.

Seeing his sister with his friend made him think of Sadie. What would being a couple with Sadie be like? Coming home has caused him to want more than he settled for in the past. He did a mental shake when he realized they were staring at him, waiting for an answer.

"There could be a network or the person could be working alone. This could connect to what's happening at the school or be completely separate. We have to look at all possibilities. I'll be upstairs in Mary Lou's room." He strode toward the staircase, deciding he'd leave Beth and Cord alone for a few minutes. His sister should at least be happy, even if he didn't know what he was going to do.

In Mary Lou's room, he began his search of the perimeter to the right of the door and moved inward. Cord came through the entrance when Ethan lifted the left corner of the mattress at the end of the bed. Nothing. He started to put it down when something caught his attention. He walked toward the headboard, raised that end, and withdrew a bottle of pain medication.

"Help me take this completely off the bed," Ethan said and waited until Cord was on the other side, then they both removed the mattress from the box springs.

Still nothing except the one bottle.

Cord's mouth twisted into a frown. "There were a lot more than two taken from the nursing home, so if she did it where are the others?"

"I think somewhere in this house. Like an alcoholic who plants liquor all over the place, she may have done the same thing."

"I'm calling in some more officers to help us."

"Choose carefully. Sadly, I've seen police officers have a problem with prescription drugs." Ethan didn't know whom to trust, and he hated that feeling.

Trust Me. Those words flitted through his mind as he continued his search. At least with the Lord, he wasn't totally alone. For the first time he also realized he wanted more from his life.

~∾∾

Sadie drove into her garage, exhausted from a long day consoling students at school. Three students dying in less than two weeks. The kids at school were numb emotionally today. They didn't know what to do or how to deal with something like that. Frankly, being an adult didn't make it any easier.

"Are you sure you don't mind me staying at your place until Mom gets through at Mrs. Winston's house?" Lexie's question broke into her thought, reminding Sadie that Kelly had been Lexie's best friend. This had to be harder on her.

"I'm positive." Sadie switched off the engine, then turned toward Lexie. "How are you holding up?"

Her stoic expression collapsed. "I haven't been able to talk much with Mom about what happened to Kelly. With the robbery, she's had to be at Greenbrier, but . . ." Her voice faded into silence.

Sadie waited a moment before asking, "But what?"

"Kelly didn't deserve what happened to her. The last thing I knew, she was going to tell Carrie and Missy how she felt about what happened to me."

"Did she know who spiked your drink?"

"She said no, and I looked her in the eye and believed her. I've known Kelly a long time, and I know when she's lying. She wasn't."

Sadie pictured Carrie and Missy at the funeral, flanking Kelly as though they were her bodyguards, which was probably what they were doing, not for Kelly's protection but their own.

"While you're here tonight, I'll help you with any of your school-work. Well, maybe not the math class but the others I can."

"I'm going to need someone to help me with Algebra II. Math isn't my favorite subject. That's the only subject I'm having a hard time with."

"My student aide in your hour is super smart, especially in math and science. Maybe I can get him to help you. Tutor you until you come back to school."

"Oliver would be great. I may need him to tutor me even after I come back to school. I've lost some ground, and I've only been gone from school a few days. I can imagine what a few weeks are going to do to me and my grades."

"Your suspension is not fair. I'm going to speak to Mr. Howard again on your behalf."

Lexie scooted toward the door. "Mom won't let me come back until Uncle Ethan solves what has happened to Jared, Luke, and Kelly. I'm not sure I want to come back either."

"I don't think much teaching is really going on right now at school. With three teens dying in such a short time, the student body is really feeling it. There are counselors all over the place, and I'm thankful to see a lot of the kids using them. Maybe you should think about talking to someone qualified, although you can always talk to me or your mom."

Lexie opened the car door and climbed out. "I talked with our pastor today. He gave me some good things to think about. I'm going to focus on the positive in Kelly's life. The friendship we shared, and maybe her death will help Uncle Ethan find the people responsible for what's been going on in Summerton."

"I hope so." Sadie shivered when she thought about catching Kalvin passing something to a student in the auditorium. The way Kalvin had hurriedly shoved the packet into his pocket and Sam snatched the money and ran, at least to her, she felt sure something was going down. She hadn't had a chance to talk with Maxwell yet to see what he'd done concerning Kalvin and Sam. She would first thing tomorrow morning, barring anything else happening. Was Kalvin involved in selling prescription drugs? That was what it appeared like to her. He was at the pill party. Who suggested having a pill party in the first place? Who suggested moving Jared's body from the warehouse? What happened to the pills the kids hadn't taken but had brought to the party?

Questions plagued Sadie as she entered her house. She would say something to Ethan later. The phone ringing jolted her and prodded her to move faster into the kitchen to answer it.

When she picked it up and said, "Hello," silence greeted her for a long, few seconds, then a raspy voice murmured, "Keep your mouth shut or . . ."

∼❧∼

Ethan parked in Sadie's driveway with Cord right behind him in a patrol car. Ethan strode toward the front porch even before Cord had turned off his engine. Why didn't Sadie call him about the phone call? Why did he find out about it from Lexie? He didn't even ring the bell but instead pounded on the door, releasing some of his anger and frustration at the cases plaguing him the past couple of weeks.

Sadie swung the door open.

"Did you check to see who I was?" Ethan asked as Cord joined him.

Sadie looked from him to her brother, then back to him. "I didn't have to. I saw your car and Cord's in the driveway."

"Why did my niece have to tell me about the call you received a while ago?" After seeing Kelly that morning, a girl who was best friends with his niece, he couldn't risk losing anyone important in his life, and Sadie was important to him. "I'm staying here tonight. You need protection."

"Let's discuss this inside." Sadie stepped out of Ethan's way.

As Cord passed her, he frowned and said, "I should have gotten a call at the very least. I'm your brother and the police chief."

"I'm aware of who you are. It only happened half an hour ago. I wanted to make sure Ashley and Steven were all right and get Lexie settled before I decided what to do. Your niece was more upset about the call than I was."

"And why is that with all that has gone on lately?" Ethan wanted to shout at her at the same time he wanted to hold her—keep her by his side until this was all over with.

"Because at the moment I can't do anything about it. If whoever called thinks I'm going to sit by and let drugs take over our schools, he doesn't know me."

Cord moved between Sadie and Ethan and got in her face. "Yes, you are. Let me do my job. You're a teacher, not a police officer." He pulled back, folding his arms over his chest. "Just what are you doing to receive a threatening call?"

She shrugged. "I'm not sure. Maybe it's because I caught someone selling drugs today at school. At least, I think I did."

Ethan stepped around Cord. "And you're just telling us this now, with the cases we're working on. May I remind you they're all tied to prescription drugs in some way? We got Kelly's autopsy back. She had tranquilizers in her system before she died."

"Then it was suicide?"

Ethan peered toward the top of the staircase and saw Ashley and Lexie watching them from the second floor landing. "Let's go into the kitchen."

A moment later, Ethan sat across from Cord and next to Sadie at the kitchen table in the alcove and lowered his voice to say, "No, I believe she was drugged before she was killed. Whoever did it didn't want her struggling. There were bruises on her upper arm most likely from her being held from behind. Recent ones. The knot used in the rope was most likely not something Kelly knew how to tie. It was a knot used by climbers. We're canvassing all the housing units facing the parking lot, and we found a latent print on the rafter not far from where the rope hung. Not your usual place to find a print. As I told you earlier, we're treating it as a murder."

"How about Luke's death?" Sadie pressed her fingertips into her temples.

"Murder. It was almost an identical scenario down to the drugs given to Lexie—tranquilizers put in his water bottle. The only difference is he went home early Tuesday rather than staying for football practice."

"So the same person went after Lexie and Luke. Is that what you're saying?"

"It's a strong possibility."

"Why would someone go after them?"

The anguish in Sadie's voice tore at Ethan. "I don't know. Maybe they're a threat to whoever is behind this somehow. So do you see now why Cord and I were so upset you didn't call us immediately?"

"This wasn't the only prank call I got this week. I received one on Monday. Someone asked if I knew where Steven was. Thankfully, he was upstairs."

With his fist on the table, Ethan surged to his feet. "And you're just now telling us this?"

"When I got the call, I thought it might be Harris or one of the kids' friends playing a prank."

"And you don't think so now?"

"I don't know what to think anymore. So far Harris has been aboveboard about everything, but what if it's an act? He fooled me once."

Ethan began prowling the kitchen. "Maybe you should stay home like Lexie until this is over with."

"That's nonsense. It was a kid trying to disguise his voice, getting his jollies at my expense."

Ethan narrowed his eyes on her. "You're taking unnecessary risks."

"Enough about me." Weaving her fingers together, Sadie clasped her hands, her knuckles white. "Who could be doing this? Three teens are dead. Murdered."

"We don't know, but it looks like he's taking care of liabilities. Greed motivates a lot of people, and there is big money in prescription drugs." Cord pushed his chair back and rose. "I'm making some coffee. Do you two want any?"

"I'll take a cup." Ethan returned to his seat. "It's not just teens. It's happening to adults, too." He thought of his sister at the nursing home, getting blood samples to test patients' drug levels and stood again. "Skip the coffee for me. I'd better go to Greenbrier. Beth might be in danger."

"Danger? Why?" Her forehead creased, Sadie came to her feet. "What's happening?"

Cord set the glass pot down on the counter. "No, let me go to Greenbrier." His gaze bore into Ethan.

Beth was his sister, but the look Cord sent Ethan spoke of deep feelings toward Beth. He knew how important it was for him to come to Sadie's house to make sure she was protected, when it could have just been Cord checking on his sister. "Get the blood samples and have one of your officers drive them to the lab and stay with them. Whoever is behind this has no problem with killing. No doubt he'll shut down his business, cover his tracks. That's what I'd do if I were in his shoes. We need to know if the nursing home is a source for him, then check the others in the area. I'll stay here and look after Sadie and the kids."

After Cord gave Sadie a hug, he left the kitchen. She stared at Ethan for a long moment then went into his embrace.

"I need you to tell me what happened at school. Who did you catch selling drugs?" he whispered close to her ear.

She leaned back. "Kalvin Majors." Then she told Ethan what occurred in the auditorium.

As he listened to her, his gut solidified into a rock. His arms tightened about her. When she finished, all he wanted to do was hold her and never let her go. "But you didn't see what was in the packet?"

"No, but the exchange of money makes it highly suspicious. This isn't the first time I've seen him do something similar. I did last week but it was way down the hall, and I couldn't get to either boy with the crowd separating us. With all that's been going on I've been extra vocal and vigilant."

"And you may be making someone nervous."

"It could have been Kalvin or Sam who called me."

"I didn't have time to talk to Brendan, Kalvin, and Zoe today with the robbery and Mary Lou, but I will first thing tomorrow morning, especially Kalvin. He's eighteen, as well as Missy. I need to talk with her without Carrie around, and they seemed to be fused at the hip."

"Yes, usually where one goes the other isn't far away. But I have Missy in class. Carrie isn't. Come to the school and talk with Missy during my class time. I know some of their classes are together but not English since Missy is a senior and Carrie is a junior."

"Good. In the meantime, I'm going to dig deeper into these kids' lives. Find a way to break through this wall around the group. I think Missy is the weak link. Tell me about her."

"You're correct. She's a perfect follower. She does everything Carrie does. I'm not sure what hold if any Carrie has over her, but occasionally I've seen this with other kids. It isn't healthy in my opinion. Missy doesn't think for herself. I have both of them on the softball team last year. Missy parroted everything Carrie did. Does that help you?"

"Yes. It confirms what I thought." And it gave him a strategy to use on Missy. He was going to make her think Carrie turned on her.

The next morning, Sadie unlocked her room at the high school and faced Ethan. "You didn't have to bring me to school and escort me to my room. It probably was Kalvin because he's upset I turned him into the assistant principal."

"Yes, I needed to. I'm stopping by the school security office and talking to the officers about keeping an eye on you. I'll pick you up at the end of the day, and we'll go get Ashley and Steven."

"I feel like I'm in the Witness Protection Program."

"No. It would be a lot worse and restrictive than what this is. I'll be back to interview Missy. I'll check in with the office, but I don't want anyone to know until I show up."

Her gaze linked with his, and the sensations of being safe inundated her as it had last night with Ethan and Cord combining forces and protecting Beth and Lexie at Sadie's house. Her home had been crowded with people yesterday evening, but she'd gotten the best night's sleep in days. "I won't say anything to anyone. Nobody wants this over with more than me."

He took her hand and squeezed it before rotating away and striding down the hall toward the outside door. He had to be tired. Ethan and Cord had taken turns staying up all night, watching over them.

When Ethan disappeared in the crowd of students filling the corridor, Sadie crossed to her desk and sat, then locked her purse in a drawer and sorted through the mail she'd picked up in her box in the office. She found the envelope from Maxwell and opened it quickly to see what he'd done with Kalvin.

She read the discipline referral, crushed it into a tight ball, and bolted to her feet. Anger surged through her. She stormed from the room, heading toward the assistant principal's office. She passed the secretary in the larger office and made her way back to Maxwell's. The door was ajar. She pushed it open, but the room was empty. He was probably on duty before school. She didn't intend to leave until she talked with him.

When she sat in the chair before his desk, her nerves jiggled. Agitated, she bounced her legs up and down. After five minutes, she rose and began pacing, unable to sit any longer. She glanced at her watch about every two minutes. Finally, she paused at the large window behind his desk and stared outside into the oval where the buses let off the students. She spied Maxwell and Jack Hughes, a teacher down the hall from her room, stopped to speak with the assistant principal. Deep lines of anger slashed Jack's face, and when the man left to come into the building, his scowling expression shouted his displeasure. Sadie wondered what had Jack so angry. Jack was one of the assistant football coaches. Did it have something to do with the deaths of Luke and Jared, both a loss to the team?

Sadie continued prowling the office, trying to figure out what she would say to her assistant principal. She needed to be calm, in control. But the second he stepped into the room, all her carefully thought out words fled her mind.

"If you're here about Kalvin Majors, there's nothing else I can do at this time." Maxwell crossed to his desk and sat behind it. "And I have a lot of work that needs to be addressed."

Sadie stood in front of him, leaning against the desk, her hands clutching its edge. "You let him go. Why?"

He looked up from shuffling some papers. "Because he didn't have anything in his pocket."

"I saw him put something in it. There had to be something there." Sadie's voice rose several decibels, and she clamped her teeth together before she made the situation worse.

"I took him directly to my office and had him turn his pockets inside out. Nothing."

"Did you keep an eye on him as you took him to your office?"

"Yes, but it was crowded in the hallway. A group of kids was coming into the building. Regardless of that, I'm sure he didn't get rid of anything."

"He had to because there was something in his pocket—front right one in his jeans."

Maxwell pinned her with a sharp look. "He turned out all his pockets and let me check his backpack. Nothing. You were mistaken, Ms. Thompson. In your passion to do something about the drug problem at the school, you jumped to a conclusion that wasn't right."

She bent forward. "I know what I saw, and I'll be keeping my eye on Kalvin. Did you talk with Sam? What about the money exchanged?"

"He owed Kalvin some he'd borrowed from him."

"They're friends? Those two don't run in the same crowd."

"There's nothing I can do, but make sure you're professional and careful about what you say and do or we'll be facing a lawsuit."

"I'll do that," she said, sweeping around and marching from the office, anger imbuing her body.

⤝⤞

"Take a seat," Ethan said, waving his hand toward a chair in the interview room.

Wide-eyed, Patti Shea sat, her back stiff, her clasped hands in her lap. "Why am I here?"

"I believe the officer who brought you in told you that some of the patients under your care haven't received their prescribed dosage of medication."

"All I can do it give it to them. I don't force it down them."

"That might be the case with one patient, but on your wing we're talking about twelve that we've tested out of twenty-four. Fifty percent. The whole nursing home is now being tested because of what we discovered. They're bringing the DEA in on this case. We'll get to the bottom of it. One patient died recently because she wasn't on the medication she needed. In pain, she freaked out when she shouldn't have if properly medicated. That woman was under your care."

"I'm only one nurse out of three on that wing who dispenses meds. I want my lawyer." Patti chewed on her thumbnail.

"That's your right. While you arrange for your attorney to be here with you, we'll be digging even deeper into your finances. You recently purchased a new car."

"My old one died on me. I need transportation. There's no crime in doing that."

"And you paid a large amount of cash as a down payment. Not a check or money order, but cash."

"Again, no law against that." Patti bit down on her thumbnail and spat it out into her hand.

"True, unless you got that money illegally. If you have nothing to hide, you have nothing to worry about." Ethan rose. "Don't say anything else until your attorney arrives. But I do want you to know the more you cooperate with us, the easier the DA will be on you. If you caused the death of that woman by withholding her medication, you're looking at manslaughter charges at the least. Maybe murder. This is serious."

Patti's eyes widened as Ethan spoke. "Murder?"

Ethan ignored the woman's question and headed for the door. "Wait."

He glanced over his shoulder, his hand on the knob.

"What do you mean by cooperating with you?"

"We can't have this discussion until your attorney shows up since you said you wanted one. Make your call and when he comes, we'll talk again." Ethan left the room before Patti could say another word.

"Do you think she's going to talk?" Cord asked out in the hallway.

"I don't know. My gut says she did it, but we need hard evidence. Have your detectives keep looking into her finances as well as her associates and friends. Search her house from top to bottom. Whoever took the medication might have been using some of it, but not all, which means she was selling it to someone, possibly a supplier. I want that supplier. I'm going to the school to interview Missy without her sidekick. Her attorney is meeting me there."

"Why not bring her back down here?"

"I want to surprise her. I don't want her talking to anyone except her attorney and certainly not Carrie."

As Ethan started down the hall, Cord said, "Say hi to my sister."

Ethan turned around, backpedaling. "Who said I would see her?"

"Just a hunch. You'll be good for her."

His friend's words stayed with Ethan the whole way to the school. It really was the other way around. Sadie was good for him. For years, he'd been so wrapped up in his work he'd neglected the other aspects of his life. Until he'd come home, he hadn't realized how removed he was from people. Even in church he'd participate but more as an observer, not truly a part of the church community. He'd seen so much pain through his job he'd thought if he held himself back, he wouldn't be a victim of that pain.

At the high school, Ethan checked in at the office with the secretary and the principal. The man set aside his conference room for Ethan to interview Missy and sent a campus police officer to escort Missy from Sadie's class with the instruction she wasn't to talk to anyone or use her cell phone. Colleen Stover sat in the conference room with Missy and called the eighteen-year-old's parents as a courtesy, although Ethan could question Missy without her parents. Missy listened to Colleen talk to them, her face paling with each word spoken.

When the girl's attorney finished the call, Ethan faced Missy across the wide table, his gaze glued to the teen for a long moment before he asked the first question, "Have you thought about my proposal from the other day? The first one who talks about what happened that night with Jared will get a deal with the DA."

"I don't know . . ." Missy pressed her lips together and turned toward her lawyer.

Colleen leaned close and whispered to her.

Missy held her necklace with a large male ring on it and rubbed it between her fingers. She shook her head, slanted a look at Ethan, then returned her full attention to her attorney.

Colleen Stover twisted forward and said, "Free from any kind of prosecution?"

"If her testimony leads to what really happened to Jared, and she isn't the one responsible for him being in the lake."

The attorney nodded at Missy.

The teenage girl stared down at the table, her lips a thin white line. Her fingers still frantically caressed the ring until she clenched it in her fist and raised her gaze to his. Her eyes shone with tears.

"We thought he was dead. We panicked. Luke didn't want Jared found at his father's warehouse, so Luke drove Jared's Porsche to the park by the lake with all of us following him. Then the guys transferred Jared from the trunk of Brendan's car to the Porsche. But when we left him, he wasn't in the water, but in the parking lot near the road that led to the boat ramp. We wanted Jared found. Just not at the warehouse." Tears spilled from her eyes. "I don't know how the car ended up in the water. None of us do. We thought some bum or bad guy must have robbed Jared and put the car in the water."

The kids hadn't been thinking clearly from the beginning. Jared's wallet had been on him, so there was no indication of a robbery as the motive. Not to mention Jared was found in his expensive car in the lake. "Who was with you at the park?"

Missy tilted her head toward her lawyer.

"You need to tell him if you want the deal."

"Brendan Livingston, Carrie Bannister, Luke Adams, Kalvin Majors, Zoe Sanders, and myself."

"Who else was at the party?"

"Just Kelly and we left her at the warehouse. She was passed out."

"That's all?"

Missy blinked. "Yes." Her answer came out slowly as though she were unsure.

"There was someone else there?"

Her eyebrows scrunched together. "I didn't see anyone else . . ."

"But?"

"I don't know. There was a time I felt like I was being watched, but when I looked around at the other kids, they weren't. I think it was that warehouse. Dark, almost menacing. I told Luke it wasn't a good place, but we needed somewhere private where no one would bother us."

"You were dating Luke?"

"Yes," Missy said in a choked voice, her eyes closing while she fiddled with the male ring on the necklace.

"Did he take tranquilizers often? According to his parents, never, but then he was at the pill party. Would he have gotten into a car after downing a large quantity of them? Would he have a reason to kill himself?"

Missy swallowed hard. "No. He was upset over Jared's death and had sworn off taking any more pills. He was scared because of what happened. He was sure everyone was going to find out about what we did."

"Would he have spiked Lexie's water to make her back off? After all, she is the one who told us about the warehouse. A warehouse that belongs to his dad."

Missy dropped her head, sliding her gaze to the left and mumbled, "No, none of us did. Why would we? You're her uncle. That would draw attention to us."

"I suggest you level with me. Right now you aren't. Could Luke have spiked Lexie's water bottle? Remember, there is no deal if you lie to me."

"Thursday night he was so angry at Lexie. He talked about all kinds of things he could do to get back at her, but I calmed him down, and I thought he was okay when he went home."

"Was one of the ways putting something in her drink?"

Missy turned to her lawyer, tears glistening in her eyes, then looked back at Ethan and nodded.

"So let's assume Luke doctored Lexie's water bottle. Would he do the same thing to himself out of remorse?"

"Luke? No, he might have a hair-trigger temper, but he had everything to live for. I believed him when he swore off taking any more drugs after his best friend died."

"So that leaves someone else drawing attention to you all? Any speculation who?"

Her mouth fell open. "You think someone is after us?"

"Or someone in your group is causing trouble no one else knows about."

"Brendan, Zoe, Carrie, and Kalvin wouldn't do that."

"Have you had other pill parties?"

Missy closed her eyes for a long moment, then nodded. "Two others at my grandparents' cabin."

"Who mentioned having pill parties in the first place?"

"Kalvin."

"What about Kalvin selling drugs? Have you seen him do that?"

"Kalvin? Selling drugs?" Missy shook her head, glanced at her lawyer then back at Ethan. "He doesn't need the money. His father is a doctor."

"With access possibly to drugs. Did you all take all the pills in the bowl that night at the party?"

Lowering her head, Missy pushed her fingers through her hair that fell forward. Finally she shook her head again. "There were a lot left over. I remember seeing them when we left to take Jared to the lake. "

"So you don't know where all the leftover pills went?"

"No. I never thought about it. Not after what happened to Jared."

"Who cleaned up the warehouse?"

"Luke, Brendan, and Kalvin."

"Then maybe they took them."

"Luke didn't. In fact, he wondered what happened to them. He thought Kelly took them. She was gone when they went to clean up the warehouse."

"No, Lexie picked Kelly up Sunday morning, and she said the bowl was empty."

Tears returned to glisten in Missy's eyes. "I don't know what happened to the pills. We panicked. Weren't thinking clearly at all. I didn't wake up until almost noon the next day when Luke called me to tell me they just finished cleaning up the warehouse."

Ethan stood. "Mrs. Stover, I'd like you to take your client to the police station to make a statement. You can have her parents meet you down there." He switched his attention to the teenage girl. "It was a smart move on your part to finally tell us what happened. Three kids from the party are dead. I'm beginning to think something else is going on here."

17

"Ashley, Steven, get your homework done now. Later, when everyone is here, it'll be too hectic to do it." Sadie said as she entered her house Thursday after school.

As Ms. Thompson's kids headed up the stairs, Lexie walked to the window nearby and looked out. "It feels odd having an officer going everywhere I go."

"My brother and your uncle are circling the wagons. They're worried."

"Do you think we're in danger?" Lexie twisted away from the sight of the patrol car parked out in front of the house.

"Maybe. I trust their instincts and abilities, but that's not to say you need to worry about it."

"Yeah, Nana used to say to me when she still recognized me that all worry gave me was heartburn and wrinkles. Then she'd tell me the Lord is much better at handling that burden."

"A wise woman, but sometimes it's hard not to worry."

"Are you?" Lexie set her backpack on the couch.

Ms. Thompson peered at her. "Yes. Not so much for me but others."

Lexie pointed at herself. "Me?"

"No, because you've got a good head on your shoulders. But some kids don't and that does worry me."

"Are you talking about Steven?"

Ms. Thompson nodded, glancing toward the stairs. "But also Ashley. Her dad is coming over to pick her up to take her to a nice place for dinner. She's all excited. I'm not."

"For thirteen, your daughter is pretty smart."

"Has she said anything about her father to you?"

Lexie thought back to the conversation she'd had with Ashley yesterday about their dads and not having them around. "There's something missing because my dad is gone. Most of the time I don't think much about him dying anymore, but every once in a while I do and there's an emptiness that's hard to fill by another. Questions left unanswered."

"Like what?"

"What would my life be like if Dad was alive? What am I missing out on? I think Ashley wonders the same thing."

"Yes, I see what you mean." When the doorbell chimed, Ms. Thompson walked toward the door. "I bet that is Oliver. He said he would be over after school to help you with your Algebra II."

"Oh, good. I need it. It'll be good to talk to another kid from school." She'd been isolated most of the time since the incident with her passing out last Friday. Other than talking with Ashley, Steven, and Kelly, she had been around adults, even at church when she helped the pastor in the office these past couple of days. She wanted to go to Luke's funeral tomorrow, but her mom had said no because of the probability he spiked her water.

When Ms. Thompson opened the door, Oliver, a pale cast to his face, stood on the porch with a uniform officer next to him. Eyes large, Oliver kept his attention on the young cop.

"Ma'am, he says he has been invited to your house to help Lexie with her homework."

"Yes. We'll be fine. Thanks." Ms. Thompson swung the screen door wide to allow Oliver into the house. "I'm sorry about that. I forgot about the officer being outside, or I would have warned you about him."

"No problem. He surprised me when he hurried up the sidewalk after me. I thought I had done something wrong."

"Oh, no, Oliver," Lexie gave him a smile, "I really appreciate you coming over to help me. I'm stuck in this whole section of the book. I need a whiz kid to help me."

Oliver reddened. "Sure. Anything I can do."

"I'll be in the kitchen trying to decide what to fix for dinner. I have tea, water, or Coke to drink."

"That's okay, Ms. Thompson, I'm fine." Oliver trailed after Lexie into the living room.

When he sat next to her on the couch, she dug into her backpack for work. As she lifted the heavy math book out of the bag and her folder, she released a long breath.

"I'm sure this is hard on you. Hang in there, Lexie. Things will turn out for the better."

Hang in there, stuck in Lexie's mind—all she could visualize was Kelly dangling from the warehouse rafter. Tears flooded her eyes. She dropped her book and folder on her lap and covered her face, her fingertips pressing into her eyes to keep the tears inside. Oliver didn't need to see her fall apart.

"What's wrong, Lexie?" His hand settled on her shoulder. "Did I say something wrong?"

She shook her head. "I just miss Kelly. She was my best friend."

"But she called you a liar and spread the rumors about you around the school."

The past couple of weeks crashed down on Lexie, and she couldn't hold back the sorrow any longer. She cried for Kelly, Jared, and even Luke.

❧

"Who just left here?" Ethan asked as he came into Sadie's kitchen later that evening.

"Oliver. He's my student aide, and I volunteered him to help Lexie with her math. They didn't get much done."

"Why not?"

"Poor guy. He told Lexie to hang in there, and she broke down about Kelly. He felt awful. He's coming back on Saturday afternoon. I told Beth not to worry, I'll be here on Saturday since she's going to be working. In fact, she'll be late which means Cord will be. I fixed a stew that should be easy for them to heat up later."

"My sister has her hands full with the DEA all over the nursing home as well as the corporate office of the company that owns the chain of nursing homes. They're working to put as many checks in place as possible, so what happened to Lucy doesn't to other patients."

"The stew will be ready in about forty-five minutes."

"That'll give me some time to challenge your son to a one-on-one basketball game. It'll do me good to exercise hard."

"He's upstairs, hopefully finishing up his homework."

Sadie stirred the stew on the stove, the aroma of carrots, potatoes, celery, and beef wafting to her. The smells reminded her of her mother's kitchen. She recalled Lexie's comments of what it felt like for her losing her dad and realized she felt the same way about her own father, and he wasn't dead.

She put the wooden spoon on the counter and went to the wall phone. Ten seconds later, her father answered. "Dad, will you come over tonight? I need to talk with you. In fact, you and Mom can come to dinner. I fixed her stew that you love so much."

"Your mom is at her book club tonight. It's my night to fend for myself."

"Then come over." She swallowed hard. "Please."

A long silence hovered between them.

"Dad, are you still there?"

"Yes. What time?"

"You can come now. Dinner is in about an hour."

"I'll be there soon. I've wanted to talk to you."

Her father's ominous words right before he hung up plagued her, making her so nervous she hardly said anything to Ethan and Steven as they went outside to play basketball. She made her way through her house, picking up any mess, even straightening things that didn't need straightening.

By the time the doorbell sounded twenty minutes later, she felt wound as tight as the dishcloth she'd wrung out in the kitchen after cleaning the counters twice. When she answered the door, she found her father approaching the porch while Harris stood in front of her. The frown carved on her dad's face announced his displeasure as loudly as words.

"Come in, Harris. Let me get Ashley." She turned to go to the bottom of the staircase to call her daughter, but Ashley charged down the steps.

"I'm ready," she said as she breezed past Sadie toward the exit.

"What time are you bringing her home?" Sadie asked Harris while her father cut across the grass toward the driveway.

"It's a school night, so is eight-thirty okay?"

"Fine."

"I saw Steven playing basketball with Ethan. I guess he's practicing for when the season starts."

Sadie peeked out the door and glimpsed her dad rounding the side of the house, probably going to see Steven. Probably not a bad idea since his least favorite person was standing in front of her. "Yeah. It doesn't take much to get him to play."

"Maybe one day," Harris said, sadness in his eyes for a few seconds before he turned toward Ashley. "Are you ready?"

"Yes." Ashley started down the sidewalk to her dad's car. "Bye, Mom. I got all my homework done."

"Thanks, Sadie, for letting me do this. She mentioned how much she liked Cattlemen's Grill. I thought she might like going with me."

When she shut the door, she put her forehead against the wood, her hand still on the knob.

"I guess there's nothing I can say to get you to send that man packing."

The sound of her father's tight voice shivered down her. *Lord, give me the grace to tell him what I want without losing my temper.*

She pushed away from the door and faced her dad, who must have come into the house through the back entrance. "Did you see Steven? Who's winning?"

"Ethan, but my grandson was rallying."

"Last time they played Steven won."

"I took a look at the stew on the stove. It smells great. Just like your mom's and my mother's." He came further across the foyer. "We need to talk."

Sadie gulped. "Yes we do. Let's go into the living room. For a little while, we're alone down here, but that won't last long."

When her dad settled on the couch, Sadie took the chair across from him, trying to remember how she had rehearsed what she was going to say to him. At the moment, not a word came to mind.

He cleared his throat. "I'm glad you called. I've been concerned about you. Cord told me he and Ethan are guarding you, Beth, and the kids until they can figure out what's going on in Summerton."

"I'm fine. Cord and Ethan are overreacting. I got a couple of prank calls, and now they're all worried. I understand why they feel that way about Lexie."

"Where is she?"

"She's upstairs lying down. She's finally realizing Kelly is gone. It hit her hard today."

"When I was a teenager, all parents had to worry about was alcohol. Now there's so much more to tempt young people."

"This isn't an easy time to be a teenager."

"Sadie . . ." He coughed. "When you left the other day, your mother let me know in no uncertain terms just how big a fool I've been. I drove you away all those years ago. When you came home, I should have set my pride aside and accepted you back with open arms. I have no defense for what I did, especially since you've been back. All I can do is ask for your forgiveness and start anew."

The only words that came out of her mouth were, "You mean that?"

"Yes. In the past weeks we've lost three young people just like that." He snapped his fingers. "It made me realize I could lose you that fast or Steven or Ashley. Life's too short to hold on to this stubborn pride. Will you forgive me?"

Sadie hurried to the couch and sat next to him. "Yes, if you'll forgive me for running away with Harris. I thought I knew best, and I was so wrong."

"Yes, honey," he choked out and drew her against him.

For the first time in fourteen years, she finally felt at peace inside. The world might be falling apart around her, but making amends with her father lifted her spirits as though a great burden had vanished.

⟶⟶

When Ethan entered Cord's office at the station Saturday morning, his friend stood in front of a white dry eraser board mounted on his wall. Ethan shut the door. "I've sent officers out to pick up Patti again and Kalvin. I think it's very coincidental that Patti is Kalvin's aunt. Even if Mr. Howard didn't find any drugs on him, Sadie is convinced she saw something going down in the auditorium."

"Not to mention he's part of Jared's group and at that pill party Saturday night. In fact, he's the one that suggested having pill parties to them."

"Interestingly the west wing is the only part of the nursing home where the patients weren't getting the right medication. The blood tests on the patients in the other wings came back fine so that leaves only a few nurses who had access to the medication on the west wing. We can rule out the late-night-shift nurses because no medication is given on a regular basis, only in case of emergencies. That leaves the four nurses on the other two shifts."

"And Patti looks the most promising of those four. At least the Greenbrier case will probably be solved soon. I can't say the same about the other ones." Cord chomped down so hard on his toothpick he broke it in two. After tossing the pieces in the trash, he faced the board again. "Okay, what do we have on Jared's murder?"

"Missy said, and the other teens involved admitted, they moved Jared from the warehouse to his car in the park. Luke freaked out and didn't want Jared found in a building his dad owned. According to each one, none of them know how Jared ended up in the lake. They didn't even buckle him with his seatbelt, but when he hit the water, he was alive. The seatbelt was around him but stuck."

"With a strong glue. Something not hard to find and effective. So, someone definitely murdered Jared. Why? He was well liked."

Ethan plowed his hands through his hair then cupped his hands at his nape. "One good thing that came from Missy's interview. We had a reason to fingerprint all the kids at the party and could match our latent prints against them."

"Yeah, but none of them match the same one we found on Lexie's water bottle, on the lighter, and on the rafter at the warehouse."

"But according to Missy, and Brendan confirmed, Luke spiked Lexie's water bottle so why was the other print on it? It isn't Luke's."

"Lexie knows the person who killed the teens? Or that person had access to her water bottle? Do you think that person threw the bottle in the trashcan?" Ethan rolled his head around to ease the tension gripping him. "I was hoping Kelly's computer would give us a lead. She was receiving some nasty emails from someone, saying they know what she did, but it originated from a cyber café. And that didn't lead us anywhere. Did she wipe the computer or someone else?"

"They were most likely from the one who killed her. That person had a reason to wipe the computer and hope they couldn't be recovered."

"Where are we with that tip about a white Chevy in the parking lot behind the warehouse the night Kelly died?"

"I have two officers watching all the traffic cameras in the area around the warehouse for Tuesday night. I hope they can catch a white Chevy or any white car and get a license number. Then we'll run them all down. But do you know how common a white car is? My mother has a white Chevy."

"At least the time is between midnight and six. It could be worse and be from noon to six."

Cord chuckled. "We take the breaks where we get them."

"It would be nice to have the same latent print on Luke's water bottle. At least what little liquid was left in it tested the same as Lexie's. If it wasn't for the type of person Luke was, we could look at that death as a suicide since we found out he drugged Lexie, but it doesn't feel right. He was too upset at her to have remorse. And certainly not enough to kill himself because Lexie was all right."

A knock at the door sounded. Cord said, "Come in."

An officer came into the office. "Both Patti Shea and Kalvin Majors are here waiting as you said in the reception area, but separated and being watched to see if they talk. Also, the hospital called. Mary Lou Winston has awakened."

"Thanks," Cord said then glanced at Ethan. "Ready. We'll let Kalvin stew for a while."

As Ethan started to leave with Cord, Bradley Montgomery appeared in the open doorway, a scowl marking his face with gravity. "I need to talk with you two."

Ethan stepped back to allow the man into the office, then shut the door. "What about?"

"I've met with the other parents whose kids are involved. We want to make it clear we want answers to who killed Jared, Luke, and Kelly. Find the murderer before another kid is killed. Tell me you are close to an arrest. My son has to be avenged. His murderer can't go free." Bradley's expression collapsed into a haggard look underscoring a man who hadn't slept in days.

The pain in his childhood friend's eyes intensified his own desire to make sure they found the killer. "I don't intend for that to happen. We have good solid leads we're tracking down. When we make an arrest and go to trial, we want the case to be airtight. Give us time."

Swallowing hard, Bradley nodded. "I've tried to stay away and give you that time, but this morning talking with the other parents, I just couldn't keep quiet any longer. I'll double the award I'm offering for any information that leads to an arrest. Use it in any way you can to get what you need."

"Thanks." Ethan moved to the door and opened it. "I'll let you and the other parents know *when* we capture the killer."

When Bradley left, Ethan made his way to the reception area to escort Patti back to the interview room. As he passed Kalvin, he slid a look toward him, Jeffrey Livingston, and Dr. Majors. The teen averted his gaze.

A few minutes later, seated at a table in room number one, Cord stood by the door with his arms folded across his chest while Ethan started. "Patti, we have you. The patients you see are under-medicated, the only ones in the nursing home. The day shift gives the bulk of the medication to these patients. Most weeks you're on the schedule for that duty five days while the other nurse during your shift only does it when you're off. With the blood tests run, the lab has determined it would have to be you taking the drugs. On top of that, you have large sums of money you haven't accounted for with the IRS. Examining your tax return from last year with your spending doesn't add up."

Her face set in a bland expression, Patti stared at Ethan as though she were in a trance.

"Patti, can you account for the money you've used to pay off some of your debts and to purchase some big-ticket items? Your husband isn't working, and you are the sole provider."

She blinked and lowered her head. "My husband and I have been doing extra work under the table so we don't have to pay taxes."

"Is that selling drugs you've stolen at the nursing home?"

"You don't have to answer that," her lawyer said.

Patti remained silent.

"Does your nephew sell them at the high school?"

She lifted her head and stabbed him with a cutting look. "No, he's a good kid."

"As we speak, we're searching your house and his. We'll find the truth. Make it easier on yourself and tell us what you can."

Patti looked at her lawyer. "I have nothing else to say to you."

Ethan stood. "Fine. I need you to stay here until after I talk with your nephew." He left the room with Cord and moved to the next one. "You want to take this one."

A grin tipped the corners of Cord's mouth up. "My pleasure."

When Ethan entered with Cord, he took the position by the door but with a clear view of Kalvin. The teen slouched in his chair, as though he had not a care in the world.

Cord eased onto the seat across from Kalvin, with Jeffrey and Dr. Majors flanking the teen. "We have your aunt in custody for stealing prescription drugs from Greenbrier Nursing Home and selling them. She's saying she has given drugs to you to sell at the high school. That you do quite well for her."

Kalvin sat up straight, his eyes flaring.

Jeffrey put his hand on the boy's shoulder and whispered in his ear.

Cord continued. "It allowed her to pay a hefty down payment on a car in cash as well as pay off some of her debts. Right now, I have officers at your house, tearing it apart looking for those drugs. We have a witness who will testify she saw you selling drugs to a student."

"No way." Kalvin brought his fist down on the table. "I wasn't selling drugs. Your—witness is wrong. I didn't know my aunt was stealing drugs. I rarely see Aunt Patti. Our families aren't speaking."

"That's right, Chief Thompson. My wife and her sister haven't talked to each other in over a year."

"That doesn't mean your son hasn't."

"I was cleared by Mr. Howard."

"Let's talk about that incident at school. What did you do with the drugs while walking from the auditorium to the office?"

"Nothing. I didn't have any drugs."

"I believe my client has been cleared. He didn't have any drugs at school."

Ethan answered a knock on the door. An officer indicated he should come out into the hallway.

When he did, the young man said, "They found about six painkillers in a plastic bag stuffed in Kalvin's sneakers in his closet."

"Just six?"

"Yes."

"Anything at Patti Shea's house yet?"

"No. Her husband wasn't there and his car was gone."

"Put a BOLO out on him."

Ethan reentered the room while Cord said, "We're bringing in Sam Travis to get to the bottom of what happened in that auditorium. It wasn't the first time Ms. Thompson saw you making a suspicious exchange at school."

"My son doesn't sell drugs. He admits he attended the pill party but only to drink beer that evening. I've taken his car away from him because of it."

Cord directed his look at Kalvin. "Well, one of you is lying. You or your aunt."

Kalvin's mouth pinched together, and he stared down at the table.

Ethan stepped forward. "If you don't sell or take drugs, Kalvin, why are six painkillers in a plastic bag in your sneaker in your closet?"

"What?" Dr. Majors asked and turned to his son.

"This is your first offense." Ethan said in a calm, reassuring voice. "You're still under eighteen. We have some room to negotiate with the DA if you come clean and tell us what went down in the auditorium. Did you go back to the warehouse and take the rest of the pills left in the green bowl?"

Kalvin's shoulders sagged forward. "I can't do this anymore." He raised his head, weariness in his expression. "Football is my life, and yet I can't play without taking painkillers. I used to have to only take one or two a day. Now it's three. I'm a tackle and sometimes the pain is so bad I have a hard time getting out of bed. I knew if I said anything to Dad," Kalvin kept his focus on Ethan standing next to Cord, "he'd make me quit football. I have colleges looking at me. I figured I'd heal after the season was over, and no one would know."

"So why are you selling the drugs? To pay for your painkillers?" Cord asked.

"I'm not selling. I was buying from Sam that day in the auditorium."

"How about the pills in the bowl at the party?"

"I took some painkillers out of it. I know what they look like. The ones I need. I didn't need the pills that were left. I didn't go back to the warehouse after we moved Jared until we cleaned it up the next morning. Brendan, Luke, and I wondered what happened but thought Kelly took them. For all I cared, Brendan or Luke had. It was none of my business."

"I want you to write down what happened at the party and afterwards. Also, what happened in the auditorium. Was that the first time you bought from Sam Travis?"

"No, I was injured in practice before school started. After my pain meds ran out, I bought mine from Sam."

"Does he sell to others?"

"Yes. For all I know, he could have come into the warehouse and taken the drugs from the bowl. He lives in the housing project near it. He could have gotten wind of the pill party. Kelly could have told the whole school. She was the new one in our group. Jared vouched for her, but I didn't totally trust her."

While Kalvin talked, Ethan studied his father's face. By the end, the doctor's expression went from shock to pain to anger. Ethan believed the teen. He wasn't the dealer at school.

As Kalvin took the paper and pen, Cord rose and left with Ethan. "I'll wrap this up with Kalvin and wait to see what's found at Patti's house before charging her. If they find drugs at her house, she may be more willing to make a deal with us in exchange for who she sold the drugs to. I'll also have an officer bring in Sam. I'd intended to talk to him anyway. Now more than ever, I want to."

"So far nothing at Patti's house, but her husband is missing. I told the officer to put a BOLO out on him. I'm going to see Mary Lou at the hospital. I'll be back in time for Sam's interview." Ethan headed down the corridor, feeling as though they finally were getting somewhere on the cases. At the end of the hall, he turned and said, "Ask Kalvin if he called Sadie the other day and warned her to keep her mouth shut."

"Definitely. I want that solved."

"Now all we have to discover is whose latent prints are on the water bottle, rafter, and lighter. Then I can breathe easier that Lexie will be all right."

"I promise not to fall apart today, Oliver," Lexie said and stepped to the side for the teen to come into Sadie's house. "I wasn't even sure you'd come back. Most guys don't like to deal with a girl sobbing."

He grinned. "I'm not like most guys." He glanced around. "Where is everybody? The other night this place was jammed packed with people."

"This is one of the quieter moments. I think Mom and I will be going back home tonight. Uncle Ethan is wrapping up some of his cases, and Ms. Thompson should be fine. That'll leave only me he's worried about."

"Because of what happened to you at school?"

Lexie nodded and walked toward the den at the back of the house. "There's a game table in here. This is usually Steven's domain, but he's gone to his grandparents' house with Ashley. Ms. Thompson is in the kitchen grading a ton of papers that have piled up these past few weeks."

"When do you think you'll be able to come back to school?" Oliver took the seat next to Lexie at the table.

"According to my suspension, in three weeks. Mom won't let me go back, though, until she knows I'm safe although she is fighting the suspension with the evidence being uncovered. The police feel Luke spiked my water, but with him dead they don't know one hundred percent sure, so Mom is being extra protective. I hope I can go back soon because I miss seeing my friends. I miss—" She pushed thoughts of Kelly from her mind before she starting crying as she did previously when Oliver came to work with her. "I've learned I don't want to be home-schooled. It'll be good getting back to school."

Oliver caught her gaze. "If you need to talk about what happened, I'm a good listener."

"Am I that transparent?"

"Just a little. Can I ask you a question?"

"Sure."

"The other day you were so upset about Kelly's death. Aren't you angry at her for what she did to you?"

"No, Kelly and I made up Saturday before she disappeared."

"After all she did to you?" His eyebrows slashed down.

"We've been friends a long time. I couldn't let one thing change that. Besides, I hated how I felt being so angry at her. It was easier than I realized to forgive her."

"I don't understand. If you're always forgiving someone for doing something bad, they have no reason to do anything right. They get away with it without any consequences."

"I did it for me. Being mad takes too much negative energy." Lexie inhaled a deep, soothing breath—the scent of smoke was in the air. "Do you smoke?"

He frowned. "No, my aunt does. I had to drop my aunt off at work this morning before coming over here. We share a car, and she smokes in it. It's a nasty habit." His nose wrinkled as though he were trying to block the odor emitting from his clothes. "I hate the smell of smoke. I'm saving my money up for my own car. One day."

"I don't blame you. The smell of smoke gets into everything, even your hair."

Oliver's frown evolved into a scowl. "Yeah, I know."

❧

After Ethan read Mary Lou her rights, he asked, "Do you understand your rights?"

"Yes," she said in a raspy voice.

"We're arresting you for stealing drugs from the nursing home. We found all of them stashed in your house. Why, Mary Lou? Were you selling them? Working with someone else?"

She closed her eyes, and for a moment, Ethan thought she had gone to sleep. The doctor said her blood test indicated she had high levels of tranquilizers and painkillers in her system. She would have withdrawal symptoms if she went cold turkey, so they were easing her off the drugs. Her doctor would move her to the psych ward later today,

"Mary Lou?"

Her eyelids slid open. "I don't have an answer for you. I was in pain and needed something for it. But the pills I took didn't seem to be enough. I needed more and more to make it through the day."

"Are you working with anyone else?"

"No. I didn't want anyone to know what was happening to me. Kelly . . ." Her head rolled away from Ethan. When she finally looked at him again, her eyes held a deep sadness. "Kelly knew although she really never said anything about it."

"So stealing the pills from Greenbrier was the first time you did it?"

She nodded.

"You don't know about anyone else there stealing pills from patients to sell or take for themselves?"

"No, but it wouldn't surprise me. A lot of drugs go through the nursing home. So what's going to happen to me?"

"You'll remain in the hospital for the time being. I suggest you get an attorney. The DA will be filing charges against you."

"I've messed up big time." Mary Lou's eyes became heavy.

"But your life isn't over with. Yes, you'll do time for what you did, but you control how you handle it. Make something of yourself for Kelly. Lexie told me she was so worried about you and just wanted you to be all right. Do that for her."

"How? I'm a mess."

"Work with the doctors here to help you with your addiction. It won't be easy, but nothing is too much for the Lord. Turn to Him. He'll get you through it."

She peered at him for a moment, her eyelids sliding lower as the seconds ticked away until she slipped into a sleep. Ethan left, praying Mary Lou could get her life together.

⁂

"Sam is gone. His uncle who he lives with said he went to school this morning but didn't arrive. He received a call from the attendance office saying Sam didn't show up," Cord said to Ethan when he returned from the hospital.

"Does Sam have a car?"

"Yes, a light gray Chevy. I had the two officers working on the surveillance tapes of the area around the warehouse go back and see if they found one like it Tuesday night when Kelly was killed. So far they haven't."

"He lives near there. It could be on the tape and not mean anything. But it's worth looking into. Also, let's get another officer on this and expand the search of the traffic cameras around the warehouse and the park on the Saturday night Jared was killed. See if we find the same car in both places. Expand it to light-colored cars. In the dark, from a distance where those apartments are, a gray or light-colored one could possibly look white." Ethan half-sat, half-leaned against a desk in the main room of the police station.

"I'll bring in an off-duty cop to join the other two. We're stretched trying to cover everything. Also, I've put a BOLO out on Sam Travis's car. The uncle wouldn't let the police come inside to check Sam's room. So they're bringing the uncle in while we're getting a warrant to search the whole apartment."

"We're close. I can feel it."

"We're checking calls on Sam's cell phone."

"I'm assuming it isn't on to track him that way." For the first time in days, Ethan felt close to getting some answers and possibly some normalcy back in his life. He wanted time to explore his growing feelings toward Sadie without everything falling apart around him. He yearned to be with her all the time, to protect her, to love . . . The realization struck him with the force of an EF-five tornado.

"Nope. If only it were that easy."

"Chief," one of the officers on the traffic cameras came into the large room, carrying a sheet of paper, "we found something. When we widened the search, we did find Sam Travis's car caught on camera a block away from the warehouse at 1:15 that night."

"Good. Check the cameras from Saturday for Sam's car. Have you gotten them yet?"

"We're getting to them next."

"I'm calling in some more help for you." Cord crossed the room to his office and disappeared inside.

"Let me see what you've got so far." Ethan took the paper from the young man and scanned the list. He came back to one name after examining the whole list.

Mr. and Mrs. Robert Wright. What is it about that name? He noted the car registered to the couple was a 2008 white Chevy and had been seen at 2:00 in the morning going away from the warehouse area.

Ethan tapped the list. "What do you have on this car? Can you get me a photo from the camera it was captured on?"

"We've just started going down this list. Let me see what we have."

Ethan's gut churned. "Give me an address and phone number. I'll check this one out."

⤌≈⤍

"I think I'm getting this," Lexie said with a big grin. "It's only taken me an hour, but finally what you've been showing me is starting to make sense."

Oliver basked in the glow from her smile. "I'm glad I can help you. Why don't you work the next two while I use your bathroom, then get us some Cokes from Ms. Thompson?"

As he rose, Lexie put her hand on his, seizing his full attention and sending an electrifying jolt up his arm. Looking up at him, she said, "I can't thank you enough. This is one class I need to be in school for. Hopefully soon."

"I hope that, too. But I don't mind helping you until then. Be back in a minute."

Oliver left the room, joy spreading through him. He'd always like Lexie and hoped one day to be more than friends. He had even arranged his schedule so he could be Ms. Thompson's student aide the hour Lexie had English with Ms. Thompson, but still hadn't found an opportunity to ask her out. Maybe helping her with her math would give him the courage to ask her for a date.

As he made his way toward the restroom downstairs, he heard the phone ring and Ms. Thompson answer it in the kitchen next to the bathroom. He started to go into the room to take care of his needs, but something in his teacher's voice stopped him. He detoured toward the kitchen, pressing his body up against the wall near its entrance from the hallway.

⟨❧⟩

Ethan stood in the Wright's living room, waiting for Mr. Wright to come downstairs to talk to him. He held his cell phone and said to Sadie, "I'm staring at a picture of the family. Oliver is in the photo. The little girl who let me in said he was her cousin who lived with them. I asked her where the white car was. She said Oliver had it. It's his car so long as he takes his aunt to work. Is he there?"

"Yes, he's been here for an hour helping Lexie with her math in the den."

"I'm coming over. Is there anything he's touched I can get a latent print from?"

"Why do you want his fingerprint?

18

Oliver stiffened when he heard what Ms. Thompson said about fingerprints. Who was she talking to about him? Her brother? Or Lexie's uncle?

He inched closer to the kitchen and peeked inside to see his teacher across the room, standing at the desk, her back to him. He crept forward, grabbing the handle on a frying pan with remnants of breakfast in it.

His teacher said into the phone, "I'm sure you're wrong about Oliver, but I'll keep an eye on him until you get here. See you then." She hung up.

Oliver swung the skillet and struck Ms. Thompson on the side of the head. He caught her as she sank to the floor and let her down gently, then took the phone and put it in its cradle.

Now what?

They were on to him.

He took his switchblade out of his pocket and cut the pull string to the blinds to use as a rope to tie up his teacher. After he secured her, he dragged her to the utility room nearby and stuffed her inside. Then he hurried and grabbed two Cokes, took out some sleeping pills from his pill party stash and crushed two. Then he dumped the contents into Lexie's drink and started back for the den. He hated giving her any medication, but he had no choice.

She met him at the door. "I've done three problems. I thought you might have gotten lost or Ms. Thompson put you to work grading papers."

"Nope, but we did chat." He handed her the doctored drink, then took a long sip of his while she enjoyed hers. "I'll check your problems, then I need to leave."

"Oh, that's a shame. Are you sure you can't stay around?" she asked and slid her paper to him then downed several more swallows of her Coke.

As he checked over the paper, he slanted a look toward her. Her eyes began to droop.

When the doorbell rang, he popped to his feet. "I'll answer it."

"But . . ." Her head fell forward then jerked back up. "Ms. Thom— " She collapsed onto the table.

Oliver made Lexie comfortable, then hurried to the door. When he peeked out and saw the officer, who sat in his car guarding the house, standing on the porch, he knew whoever called Ms. Thompson alerted this cop.

He rang the bell again. Oliver rushed back and grabbed his jacket. Then he returned to the foyer, slipping on the coat. When he opened the front door, the officer had his hand on his gun.

"Sorry, it took so long. I told Ms. Thompson I'd answer the door on my way out." He pushed the screen open for the officer to come inside. "She's in the kitchen."

The young cop entered, drawing his gun from its holster. Before he pulled his weapon completely out, Oliver leaped forward and plunged his knife into the man's stomach. The young man crumpled to the floor, clutching his gut while blood flowed out. Oliver leaned over, withdrew the gun, and went back for Lexie. He wasn't leaving without her, even if he had to carry her to his car.

❧

On the twenty-minute drive across town, Ethan received confirmation from the officers working on identifying the cars Tuesday and Saturday night around the warehouse. They identified Oliver's white Chevy on footage from a camera on Sixth Street as well as one near the Red River City Park where Jared died. He'd figured out who was behind the killings. He needed to find the teen before someone else died.

When Ethan arrived at Sadie's house, Oliver's vehicle was gone and the patrol car was vacant. He ran toward the house, fumbling for the key Sadie had given him in case there was trouble. And this was certainly the time. Another officer pulled up to the house and got out of his car.

When Ethan started to use the key, he realized the door was unlocked. Every sense became alert as he moved into the foyer, his gun drawn. On the floor lay the officer guarding the house. The man's gun was gone along with his handcuffs. Ethan knelt next to him and felt his throat for a pulse.

The officer arriving right behind him charged through the door, weapon up.

"He's alive. Call 911. I'm going to secure the house." Ethan rose.

His heartbeat pounded a quick tempo against his ribcage as he neared the kitchen. This was where Sadie had been grading papers when he'd left for the station earlier. His mouth went dry as he held his gun up and swung into the entrance.

Empty.

Where's Lexie? Sadie? Please, Lord, keep them alive. I can't lose them. The den. That's where Sadie said Oliver and Lexie were.

He crept toward the room as the sound of sirens cut into the eerie silence in the house. More backup arrived here. When he reached the den, he went in with his weapon clasped between his hands. As in the kitchen, the emptiness mocked him. But spread out on the game table were Lexie's papers and textbook.

As officers and Cord flooded the house, Ethan told them what he'd found when he arrived. Cord issued a BOLO out for the white Chevy and directed his men to search the place thoroughly.

Think! Where would the kid go? But Ethan didn't know much about the teen other than what his uncle had told him about Oliver. Quiet. Would never have anything to do with prescription drugs or anything like that. His mother had died from an overdose of sleeping pills, and his father shot himself the day of the funeral. They took Oliver in, but he stayed to himself. He'd been living with them for eight years.

"Ethan, come in the kitchen. We found Sadie."

Cord's words sent hope and fear through Ethan at the same time. He hastened from the den to find Cord kneeling over his sister on the floor near the utility room.

"Is she—" a lump captured Ethan's next words.

"She's alive, and I've called for another ambulance. But she has a nasty bump on the right side of her head."

Ethan stooped next to Sadie, taking her hand and laying his fingers on her wrist. He had to feel her pulse. Its faint pulsating beat gave him the hope he needed. *Please, God, the rest is in Your hands.*

Holding Sadie's hand and feeling helpless, Ethan tried to rein in his anger. It would get in the way of finding the teen responsible for this.

One of the officers reported to Cord the house was clear. No one else was in it.

"Which means Oliver must have taken Lexie hostage." A vision of Kelly hanging from the rafter still haunted Ethan and gripped him with fear.

"We'll find him, and he'll pay for what he has done," Cord said between gritted teeth.

As the paramedics came into the kitchen with a gurney, Ethan and Cord stood back to let them work on Sadie and prepare her for transport.

"I'm going back to the uncle's and find out everything I can about this kid. Where his favorite places are? Relatives or friends nearby? Anything to help us find out where he went with Lexie."

"Go. If I hear anything, I'll give you a call. I'll let Beth know about Lexie. You focus on finding Oliver and Lexie. I'm calling in every cop I can get hold of. I'm flooding the streets with people looking for the white Chevy, and I'll alert the radio and TV stations. He won't be able to show his face anywhere without being recognized."

Ethan followed the paramedics taking Sadie to the ambulance. The sight of her being put into the back of the vehicle, then one of the EMTs shutting the doors closed scared him more than when he was ten and watched them take his father away. Back then, he'd thought his dad would be okay and come back to him after the doctors fixed him up. Now he knew that wasn't always the case.

$$\approx \circlearrowleft 2$$

Lexie opened her eyes halfway, her cheek pressed into the softness of a pillow. What happened? Her brain foggy, she lifted her head a few inches and looked around. Where was she? Not Ms. Thompson's house? Or her home? A cabin? She moved to get up and realized he had handcuffed her to a bed. Panic bolted through her as she pushed to a sitting position, one arm stretched out toward the post on the headboard. Handcuffs secured her wrist to the post.

She yanked her arm with all her strength and only succeeded in making noise and chafing her wrist.

The door banged opened. Oliver came into the rustic bedroom. He smiled. "I wouldn't do that if I were you. You aren't going anywhere."

"What have you done? Why?"

"I've taken you hostage. I'd hoped to get out of town but couldn't, so we're staying here until things die down."

"Why?"

"Because your uncle forced me to hurt a police officer." He took the chair a few feet from her, laying a gun in his lap and relaxing back as though what he was doing he did everyday.

"I don't understand. What does my uncle have to do with this?" With her free hand, she rubbed her eyes, trying to get them to focus clearer. "We were doing math. You gave me a Coke . . ." Her gaze shot to Oliver. "What did you put in it? Did you put something in my water bottle at school, too? I almost died." She tried to stamp down the fury rising within her, but as it slowly dawned on her what kind of trouble she was in because of this boy, she fluctuated between anger and fear.

"I wouldn't do that to you. No, that little stunt was Luke. I saw him take the water bottle from your backpack and throw it away when Ms. Thompson left the room to go to the restroom before she left school that day. He tossed it in the trashcan. But he paid for trying to kill you. I couldn't let him get away with it."

"What did you do?"

"What he did to you. I'm quite good in science. It wasn't hard to figure out what pills he put in your water."

"You killed him!" Rage momentarily surpassed all caution in Lexie. She shuddered. A chill encased her from head to toe. She crossed her free arm over her middle, trying to stop the quaking.

"Not really. He killed himself by getting behind the wheel of a car when he was drowsy. He should have known better."

Who are you, she wanted to shout at Oliver, but she had to calm down and think. Not make him mad at her. "How about Jared?"

"I'd heard about these pill parties happening at school. I couldn't believe kids were so stupid to do something like that. Our leaders at school. They were taunting death. They thought that was fun. I decided to show them the consequences of taking different pills for fun."

"And Kelly?" Her throat swelled around her friend's name. She missed her so much.

"She spread false rumors about you. Kids were shunning you. I saw how sad you were. Besides, she took drugs like her boyfriend. I tried to warn her about what she was doing, but she ignored my emails.

"So you wiped her computer clean."

"Had to. No sense leaving a trail to my doorstep."

Chills flashed down Lexie's spine at the sensible sounding voice spewing from Oliver as though he were discussing the weather, not people's lives. "She was my best friend. She was confused and trying to figure things out. We made up. You didn't have a right."

"I didn't mean to hurt you like that. I thought you were angry at her."

"What are you doing now?" She rattled the handcuffs. "This is hurting me." She glared at him. "You drugged me like Luke. I hate taking anything. I've seen what it does."

"I do, too, and I didn't plan on doing that. Everything has gotten out of control. I didn't mean to hurt you."

"But you are."

"Not for long."

His words struck terror in her heart.

⁂

After talking again with Oliver's uncle and aunt, Ethan headed back to the police station to coordinate with Cord. The chords of "The Eyes of Texas" sliced through the quiet in the SUV. He clicked his cell on. "Stone here."

"Missy's grandparents who own a cabin by the lake said the silent alarm has been tripped. Someone who shouldn't be there is in their place," Cord said.

Ethan gripped the steering wheel tighter. "Are you thinking what I'm thinking?"

"Oliver might have gone there to hide with Lexie. It's off the beaten track, tucked back from the road. If he'd been watching those kids, he might know about the cabin."

Ethan turned left at the next stop sign and made his way toward the east end of Summerton Lake. "I'll meet you there. I know the approximate location. Can you give me specific directions?"

After Cord did, Ethan hung up and stepped on the gas. Knowing what Oliver was capable of, he felt Lexie's time slipping away. He would not go to Beth and tell his sister her daughter was murdered.

Lord, all things are possible through You.

⁂

Tears came to Lexie's eyes as she watched Oliver pace the bedroom at the cabin. He carried a gun, his arm straight at his side, the barrel pointed toward the floor. But the sight of the weapon empha-sized how grave the situation was. Oliver had killed—three times. As he prowled, his movements became more agitated. He hadn't said a word for the past fifteen minutes and Lexie was afraid to say anything to him.

One tear after another began to fall onto her lap. She couldn't stop them. She tried to cry quietly, but a sob escaped her mouth.

Oliver stopped.

Her breath trapped in her lungs, she furiously wiped the wet tracks from her face.

He whirled toward her. "Don't cry. Please."

"I'm—I'm try—ing not to. I'm scared."

He lifted the gun and tapped his chest with its barrel. "Of me? I won't hurt you. I care about you. Have for a long time."

"Then why am I handcuffed? Why did you take me from Ms. Thompson's house? Is she okay?"

Oliver blinked, his shoulders drooping. "I don't know. I hit her with a frying pan. I just reacted."

Lexie gasped, the tears renewed.

"I'm sorry. I didn't know what else to do. They were coming after me. I had to get away." He scanned the room. "But this isn't what I planned."

Lord, help me. Oliver frightens me. I don't want to die like the others.

With the weapon in his hand, he combed his hair back from his face. "I've got to figure out what to do."

Lexie sucked in a shaky breath and said, "Sit. Talk to me about what you're thinking." Somewhere on TV, she'd seen where a hos-tage connecting with his kidnapper could decrease the likelihood of being killed by the criminal. She didn't know what else to do.

Oliver plopped into the chair he'd occupied earlier. "All I wanted to do was let teens know how deadly taking drugs can be."

So he killed Jared to show them? "I agree with you. My mother is a nurse and has told me about cases where people get hooked on a medication and can't get off it. Like taking heroin, except their doctor gave it to them for pain. For some that can become an addiction if they aren't careful."

"Yes. You're so right. But it isn't just pain meds. It can be tranquil-izers or sleeping pills. Some people become dependent on them and can't stop. My mother was like that. She killed herself when I was ten. She just kept taking more and more until she didn't wake up."

"I'm so sorry, Oliver." Through her blurry vision, she watched him fix his gaze on her and tilt his head to the side.

"You do understand. You care. My father didn't. Right after the funeral he killed himself. He left me alone. And now I'm in trouble. I don't have . . ." His voice faded into the silence, and he hung his head.

***

Ethan pulled up to the cabin and parked back behind a hedge of wild bushes. He took out his binoculars and panned the area. He saw the back end of a white car behind the cabin. He called Cord.

"How far are you away from the Collins's place?"

"Ten minutes with several others behind me."

"I believe they're in there. I'm going to try and get closer. All the blinds on this side of the cabin are closed. I'll check the other sides. If I can see in, I might know what's going on."

"Be careful. On a good note, I got a call from the Highway Patrol. They caught Sam heading for Oklahoma. They found a lot of drugs in his car. They're escorting him back here for us."

"See you in ten."

Ethan put his cell phone on vibrate and stuck it in his pocket. If he could work his way up closer, he didn't want it ringing and alerting the teen he was outside. Soon enough Oliver would know.

Running low to the ground, he hurried across an open space and ducked behind some thick brush. He had a different view of the cabin and noted the blinds were drawn on the left side of the cabin as well as the front.

When his cell phone vibrated in his pocket, he quickly retrieved it. The call came from a Ned Collins. "Stone here."

"Stay back, if you know what's good for your niece."

"Is this Oliver?"

"Yes, but you already knew that. Don't come any closer. Stay back by the road. Remember, I have Lexie with me."

"Ms. Thompson and the officer will recover, Oliver." At least, Ethan prayed they would. Thoughts of Sadie started to intrude, and he pushed them away. He had to focus on the situation before him. "This won't end well if you don't give yourself up. I know you care about Lexie. Let her—"

Oliver hung up.

Ethan tried the number, but it kept ringing until it went dead.

ﾂﾐ

Through the open door, Lexie watched Oliver. He yanked the phone from its jack, picked up his glass of water, and marched into the bedroom. "Was that my uncle?"

"Yes. He wants me to turn myself in."

"What do you want?"

"Peace. This over with." He sat on the other side of the bed.

Lexie twisted around, her movements limited by the handcuffs. When he popped something into his mouth and washed it down with water, she asked, "What are you doing?"

"I don't want to live anymore." He opened his hand to reveal a fistful of pills, two different colors and sizes.

As he proceeded sticking a couple more into his mouth and taking a long drink, Lexie cried out, "Don't. That isn't the answer. You need help."

He ignored her and finished the rest of the pills, one quickly after another. "Maybe my mother was right after all."

"No, Oliver. What did you take?"

"A nice mixture of tranquilizers and painkillers. Not something you should combine, but then the kids at the pill party could have done that and not even known it." Oliver put the weapon from his waistband on the nightstand near him, then lay down on the bed.

Lexie jerked and pulled on her handcuff. She needed to get him help. She had to do something.

"Don't be upset, Lexie. I'm going to see my mom and dad again." He closed his eyes.

What can I do?

She frantically searched the room for something to help her. She tried to make her hand smaller so she could slip it out of the steel ring. She couldn't.

Gripping with both hands on the bedpost, she used all her strength to yank it loose. After five minutes of losing the battle with the headboard, she turned back to Oliver and felt for a pulse. A faint one beating beneath her fingertips urged her to do something else.

Her gaze focused on the window a few feet from the bed. If she could reach it and open it, she could yell for her uncle. From what Oliver said on the phone, Uncle Ethan was outside by the road. Maybe he'd see her break the glass or hear her shout.

But as she tugged on the bed, it only budged a little, the frame heavy and made of solid wood. Why hadn't she lifted weights or something? She was so weak.

Inch by inch she dragged the bed toward the window. Exhausted, the effects of the sleeping pill he'd given her still making her groggy, Lexie made it to the side of the blinds and opened them. She still had some more to go to raise the window up, but every part of her protested. Weary to the bone, she sank on the mattress and glanced at Oliver.

His face evened out into a peaceful countenance. *Is he dead? No, it's too soon.*

She launched herself off the bed and stretched as far as her body would allow. A hand length away was the latch to open the window.

Please, Lord, I need Your strength.

Her hands clasped around the post, she hauled the bed a few more inches. Then some more. Until her fingers clasped the knob and twisted it. When she tried to lift the wooden sill, it wouldn't budge. Frustration put a stranglehold on her. She wanted to pound her fists into the glass. The thought spurred another, and she peered around her for something to use.

Her gaze riveted on the pillow. Maybe she could use that. She snatched it up and put it against the pane, then smashed her fists into the pillow until she heard the glass shatter. She kept doing it until a large ragged hole appeared.

"Help! Uncle Ethan, help!"

Cord and three other officers arrived at the cabin. Ethan headed back toward the cluster of cars at the end of the road to the cabin.

"Help," he heard when the sound of the engines went silent.

Ethan stood straight, waved his arms at Cord, and yelled, "Quiet."

"Uncle Ethan, Oliver is passed out."

Ethan rushed toward the noise, rounding the back of the cabin to find a window broken and Lexie standing at the side of it. "Where's Oliver?" he asked as he moved closer and peeked into the bedroom.

"On the bed. He took a lot of pills. He wanted to commit suicide. Please get him help."

"I'm coming around to the door. Be right there." Ethan raced back toward the front and met Cord halfway there. "Oliver has overdosed. He's out."

Cord shouted at one of his officers, "Call 911," while he rushed with Ethan to the entrance into the cabin.

Kicking at the sturdy door didn't budge it. But one of the officers brought a battering ram, and they used it to break into the cabin.

Ethan was first into the bedroom, embracing Lexie, while Cord went to see about Oliver.

"He's still alive," he said to Ethan.

Lexie sobbed against Ethan's chest. "You're okay, Kiddo. Your mom will be glad to see you." She was shaken but safe. He thanked the Lord.

But what about Sadie?

Sadie's father leaned down and kissed her forehead. "I'll leave you alone to get some rest, but your mom insists on staying."

Sadie smiled. "I know. I've been trying to talk her into going home. I'm going to be fine."

"Mom. I want to stay," Ashley said from the small couch. "I can sleep on this."

Sadie scanned the faces of everyone in the room. *Where's Ethan?* Sadie lay in the hospital bed, pain tap dancing against the sides of her skull. "I want you and Steven to go with Grandpa. The doctor said I'll be able to go home tomorrow." She then turned to her mother. "I want you to go with Dad. Really I'm fine."

"But I should—"

"No, Mom. Go."

Her mother grumbled something under her breath but squeezed Sadie's hand. "I'll be back first thing tomorrow morning."

As she followed the rest to the door, it opened. For a second, Sadie's breath caught in her throat. Ethan? Instead, her brother came into the room.

When Cord stood by her bed, she asked, "Where have you been? Mom and Dad couldn't tell me much of anything with the kids here. How's Lexie?" *Where's Ethan?*

"She'll be okay. She was checked out by the doctor and is now home with Beth. I'm going over there after I see you."

"Is that where Ethan is?"

"Yes, then he's coming here."

"Tell me what happened."

"We have closed a couple of big cases today. Patti Shea along with her husband who was selling the extra drugs from the nursing home on the street will go away for a long time. The nursing home is going to institute random blood tests on employees and patients in the future to keep this kind of situation from happening again."

"I can't believe Oliver hit me with a frying pan." Although the pain in her head made it very real.

"Oliver didn't make it. He died on the way to the hospital, but he told Lexie he killed Jared, Luke, and Kelly because they were involved with drugs. Rather, that's the reason he did Jared, but Luke was in retaliation for spiking Lexie's drink, and Kelly was because she turned against Lexie. It seems he had a crush on Lexie."

"I never knew it."

"Neither did she. But we found out he bought some flowers from the grocery store around the time she received a bouquet from a secret admirer."

Sadie closed her eyes for a few seconds. "How about Kalvin?"

"He wasn't selling, but using. It was Sam selling at the high school and Sam's little brother dealing at the middle school."

"They probably aren't the only ones."

"I agree, but Mr. Howard is determined to crack down on drugs at school. This has really opened his eyes."

"Good."

"Sam did admit to calling you and leaving those threatening messages. He didn't like how nosy you were getting."

"I'm glad to have that figured out." Sadie looked at the wall clock. *Where's Ethan?*

"Ethan was here earlier when you were pretty much out of it. He'll be here—"

The sound of the door opening drew Sadie's gaze toward it. Ethan entered.

"And that's my cue to leave, little sister." Cord strode toward Ethan. "How are Beth and Lexie?"

"Doing fine, under the circumstances. My niece is amazing. All she wanted to know was how everyone else was."

When Cord left the room, Ethan approached her, his eyes fastened to hers. "I tried to get here as quickly as I could when your mom told me you were awake. I didn't realize how many loose ends had to be tied up."

She held up her hand. "Come here and kiss me."

He laughed. "That's the first thing you say to me?"

"Yep. I need something to focus my mind on rather than the pain."

He was at her side, cupping her hand between his. "Anything to oblige someone hurt."

He bent down and brushed his lips over hers, a gentle possession as though he were afraid to hurt her further. She slipped her hand from his grasp and hooked it behind his neck to pull him closer and deepen the kiss. The sensation of his mouth on hers wiped everything from her brain but him.

"I'm not that fragile. I'm so glad this is over with."

"And you and I can move forward," Ethan murmured, his breath fanning her lips.

"I like the sound of that. You know I've had a crush on you since I was a teenager."

"That's the rumor I heard."

"So Texas Ranger Ethan Stone, what are you going to do about it?"

He claimed her mouth in another kiss, declaring her his.

Discussion Questions

1. Have you ever trusted someone who did something to hurt that trust? What did that person have to do to regain your trust?

2. Prescription drugs can be good for us and heal what is wrong, but they also can be bad if used in the wrong way. What do you do with the prescription drugs you don't finish or keep on hand at your house? Do you keep track of what drugs you have? Why is it important for a person to be aware of what drugs they are taking and why?

3. Sadie and Lexie had to deal with forgiveness. Sadie finally decided she had to let go of her anger toward her ex-husband if she were going to move on. Do you have someone you need to forgive? What did they do? Why are you still angry? Who is that anger hurting the most: you or the person you can't forgive or someone else?

4. What would you do if your child were taking prescription drugs illegally? Why would you do that?

5. Do you know anyone who is addicted to prescription drugs? How can you help them?

6. Do people change? Should Sadie give her ex-husband a second chance with his children? Why do you think yes or no?

7. Mary Lou became so desperate for drugs that she broke into a nursing home and took the medication. Have you ever been so desperate that you've done something you regretted? How could you change that situation?

8. What are some things schools can do to help with drug abuse? Is this happening in your area?

9. Kelly wanted to be part of the "in crowd" to the point that she did things she knew she shouldn't. Have you ever done that? How did it work out for you? How could you have done things differently?

10. Steven drank a bottle of cough syrup with codeine in it. It was a cry for attention, a protest concerning something happening to him. Have you done something stupid because you were upset? Did it work out okay for you? If not, what happened? How could you have handled the situation better?

If you enjoyed *Severed Trust*, you will love all three books in Margaret Daley's Men of the Texas Rangers series: *Saving Hope, Shattered Silence,* and *Scorned Justice*. Here's a bonus chapter from the first book of the series, *Saving Hope*.

Saving Hope

Book 1 of Men of the Texas Rangers Series

∼♋∼

1

*R*ose gripped her cell phone so tightly her muscles ached. "Where are you, Lily?"

"At—Nowhere Motel." A sob caught on the end of the last word. "Help—me." Lily's breath rattled, followed by a clunk-ing sound as though she'd dropped the phone.

Rose paced the small bathroom at Beacon of Hope. "Lily?" Sweat coated her palms, and she rubbed her free hand against her jeans.

Silence taunted her.

What have you done? But the second that Rose asked that question, an image came to mind of her friend lying on the dingy gray sheets in the cheap motel, wasted, trying anyway she could to forget the horror of her life.

"Lily, talk to me. Stay on the line." Pulling the door open, Rose entered her room. When she saw her roommate, she came to a stop.

Cynthia's wide-eyed gaze fixed on Rose for a few seconds before the fourteen-year-old dropped her head and stared at the hardwood floor. Rose crossed to her dresser, dug into the back of the top drawer, and grabbed a small, worn leather case. She pushed past her roommate and headed into the upstairs hallway.

Striding toward the staircase, Rose dismissed her room-mate's startled expression and focused on the crisis at hand. "Lily, are you still there?"

A sound as though someone fumbled the phone and caught it filtered through the connection. "Rose, I need—you."

"I told you I would come if you wanted to get out. I'll be—"

A click cut off the rest of Rose's words. *No, Lily. Please hang on.*

Rushing down the steps to the first floor, she quickly redialed the number and let it ring and ring. When she approached the program director's office, she finally pocketed her cell, took out her home-made tools, and picked the lock, a skill she learned to give her some sense of control over her life. In the past she'd done what she had to in order to survive.

Guided by the light through the slits in the blinds, Rose entered Kate's darkened office and switched on the desk light. A twinge of guilt pricked her. If Kate found her in here after- hours, how could she explain herself? Especially with what she was going to do next to the woman who had saved her and taken her in.

Kate's gonna be so disappointed in me for stealing—no, borrowing—the van. She's put so much faith in me. But I've got to save Lily. I promised her. When I bring Lily back here, Kate will understand.

Rose used her tools to open the locked drawer on the right. Pulling it out, she rummaged through the papers to find the set of keys at the bottom, then bumped the drawer closed with her hip.

I have no choice, Kate. Please forgive me.

The memory of the words, *I need you,* spurred Rose to move faster. She had to get to her friend. Get her out . . . finally. Bring her to Kate.

Clutching the keys in one hand, she turned off the lamp and carefully made her way to the office door. She eased it open a few inches and peered out into the short hallway. The empty corridor mirrored the feeling inside her.

When would it go away? When will I feel whole?

After she checked to make sure the office door was locked, she hurried toward the side exit of the building that housed the residential program for teens like her. Outside the summer heat blasted her in the face even though it was past midnight. Her heart pounded as hard as her feet hitting against the con-crete. Sweat beaded on her forehead as she rushed toward the parking lot to find Beacon of Hope's van. The security light cast a yellow glow on the vehicle at the back of the building. Visions of her friend slipping into drug-induced unconsciousness, no one there to care whether she died or not, prodded her to quicken her steps.

I won't let you down, Lily. She was the reason her friend was where she was right now, stuck in a life that was quickly killing her.

As Rose tried to unlock the white van, her hands shook so badly the keys dropped to the pavement. Snatching them up, she sucked in a breath, then another, but her lungs cried for more oxygen. With her second attempt, she managed to open the door and slip behind the steering wheel. Her trembling hands gripped the hot plastic. After backing out of the parking space, she pressed down on the accelerator and eased onto the street in front of Beacon of Hope. With little driving experience, she would have to go slower than she wanted. She couldn't get caught by the cops. This was her one chance to save her friend. If all went well, she could be back here with Lily before morning.

She tried to clear her mind and concentrate totally on the road before her. She couldn't. Memories of her two years as a prostitute tumbled through her mind, leaving a trail of regrets. One was having to leave Lily behind.

Nowhere Motel—her and Lily's name for one of the hell-holes where they'd had to earn their living. A place—one of several used when they were brought to Dallas—near the highway on Cherry Street. A place where inhuman acts hap-pened to humans—young girls who should be dressing up for their prom, not their next trick.

She'd escaped only because she'd been left for dead on the side of the road when a john discarded her like trash. But the Lord had other plans for her besides death. A judge had seen to it that she came to the Beacon of Hope program, and Kate had given her a glimpse of a better life.

And I'm gonna start with rescuing Lily. I'm not gonna let her die. She's gonna have a chance like me.

Rose slowed as she neared the motel, two rows of units. Bright lights illuminated the front rooms, which maintained an appearance of respectability, while the rooms in the back were shrouded in dimness.

After she parked across the street from Nowhere, she sat in the van staring at the place, its neon sign to welcome travelers taunting her. Sweat rolled down her face, and she swiped at it. But nothing she did stopped the fear from overwhelming her to the point of paralysis. Memories of what went on in the back rooms of the motel threatened to thwart her attempt to rescue Lily before it began.

I owe her. I have to make up for what I did to her.

She pried her hands from the steering wheel and climbed from the van. After jogging across the two lanes, she circled around to the second building that abutted the access road to the highway.

The sounds of cars whizzing by filled the night. People going about their ordinary life while some were barely hang-ing on. A loud, robust laugh drifted to her as she snuck past the first unit, heading for room three, the one Lily always used at Nowhere. Someone opened a door nearby and stepped out of a room ahead of her. Rose darted back into a shadowed alcove at the end, pressing her body flat against the rough cin-der block wall. Perspiration drenched her shirt and face. The stench of something dead reeked from a Dumpster a few yards away. Nausea roiled in her stomach.

Two, sometimes three, of *his* guards would patrol, making sure the girls stayed in line. She wasn't sure this was a guard, but she couldn't risk even a quick look. She waited until the man disappeared up the stairs, then hurried toward the third unit. With damp palms, she inched the unlocked door open and peeked through the slit.

Dressed in a little-girl outfit that only underscored Lily's age of fifteen, she lay sprawled on the bed, her long red hair fanning the pillow, the sheets bunched at the end. Her friend shifted, her eyes blinking open. Groaning, she shoved herself up on one elbow, only to collapse back onto the mattress.

Footsteps on the stairs sent a shaft of fear through Rose. Her heartbeat accelerated. She pushed into the room and closed the door, clicking the lock in place. She almost laughed at her ridiculous action as though that would keep anyone out. But she left it locked.

The scent of sex, alcohol, and sweat assailed her nostrils and brought back a rush of memories she'd wanted to bury forever. For a few seconds she remained paralyzed by the door as memories bombarded her from all sides. Hands groping for her. A sweaty body weighed down on top of hers. The fog she'd lived in to escape.

She shook them from her thoughts. *Can't go there. Lily is depending on me.*

Turning toward her friend, she started across the room. Lily's glazed eyes fixed on her. For several heartbeats, nothing dawned in their depths. Then a flicker of recognition.

She tried to rise, saying, "Rose, so sorry . . ." Lily slurred her words as she sank back. "Sor—reee."

"I'm here to get you out." Rose sat on the edge of the bed. "You've got—"

A noise behind her and to the left cut off her next words. She glanced over her shoulder as the bathroom door crashed open, and *he* charged into the room.

"Did you really think I'd let you go?"

His gravelly voice froze Rose for a few seconds. King never came to Nowhere Motel. Too beneath him. He should be—

Finally, terror propelled her into action. She scrambled off the bed and ran for the door. She grappled for the lock, her sweat-drenched fingers slipping on the cold metal.

King slammed her against the wall beside the door—her only escape route. He pressed her back to hold her pinned, the scent of peppermint sickening her. He loved to suck on pep-permint candies, and she'd come to hate that smell. The aroma enhanced her desperation.

Words from her street days spewed from her mouth. She twisted and tried to buck him off. He thrust her harder against the wall until she couldn't catch her breath. Lightheaded from the lack of air, she went still.

"You'll always be mine. That john paid for losing you." Her pimp threw the lock on the door and opened it. "Tony."

Oxygen rushed back into her lungs and with it returned the frantic need to get away.

But before she could make a move, King's fingers clamped around her upper arm so tightly she thought he would break it. A six-foot-tall guard appeared in the doorway as King dragged her across the room and flung her on the bed. One of her arms flopped then bounced on the mattress near Lily. Her friend's head lolled to the side. Her eyes closed.

"Hold her." King withdrew a syringe, filled with a clear liquid, from his pocket.

"No," Rose screamed and scrambled over Lily's body. She *had* to get away. She wouldn't go there again.

Tony lunged across the bed and grabbed her leg. His fingers dug into her ankle. Inch by inch he hauled her to him. Lily moaned as Rose slid across her, but Lily's eyes stayed closed.

Can't give up. Rose kicked free and launched herself at the guard, raking her fingernails down his cheek.

He struck her face with his fist. Pain radiated outward from her jaw. Her vision blurred. A metallic taste coated her tongue. The room tumbled through her mind, as if she'd been stuffed into a dryer in the middle of its cycle. The ringing in her ears drowned out what Tony said. Throwing his body over hers, he trapped her on the bed.

Can't—

Her pimp loomed over her. Through the haze, she saw the malicious grin as King gripped her arm and yanked it toward him.

When he held up the syringe, her heart beat so fast she thought she would pass out from the hammering force against her ribcage. She gasped for a mouth full of air, but it wasn't enough.

"No, please not that," she whimpered as he jabbed the needle into her arm.

Want to learn more about author
Margaret Daley and check out other great
fiction from Abingdon Press?

Sign up for our fiction newsletter at
www.AbingdonPress.com
to read interviews with your favorite authors, find tips
for starting a reading group, and stay posted on what
new titles are on the horizon. It's a place to connect
with other fiction readers or post a
comment about this book.

Be sure to visit Margaret online!

www.margaretdaley.com